BIRTHRIGHT

BIRTHRIGHT

BIRTHRIGHT

A NOVEL

Alan Gold and Mike Jones

ATRIA PAPERBACK

NEW YORK LONDON TORONTO SYDNEY NEW DELHI

ATRIA PAPERBACK

An Imprint of Simon & Schuster, Inc.
1230 Avenue of the Americas
New York, NY 10020

Originally published in 2013 as *Stateless* by Simon & Schuster (Australia) Pty Limited.

First Atria Paperback edition August 2015

ATRIA PAPERBACK and colophon are trademarks of Simon & Schuster, Inc.

For information about special discounts for bulk purchases, please contact Simon & Schuster Special Sales at 1-866-506-1949 or business@simonandschuster.com.

The Simon & Schuster Speakers Bureau can bring authors to your live event. For more information or to book an event, contact the Simon & Schuster Speakers Bureau at 1-866-248-3049 or visit our website at www.simonspeakers.com.

Manufactured in the United States of America

10   9   8   7   6   5   4   3   2   1

Library of Congress Cataloging-in-Publication Data is available.

ISBN 978-1-4767-5986-9
ISBN 978-1-4767-5987-6 (ebook)

Terrorism is the tactic of demanding the impossible, and demanding it at gunpoint.

— Christopher Hitchens

BIRTHRIGHT

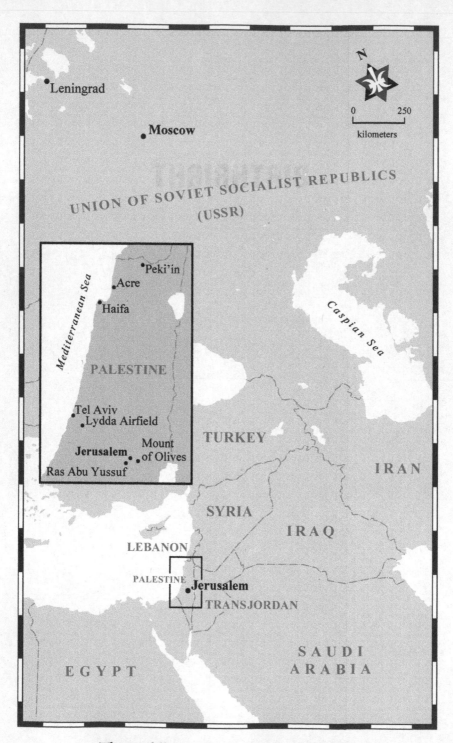

The Middle East Crisis Areas, 1933–1948

PART ONE

PART ONE

Kibbutz Beit Yitzhak,
Northern Palestine

1931

FOUR-YEAR-OLD SHALMAN ETZION ran as fast as his little legs could carry him and hurled himself into the void as the ground disappeared beneath him. He plummeted like a diving bird, arms and legs akimbo, screaming as he flew through the air. He felt the air hurtling past as he plunged over the edge of the sand dune, exhilarating in the heat of the sun and the acrid perfume of salt and sea spray. Neither his mother nor his father, seated nearby, turned as Shalman shrieked into the wind.

His body landed with a thud and nearly disappeared into the soft white powder as he slid with the sand, gliding down to the bottom where his parents, dressed only in their swimsuits, were sitting on a blanket eating hummus, t'china, and pita bread.

"Shalman," said his mother, Devorah, turning when she heard him stand up and laugh, "come eat. You'll hurt yourself one day. Come, bubbeleh. Have some food."

The boy brushed the sand off his body. Ari, his father, continued to read his copy of the *Palestine News* but said softly to his wife, "Devorah, leave the kid alone. He's having a good time. He'll eat when he's ready."

Shalman was ready. Spending all of Saturday at the beach was the greatest fun in the entire world, and even though his week was filled with learning to read and write and singing songs and playing with his brothers and sisters on the kibbutz, there was nothing he loved more than when he had his abba and imma to himself. Sometimes the family came to the beach for a picnic with other families from the kibbutz, and then the fun would be multiplied as all the kids ran wild across the sand. But there was something special on a Shabbat morning when his abba was given permission by the kibbutz director to borrow the organization's truck and drive his family to a beach.

And this beach, some thirty miles south of Haifa, was the one he enjoyed the most. There were beaches that his kibbutz faced, beaches where the cultivated land and the orange and grapefruit groves gave way to the sand and then to the sea. But this beach, a half-hour drive away from his kibbutz, had towering dunes that curved so that when large waves thundered down on the sand, they sent up white clouds of spray and salt. It was incredibly exciting.

Shalman, hair tousled and full of sand, walked to the blanket and sat cross-legged as his mother put a plate of the pastes and bread in front of him. He turned up his nose, which his father noticed. He knew there was chicken and coleslaw and didn't want to waste his time eating this grown-up food.

"Stop it, Shalman. Do you know how lucky you are to have good food? Little boys and girls in Europe are starving. You should eat everything and be grateful."

"Why can't they come here, Abba?"

"Bubbeleh, it's easy for people like you and Mummy and me to travel—we just get into the kibbutz's truck and drive. But it's not so easy for others. The British have stopped many of our people from coming here, and many have died trying."

Only a few years had passed since Jews in Palestine were barred access to the temple in Jerusalem amid riots and violent bloodshed between them and their Arab neighbors. This had prompted the British, who administered the land of Palestine under the mandate, to crack down and restrict Jewish migration.

Devorah interrupted. "For God's sake, Ari; he's a child. Don't tell him such things."

"No!" said Shalman. "Tell me now, Abba. Tell me. I hate the British. I want to kill the British. And the Arabs."

Devorah was shocked. "Don't say such horrible things! You mustn't talk about killing and murder." She looked at her husband. "Where does he learn these things?"

Ari shrugged. "It's a kibbutz. Kids talk. They repeat what they've heard their parents say. But what am I supposed to tell him? The British and the Arabs are our best friends?"

"He doesn't have to learn hatred while he's a child. He can be different from us," Devorah replied.

"It's important that he knows his birthright!"

"He'll learn soon enough. When this is our country, then—" A sudden gust of wind carried her words away.

But Ari's attention was drawn to something in the distance. His expression hardened and his mood changed, which little Shalman noticed.

Ari had heard the noise of a vehicle. "Quiet!" he ordered. Devorah and Shalman looked at him in concern as he stood and scrambled up the dune. The road from Haifa to Tel Aviv was fairly busy, but there were very few cars or vehicles that turned off on the long side road that led to the beaches. And these beaches were too far from villages or other centers of population to be visited by many people.

Ari popped his head up just above the line of the dune so he could see the kibbutz truck he'd borrowed. It no longer stood alone; parked beside it was a military vehicle carrying four British soldiers.

With a sinking heart, Ari watched them walk toward the beach, two carrying their .303s and one carrying a new Bren gun. The fourth soldier, a sergeant, carried a side revolver.

Ari didn't know what to do. He could climb up over the dune and greet them, and dressed in a swimsuit, he would appear patently unarmed. To better protect his family, he crawled back down to where Shalman and Devorah waited. "The British. A four-man patrol. Armed. Just sit and eat like everything is normal."

"Everything *is* normal, Ari. We're just having a picnic." But her words were more for Shalman than her husband.

Shalman turned toward the dune, but Devorah said urgently, "Bubbeleh, just look this way, toward the sea. Keep your eyes on Abba and Imma."

Ari said loudly in English, and somewhat too theatrically, "Well, I see that you're both eating the kibbutz food. It's really good, isn't it?"

Devorah glared at him. "Stop pretending, idiot. You're no actor. You sound like a *meshuggeneh*."

The four soldiers, weapons ready, appeared at the top of the dune. Ari glanced up and smiled and nodded. "Good morning, gentlemen."

The soldiers didn't return the greeting. Instead, the sergeant pointed to the basket and said loudly, "You. Missus. Open the basket very slowly and show us what's inside. Very bloody slowly." As she moved to follow his order, one soldier leveled his .303 from the hip, pointing it directly at Devorah, fearful that she might draw a weapon. In Palestine, anything was possible.

Devorah moved to open the basket, lifted it, and showed it to the soldiers. Then she put it back on the blanket and slowly took everything out: first the chicken, then some salad, then two bottles of water. When she'd done so, she turned it upside down to prove that there was nothing else inside.

The sergeant nodded. "What are you doing here? Why so far from town? Where are you from?"

"We're from Kibbutz Beit Yitzhak, about ten miles south. It's our day of rest, so I'm here with my wife and son, having a picnic."

One of the other soldiers, standing next to the sergeant, whispered into his ear. The sergeant nodded. "My corporal's going to come down and make sure you're not hiding weapons under your blanket. Don't make any moves. Understand?"

The younger man descended the dune, slipping on the sandy surface, and walked over to the family. He pointed his .303 at them. "Move off the blanket. Now!"

Shalman involuntarily let out a whimper, the quiet of the beach seizing him with uncertain fear. But the Tommy was unmoved and continued to point his rifle at them. Ari picked up Shalman, and they moved onto the sand. The corporal poked the blanket with the barrel of his gun, but it was obvious that nothing was hidden beneath. He looked up and nodded to his sergeant. The other three men descended the dune, and the sergeant smiled at Ari and his wife.

"Sorry, mate, but you Jews are causing us no bleedin' end of problems these days. You never bloody know who's going to stab you in the back at the moment."

Silently, under her breath, her face turned away from them toward the sea, Devorah whispered to herself, "Nobody trusts anyone anymore . . ."

Moscow, USSR

1931

LITTLE JUDITA LUDMILLA hid beneath the table, but try as she might, she couldn't stop herself from crying. While her older brother and sister were hiding under the sheets of the single bed the children shared, the two-year-old tried to block out her father's stentorian voice rebounding off the walls of their tiny apartment. It was the third time this week that Abel Abramovich was shouting at his wife and three children. His thundering voice was punctuated by the sounds of his fist pounding on the table and furniture being kicked over as he stumbled drunkenly across the room.

The little girl, perpetually hungry, limp, ragged, and exhausted, squeezed her eyes shut to block out the sight of her father's teetering body. She was frightened that he would do to her what he did to her mother. Sometimes the marks on her mother's face and shoulders didn't disappear for a week. Her mother would make excuses to stay in the house then, but when she was older, Judita would understand that her mother was ashamed.

Abel Abramovich reeked of vodka, there were borscht stains on his work clothes, and he was covered in concrete dust from his construction site. From under the table Judita could hear her mother, Ekaterina, trying to calm her husband. But her mother's shallow voice was no match for the bombast, and her attempts just made him more furious with the world.

"That Stalin cocksucker! He made me like this. A pauper. A fucking pauper! A Jewish fucking pauper! And you . . ." Judit didn't have to see her father to know that his huge stubby finger was pointed at her mother. "You just fucking complain. And look at this house! A shithole. I work for nothing and you do nothing!"

Little Judita didn't really understand what her father was saying, but she knew from the terror in her mother's voice that it was very bad.

"Quiet. You'll have us all arrested!" As her mother's tears distorted her words, Judita could make out only "Siberia" and "gulag" again and again.

Ekaterina, Abel's wife of seventeen years, was terrified when he came home in one of these moods. Abel never laid a finger on her when he was sober; in fact, he was rather quiet and somber. But the moment he was drunk, which was often daily, Ekaterina knew what was to come. She would comfort the children when Abel Abramovich was asleep, telling them not to worry and that their daddy was only joking, but none of the children believed her. They'd lost faith in her words of reassurance long ago.

At the end of his working day, it had become a tradition that he'd go into a drinking circle around one of the bonfires on the building site, and the bottles of cheap vodka would be passed around, along with the even cheaper cigarettes. The workers bought bowls of soup from an old woman trundling her cart from site to site, corner to corner. Cheap booze, cheap borscht, and hours sitting on the filthy ground smoking and drinking with his comrades until the freezing cold drove them home.

Ekaterina wondered if her husband sounded off so vocally to his drinking friends about his disdain for Stalin. She suspected not. Such words were death. The OGPU, the secret police run by Vyacheslav Rudolfovich Menzhinsky, had ears everywhere; even children were known to report their parents. No, Ekaterina knew her husband saved these dangerous rants for when he got home. She also knew how thin the walls of their tiny two-room apartment were, and feared his voice more than his fists. His blows hurt only her, but his words could be the death of them all; they would simply disappear in the night, leaving behind just the whispered rumors of their neighbors. It was these thoughts that brought strength back to her voice.

"Abel, shut up," she hissed over the noise of the children's whimpering. "Shut your mouth or you'll get us all killed."

Abel was stunned by his wife's admonishments and opened his

mouth to reply but was silent. He stared at her, blinked several times, tried to remember what he was going to say, and then fell forward onto the floor like an overbalancing statue. His huge frame hit the wooden boards, and the room descended into sudden silence.

Judita redoubled her efforts to hold back her tears. On this night of all nights, she realized that she hated her father. In turn, with her child's logic, anything her father hated must be something good. She'd grown up to fear the uniforms of the police, but now, with the sounds of her father's bellowing still echoing in her ears, she found herself imagining the uniformed police dragging her father away. And she smiled grimly.

Ekaterina didn't try to move her husband. He was too big, too bulky; she let him sleep where he'd fallen on the floor. She reached under the table and pulled out little Judita Ludmilla, comforting her with kisses and a soft Yiddish melody she'd learned from her own mother. She stroked her hair gently, kissed her on the cheek, the neck, and blew softly into her ear. Then she walked into the bedroom, pulled back the bedclothes, and gently lay Judita alongside her older sister and brother, who had crawled out from under the sheets.

"Father is sleeping," she said. "He's very tired after a hard day's work. You must understand, my little ones. Your father works to support us all."

The children nodded, and Ekaterina lay down beside them. They all snuggled into her body, and her son, Maxim, whispered, "I don't like it when he shouts. And when he smells like that."

"I'm frightened as well," said Galina, Maxim's younger sister.

"Then let me tell you a story," Ekaterina said. "A nice story about a nice place. A story about Israel, where it's always warm and there's lots to eat. That's the place where the Jewish people came from. That's our real home, my children, not Moscow. And one day I'm going to take you back so you can enjoy your heritage. Do you remember me telling you about Israel? Do you want to hear that story, my babies?"

Judita scowled. "I'm not a baby, Mama."

Ekaterina smiled. She closed her eyes and held her children even tighter. It was hard to picture a land of warmth and security, but she tried. It was a place she'd never seen with her own eyes, only in picture books. She tried to remember what the images looked like. There was a seashore, and sand dunes, and a city of white stone with a beautiful golden dome in the middle.

Ekaterina took a deep breath and began. "In a city called Jerusalem, there once lived a man called King David. And he had many wives, as happened in those days. But one day on the roof of his palace, he looked down, and there he saw another beautiful woman called Bathsheba . . ."

The town of Yavne, Roman province of Judea

161 C.E. (first year of the co-emperorship of Marcus Aurelius and Lucius Verus)

TZADIK BAR CAIAPHAS flicked away a fat and lazy fly that had just landed atop the scrolls resting on his desk. Tzadik was the exiled high priest of Jerusalem, but as the city had been occupied as a Roman military base for decades, he, like all Jews, was forbidden for all time from freely entering Jerusalem, so his home was made beyond the city walls.

The insect, black and bloated from feasting on rotting summer meats left in the refuse heap on the outskirts of the city, rose to the ceiling the moment the priest's hands approached. It buzzed around the smoking oil lamp, then settled upside down on one of the wooden beams. Tzadik looked at it in wonder; why had the Lord Almighty created a creature that could spend its days living the wrong way up?

Tzadik had lost count of how many flies and midges and other irritating insects had interrupted his thoughts while he was working. It was a fiercely hot day, and although the drawn shades kept the blistering rays of the sun from entering the office, nothing could stop the enervating heat from draining all of his energy. It was like working in a tar pit. Beneath his robes of office, his golden turban, and his prayer shawl, his body was prickling in the airless cauldron that was his room. But he had work to do, and nothing must distract him.

These were troubled times. Things in Judea were always fraught, but during the past few weeks, it was as though the very fabric of the nation were the skin of a drum and some manic musician was pounding out an erratic and unpredictable beat. The death of one Roman emperor had seen the enthroning of two in his place: a conjoined rule between Antoninus's adoptive sons, Marcus Aurelius and Lucius Verus.

Tzadik and his fellow priests were well used to the tides that flowed through the fractured and torn cities and towns of the Roman province and, by and large, knew how to ride their rise and fall. The priests of Judea were nothing if not pragmatic. But the end of one reign and the beginning of another was always tumultuous and posed many questions for the priest. How would the new emperors treat their captured peoples? Would war begin in the north against Syria or the restive Mesopotamia? Would the new reign of the two emperors be filled with anti-Jewish edicts, new commands, new decrees, that would further damage his people?

Above all, would this new emperor allow them to enter the city of Jerusalem once more? The once beautiful city that King David and King Solomon had built had been destroyed by the emperor Titus to little more than piles of rubble. The emperor Hadrian had rebuilt it but as a Roman command post and without the temple that was the center of the Jewish world. Would they one day be allowed to rebuild the temple?

These were the questions that filled the mind of the priest, though he was not so removed from the truth of the world as to be ignorant to the reality faced by his people. Roman soldiers who would thrust a spear into a Jew just for the pleasure of it. Constant skirmishes between their Sadducee brethren and the Pharisees, from the remnants of the Zealots who still dreamed about an Israel free of Rome, from those who wanted to live in peace with the Romans, from those who wanted to worship the gods of other peoples, and from those who demanded that only Yahweh be worshipped. This was the cacophony that troubled the nights of Tzadik bar Caiaphas, and he had set himself to accommodating the Romans as best as possible so there was no repeat of the massacres that had decimated his people in the past.

The Romans were good administrators and terrible enemies. Provided that neither he, as high priest, nor any Jew in the nation went against a Roman decree, his people might be left alone. The Romans had many problems on the distant borders of their empire and were ruthless at crushing dissent.

It was a fine balancing act, but if he plied the road between the ambitious Romans and the intemperate Jews, acting as the water that doused both furnaces, then perhaps peace and hope could be maintained.

To that end, it had been peaceful in Judea for the past twenty-five years, since Simeon bar Kochbar had revolted against the Roman emperor Hadrian. So surprised were the Romans by the bar Kochbar rebellion that Hadrian had ordered his general Sextus Julius Severus to leave Britain and crush the rebels. And crush them he did, killing hundreds of thousands of people until the very rocks themselves cried out in grief.

The destruction of Jerusalem in the wake of the two rebellions was so great that even now, a quarter of a century later, the blood of the Jewish martyrs still stained the white walls of what remained of the city. And the Romans took great pride in the rebuilding of their quarters on what had once been Jerusalem, using those bloodstained blocks of stone.

It was after bar Kochbar's revolt that Hadrian had renamed the country Syria Palaestina, but Tzadik would never call it by that except in the presence of Romans.

For all the violence and bloodshed he had wrought, Hadrian had died peacefully in his bed, and his place was taken by his adoptive son Antoninus Pius. Though he continued to forbid the Jews to enter Jerusalem except on one day of the year to mourn their temple, life was at least peaceful. The persecution of the Jews, which had given such pleasure to Hadrian and his soldiers, was stopped, as was the depopulation of the cities.

During the reign of Emperor Antoninus, the Jews had slowly returned and the intellectual and social life of Israel resumed. Antoninus even repealed those edicts of Hadrian that denied burial of Jewish soldiers and martyrs who had fought the Romans, and whose bones had lain on the battlefield.

Tzadik bar Caiaphas sighed as he struggled to read his scrolls, his eyes misted by sweat from the burning heat of the day. He stared out the open window in the airless atmosphere and recalled the days of his youth. They were not pleasant memories. The stench of decomposing bodies; the ravaging dogs and wolves that roamed the streets with impunity, tearing rotting limb from rotting limb, crunching on bones that once were worshippers. Even prides of lions marauding.

Whenever he began to recall these events, he deliberately stopped his thoughts and instead contemplated his responsibilities now that he was high priest, acting under sufferance from Rome.

He sighed and wiped the sweat from his eyes. He was roasting and had to leave his office to find some sanctuary from the burning heat.

Carrying his scrolls under his arm, Tzadik walked out of his house and into the garden, where a breeze from the distant sea rustled the leaves. He headed toward a desk that his servants had set up the previous day underneath the gigantic canopy of a cypress tree. As he walked through his garden, he saw movement behind one of the bushes in the distance. It looked like the shadow of a very small man.

"Who's there?" he shouted. "Come out. My servants are nearby."

He stood and waited, and after a moment, the shadow revealed itself as a boy, seemingly ten or eleven years old. But as he walked nearer, Tzadik saw that he was older, perhaps fourteen or fifteen. A man but still a boy. A boy dressed in rags, his sandals broken, his clothes torn and filthy.

"Who are you?" demanded Tzadik.

The boy came closer, obviously in awe of the high priest's sumptuous regalia, his jeweled turban and heavy golden seals of office hanging around his neck. The child was looking up in amazement at Tzadik's head. The high priest understood that the boy's incredulity was because he came from the country and probably had never seen such dress—or any priestly garments.

"What's your name, boy, and why are you in my garden?"

"I'm Abram ben Yitzhak. I've walked from the north of Israel—"

"Silence, child."

Tzadik knew he was alone and safe but still cast his eyes about involuntarily to ensure that no one had heard the name the boy had called the Roman province. "Israel" was never to be used. It was death.

When Emperor Hadrian had crushed the Jewish rebellion, he had set about ensuring the dissolution of national identity that could lead to such rebellions. Hadrian had attempted to rob the Jews of their sense of self by making it a crime punishable by death to even call the land by its ancestral Jewish name. It was known to all as Syria Palaestina.

"Never use that name, boy."

Abram looked at the priest with curiosity.

"What do you want here?" Tzadik asked.

"I've been told to come and see the high priest of Israel to bring him greetings from—"

At the repeated transgression, Tzadik cut the boy off. "Who told you to seek me out? And what do you want with me?"

Abram looked up at the high priest. At first he hadn't been in awe, but the man's imperiousness did make him nervous. Despite the privations and hardships of his three weeks' walking from the Northern Galilee to the coastal city of Yavne, the constancy of his hunger and fear of bandits and nocturnal animals, he'd maintained his confidence and courage until now. Suddenly, he was tongue-tied.

"Well? Speak, boy; I'm a busy man. Who sent you to see me?"

"My friend. Rabbi Shimon bar Yochai."

High Priest Tzadik stared at the lad in shock. "Shimon . . . Shimon? He sent you?"

Abram nodded.

"You mean he's alive? He lives? Is he well? How does he fare? Where is he?"

"Of course he's alive. I fetch him food every day. He lives in a cave near where I live. I have come from the village of Peki'in in the Galilee on a mission given to me by Rabbi Shimon. He told me to come here first, master, and to see you. He said that of all the people in Israel, you were the only one I could trust to help me."

Tzadik grasped the boy urgently by the arm and led him to the desk in the shade of the tree. Abram didn't struggle against the high priest's firm grip. They sat, and Tzadik poured the boy a drink of freshly made pomegranate juice, which he drank eagerly to slake his fierce thirst. It was obvious to Tzadik just by looking at the boy that he was malnourished, so he uncovered a tray of honey bread and offered it to him. He then waited patiently while Abram ate five slices and drank another whole glass of juice.

Abram smiled at Tzadik. "You are the high priest, aren't you?" he asked softly.

Tzadik nodded. "Tell me of Rabbi Shimon. For many years, I thought he was dead. He was arrested by the Romans. I had heard he'd escaped, but nobody knew where he went. We all assumed the worst."

"He's alive. He lives in the cave with his son, and only I know where it is." Abram had a fierce determination to him. A resolve that defied his size and means.

"And what do they do in his cave, Rabbi Shimon and his son?"

Abram shrugged. "They talk and shout. I sometimes listen outside the mouth of the cave, but I don't understand what they're saying or the words they're using. They're always talking about shining lights and spirits and radiance and—"Abram shoved another slice of honey bread into his mouth and spoke while chewing. "I don't understand a thing, but they're always so serious. Until I come with the food. Then they laugh and joke with me. But when I leave, I hear them starting to shout at each other again. I don't think they like each other."

The high priest smiled. "It's just their way. They're mystics and don't think of this world but of the world of God. But Abram, tell me about the mission he gave you. What was so important that he'd risk the life of a boy your age in a land under the heel of the Romans?"

The boy stopped chewing, swallowed, and looked the priest up and down as if appraising him, judging him. The scrutiny annoyed Tzadik, annoyed and in other circumstances he might have berated the boy for his insolence. But the priest sensed what the boy had to say was not going to be good news.

Abram slowly took a ragged piece of cloth out of an inside pocket of his torn shirt. He unwrapped it on the table and exposed a seal, words written into once burning white alabaster, once beautifully radiant but after a millennium bearing stains of age. Tzadik picked it up gingerly, turning it in the sunshine to expose the writing that had been etched on the stone a thousand years earlier.

Tzadik closed his eyes and lifted his head to heaven, whispering a prayer. Then he looked at Abram. "Have you read these words?"

The boy shook his head. "Is the writing old? What does it say? Rabbi Shimon didn't tell me."

"Yes, my son. The writing is old, but the words are still what we say today. They were written a long, long time ago. It is a style of writing that we Jews haven't written for centuries. They say, 'I, Matanyahu, son of Naboth, son of Gamaliel, have built this tunnel for the glory of my king, Solomon the Wise, in the Twenty-second year of his reign.' Imagine that, Abram!"

The tunnel was one that ran from the floor of the Kedron Valley to the top of the mountain, coming out at the very foot of the temple. It created a water course to sustain the city.

"But the temple is no more. Rabbi Shimon said to me that Solomon's temple was rebuilt when the Jews returned from their Babylonian exile, but then King Herod rebuilt it and—"

"Yes," interrupted Tzadik, "the Temple of Herod is no more. All that remains standing is the Western Wall." The priest reverentially turned over the seal. "But our god Yahweh is still there. He remains, even though the stones no longer sit one on top of the other. He waits for us to rebuild."

The boy nodded. He didn't fully understand how Yahweh could still be in the temple if the temple was no longer standing, but there was much that he didn't understand. All he cared about was completing the task that the rabbi had set him: The alabaster stone must be returned, and Abram was to let no one stand in his way.

As if reading his mind, Tzadik looked up from the stone and into the eyes of Abram. "And your mission?" he asked the boy.

Abram hesitated. He felt nervous that the stone was no longer inside his shirt, where the rabbi had told him to keep it hidden and safe.

"To return it to the tunnel and hide it from the Romans, so that only Yahweh will see it, and then He'll know who built it. Rabbi Shimon says that this will mark the beginning of the rebuilding of the temple."

Tzadik reeled back in shock. "Return it to Jerusalem? Impossible. It's certain death for you. No Jew is allowed to enter Jerusalem, on pain of death! Only on the Ninth Day of the Month of Ab, just one day, and then the Romans watch everybody like hawks.

"No, my child, the revered Rabbi Shimon obviously isn't aware of what's happening in the world outside of his cave. No, you will not go to Jerusalem."

This was what the rabbi had warned him about. Not to trust anyone who would stand in his way. Yet the one person Rabbi Shimon had said he could trust, this high priest, was now one of those who would stand in his way. He didn't understand, but his immediate desire was to reach out and snatch the stone back from the priest and run. However, caution told him that he should resist and try to reason with him.

"But he told me to. And he told me that you could help me. That's why I've come here. Now you want me to return without my mission being a success. I can't return. I can't go back to Peki'in and tell him that I didn't do what he told me."

The high priest smiled and reached over to hold Abram's hand. "My boy, rest here, bathe, and when you're ready, return to Rabbi Shimon. I will keep this seal. It will be safe with me."

Abram looked at the high priest sternly. "No!"

The priest was shocked. No one ever said no to him, least of all a child.

"I must do as the rabbi ordered."

Tzadik sighed. "Then, like so many of your brothers and sisters, you will die at the hands of the Romans. No. I will not have your blood on my hands. The seal will stay with me . . ."

• • •

Abram was young but smart and careful and cunning. It was these traits that the old rabbi in the cave had recognized and that had encouraged him to entrust the boy with the task of returning the seal. Abram demonstrated all these qualities as he waited and watched in the dark while the lamps inside the home of the priest were, one by one, extinguished for the night.

Tzadik had wrested the seal from his grasp, and now he needed to get it back. The priest had offered him food and drink and water to bathe. He had even given Abram fresh clothes for the journey home. The boy had accepted all of these while watching carefully and waiting. The priest had also offered a bed for him to stay and rest in until he was ready to return. Abram agreed and had been shown to a small room at the back of the house where the servants lived.

He hadn't stayed in the room long before he gathered his things and as much food as he could carry and slipped out of the window. He doubled around through the dark to where he now crouched beneath the window that looked onto the high priest's study.

Once all the lamps had been extinguished in the house, he pushed himself up and over the ledge and into the study.

He crouched low and felt with his hands to orient himself. He could see nothing—the room was entirely blanketed in darkness—but he had known this would be the case once the servants had turned in for the night. He had studied the room carefully for an hour earlier in the evening, so he had a mental map of its layout.

Abram's hands found the wall and the stool that rested near it to his right. This told him that the priest's desk was directly ahead. The young man got to his hands and knees and crawled, counting off the distance in his mind. With one hand extended, he felt for the timber of the desk until his finger touched the wood, then he stopped once more. Abram listened carefully but could hear only his own breath and the beating of his heart. He'd never been a thief. He'd always followed the injunctions of the Bible. Now . . . this . . .

Old Rabbi Shimon back in Peki'in had said to seek out the high priest but had also warned him to trust no one else. These thoughts commanded the boy's mind as he turned left at the desk, still on his hands and knees, and headed toward the shelves of scrolls and parchments against the far wall. It was here that Abram had watched, with eyes barely above the lip of the windowsill, as the priest had hidden away the seal Abram must now retrieve.

The lad was aware of the sins he was about to commit. The priest had taken the seal away from him, but in Jewish law, did that mean that it belonged to Tzadik? And if it did, was Abram about to break one of Father Moses's commandments? What would the priest do if he was caught? Would he be beaten or whipped or worse? Was it an even greater wrong to defy a priest? Tzadik had been explicit in his decree that the seal should stay with him and Abram was to return home without fulfilling his charge. And yet Abram knew that his only true loyalty was to the rabbi and the mission on which he had been sent.

"Trust no one . . ." The words of the rabbi echoed in Abram's mind and gave him courage enough to defy the high priest and break the commandments.

Abram's extended hand came into contact with a loosely wound parchment scroll. It was thin and light, and the small pressure from Abram's hand knocked it from the shelf. It clattered off the ledge and rattled against another, larger scroll. The two together tumbled off the shelf in the dark, falling to the floor.

The sound would not have been so loud had the night not been so deathly quiet. To Abram's ears, the falling scrolls sounded like a short, sharp spasm of rattling bones. He froze and turned his head, but there was only darkness. He listened for the sound of footsteps and opened his eyes wider to find any light from newly lit lamps that might have been coming his way.

Long slow moments passed and then a distant shuffle, somebody moving in another part of the house. He had to move more quickly. He turned back to the shelf to find the small wooden box he'd seen the priest pull from the top of the shelf where he'd placed the precious seal for safekeeping. Abram drew himself to his feet and pushed himself up onto the tips of his toes to try and reach the top shelf.

Behind him and beyond the door, the rustling was combined with a swishing—feet on the floor and the swirl of clothes. Abram dared to turn his head and saw a small soft glow down the hallway. Someone was coming.

Abram pushed himself higher, one hand holding on to a shelf to help force his free hand higher. His fingers traced the edge of the shelf for the corner of the box.

The sound in the hallway turned from rustling to footsteps, and the glow of the lamp the person carried began to illuminate the room. Abram could now see his fingers, and they were but a fraction away from the box. With a last effort, almost a jump, he grabbed the corner of the box, sliding it off the shelf and catching it with his other hand.

The lamplight grew brighter and the footsteps beat on the stone floor; the person would soon turn the corner into the room. With the box in his hand, Abram spun to the window, then turned back to the doorway. The distance was too great; he wouldn't make it to the window before the servant rounded the corner and entered the office. Between him and the window was the desk of the high priest, covered in scrolls and with parchments heaped up around it. It was his only choice. Abram dived under the table, clutching the box to his chest, and lay as still and silent as he could, his eyes never leaving the doorway.

The lamplight grew brighter, spilling a yellow glow into the office until a foot appeared, followed by legs and a long gown. Abram held his breath as he saw the feet stop. He knew the desk would not fully conceal him; it was only a matter of time before the man would see some telltale sign of him, raise the alarm or a weapon, and then . . . .

Abram trembled. It was dark under the desk, but the light from the lamp would soon reveal him. The boy's mind raced as he considered running, or staying and facing his accuser. He felt the muscles of his legs tense beneath him and his fingers bind tighter around the wood of the small box in his hands.

The feet moved closer and then, as the light swung around, stopped.

Abram's heightened senses heard an intake of breath. It was all that the boy needed to act.

His cramped legs surged upward, pushing his body as he extended his hand above his head. He heaved on the underside of the table with all his might. It was not a large table, but it was dense and heavy. Abram's small frame barely lifted the table's feet off the floor, but they did lift it off center and, with all the force of his legs uncoiling, heaved it over on its side. The table tipped its contents at the man with the lamp and crashed with a booming thud so close to his bare feet that he was forced to leap back or else have his toes crushed.

The man dropped the lamp to the ground, breaking the pottery and spilling oil over the floor. The burning wick instantly caught the vapor of the oil and swished into flame.

Abram turned toward the window and bounded across the remaining space to escape. Behind him he heard the man yelp as the flames licked at the dry, flammable parchment.

"Fire!" screamed the old man. Abram ran but felt relief that the word had not been "thief." He heaved himself out of the window headfirst, one arm extended to cushion the blow with the ground, the other tightly gripping the box pressed against his belly.

Abram rolled on the ground and quickly scrambled to his feet. He allowed himself a moment to cast his eyes back to the house and saw the bright glow of flame through the window cavity and the scrambling efforts of the man to douse the flames and save the scrolls. Then Abram heard the sounds of the house waking up in panic and the high priest bellowing, demanding answers from the Almighty for what had just happened.

He'd never intended to start a fire, but as he ran down the hill and into the enfolding darkness, he knew that it would buy him time to escape. The servants would be intent on dousing the flames and not on chasing him.

Abram ran faster than he had ever run in his life. In Peki'in, life was never spent running, not since he was a child. People walked slowly past Roman columns, people walked cautiously. Now he was running, not because he was a thief and not because he was an arsonist but because Rabbi Shimon had entrusted him with a sacred mission, and even though he might have to break some of the Almighty's commandments, he'd put the seal back in the tunnel in Jerusalem, whatever the cost.

As he ran farther and farther from the high priest's house, Abram's mind began to clear. Reason took over from panic. He stopped when the house and the flames were no longer visible, and sat on the ground, breathing heavily. Rabbi Shimon had told him that the high priest was the only man he could trust; yet he'd taken the seal and told Abram to return home. Rabbi Shimon had told him that this seal, which had come from the hands of a man who knew King

Solomon, was of great value to his people and must be returned for the sake of all.

If he couldn't trust the high priest, whom could he trust? He was all alone in the land of the Romans, far from his mother and father, far from Rabbi Shimon. He had nobody to ask. All he could do was rely on himself. And that frightened the youngster more than anything.

Kibbutz Beit Yitzhak,
Northern Palestine
1941

NOBODY ON THE kibbutz paid any attention when the truck coughed and spluttered its way up the hill and finally, like an old asthmatic straining for air, crawled through the kibbutz gates. It was so ancient, some joked that it had been used by Moses to deliver the Children of Israel over to the other side of the Red Sea to escape the Pharaoh.

The kibbutzniks could always hear, and sometimes smell, its arrival minutes before it came into view. It was on its last legs but beloved by all.

Young Shalman straightened his back when he saw the truck arrive. Working in the henhouse was smelly, especially in the heat of summer, but the kids on the kibbutz helped their parents in the day-to-day work, and he enjoyed ensuring there were enough eggs for breakfast. He watched as the driver jumped out. These were only short breaks, but they refreshed his mind and eased his body from the hard work that he and the other kids of the kibbutz, his brothers and sisters, had to do to stay alive.

Dov, the driver, dropped out of the cabin onto the dusty ground. He was a short and wiry man, but there was an invisible strength in his body, and nobody messed with him. Dov, like Shalman in the henhouse, straightened his back after the long drive and looked over at the group of men and women in the fields. They were preparing the land for next season's crop. Some of the women, wearing the traditional gray trousers, flannel shirts, and scarves, were using long-handled hoes to weed ahead as the men, in shirts and shorts and pointed blue-and-white hats, were hand-planting the seeds behind them.

Dov had been the kibbutz's truck driver for years. In Germany, before the war had begun, he'd been a railwayman in Berlin, which somehow qualified him to drive "Adolf the Beast," as the truck was affectionately known. Dov had managed to escape Germany with his wife and six children just before the closure of the borders. It was an act of daring and courage that had saved his entire family from the gas chambers.

The other thing for which Dov was renowned was being a thief. It was he who went on nighttime stealing missions. He and a few others would park their truck a long way from where the British Tommies had set up camp during maneuvers, then crawl on their hands and knees and stomachs, sometimes for a mile or more. In total silence, they would steal rifles and ammunition inadvertently left against a rock or a tree after a patrol by exhausted British soldiers prostrate in the heat of Palestine.

Dov had managed to steal more than forty rifles and thousands of rounds of ammunition from the British in the years he'd been the kibbutz's "lifter." An amiable fellow, he was well liked by his comrades and had friends in many other parts of Northern Palestine. He'd even befriended the inhabitants of the nearby villages such as Peki'in, where he would trade the produce of the kibbutz for supplies.

Everyone in the kibbutz knew what Dov did, but that didn't stop the wiry little man from scanning to see if anyone was watching before he peeled back the tarpaulin cover. However, Dov didn't see that Shalman had crept up around the front of the truck and was visibly shocked when he heard the boy say: "What did you find, Dov?"

"Hell, don't go sneaking up on me like that, kid."

Shalman was unperturbed. "What did you find?"

Dov smiled, looked around once more to make sure it was just him and the boy, then pulled out from the truck bed an object wrapped in an oil cloth.

"What is it?" asked Shalman.

"Not something your dad would want you playing with." Dov flipped the cloth open to reveal a revolver in shiny gunmetal gray. "Know what this is?"

"A gun," replied Shalman.

"It's a pistol," corrected Dov. "It's an officer's pistol. A Webley. I took it from a British officer."

"Did you kill him?" asked Shalman without emotion, only genuine curiosity.

"Whoa, now, that's a question your imma wouldn't like you asking and certainly wouldn't like me telling. Even if it were true . . ." Dov gave the boy a wink and Shalman smiled. "You can hold it if you want."

The lad held out his hand eagerly and Dov placed the pistol on his palm. The weight surprised him, but Dov deftly reached over and showed him how to do it. "Hold it tight, boy. You never know when you might need a gun like that. We've got Brits and Arabs on all sides, Shalman. You never, ever forget that."

From the field where he was tilling the soil, Shalman's father, Ari, straightened up, stretched out his back, and noticed his son talking to Dov. He saw something in Shalman's hand and felt a moment of concern. It was probably Dov's latest acquisition. Ari shook his head. Why was Dov always showing the guns he stole to the children of the kibbutz? Didn't they deserve a normal childhood in this war zone of a land? Hadn't the Jewish people learned enough about guns, now that they were being forced to fight against the British and were the victims of these Nazis in Germany?

There was a squeal of children's voices as a gaggle of six young ones came running toward Dov, arms outstretched, ready to embrace their father. Ari couldn't help but smile even as he saw Dov quickly hide the pistol away in his coat and kneel down to embrace his kids. The throng of small bodies knocked Dov off his feet and sent him sprawling in a mass of tickles and giggles onto the ground.

The peace of the moment was short-lived. Suddenly, four British army Jeeps and a large truck roared furiously through the front entrance of the kibbutz, still open from when Dov arrived. Everybody working in the field looked up in shock as the vehicles screeched to a halt, throwing up stones and clouds of dirt. Ten British soldiers jumped out and fanned in a protective line in front of their vehicles, rifles pointing at the kibbutz inhabitants.

Shalman's eyes turned back to Dov and saw him quickly push the children off, stand, and move sharply to his truck so he could pull the cover over the back. He then ordered the children to return to their mother.

Last out of the vehicles was the commander of the group, a man Ari already knew; he was the senior officer who had remained sitting in the Jeep while his NCOs had intimidated the family when they were having a picnic on the beach ten years earlier. Though Ari wasn't the kibbutz leader, he walked slowly out of the field, as though this were a daily occurrence, and meandered over to the commander, his hand outstretched in greeting.

Reluctantly, the major took it. A nod was his only greeting before he said, "That truck"—pointing to Adolf the Beast—"who owns that?"

Ari didn't turn to face any of the kibbutz residents who gathered around. But he knew that Dov was standing near the truck beside Shalman.

"This is a kibbutz, Major. We all own it," said Ari. With a smile, hoping to remove some of the tension from the air, he added, "It's a piece of junk. We'll pay you to take it away."

The major didn't appreciate the joke. His face remained stern. In a clipped voice, he said, "I'll ask the question again. And don't mess about. Understand? Now, who was driving that truck?"

By this time more of the community had gathered around. Women pushed children behind them, but all stood and watched the soldiers. In turn the soldiers gripped their rifles more tightly. Ari sensed all this and sweat beaded his brow.

"Can I ask what this is all about? We've done nothing wrong. We're farmers."

"Answer my question. Who was the driver of that truck?"

Ari turned his head to look briefly at the people gathered nearby. All knew the answer to the question, but none knew what Ari would say. Dov had retreated into the crowd, his children, frightened, gathered about him—all six holding on to a hand or a pant leg. Dov's eyes met Ari's, wide and still and uncertain.

"Now! Right now! Who was driving?" commanded the major.

One of the soldiers behind the officer nervously raised his rifle and a woman nearby let out an involuntary whimper. Dov's eyes darted back and forth like a trapped animal's, but he didn't move. Then Shalman stepped from the crowd toward his father.

"Stay back, Shalman," said Ari, raising a hand to ward him off.

"I won't ask again, farmer," the major said. There was no mistaking the menace in his voice.

"Abba?"

The silence weighed leaden in the air as Ari looked once more to the mass of frightened children about Dov's legs. Dov's six young children.

"It was me," Ari said softly. He heard a gasp behind him. So did the major, who continued to stare deeply into his eyes before he turned and barked an order.

"Search it."

Three of the soldiers ran over to the truck, and the people nearby parted like a field of reeds. The soldiers threw back the cover while the other soldiers stayed where they were, pointing their rifles at the men and women in the field as though daring them to move.

Ari wanted to say something, but there was nothing to say. He knew what the soldiers would find.

"Sir!" shouted one of the privates. "Here, sir. Look at this, sir."

The major walked over, and one of his men handed him a rifle pulled from the truck and hidden under a blanket. He turned back to Ari with a look of disgust and incredulity. With a raised eyebrow, he said, "Once more! Just to be absolutely clear! Were you the driver of this vehicle? You understand the consequences of your answer, don't you?"

Out of the corner of his eye, Ari saw Dov begin to move forward.

"Yes, it was me. Only me."

From a short distance away in the field, Devorah cried, "Ari. Don't!"

He turned and smiled and nodded. "I'll be all right. I'm just going to clear up a misunderstanding. I'll be home soon."

The major stepped forward and whispered to Ari, "Don't be a fool, man. I can smell the field on you. We both know you weren't driving. And you know the consequences if I take you away."

Ari looked into the eyes of the major and shrugged. Softly, he repeated, "It was me."

The major stepped back a pace and said to Ari, "Oh well, one Jew's as good as another."

The entire group of men and women in the fields, knowing what was about to happen, began to murmur and move toward the British soldiers, who immediately raised their rifles from waist height to shoulder height, pointing them at the kibbutzniks.

Ari feared what might follow and shouted, "Stop. Everybody. Don't be stupid. I'll go with these soldiers. I'll be all right."

Two soldiers came forward to seize him by the arms. Ari turned to look at Shalman, who stared back up at his father. Ari went to say something to his son but turned his eyes to Dov. "Look after Shalman, will you, Dov? Treat him like you treat your other children. I'm making him your responsibility."

And with that, Ari was driven away in a cloud of dust. It was the last time that Devorah saw her husband and the last image that young Shalman had of his father—driven off as a prisoner between two British soldiers.

MOSCOW, USSR
1943

FOURTEEN-YEAR-OLD JUDITA TRIED to stifle her yawn but failed miserably as the elderly rabbi looked up from his Talmud just as she was putting her hand to her mouth. The rabbi looked closely at her to see whether there were any marks remaining on her face. Two weeks ago she'd appeared in his class looking like a whore with cheap makeup plastered all over her eyes and cheeks, an unsophisticated way of covering up the black eye and slaps her father had given her the night before. The rabbi sighed. Such a brilliant girl; such a beast of a father.

And somehow it was worse when it happened in the dreadful winters of Moscow. Children couldn't leave the house, and so the tensions caused drunken fathers to flare up, and so many wives and children were beaten. The rabbi thought of this as he pondered another problem with the winter months in Moscow. The windows of the basement where he taught the children were closed and opaque from condensation, yet the paraffin heater made the room horribly stuffy. Judita wasn't the only one yawning, but somehow she was always the one Rabbi Ariel saw, the one he always looked at first when he glanced up from reading.

His half-moon glasses were perched on the end of his nose, his huge gray beard permanently curled from his constant stroking when he was talking or listening, his battered hat askew on the back of his head. Reb Ariel treated Judita more strictly than any of the other students in the tiny classroom. But she knew, because he often told her parents, that his discipline was harsh because of her potential; she was by far the brightest student in the small school, and he was determined that she would become a great figure in the Russian Jewish community, even though she was a girl.

Classes were held in the basement of a public theater on Bolshaya Bronnaya near Tverskoy Boulevard. The building was once the Lyubavicheskaya Synagogue until it was appropriated by the Soviet authorities for nonreligious public entertainment. Though the students were all the same age, some were barely able to read a word of Hebrew. But Judita was able to read the Hebrew words as though they were as familiar to her as Russian. She was a natural linguist and could speak a few words of almost any language just by listening to two people speaking it. Similarly, she could speak and read fluent Yiddish and enjoyed smatterings of Polish and German.

A young boy was reading aloud, wrestling with the words, and had already spent long minutes trying to get his tongue around the phrases. The rabbi shook his head sadly and said, "Moishe, listening to you, I'm sure that the Messiah will decide not to come to earth for another generation. Your Hebrew is terrible. Learn, child. Learn! Practice. Now, Judita Ludmilla, read the next section."

Without looking up, flawlessly, and in a voice that was both strong and commanding of attention, the tall, thin, handsome girl began to read the Hebrew as though reading a novel by Pushkin. "*By your messengers you have defied the Lord, and have said, 'With the multitude of my chariots, I have come up to the height of the mountains, to the innermost parts of Lebanon; and I will cut down its tall cedars, and its choice fir trees; and I will enter into his—'*"

Judita abruptly stopped reading and glanced up. In the silence, the entire class looked at her, very few of them really understanding more than the odd word of Hebrew she'd just read but comprehending that she had stopped short of finishing. The rabbi also raised his head and felt doom descending. He knew that expression. Judita understood the Hebrew and was about to ask one of her philosophical questions.

"Rabbi, why does it matter where the wood came from?"

The rabbi looked at her curiously, as if failing to understand the question. Judita continued. "I mean, I understand the story, but we live here in Russia. Why should this story matter?"

The rabbi was used to Judita's questioning, but this was more blunt than he had anticipated. He pushed out a reply: "These stories tell us who we are, where we come from, our faith that God has chosen us—"

Judita cut off the rabbi by changing tack. "But Comrade Lenin said that all modern religions and churches, every kind of religious organization, are always considered by Marxism as the organs of bourgeois reaction, used for the exploitation and stupefaction of the working class."

The rabbi was speechless as the class drew a collective breath. He smiled, trying to brave her communist leanings. "Yes, child. All *modern* religions. Ours isn't a modern religion. Ours is the oldest and best and—"

Judita pushed on bravely. "If what Comrade Lenin said is true, and of course it has to be, then should we not reject these stories? What does it matter if we are Jewish?"

The rabbi was unused to being subjected to an inquisition by a fourteen-year-old girl, dealing with the difference between the doctrine of the state and the doctrine of his faith. He banged his fist on the table, yelling, "Judita!"

But as soon as her name left his lips, he regretted it. The harsh booming of his voice shocked the class, and even plucky Judita cowered for an instant. He realized in the shock of her face that he reminded the poor brilliant child of her father. At the same time, he was furious that here, in the confines of his school, a Jewish girl could reject all that he represented, all that he was.

The distant noise of a door creaking made all of the students shift their attention from Judita to the front of their classroom. With the secret police everywhere, any unexpected noise could herald danger. They all looked at the rabbi, who smiled and nodded to give them confidence, but they knew from his forced smile that he was feeling as ill at ease as they were.

The students listened intently to steps on the upper floors walking in the direction of the basement room. Then the steps—two or three or even more men—could be heard descending the stairs. The rabbi put his finger to his mouth and whispered, "Quiet, children. Silence."

All the boys and girls, as well as Rabbi Ariel, looked in fear to the door. Any interruption these days almost always spelled trouble. The door burst open, and three men stood there dressed in the uniform of the NKVD, the Soviet secret police: brown army jackets, brown trousers, heavy black boots, and a cap of purple and red stripes above the shiny black peak.

A tall man with a bushy mustache like Comrade Stalin's stepped forward into the room. He was followed by the other two men. All the soldiers were wearing mustaches. Without even glancing at the rabbi, the first man surveyed the boys and girls slowly, letting them know that he was in command of the room. Only then did he turn and acknowledge the rabbi, who was staring wide-eyed at the three newcomers.

NKVD officers usually came at night to a person's home. They never knocked but pushed the door in with their feet, dragged the oc-cupants out to a truck, and then drove off. The householders were never, ever seen again. A new family would be in residence the fol-lowing day, as though they'd lived there all their lives. Rumors said that hundreds of thousands, perhaps millions, of people disappeared, never to be seen again. No explanation, no comments from the neigh-bors, and certainly never a mention of the family who'd lived there the day before.

The rabbi started to speak, but the leader glared at him in such a way that all he could say was "What can I . . . ?"

"You have a pupil. Judita Ludmilla Magidovich, daughter of Abel Abramovich Magidovich and his wife, Ekaterina Davidovna Magi-dovich. Where is she?"

The rabbi gulped and shook his head.

Without realizing the implications, everybody in the room stared at Judita the moment the Russian policeman mentioned her name. She tried to diminish the size of her body. Ignoring the rabbi, the cap-tain of the NKVD said, "Judita Ludmilla?"

She stood, and the rabbi tried to catch her eye, shaking his head fiercely, silently begging her to sit down. But she didn't.

"Excellency?" she asked. "Why do you want me?"

He examined her. Most people whom he confronted, either at night in their homes or in the prison cells of the Lubyanka, looked at him in utter horror. But this girl looked him directly in the eyes and didn't flinch at all.

"Come with me."

She didn't move. After a long moment, she asked calmly, "What have I done?"

"I said come with me."

"And I asked what I've done."

The students, the rabbi, and the other soldiers looked at Judita in astonishment. Nobody ever questioned the orders of a commanding officer, especially not a schoolgirl. And a Jewess. Instead of drawing out his gun or screaming a command at her, he said, "Your country needs you. Now, don't dawdle, girl. Follow me."

Judita looked at the rabbi, who stood and said, "Excellency, surely you've made a mistake. Look at her. She's only a child. Let me go with you instead. I'll answer all your questions. Let me send these children home, and—"

"Silence!" said the officer, and he nodded to the other men in his troop, who walked aggressively through the rows, pushing desks out of the way, and grabbed the young girl's arm to hurry her to the door.

Before she left the room, she said to the rabbi, "Please, Reb Ariel, tell Mama and Papa that I'm fine and that all will be well. This is Russia . . ."

Once outside the school, Judita found herself in a truck on the way to the center of Moscow. She sat quietly on the seat between the captain, whose name she didn't know, and the other men, who were never identified.

"Where are you taking me?" she asked softly.

"You're going to the Lubyanka," the captain said, looking out of the window at the empty streets of the nation's capital.

She gulped. Every Muscovite, every Russian, was terrified of the Lubyanka, even if they'd never been to the center of Moscow. It had a fearsome reputation. It was a place people went and never emerged, never returned. Some people said at night you could hear screams from inside.

"What have I done?" asked Judita, desperate not to cry.

The captain finally turned and looked at her. "To ask a question like that, Judita Ludmilla, indicates a guilty conscience."

Judita held her breath and fell silent. She knew she'd find out soon enough.

• • •

Comrade Lavrentiy Pavlovich Beria walked the cold Moscow streets with his coat pulled tight around him. It wasn't a long journey to the Kremlin, perhaps a couple of hundred yards at most, but it could be the most dangerous journey in the world. Not because of criminals or car traffic. Nor because of the numerous checkpoints that were a constant threat to Moscow citizens. Beria was the state security administrator and chief of the NKVD, instantly recognizable to any soldier and therefore safe in that respect.

No, the reason the fifteen-minute walk was so dangerous was because he never knew whether he would return to his office or be murdered at the whim of his leader. Beria was powerful and influential but always walking the tightrope plucked by Iosif Vissarionovich Stalin, always in danger of being tossed into the abyss.

The walk was from the hill on Teatralnyy, down the street from Beria's office in the Lubyanka, past the Bolshoi Theater and the Metropol Hotel and through the massive gates that punctuated the Kremlin's red walls.

Earlier that day his telephone had rung with the summons to meet with the general secretary of the Central Committee of the Communist Party of the Soviet Union. Beria assumed a particularly stern voice to the leader's assistant, saying that although he was very busy dealing with great matters of state, he would make time to see the general secretary and would be there as soon as possible. The truth was that the moment the telephone's bell sounded, apprehension had gripped him. He could have ordered his car and chauffeur, but he needed the walk. He needed to be focused. He needed to think over the past couple of meetings with Stalin and try to work out if he'd done something that might have angered the man. But what? Nothing! Or possibly . . .

He walked through the private entrance in the massive red walls of the Kremlin and found his way over the vast courtyards to where the nation's most powerful man lived. While he was climbing the stairs to Stalin's office, he pondered the deeply divergent paths the meeting might take. If Stalin was in one of his jovial moods, the two Georgians would sit for hours eating piroshky and drinking vodka and Alazani wine until the general secretary fell asleep in his chair and Beria could stagger home or to the apartment of one of his mistresses.

But if Stalin needed to be told something, often for the third or fourth time, Beria would have to pretend that the question had never been asked and answer with enthusiasm, praising the leader for his perception. On occasion, if he was lucky, Stalin only wanted his advice on something or confirmation of an order, and then he'd be dismissed, always with thanks. These were some of the better scenarios of how the meeting might go. Sometimes on his way to Stalin's offices, Beria would stop off at the GUM department store, opposite the Kremlin walls in Red Square. There, he'd be shown into a private room where his usual Georgian vodka would be ready on ice, along with some Beluga caviar. This time he obeyed the call of his master.

He was ushered immediately into Stalin's offices and found the leader sitting at his desk. Beria tried to see what he was looking at, but the general secretary's eyes were dead. Expressionless. It was impossible to tell what he was thinking. His entire face was like a death mask. It moved only when he spoke, and then his lips barely enunciated the words.

Beria sat and pondered Stalin as though Medusa the Gorgon were on the opposite side of the desk, waiting on his master to acknowledge his presence. Yet Stalin sat reading, making notes. Then he looked up and out the window, staring around the room, looking through Beria, not at him, as though he were invisible. Did ten minutes pass or an hour?

Beria surreptitiously glanced through the window at the onion domes of St. Basil's Cathedral. It gave him comfort. Not because of any sentimentality for his Russian Orthodox upbringing but, rather, because of his latest stratagem. He'd spent many weeks going over maps of Palestine and the entire area of Arabia, reading the documents of the Jews and Arabs who lived there and the details of the British mandate that enabled the effete government in London to rule the region.

In his readings and study, he'd been surprised to learn that the very church just across the way, the church on the grounds of the Red Square and others in the center of Moscow, were viewed by the Russian priesthood as the equivalent of the holy city of Jerusalem. They even believed that St. Basil's Cathedral was the very Temple of Solomon itself. This seemed an odd idea. Did these idiot priests have any idea just how far the sun-drenched white stone of Jerusalem was from freezing soil and the iron sky of a wintry Moscow? How much would the stupid Muscovite priests, still faithful to the god banished from Russia by Marx, love to be part of a global plan where Moscow would become the new Jerusalem?

Eventually, waiting for Stalin to acknowledge his presence in the office became too much and Beria coughed apologetically. It was a cautious cough, not enough to be heard but enough to make a disturbance in the funereal quiet of Stalin's office.

Suddenly aware of the disturbance, Stalin stopped writing and looked slowly up at Beria, sitting opposite him across the desk. "Good afternoon, Lavrentiy Pavlovich. I've kept you waiting. I had to finish this communication. Now, you wanted to see me."

Beria swallowed, though Stalin's forgetfulness and confusion were not unusual. The general secretary had summoned him, but in the half hour it had taken him to arrive, Stalin had forgotten the reason he'd sent for Beria, or seemingly that he'd summoned him at all. Beria made no indication of this and pressed ahead.

"Comrade Chairman, if you remember, you and I had previously discussed the use of Jewish operatives in Palestine. To this end I have begun the process and brought in the potentials. As of yesterday, I am delighted to inform you that the last Jewish spy to be trained has just been put into place. She's a very young woman, little more than a girl, but utterly brilliant. A real asset. Once she is trained, Operation Outgrowth can begin."

"What?"

Surely he remembered. It had been discussed last week. Beria spoke again. "Operation Outgrowth. The plan that you approved yourself last year. We've been searching for the right personnel, and during this year we've identified them. Now we've drawn them together. Twelve of them in total. Like Jesus' disciples. All young Jews, utterly loyal to Mother Russia, but gifted in the language and cultural knowledge of the Jews."

Stalin continued to stare at Beria, who found the heat in the room overwhelming and began to sweat. Was it all going wrong? Why didn't Stalin react? Stalin's face was still a mask. Beria couldn't tell whether or not he understood, or agreed, or was about to explode with rage.

Nervously, Beria continued. "Allow me to detail the context for your approval. You suggested that as the war against the Nazis was at last turning in our favor, it was time to look beyond the boundaries of the glorious Soviet motherland and think of a new Europe without the boundaries that were in place before the madman Hitler's adventure. We know, when Germany is defeated, that we might absorb Poland, Czechoslovakia, Hungary, and the petty principalities of Bosnia, Herzegovina, Albania, Romania, and so on. But there is also the matter of our navy . . ."

Beria looked at Stalin expectantly, but the chairman's face remained like granite. Did he understand? Did he remember? It was impossible to read Stalin's mind. He might be forgetful—except where his enemies were concerned—but he was also cunning and guileful and so deadly dangerous.

Again Beria swallowed before speaking. "Might I respectfully remind you, Comrade General Secretary, about the outcome of the Moscow Conference that we've just concluded. This did more than agree on an allied pact against the Nazis. Britain's Anthony Eden, the American Cordell Hull, and our own Vyacheslav Mikhailovich Molotov all agreed on ways to bring this war to a just and glorious conclusion. We must also prepare for the disposition of the world after Hitler and his fascists are destroyed and become a footnote in Russia's long and glorious history.

"The British and Americans think they'll be able to acquire territory, so we must be prepared to expand before them. In this, you believed it was the sands of Persia, Arabia, and the oil that lies beneath that should be our focus. But you also thought much further; it was your idea to create a permanent base for our Soviet navy in the warm waters of the eastern Mediterranean."

He hoped the phrase would alert Stalin's memory. He waited for some response, but Stalin continued to stare at him. He wondered whether the man had fallen asleep with his eyes open, knowing that Stalin slept one or two hours a night and catnapped during the day.

Beria persisted. "So that we can remove our navy permanently from the Black Sea and base it in the open waters of the Mediterranean . . . so that we're never again bottled in by Turkey."

Stalin didn't blink, frown, or move a muscle of his face. For Beria, it was like talking to a brick wall.

Beria now felt desperate. "Comrade, when Russia is victorious in this evil fascist war, the time is ripe for us to make great gains in the territory of the Middle East. For its oil. For the warm-water port that Mother Russia has always been denied. Palestine is a hotbed of internecine warfare, with Jews fighting Arabs fighting the British. We know that the mufti of Palestine has allied himself with Hitler, so when Hitler is defeated, the Jews will fight the Arabs. And both will no doubt turn on the British. This is a chaos we—" Beria caught himself. "This is a chaos you clearly saw our ability to exploit."

Stalin nodded. A nod so small and subtle, many would not have seen it at all. But Beria saw it.

"Comrade Chairman, this is how I . . . you . . . proposed that we use our Fifth Column Jewish spies within Palestine. To lever our influence and create a Jewish communist puppet state and satellite of Moscow when Palestine gains its independence from its British colonizers, which will give us a warm-water port in the Mediterranean for our glorious navy."

Suddenly, to Beria's surprise, Stalin came to life, stood from his chair, and walked over to a huge map of the world hanging on the wall of his office. The moment he stood, Beria sprang out of his chair and stood to attention. Stalin said nothing but simply regarded the map, silently inviting Beria to continue. Beria walked over and tried to make himself slightly smaller than Stalin, who himself was short;

there were no men taller than Stalin in his command structure. All the tall men had been removed.

Beria looked at the map and cleared his throat. "Here," he said, pointing to the Black Sea and the port of Sevastopol, "is where the Russian fleet is currently moored. But we are in danger of our fleet being locked up from winter ice here in the north . . ." Beria pointed to the Russian Baltic ports on the border of the Arctic. "And on the other side of Russia," he said, moving his hand over the enormous expanse of the nation to the far eastern city of Vladivostok, "the ports are frozen six months of the year. And while our navy is moored in the Black Sea, it's in danger of being bottled up by the Turks in Istanbul. Operation Outgrowth is a concept that aims to deliver us a permanent warm-water port in the Mediterranean where we can come and go at our will. Our Russian navy will be a foil to the U.S. navy, which feels it can roam the globe freely, as it will be to the British and the French and whoever else underestimates our strength."

Slowly, Stalin nodded once more and said, "It is a good plan, and you have understood my directions well."

"Thank you, Comrade Chairman."

It was Beria's plan, one born of a keen intellect for strategy and covert operations. A plan that he had brought to Stalin those many months ago. But he played the part that must be played.

"The world will come to recognize your genius once our glorious Soviet fleet has sailed out of Sevastopol and is moored safely in the warm and welcoming waters of Haifa and Jaffa in a new country that will be called Israel."

Stalin nodded again and then added, "You said something about a girl. What girl?"

Beria was somewhat surprised by the question but quickly responded, "We acquired her from her religious school. She speaks the Jews' language of Hebrew well, and she's intelligent. Very intelligent. And she is"—Beria looked for the right word—"she's receptive and will be totally, unquestioningly loyal to the state and the Soviet socialist cause. Once her training is finished, she'll be my thing."

At this, Stalin raised a thick eyebrow. Beria continued. "We're about to begin training her with the other young men and women in weaponry, spycraft, urban warfare, geopolitics, and Marxist ideology. Once her training is complete, she'll be deployed into greater Palestine."

Stalin looked back at the map, then at Beria. He nodded. "Yes. Good." He turned his attention back to the map. "Remind me of the location of Jerusalem."

Central Israel

161 C.E.

ABRAM WAS EXHAUSTED and starving.

The road south from Yavne had taken the lad across the coastal plain that led down to the Mediterranean Sea. Living in the mountainous Galilee, he had never been to the seaside, though from a high hilltop, he'd once spotted the ocean.

Now he was fascinated by its vastness, its constantly changing moods and smells. At daybreak, it filled the air with the fresh and perfumed tang of a mountain forest. At the height of day, it was salty and rancid, smelling more like the carcass of a dead animal. As the night fell and the stars flooded the firmament, it smelled like a freshly washed blanket.

For the first few days, he had enjoyed these sensations. Through his journey south, he had skirted settlements and villages, frightened as much by meeting local villagers as he was of encountering a troop of Roman soldiers. His mind remained fixed on the seal inside his shirt and the city of Jerusalem where he must deliver it. It was a goal that had sustained him on little food, water, or sleep. It was what had caused him to become a thief, cause a fire in the high priest's home, and steal away in the night. It was what had made him feel ashamed of who he was.

But after three days of walking, the food he'd stolen from the priest's home was gone. This meant stealing again, this time from an orchard of fruit trees or a field of growing vegetables or gathering God's bounty of free wild berries, mushrooms, and other edible produce of a forest. But unlike the Galilee, where Abram knew how to gather supplies and could live for days without meeting another person, the vegetation and bounty of the seashore was strange to him.

So he headed inland and the air grew drier and hotter and his water ran out. Abram lost direction and could not focus his thoughts. His instincts and distrust had him hiding when he saw strangers ahead instead of pleading for help.

And now Abram was near breaking down. He just needed to rest. Only a morning or two to regain his strength. Simply to lie down in the welcoming grasses and close his eyes and feel God's sun on his face; to sink into sleep and dream about the cool air of the Galilee, the breezes of the mountaintops, the sparkling water, and the joy of hearing his parents' voices.

The sky ahead was bleached white like the bones of a large fish washed up on the shores of the sea. Now his head spun and he smiled, because he was swimming in warm water, refreshing water. He lay down and closed his eyes as his body was swept away by the warmth of the tide washing over him. He tried to turn his body, but he felt himself sinking further and further into the warm water. He knew he was smiling. He didn't know that he'd collapsed face-first into the dirt at the side of the road.

• • •

Had he not been delirious, Abram would have seen that he was within sight of a village sheltered in the lee of a high hill. Soon one, then two, then before long half a dozen people came toward him and silently surrounded his semiconscious body, covered in the dirt of the ditch.

Abram struggled to open his eyes as the people around him shaded his face from the sun.

"Brother," said a tall and bearded man. "Who are you?"

And then darkness.

• • •

When Abram awoke, it took him a few moments to realize that he had been laid under the shaded protection of an olive tree. His face was wet and he felt his skin itching. His head pounded. The nozzle of a water skin was pushed to his lips and he drank deeply. Around him were seven people, all looking at him with questions and concern in their eyes.

"Why have you come to our village?" asked one of the men.

Abram could feel an unease in the villagers who stood before him. There was suspicion in their faces, and in these days of Roman control, suspicion could quickly turn to hostility.

He tried to speak, but his voice rasped. He coughed and whispered, "I'm traveling to Be'er Sheva."

Despite his headache, the boy knew he had to be cautious. That was all Abram could, should, say, knowing that he had to keep from everybody the reason he was journeying to Jerusalem.

His answer didn't satisfy anybody. "Then why come along this road? Why did you come here? Why to us?" asked the man.

He had no answer.

A woman pushed through the crowd and said harshly, "Abimelech, stop this nonsense. He is just a boy. He's exhausted and hungry. The poor child has collapsed. Look at him; he's suffering from the heat of the sun and thirst. How can you treat him like this?" She reached over and held Abram by the arm. "I am Elisheva of the House of David. What is your name?"

"Abram," he said softly, his throat still hurting despite the water he had swallowed.

"Come with me, brother Abram, and have some food. And a wash. You look as though you need both."

As Elisheva helped him to his unsteady feet, supporting him to the house where she and her husband lived with their three children, the rest of the village stared after them. But then Abimelech, the episcopus of the community and the one to whom others deferred, shrugged.

"Let us hope that young Abram isn't a spy for the Romans. And let us pray, my brothers and sisters, in Jesus Christ our Lord's name, that he might see the light of our Lord, and become one of us . . ."

Inside the modest home, Elisheva sat Abram at a roughly hewn table and put a bowl of stew in front of him, fresh from the fire. She handed him a goblet of water, which he drank greedily.

"Not too quickly, my child," said Elisheva. "When you're so thirsty, you must drink slowly at first, or you'll become sick."

Abram ate the stew ravenously. It was full of chunks of lamb and

vegetables, of lentils and herbs. The smells of the food caused Abram
to remember the meals his mother had prepared for Rabbi Shimon,
which he'd taken to the cave in the hills. And from that memory a
great sadness descended on him, which Elisheva recognized.

"What are you doing, Abram, wandering these roads alone? In
these troubled times, my son, it's not safe."

Abram looked at her, wondering whether to trust her. She had
shown him kindness, and Abram was aware of how easily he might
have been left by the side of the road to die. Yet she was still a stranger,
and he could not ignore the instructions of the rabbi.

"I'm going to visit my uncle in Be'er Sheva," he lied.

She smiled and reached over to hold his hand. "If that's your mission, then you'll need to eat and put on weight, because it's a long
way from here into the Negev Desert. The roads, what roads there
are, teem with bandits and men you really don't want to meet."

Abram frowned. "But I was told that the people in the desert
were friendly and welcomed strangers." It was a lie. He'd never discussed the people who lived in the desert. He hated lying. He hated
stealing. Look what he'd become since he'd left his parents' home.

Elisheva shook her head. "Some of the desert people are friendly,
others are dangerous. Those from ancient times who plied the caravan routes in their tents were hospitable. But for a long time now, another people—who call themselves A'raab, inhabit the desert with
their camels and goats and sheep, and they are tribal and fierce. They
have a saying: *I against my brother, my brothers and I against my cousin,
and then my cousins and I against strangers.* We hear stories about travelers who disappear when they come across these tribes who wander
the sand dunes of the desert.

"No, Abram, the desert is not a safe place, especially not for a
young man like you, alone and far from his home."

Abram looked down at his plate, his appetite sated. But Elisheva
hadn't finished. "And there's always danger from the Romans. The
Roman emperor has just died, and we don't know what the new rulers in Rome will do to us. We hear stories that involve very terrible
persecution against our people."

"But haven't the Romans always hated us Jews?" asked Abram.

Elisheva smiled and shook her head. "No, in the time of King Herod, we were friendly with the Romans. But now they are against the Jews, as well as against us, the Christians, the followers of Jesus of Nazareth."

"Who's Jesus of Nazareth?"

"He's our Lord. The son of our God."

Abram could not hold back a brash laugh. "God has a son?"

Elisheva nodded patiently, but the look she gave Abram unsettled him. "Yes, the Lord God sent His son to earth to create the Kingdom of Heaven. He was crucified and he rose from the dead. He is our Messiah."

Abram ate another spoonful of the stew while he considered what Elisheva had said. "My rabbi said there are many men who say they are sent by God. They all call themselves messiahs, from our word 'to be sent.' My rabbi said I should ignore them as madmen. Was your Jesus one of them?"

Again, Elisheva remained patient and smiled. "Jesus is the only true Messiah, Abram. He is truly the son of God, and we know this from the miracles he performed. You see, Jesus has done what no man before him has done. He rose from the dead and came back to us alive, three days after he was crucified."

Abram shook his head. He didn't understand. "How can a dead man come alive again?"

"He is not a man, my dear. He is our God, and we worship him."

Abram pushed the empty bowl of stew away as if pushing away the bizarre logic.

Elisheva then poured Abram a cup of goat's milk and slid it toward him. Abram looked at the cup as if it were a foreign object, not to be trusted. Jewish law forbade the drinking of milk after a person had eaten meat.

Elisheva saw Abram's reaction. Softly, she told him, "My son, Jesus told us, his followers, that we need no longer obey the rules about food that are written in the Book of Levi and the Book of Deuteronomy. Jesus, our teacher and master, told the apostle Mark that we need no longer follow the old ways. We are free of the restrictions of the priests of the temple now that there is no longer a temple. This is a new world, Abram. Yes, it is controlled by the Romans, but as we grow, we will ascend and sweep away the old and replace it with the gift of Jesus and his teachings."

"You'll fight the Romans," Abram said in astonishment.

Elisheva smiled. "Dear boy, we Christians don't fight. We are a peaceable people. Our weapons are those of love and fellowship. This is what Jesus and his apostles taught us."

"What's an apostle?" asked Abram.

She reached over again and held his arm. "Oh, Abram, we have so much to teach you."

Abram wasn't sure he liked the sound of that and stood up from the table without drinking the milk. But as he did, his head swam and his knees buckled, causing him to stumble backward. He caught himself by grabbing at the shoulder of Elisheva, who had stood quickly to assist him. But then his stomach pitched and yawed and he doubled to vomit all over the floor, his partially digested stew spilling out in a liquid pool at his feet.

Then Abram passed out.

Every day since then, with the seal tucked inside his shirt, Abram had felt compelled to be on his way, to fulfill the task he had been set, and find his way to Jerusalem. But for some time he was too weak and too ill to leave the home of Elisheva and her husband, Abimelech.

They fed him and washed his clothes and gave him a corner of a room in their small house with straw for a bed. They were generous and kind, but Abram did not trust them. It wasn't just the warning of the rabbi to *trust no one until the seal is returned* but something else about the people caring for him that made Abram ill at ease.

For two weeks, as Abram recovered, Abimelech, who was the episcopus of the local community, told him stories about the man called Jesus of Nazareth.

Abimelech was a leather maker with a workshop next to the house. But he seemed to have endless time to spend with Abram and talk. The young man learned many things about this Jesus, who the whole village seemed to believe was the son of God. For his part,

Abram asked many questions and felt gratified that in the answers he sought, he was treated like an adult.

Back in his village of Peki'in, the rabbis had treated him with love and friendship but never respected the questions he asked. Instead, intent on exploring the depths of their own mysticism, they treated his questions with bemusement, telling him that when he was older, he would understand.

Abimelech appreciated every inquiry and often took great pains to fully consider the question and answer. The answers were nonetheless often difficult to comprehend and seemed to conform to a logic that the pragmatic Abram found hard to grasp.

Abimelech told Abram of the crucifixion of Jesus. It surprised the boy, who said, "I thought that only slaves and traitors were crucified by the Romans."

Abimelech smiled and nodded. "That's how much they hated the son of God . . . that they would treat him like the greatest threat to themselves."

He then told Abram how the Jewish priests had tried Jesus for heresy and taken him before the Roman governor Pontius Pilate, who condemned him to death. After death, Jesus had risen from the grave.

To the cautious and pragmatic Abram, the idea that God letting His son die should somehow change the fortunes for the Jewish people and make their lot better seemed strangely unconvincing. He had been around the whole village during his recovery and saw nothing of a life of ease. The people were still afraid of the Romans and eked out a bare living with brutally hard work that would never see them emerge from poverty.

Surely, if God had sent a messiah, He would be able to do more to help His chosen people than simply offering up a sacrifice that, as far as Abram could tell, hadn't achieved very much. But he said nothing of his doubts to Abimelech.

The couple caring for him seemed intent on his well-being but equally intent upon his believing what they believed, and this was a puzzling idea for Abram.

More confusing still was the anger that Abimelech felt toward the priests, the rabbis, and even his fellow Jews. It seemed he hated them more than the Romans. He even singled out the high priest from whom Abram had retrieved the seal many weeks ago.

"Tzadik bar Caiaphas hates us and has sworn to destroy us, to destroy all Jews who follow the teaching of Jesus of Nazareth. He says that we're Jewish heretics, no better than the Zealots, and that we should be convicted by the Sanhedrin. He says all of us should be put to death. Thank Jesus there is no longer a Sanhedrin, no Jewish court. Tzadik has become powerless as more and more Jews leave this land of Israel because of the Romans, to live in other places, and more and more Jews are converting to the new Judaism, the Judaism of Jesus of Nazareth."

The more Abimelech spoke of Tzadik, the angrier he became, until Abram asked cautiously, "You hate him?"

"I do."

"But didn't you say Jesus teaches us to love our neighbor?"

Abimelech's eyes narrowed and he didn't answer the question. Abram noticed a sudden twinkle in Elisheva's eyes.

• • •

Later that night Abram sat eating the evening meal at the table. They ate largely in silence, and despite his hosts' abandonment of the usual rules about what food could be consumed, Abram tried to keep to what the rabbi would approve of and hoped his hosts wouldn't notice.

Abram's strength was returning daily, and he often found himself at night thinking about when he would be able to leave and continue his journey. As he entertained these thoughts at the table, he absently fingered the stone seal through his shirt. When he stood to clear the table, the seal came loose from the inside pocket and dropped to the floor with a thump. The sound caught Abimelech's attention, and he quickly leaned down and scooped up the talisman before Abram was able to.

Seeing the ancient seal in the hands of another made Abram nervous. He reached out to take back the seal, but Abimelech continued to finger the object and turn it over in his hands, ignoring Abram's outstretched hand.

"What is this, my boy?" he asked.

"Nothing," said Abram without emotion.

"It doesn't look like nothing. It seems to be very old." Abimelech read the inscription on the seal, but his expression remained impassive, and he looked up at Abram. "Where did you get this?"

"I found it," Abram lied.

"It is from the old time and belongs to the old ways . . ." He held it up. "Jesus has shown us we can move beyond the priests and the temple and the trinkets of ancient rituals. We are no longer in the days of Moses, who gave the ancient laws, but in the kingdom of tomorrow, and we obey Jesus' new laws. Our Lord said that it is not stones and bricks but He who is the Kingdom of Heaven. Adornment or veneration of such things will not let you enter our kingdom, Abram, which is the only kingdom."

With the same dexterous movement by which Abimelech had snatched the seal from the floor, he snatched Abram by the arm. The grip was so hard that the boy let out a small yelp.

"For those Jews who do not believe in Jesus, death is an end with little but dust and decay. But we, the followers of Jesus, look forward to the joys of heaven for all of eternity. For us, and soon for you, life begins after death."

Abimelech stared at Abram for a long and uncomfortable moment. The words "soon for you" resonated in Abram's mind, and for reasons he couldn't quite grasp, he was afraid. But in the moment of the stare, Abram took his chance and seized the seal from Abimelech and clutched it in his fist, moving his arm behind his back and out of reach.

Abimelech smiled at the boy, a broad but considered smile, patted him on the shoulder, and turned his attention back to his meal.

Abram made his way over to his corner of the one-room house with the seal still clutched tight in his fist. He settled down on the straw as Elisheva cleared the plates and began to blow out the lamps for the night. He lay down his head but kept his eyes on Abimelech as the man lifted up a heavy wooden plank at an angle to the door of the house to prevent anybody from entering at night. He slammed it home into place with a blow from his fist. But it was odd. In the time

Abram had been in the village, he'd seen it as an open and welcoming community, and he'd never known Abimelech to bar the door. The man's action made him nervous.

Abimelech then turned to Abram. "It is time. Tomorrow, Abram, you shall become one of us. You will be baptized."

Then Abimelech blew out the last oil lamp and the home fell into darkness.

•   •   •

The night passed slowly for Abram as he lay awake, apprehensive of what the dawn would bring.

Abimelech and his wife said very little to him when they woke and prepared to leave the house, only that they would take him to the river and the whole community would be there to see him reborn. The followers of Jesus had told him of the ceremony by the river, which they called baptism. It sounded exactly the same as that which his mother did by the river in his village of Peki'in when she'd finished her monthly bleed, and what his father did after he had enjoyed sex with Abram's mother. So the youngster wasn't particularly concerned about the ceremony of the Jews who called themselves after Jesus. After all, they were Jews, if strange ones who drank milk after eating meat and believed that God had a son and that a man could die and then live again.

Abram was even looking forward to his immersion in the river. Since his illness, he hadn't been able to wash properly, though in Peki'in, he'd been scrupulous about his cleanliness by bathing in the river when he could.

What caused him doubt was that he was being told by Abimelech that the ceremony would enable him to be reborn. He was already born.

Abram pondered the word "reborn" and all that it might entail. Reborn as a follower of Jesus? Would he still be Jewish? Abimelech had called it the "New Judaism," and Abram wondered what that meant. The man had spoken of how many Jews were "converting" to be free of the control of the priests and their laws, but the very idea of "conversion" to something else appeared very foreign to the lad.

Either you are or you are not. In the old days, when the Jews controlled their land, many people converted to being Jews, and their whole body was immersed in the water of the *mikveh* as the final act. But since the time of the Romans, nobody converted to being a Jew—who would want to? In turn, the priests and rabbis had no interest in converting anyone. Yet these followers of Jesus seemed passionate about the idea of changing who people were. Abram couldn't work it out.

Perhaps he should run away, as he'd run from the high priest's house. But he was still weak from the illness, and these Jews had been kind to him. Perhaps the ceremony would benefit him, make him stronger, able to complete the task that Rabbi Shimon had sent him to Jerusalem to perform. Yes, he thought, he would go through the ceremony of baptism and see what happened afterward.

It was at midday that Abram walked with Abimelech and Elisheva through the tiny village. They were slowly joined by other people from the community. No one spoke; they simply fell in beside and behind, walking with them toward the river.

Abram was afraid. The seal was still clenched tight in his fist. He did not know what would happen at the baptism other than he would have to be covered by water and could not take the risk that the seal would be lost in the current.

His eyes darted about him as the procession moved slowly out of the village and down the hill. He looked for a place to hide the seal, someplace safe he could secret it and return for it later, someplace marked that he could remember. Finally his eyes landed upon a large stone marker, a milestone etched in Roman numerals showing the distance of the road. The milestone had a collection of Roman letters that he could not read, but one stood out, an X, and Abram knew that this would be a mark he could remember.

With quick thinking, and before they could pass by the milestone, Abram moved his right foot too far over in front of his left and forced himself to trip and stumble to his knees directly in front of the marker. He pushed his hand out in front of him to catch his fall; in that hand was the stone seal. With the weight of his fall, he pushed the seal as far into the sandy earth as he could.

Almost immediately, Elisheva bowed to his side. "Are you all right, Abram? Are you hurt?"

"No. I am fine. I just tripped," Abram said softly, but it was loud enough for Abimelech to hear.

"And so did our Lord Jesus trip and stumble as he carried the cross." Abimelech reached down to help Abram up, but before he rose, the lad took one last opportunity to push the stone seal deeper into the sandy dirt at the foot of the milestone and offered a silent prayer that it was well hidden.

Abimelech whispered into Abram's ear, "It is the old ways that make you stumble, my son. You walk toward a new life and your old life still clings to you, wanting to drag you down. But we shall not let it." He gripped Abram's arm so hard his nails dug into his flesh. "You will be baptized. You will be one of us. It is the only way you can be saved."

They came upon the bank of the river and saw the water moving swiftly, in places bubbling over submerged rocks or tree trunks. It wasn't the clear waters of mountain streams that Abram relished near his home but, rather, brown and opaque. As his feet entered the water, they immediately disappeared from view. The people from the village began to gather at the bank, forming a semicircle around Abimelech and Abram, now standing shin-deep in the river. They began to sing a rhythmic chant that Abram didn't recognize.

Abram surveyed the scene as his mind began to panic and look for a way out. This didn't feel right. In his home, the water was clear and cold and sparkling; this water was brown, and the people looked at him in what Abram feared was a menacing way. He looked up at Abimelech and the man's zealous expression frightened him even more. Why was he gripping his arm so tightly? Was it so that Abram didn't run away? What was happening?

The semicircle of onlookers appeared to him as a barricade of guards blocking his escape. Abimelech took him by the hand and led him out farther from the bank and into deeper water; the water was warm, like a broth, and it frightened the boy even more.

Fear continued to rise higher and higher in Abram's mind as the water grew deeper and the distance from the shore grew longer, and the prospect of escape receded. As the water level rose to his knees, and his feet sank deeper into the muddy bottom, he felt the pressure of the current and gripped Abimelech's arm to keep from falling over.

"Come deeper, my son. You must be submerged and cleansed and arise anew."

Abimelech led Abram deeper until the water came to his waist and the force of the current threatened to carry him away. The streams of the Galilee were not as deep; he was scared. Then the man put a firm hand on the back of Abram's neck as he spoke to the crowd on the shore. Their chanting stopped.

"Today," shouted Abimelech, "we deliver another into the arms of God through His son, Jesus. The death of the old self and the rising of the new from the purifying waters . . ." Abimelech's gaze turned to Abram. "All your guilt, all your corruption, all the wrongs you have thought and done will be washed away."

Abram realized that the man was going to drown him. Was this what the Christians did to Jews? They drowned them?

Abimelech lifted his other hand to place it over the face of Abram, almost smothering him as he raised his impassioned voice. "You will be saved as we have been saved. You will be welcomed into the next life when this life has passed . . ."

Abram's mind spun as he felt the water swirl around him. His mind raced for a way out. Abimelech was larger and stronger and held him fast. He could not escape from these strange Christians, who he realized meant to kill him like Jesus was killed, so that Abram could rise again. The words of the rabbi, "trust no one," haunted him as he stood waiting to be pushed beneath the water, waiting to be drowned.

"You will be with our Lord, the son of God, Jesus . . ."

Abram heard these final words and then was forced down into the sluggish brown water by Abimelech's powerful hands. As he was immersed, he felt the strong current try to carry him downstream to the sea. The moments felt like an eternity as the water filled his nose and his eyes. He tried to keep his mouth closed, but the sudden downward push had forced it open and water cascaded into his mouth and throat.

Abimelech was going to drown him. And that meant he'd failed the rabbi. Was this the end? The stone seal lost in the dirt at the foot of a Roman milestone, never to be returned to the place it belonged so that God Almighty would save His people, Israel?

Abram wanted so badly to live and not to fail. The task had given him purpose and meaning. His young life had been of no consequence until the moment the rabbi had entrusted him with the mission. Now a Christian was trying to drown him.

And so Abram kicked.

He kicked with all his might. He lashed out his legs, digging his heels into the muddy bed of the river. He kicked and pushed with all his strength and felt the deathly strong grip of Abimelech slip away from his neck and relinquish its hold on his arm. Abram kicked and pushed his body into the river, deeper into the current, held his breath, and let the rush of water sweep him away.

Palestine

1943

IT HAD BEEN two years since Shalman's father had been led away by the British, never to return. They knew he'd been taken to the fortress at Acre, but all they'd been told was that he'd died accidentally during interrogation; the British authorities said that he'd slipped and fallen down a flight of stone steps. They were sorry.

Later, the story was that he'd been found guilty of terrorism and hanged. His family and friends had been dismissed, as though the rule of British law were nothing more than a joke.

The people of the kibbutz didn't speak about that day, and neither did Shalman's mother, Devorah. On a kibbutz, everything was shared, and the community worked and cared for all. But one member of the kibbutz never recovered from the guilt of sending Shalman's father to his death.

Dov had honored Ari's request and treated Shalman as one of his own, though as he grew into young manhood, Shalman never really felt close to Dov's other six children. He saw his mother retreat into an increasingly thick shell now that her beloved Ari had been taken; she still cared for Shalman but no longer with the warmth and depth he'd known when he was part of a family, playing on the beaches as a young boy. As the months rolled away, Devorah became increasingly locked into her own world of perpetual despair, distant and cold, not just from Shalman but from everybody.

Anger grew like a cancer in the young man's breast. Every time the British army vehicles rolled past, or the people of the kibbutz were stopped at a checkpoint, Shalman felt anger. But it was anger that had no outlet until the day Dov handed him a small heavy package in an oil rag.

Since the day Ari had been taken away, Dov—like Shalman's mother—had changed. Where he had once been jovial and energetic, he became focused and solemn. And with his change in demeanor came a change in his activities. Dov was still the kibbutz's resident thief, but as he trained others in the tasks at which he was so skilled, his activities took on a higher, more directed purpose, separate from the kibbutz, and he grew increasingly distant from his *chaverim*, friends he'd known for years.

When Shalman unwrapped the package he found the heavy, shining, gunmetal-gray pistol he'd seen the day his father had been taken away.

"You're old enough now to use that," said Dov. It wasn't a statement of intent, just one of fact.

Shalman weighed the pistol in his hand with ease, no longer fearful of dropping it as he had been a couple of years before.

"If we're to keep this land, we have to fight for it. We have to take it, Shalman."

The teenager looked at Dov, shifting his grip on the pistol into a position ready to draw and fire. But Dov said nothing more. Just squeezed his shoulder and walked away.

Now, with the pistol, Shalman was a Jewish warrior. Weeks after giving him the gun, Dov introduced him to some people who seemed to like him. They bought him a beer, treated him like a man. On the second occasion, when he met with them in a café on the side streets of the northern port city of Haifa, they told him they were part of Palestine's defense force. They were members of Lehi, the gang of anti-British freedom fighters created by Avraham Stern three years earlier. The British, who called Lehi "the Stern Gang," hated the group, which was responsible for thefts of armaments and the assassination of British soldiers.

Shalman was surprised that the people he was meeting were so pleasant. The *chaverim* on the kibbutz hated Lehi and disparaged them at every opportunity. They called Lehi members "animals." It was because the founder, Avraham Stern, had tried to form an alliance with the Nazis of Germany and the Fascists of Italy against the

British, even though everybody now knew about Hitler's concentration camps, and even their death camps were becoming known. Stories were seeping out of Germany, so such an alliance would have been a pact with the devil himself.

Stern had been shot dead by the British, and since then, for some reason, the leadership had turned to Stalin and Moscow for an alliance against the British.

Dov made Shalman promise not to tell anybody on the kibbutz that he'd met with men from Lehi; within a month, the youngster agreed to join. He was trained in the use of a rifle and covert activity, and this night, the first in his life, he was lying on a rooftop, about to kill a human being. He thought back to the details of his training as he secured the rifle butt to his shoulder and aimed down the sight to the uniformed British officer in the distance.

Shalman's hands were sweating; he was trembling. He had to blink twice because the sweat on his brow was dripping into his eyes. Not that the weather was warm; it was a chilly night.

In his mind he envisioned what would happen, what he must do. He imagined the bullet erupting from the barrel and flying at the speed of sound across the space to thud into the flesh of the British soldier. It would tear his uniform, puncture his skin, rip his muscles to shreds, and spill blood on the ground.

Shalman felt sick.

When he'd lain on his stomach in the training sessions and aimed at distant bottles, squeezed the trigger, and watched them explode into a million shards of glass, his hands hadn't been shaking or sweating. So why now? Because it was dark? Because it was cold? Because he was alone? No, he'd been alone in the dark before he became a soldier with a rifle, on missions for Lehi, missions that were part of his training . . . now that he was sixteen, they'd told him to go out and get his first kill.

Shalman, at Dov's urging, was set to become a willing participant in the activities of the Stern Gang, relishing the sense of place and empowerment it gave him, helping to emancipate him from the haunting memories of his father being taken away.

Focusing again on his target, Shalman saw the face of the British officer illuminated by a brief yellow glow as he lit another cigarette. Down the rifle sight, Shalman saw that face and felt a coldness within him that he had never felt.

He'd been told by the intelligence people in Lehi that this British officer worked in strategic command and that his removal would cause disruption. It was disruption that Lehi sought. British time in Palestine was limited, and the more disrupted it became, the shorter their stay would be. The British were already exhausted from fighting the war against the Nazis; a growing battlefront in Palestine wouldn't be tolerated by the British public, and that should lead the Houses of Parliament in London to withdraw their troops.

Shalman knew he had to pull the trigger, he knew he was a good marksman, and he knew he could hit the target when it was an empty bottle of beer. But still he could feel the sweat on his brow.

Then a voice in bad Hebrew said, "What the hell you doing? Why not shoot? Why stop? What the fuck?"

The voice came from a man sliding up on his belly in the dark to lie next to him. It was a distinctly Polish accent. The man had been assigned as Shalman's supervisor and acted as lookout for the operation, though Shalman was yet to learn his name.

"Fucking shoot or go away. If you can't, I do."

"I'll do it," whispered Shalman defensively. "I'm just waiting for the right shot."

"Bullshit!" said the aggressive man. "You fucking coward. I been watching. Plenty shots. You scared. Yes?"

Shalman turned his attention back to the gun sight.

"You never kill man before. First kill difficult. Next kill easy. Now you do first kill."

Shalman shook his head.

"Okay, give me rifle. I kill. You take credit. Then others don't know how you coward. Tomorrow you grow balls. Tomorrow we talk. I teach you how to kill. Today we must act. Yes?"

The man took the rifle from Shalman's hands, aimed, and within moments, the quiet of the night was pierced by a sharp crack as the bullet tore out of the rifle and penetrated the officer's chest. Before the body of the target had even hit the ground, the Polish man said, "Quick. We go. Now!"

He stooped and ran with the rifle back to the vehicle. Shalman followed.

• • •

The following night, Shalman and the man with the Polish accent met in a café on Ma'alot Ir David, close to the center of Jerusalem. The older of the two, though himself only twenty-two, nodded without smiling to Shalman as he entered the café. It wasn't until he stood near the table before sitting that Shalman realized how diminutive the man was. Not that Shalman was particularly tall, especially compared to the British soldiers, but this young man only reached Shalman's shoulder. Shalman knew that it was the difference between the healthy life and food on a kibbutz and the dark, claustrophobic, and sunless world of a European ghetto where Jews were locked into walls like animals in a pen.

They looked at each other, not speaking a word, the man's face a mask of indifference. A waiter came up, and the Pole said curtly, "Wodka. And falafel." The waiter looked at Shalman, who said, "Just a falafel, thanks. Oh, and a black beer."

Shalman was unsure what else to say. The Pole had asked to meet for a drink, and Shalman could find no reason to say no. As he pondered what to say, the man took the lead.

"Last night. Big problems caused by you. Disobey order. Bad for you, bad for comrades. If this were normal war, you'd be shot. But this no normal war . . ." He shrugged casually and threw back the vodka the waiter had just placed on the table.

Shalman made no response, though his hackles rose at the idea of being thought a coward.

The Pole pressed on, not waiting for Shalman to reply. "I could report you, but you're a kid." Then he looked around the room before leaning forward and lowering his voice. "Why are you doing this? Why not stay school or kibbutz? Why join gang?"

"Same reason as you," Shalman said, adjusting to the Polish man's awful Hebrew. He looked around the café to see if anybody was listening, but all the other people seemed to be eating and drinking or engaged in intense conversations. He then said, "To kill British."

"Hmmm," said the Pole. "Not for country, not for people? Just for killing?"

Shalman wanted to object, to explain his nationalism, but instead said, "Your Hebrew is terrible. Would you prefer to speak in Polish?" Shalman's kibbutz was made up of people from all over the world, and he'd picked up a workable command of Polish as a kid.

The Pole nodded. "I've only just started to learn Hebrew. It's very difficult."

"You didn't learn any Hebrew in Poland?"

"I went to school in Ruzhany before the Soviets came. But I liked girls and other things too much." The diminutive Pole gave Shalman a wry wink.

As well as languages, Shalman had learned many other things from life on the kibbutz, especially stories of escape. Everyone who came to the community had a story. Some were full of adventure and funny circumstances that would have everyone rolling with laughter in the evenings over dinner. But most were dark and full of despair. So when the Pole said the simple words "before the Soviets came," Shalman knew what that meant.

At the start of the war, the Soviet secret police deported hundreds of thousands of Poles to the gulags in the frozen north. It wasn't the forced labor that was terrible so much as the cold. Many lost fingers, legs, and arms to frostbite, and many more simply died of exposure. Shalman recalled a story of a man who wrapped his fingers and hands and feet in straw and horse shit, so as it rotted, it warmed the flesh. Shalman involuntarily looked down at the hands of the Polish man in front of him, saw the fingers intact, and wondered if he'd done the same.

Such stories and images were the intimate personal details of much larger political maneuverings. When the Nazis broke their non-aggression pact with Russia, Stalin was desperate for allies, knowing that the German war machine was about to be unleashed toward Stalingrad. He signed the Sikorski-Mayski Agreement, and overnight all those Poles who had been rounded up into forced labor by the NKVD found themselves soldiers in the service of the Soviet Socialist Republic and formed into a ragtag Polish army some twenty-five thousand strong.

"Some of us were made officers, given shiny uniforms and extra food. But not me. I couldn't be bothered. I just wanted to kill. Russians, Germans, Arabs, British. I didn't care. Everybody was my enemy," said the Pole as he washed down the falafel with another shot of vodka.

Shalman wanted to ask questions but held back, unsure of the intentions or motives of his companion. He didn't even know the man's name. So he asked.

The Polish man merely looked at him and said, "Names are for the bourgeoisie. No better than lord or earl or sir or mister. A man should be identified by his deeds. I'm known to my comrades because I can kill without blinking an eyelid, not because of what I'm called. So you call me comrade, or in Hebrew, *chaver.*"

Shalman shrugged. He'd find out from the others. In the meantime, he thought of what his new comrade had told him about the life of Poles in Hitler's Europe and Stalin's Russia. He found himself connecting this man's stories to the flood of Poles into Palestine in recent years.

The Pole continued: "Anyway, the Russians couldn't feed us, so Stalin shipped most of us out to Iran to serve with the British." He sneered as he said it. Shalman had no doubt that had they been outdoors, the man would have spat alongside the words. "You know, we had to walk all the way, in the freezing cold and across mountains, without food and drink, from southern Russia to Iran. Can you believe it? Thousands died. Starvation and sickness. We couldn't bury them. We just had to keep on marching. At least the vultures had a good feast." The broad smile at his own joke unsettled Shalman because it seemed genuine. "And that's how we got here. Poles all over Palestine."

Shalman nodded, beginning to understand the anger of a young man who'd traveled so far from his home, with so much violence and hardship, and just why he was able to kill without any compunction.

The Polish man sat quietly for several moments, then threw back another glass of icy cold vodka, as though clearing his throat of the filth of the road he had to travel to get to Palestine. Then he turned to Shalman and said, "You want to know my name? It's Yitzhak. Yitzhak Shamir."

Leningrad, USSR
1944

DURING THE YEAR since she was escorted from the school by the tall and terrifying NKVD men, Judita had embraced her training. Initially, it had taken place in Moscow, but the later training in more advanced spycraft was conducted in one of the most spectacular palaces in Leningrad, a city just beginning to recover from the murderous siege of the Nazis.

Judita had turned out to be a brilliant student, absorbing all the facts and figures, the philosophies of communism, and the geopolitics of the world like a sponge. She'd been trained well. Languages came naturally to her, but as she soon discovered, so did many other skills. Photography, cryptography, forgery, weaponry, ballistics, covert communication, dead-letter drops, and much else of spycraft all spoke to her agile intellectual mind. It was her newfound affinity with marksmanship and the handling of firearms that surprised not only her but also her handler.

Anastasia Bistrzhitska had watched over Judita as her protégée. A beautiful but severe woman, ink-black hair pulled tight back from her forehead in the bun of a Leningrad Kirov ballet dancer, she felt an empathy with the young Jewess, more so than with her many previous students.

Judita relished Anastasia's companionship, which provided a friendship and a depth of trust she had never found in her own family. Judita had loved her mother with all her heart, but as the girl grew into a young woman, she came to resent her mother's lies. Lying about her husband's violence, lying about how everything would one day be all right. These lies, however well intentioned, broke the trust.

But with Anastasia, trust was clear, trust was expected, trust was not to be questioned.

Along with the skills she would need as an NKVD agent, Judita was also schooled in Soviet socialist policy, the doctrine of Lenin, and the values and aspirations of the workers' republic. Judita had been a student of schools of the state and was a believer before being caught up in the NKVD; but her time in training, with the resources she was afforded and the knowledgeable teachers who lectured to her and the others, expanded her love of the Soviet.

Her father's drunken rants about the failings of the Soviet state only validated her trust and faith in the communist system of which she was now an integral part. Whatever he hated must be good.

All this had delighted Anastasia and transformed her student into a protégée. While Anastasia encouraged all the other students, even though they were Jews and many of them were exceptional, Judita's knowledge, skills, and dedication had caused Anastasia to form an unusually close bond with her. But now the time was approaching when the training and shelter of the NKVD would end and Judita's real purpose would begin. Today she was to meet Comrade Beria, the chief of the NKVD and, next to Stalin himself, the most powerful man in the country. In thinking about the meeting, Judita had asked Anastasia what skills, of all she had learned, would be most valuable in the tasks ahead. Anastasia had put a hand on her shoulder and said simply, "Disguise." It was this word Judita pondered as she stood in front of the ornate door that led to the office of Comrade Lavrentiy Pavlovich Beria.

Judita knocked on the door, clear and firm, and within moments it swung open. Her heart was beating fast, and she was surprised to see Anastasia standing there, smiling and nodding encouragement. Anastasia leaned forward to whisper in her ear, "Don't be frightened, my little dove."

Judita walked into the massive room. It was in the center of Mariinsky Palace, where Beria housed himself when he came to Leningrad. Around the colonnaded walls hung exquisite paintings, portraits of noblemen and -women, massive pictures of soldiers on horseback and elegant ladies in ball gowns. She was surprised to see the portraits of the nobility. When she'd been to museums in Moscow, such pictures had been removed, replaced by Soviet heroes and heroines.

Anastasia noticed her look of surprise, and as they walked forward, the older woman whispered, "Comrade Beria likes to keep these portraits on the walls so that he can sit in the chairs and work at the desks these parasites once used and remind himself and others of how these so-called aristocrats once ruled our land while their peasants starved."

Judita nodded and smiled. She continued to survey the room, and she walked toward the desk where a man whose face she knew all too well from the newspapers was seated. He was surrounded by men in the dress of senior army officers. All were watching as she and Anastasia walked down the length of the reception room.

Yes, she was frightened. Everybody was terrified of Beria. His balding head reflected the lights in the ceiling, and it was impossible to see his eyes because of the reflection in his rimless glasses. But she knew with absolute certainty that he was examining every step she took.

They stood in front of the desk, and Beria continued to look closely at Judita. He didn't say a word but simply stared at her. Was he trying to make her nervous, uncomfortable? Her training had prepared her to steady her mind and focus. She drew on that now and waited.

"So, you're the young Jew who has excelled in our instruction," he said. His voice was higher than she'd anticipated, and from his position in the huge chair, it was apparent that he was also a lot shorter than she'd realized. It was well known in Russia that the diminutive Stalin had a hatred of men taller than he, especially in the upper echelons of the military and the government.

"Yes, Comrade Beria."

"My wife was born Jewish, though of course she eschewed her religion, as have all right-thinking communists."

"Yes, Comrade Beria."

He looked down at the dossier on the desk and read a few paragraphs. "Top in logistics, top in languages, top in spycraft, top in . . . top in . . . top in . . . You're a very good student. You excel. Have you always excelled, Judita Ludmilla?"

"I've always tried to excel for the good of Mother Russia," she said.

Beria nodded. "There is a task you must do. For the first time since you arrived here, you will be out of our sight. You have been briefed on your mission?"

"Yes, comrade."

"Do you understand what is expected of you?"

"Yes."

"And do you understand that you must succeed in everything we ask of you? That there are consequences for failure?"

"Yes, Comrade Beria."

For a long moment Beria continued to stare at Judita, but she did not flinch or look away and indeed tried very hard not to blink. Finally, Beria gave a curt nod to Anastasia and said, "Good. Then I wish you fortune, in the name of the Soviet Socialist Republic. You will be flown today to Moscow, where you will undertake your mission."

He looked down again at her dossier. The interview was over. The warning had been given.

She turned and walked out of the room without another word.

• • •

Later that night, as she was driven through the Moscow streets in a black car with darkened windows, Judita pondered what Anastasia had said about the skill she would need the most: "Disguise." True to that word, she was in disguise tonight. Though she was only fifteen, she had the body of a grown woman, a body now clothed in an expensive dress, high heels, and stockings, with her face painted in expensive cosmetics the likes of which she'd never seen but knew were used by the wives of the party leadership. Both her age and her true purpose were clearly disguised.

Her training had been the best possible, and she knew what was expected of her, but how she'd achieve the result, given the unpredictability of the situation, was something for which she couldn't be trained. She would have to rely on her intelligence, her instincts, and her natural cunning.

"You're a child of the Moscow streets," Anastasia reminded her. "Cunning is in your blood. That's part of the reason you've been chosen for your mission. The other Jews in your class have been taken to their home cities for their missions."

Judita had been told that the American diplomat was in the consulate in Moscow alone and away from his wife and children. And he was known to be a womanizer. No American diplomat's family was sent to Moscow during the war. He'd been sent here in November 1941, shortly after Operation Barbarossa was launched by Hitler to invade Russia. During the three years, the people of Moscow and Leningrad had fought bravely, despite hideous losses.

Now the Germans were being pushed back, and Russia at long last could begin to breathe freely again. But the movements of troops and battlefronts were not things of her concern. Judita's task was specific and focused. The target was not an army or a strategic piece of land but a single man and the information he held. Anastasia told her the Americans had a name for it: a "honey trap."

The leaders of England and America, Churchill and Roosevelt, were to meet in Yalta in the Crimea in a few months' time, and there they would make plans to carve up Europe after the war. The diplomat who was Judita's target held information about that meeting.

Anastasia dropped her off by car at the hotel the American diplomat was known to frequent. As Judita entered, she blinked at the heavy clouds of smoke in the air and found her way to a table. It was past eleven, and the bar was half full of Muscovites, reporters from America and Britain and Canada, and the usual sprinkling of prostitutes, both male and female.

Judita ordered a vodka and tomato juice from the waiter and when he returned, she took out her purse, full of rubles from Anastasia, and gave him some money. It was far more than the drink cost, but she smiled at him and said, "Keep it."

He looked at her in surprise. "I owe you an apology, miss. I thought you were a barfly."

She laughed. "How do you know I'm not?"

"Girls who work here don't tip the waiters. They usually start off with cheap soda water and wait for men to buy them expensive drinks."

The waiter turned to leave, but Judita caught his hand with a gentle but firm touch. He stopped and she lowered her voice to a whisper. "I'm a widow. My husband was killed in Leningrad. I'm looking for someone to help me." This was one of the many rehearsed scenarios imprinted in Judita's mind. "I'm looking for a fresh start somewhere else. Maybe America."

The waiter smiled and looked Judita up and down before saying, "Avoid the reporters. It's the diplomats who have real power," and he nodded in the direction of a tall, muscular, but aging man on the far side of the room. "Just don't hold your breath. Promises are nothing. They'll tell you anything to get you into bed, but you'll wake up alone and ashamed. If you take my advice, young lady, you'll go home and suffer like the rest of us. I'm sorry, but whatever promise you hear from the mouth of an American diplomat, assume that it's a lie."

Judita stroked his hand softly. "Thank you for your concern, but I know what I'm doing. All I need is for you to point out a diplomat. I'll do the rest."

• • •

Two hours later, Judita was sitting at a table, one arm around the shoulder of Henry Clifford, the American diplomat who was her mark, the other arm fending off his attempt to put his hand up her dress.

After ten glasses of vodka, his spectacles were askew, his tie pulled down, his shirt no longer tucked into his trousers. Judita's waiter looked at her in concern and mouthed, "Shall I stop him?" but she shook her head and gave him a wink.

Henry was tall and strong, but the drink had weakened his concentration, and his words of affection and less than subtle innuendo—delivered in poorly constructed Russian blended with English—were slurred. Judita had coyly shared with him her story of being the young widow of a Russian academic killed by that "monster Stalin," and the narrative seemed to be holding up.

She allowed his hand to remain at the top of her stockings, but held it firmly so that it went no higher. She whispered in his ear above the din of the room, expanding on her story. "I spent time with my husband in New York, and it was glorious. I just want to go back there, to the white picket fences and the roses in the gardens and the way the leaves turn red in the fall."

Henry swayed and slurred and attempted to grope Judita's breast. She allowed it for a moment and then playfully swatted him away. She judged he needed to know the honey was on offer if he was to open up.

"Take me away with you," she said in lighthearted Hollywood-esque fashion, and kissed him on the cheek. It was her toe in the water to see how he would respond.

Henry dropped into English, the alcohol dissolving what was left of his Russian. "Honey, you would love it in the States. Girl like you, you could go to Hollywood. I could make you a star."

"Do you know people in Hollywood?" Judita asked in apparent awe.

"Of course. I know all kinds of people," he said, again moving his hand up Judita's leg.

"Then take me." She phrased the word for all its double entendre.

"I'll put you in the diplomatic bag," he said, then started to giggle to himself. It was the funniest joke he'd ever told. And Judita laughed, judging the moment, counting his drinks, watching his eyes.

"I'd be very, very grateful . . ." She let the last word hang in the air.

"You wanna show me your gratitude now, babe?" he said.

She thought she'd rather jump into the icy Moskva River than have him kiss her. But she remained focused. "Sure," she said, and started to fondle him. He opened his mouth like a fish dying on a riverbank, and moaned. She glanced over to the bar and saw the waiter staring at her, shaking his head in warning. But she winked again at him.

Judita whispered into Henry's ear, "Can you get me to America next February? That'd be the most wonderful thing. Then I'll really, truly show you my gratitude."

From the depths of his drunken fog and his urgent need for sexual release, something stirred in his mind. "February? No. Not a good time. That's when Roosevelt . . . oops . . . shouldn't say too much."

"My God," she said in wonder. "You know the American president. You're that important?"

He looked at her, trying to focus. She was so utterly beautiful, young, and innocent. And her big eyes opened wide when he dropped the name of the president. He nodded and put his finger to his lips. "Shush . . . mustn't say. Very confishential . . . I mean con-fid-ential." He slowed the word down to get it right.

"What's confidential?" asked Judita, sensing she was close, though what information he might offer, she didn't know.

"The conference. Very secret. Shhh." And he giggled at himself.

"Will you be there?"

"Sure I'll be there, baby. I'll be leading the discussions."

He smiled to himself. She'd been briefed that he was a rather junior diplomat, a pen pusher who'd risen to a senior position more by the necessities of war than by merit.

"Will you meet Roosevelt? Will you meet Stalin? What will they say to you? Oh, Henry . . . I never dreamed I'd meet somebody as important as you."

He thought for a moment, blinked and tried to focus, then said, "Don't say anything to anybody . . ." He held her hand and leaned so close to her face that she felt she could almost become drunk from the fumes from his mouth. "We're going to put Europe back together again when this war's finished. That's what I'm going to be talking about with your great leader Stalin and my boss . . . put the whole shooting match back together again. Yep!"

"But how? Isn't Hitler winning?"

Henry snorted. "You kidding, babe? That Nazi asshole is staring at the end. As soon as this thing is over and ol' Adolf is captured, we're gonna try him. American justice! And we'll carve up Europe so that Germany ain't no more . . ."

"And what about here? What about Russia? What do you plan to do with little ol' us?" said Judita, feigning the accent of an American Southern belle. She'd never seen nor heard such a person with such an accent. But her training had been thorough, including American movies and culture.

He shook his head and said softly, "You'll do okay. Ol' Uncle Joe Stalin will get the scraps from what we have left over. Germany, Hungary, and Czechoslovakia, the Brits will get the Balkans, and we'll throw some scraps to France. They can have the fucking Ruhr if they want it!"

"So shall I stay here in Russia without you, Henry? If everything is as good as you say it will be?"

"No, baby. Let Uncle Henry take you outta here. I think your uncle Joe is gonna be so pissed off with what we leave him that all hell's gonna break loose. Maybe even another war."

It was in this moment that Judita understood. This was not a mission so much as a test. The diplomat gave up little that the NKVD wouldn't already know—just motives and objectives rather than tactics. So as she excused herself, telling Henry that she needed to go to the bathroom and with the promise of something "special" when she returned, she wondered if she had done enough to pass the test. Had she performed in a way that would make Anastasia proud?

Judita slipped out of the doorway and into the freezing night air. It had been snowing, and her footprints in the fresh powder caused her concern, should the idiot attempt to follow her. But the moment she appeared on the street, the black car she had arrived in roared up beside her and the door opened.

The cabin of the car was deliciously warm, and in the dull light she saw Anastasia Bistrzhitska sitting in the backseat. "Well, little one?"

Judita nodded and recounted to Anastasia the entire conversation from her extraordinary memory. Every detail. Every word. She did so without emotion or embellishment. Pure reportage of what the diplomat had said. All the while watching Anastasia's face for signs that she had done well and that her handler approved.

Finally, Anastasia smiled and said simply, "Well done, my little dove. You're set for great things, Judita Ludmilla, for the motherland, for the Soviet Republic, and for the glory of the Russian people."

"You already knew everything I've told you, didn't you?" said Judita.

Anastasia smiled. "Of course."

"So it was nothing more than a test to see if I was ready."

The interior of the car was dark, but Judita knew that Anastasia nodded and was smiling.

"And did I pass?"

"Oh yes, my little dove; you passed with flying colors."

Judita remained quiet as the car drove back to the Lubyanka. As it crossed the Moskva River and went right on Borovitskaya to pass Red Square and the Kremlin, Judita said quietly, "Oh, you'd better drop me off here. I had a note earlier today to meet tonight with Comrade Stalin." Out of the corner of her eye, even in the dim light cast by the streetlamps, Judita could see Anastasia turning toward her in shock. "He wants me to teach him Hebrew," she said.

Anastasia said nothing. Her mouth was open. She was incredulous.

"Just testing you," said Judita, trying not to laugh.

Anastasia burst out laughing and threw her arms around the young woman. She kissed her on the cheek and lightly on the lips.

"So you think I'm ready for my mission?" Judita said softly.

Anastasia was still laughing but managed to say, "Soon, my dove. Very soon. But not quite yet . . ."

Moscow, USSR
December 1944

JUST WEEKS AFTER she'd passed her initiation test with the American diplomat, Judita rode through the streets of Moscow in the backseat of a car driven along the river, parallel to the magnificent embankment. The streetlamps bathed the white snow in sepia. Next to her was Anastasia.

"Where are we going?" asked Judita, turning toward the imposing woman beside her. Beautiful, powerful, confident, and cold, Anastasia was everything Judita had been shaped to admire.

"You will see" was her only answer, given without turning to face her protégée.

Judita knew better than to ask further and turned her attention back to the snow outside.

• • •

That day when NKVD agents had come for her at the school in the basement of the old synagogue seemed so very long ago. A different time. A different life. A different Judita. When she thought of herself then, it was like thinking of a stranger, someone distant and unfamiliar. Much more significant than the change she'd undergone from girl to woman, Judita now saw the world differently. The lessons she had been saturated in—communist theory, philosophy and history, spycraft and languages—all changed her sense of self and her place in the world. And yet as she watched the city of Moscow drift by the window, she felt its familiarity, a connection older than the self she knew now. She had been a Jewish child in these streets before she was a Soviet woman. She'd thought the training had knocked that out of her, but it was a memory she couldn't remove.

She had passed her initial training as an NKVD agent and been handed over to specialists. Anastasia remained her lead handler, but her world had shifted and changed yet again since the meeting with Beria, since her test with the American diplomat. Of the initial fifteen young and middle-aged Russian Jews who had been selected from all over the Soviet Socialist Republic, only a handful from her group had been chosen for further training.

Now she and her colleagues were studying Jewish and Arab languages, history, imperialism, collectivism, government structure and its intersections, the inefficiencies of officialdom, and the personal weaknesses of key members of the Jewish Assembly of Representatives, a new governing body in Palestine. Lectures were conducted every morning and afternoon, six days a week, and tests were given every evening.

It also meant that every Sunday, she and the others were free to wander the streets of Moscow and marvel at the buildings, the wide boulevards. Lighthearted on a Sunday morning after a concentrated week, the young men and women would walk along the banks of the river, accompanied by a number of guards to ensure that they didn't wander away.

On one particular day the group had passed a café, and Judita glanced inside to see a number of customers sitting at tables, sipping drinks, when something caught her eye. She looked in again; then she peered deeper into the shop, much deeper. To her utter amazement, two of the people sitting there looked more than familiar. The sun was playing tricks on the glass window, but Judita stared carefully and was certain she could see her father and mother at one of the tables, sitting opposite each other, talking animatedly, silhouetted against the dim lights of the interior.

She began to move away from the group to go into the café, but the guard prevented her, telling her to keep up with the others. She started to argue, but the guard, as though under instruction, uncharacteristically became aggressive and forced her to move forward. For the next ten minutes, as they were virtually frog-marched along, Judita continued to turn back and stare in the direction of the café, but nobody emerged.

• • •

The car came to a stop and Judita leaned toward the window to ascertain where they had arrived. It was a place she'd been many times in her youth; she had played there as a child the few times her mother had the time to spend with her and her brother and sister. She turned to Anastasia. "What are we doing here?"

"You're a Muscovite; you should know well enough why people come here. To walk and talk and enjoy nature."

"What do you want me to do?" asked Judita, her instincts making her focus and gain clarity on the situation and her orders.

Anastasia's face and body didn't move, but her lips parted just enough to say, "I want you to kill someone." Then she stepped out of the car.

Judita tried to hide her shock, but she had known such a task would be asked of her one day. She'd been trained for it. But knowing the moment was coming and feeling its arrival were very different things. Shooting targets and distant bottles on rocks wasn't the same as shooting a human being in cold blood. But Judita had no time to ponder and quickly pushed the car door open to follow Anastasia.

The two women stood at the front of the vehicle. Before them was the enormity of Gorky Central Park. It was surprisingly empty except for two people sitting on a bench about two hundred meters from where they were standing. Judita glanced at the couple and then back to Anastasia. "Who are they?" she asked.

"Does it matter?" replied Anastasia. "I'm about to order you to kill an enemy of the state. That's all you have to know."

Judita nodded. She knew this was the only answer expected of a loyal officer of the state.

But Judita did look closer. Her keen eyesight, so used to rifle sightings, traced the figures across the park and observed their movements. She was familiar with the way they sat, moved their arms, inclined their heads. She'd known them since she was a baby. Her heart sank. Her childhood flooded into her mind as she blinked, trying to remove the distant man and woman from her view. But they remained. Even from this distance, she was certain of who they were, from the way the woman held her head at a slight angle to the ground and how the man appeared to be telling her what to do.

For a moment she forgot herself and turned to Anastasia. "But it's . . . they're my . . ."

It was all she was able to say before her tongue fell silent and her gaze went quickly back to the couple.

Anastasia, to Judita's surprise, put her hand on her back, the closest thing to an embrace from the woman who was at one time her friend but now her commander.

"Where lies the highest duty of every child in Mother Russia?" Anastasia asked in a near whisper.

"To Comrade Stalin. To the Supreme Soviet. To the state. To the Praesidium."

"And this is your order. This is your command from the state, from the Supreme Soviet. And from me."

Judita's eyes didn't leave her parents, sitting on a park bench in the distance. "You want me to kill them? You want me to kill my mother and father?"

"Your order is to kill one of them. One only."

"Which?" A simple but horrifying question.

"Of that there is no order. Only choice. Your choice."

As if on cue, the chauffeur approached them with a Mosin-Nagant sniper rifle and a telescopic sight. It was the weapon made famous by snipers during the Nazis' siege of Stalingrad, and it was one Judita knew well. But as the chauffeur thrust it into her hands, it felt foreign and awkward, as though she were holding something she had never seen.

The chauffeur disappeared into the car, and so did Anastasia, leaving Judita alone.

With a strange panic rising inside, Judita tried to remember her lessons. Detachment. Personal feelings must never count. The object was the well-being of the state, and nothing else mattered. But while these mantras focused her for the act of killing, they did not help her with the choice. If it had been an abstract scenario for class debate in her lessons, she might have reasoned between knowledge of the father's alcoholism and violence against his sole ability to support the family. If the mother were to die, the father could still work and feed the children. To kill the father would be to make paupers of the whole family.

As she positioned herself on the ground, flat on her belly with the rifle snug against her shoulder, she found the rational practicality ill at ease with the reality of the choice. She had hated her father and grown to resent her mother, but as her gun sight framed them both, the choice was impossible.

Judita drew upon the steely determination she'd shown in all the other tests. She bit the inside of her lip and felt the rifle in her hands, cold and indifferent. She adjusted the telescopic sight until both of her parents were clear and sharp. Then she aligned the crosshairs until her father's chest was filling the entire circle, the intersection of the black lines crossing his heart.

She paused. Thoughts of her siblings, of their life without the income of a father, came to her, and almost without physical intention, her gun sight shifted so that it was in place over the heart of her mother.

Was living with violence better than dying of starvation? Was this the choice Anastasia was asking her to make? Was this the purpose of the test? No doubt Anastasia knew about her father, his violence, his drunkenness. No doubt her handlers knew more about Judita's childhood than even she remembered. This was a test, but what was it testing, and what was the answer?

Judita steadied herself again, but the crosshair drifted—from the heart of her mother to the heart of her father and back. The order was clear, but the choice was not.

By reflex, Judita found herself saying a short Jewish prayer: something she had not recalled in what felt like a long time, but it was imprinted on her soul. She drew in a breath, holding it as she was taught, feeling her heart's pulse in her temple.

She remembered hiding under the table, she remembered her childhood fear, her mother's cries, the bruises on her face . . .

The crosshair centered and held firm over her father's sunken chest, and she squeezed the trigger.

But there was no sound. No percussive pop, no kick in her shoulder from the recoil, only a dull metallic click. Through the viewfinder her father, still sitting there, talked animatedly at her mother's bowed head. She pulled the trigger again, but still the dull click. She felt the presence of a woman, warmth and perfume enveloping her. Anastasia reached down and took the rifle from her hand.

"Come, Judita. No more tests. You've passed. And I'm so very sorry to have had to put you through this. Your loyalty is unquestionable. It's time to go, my little dove."

• • •

Inside the car, threading back through the Moscow streets, Anastasia and Judita sat in silence until Judita could bear it no longer. "Don't you want to know who I chose?"

Anastasia turned to her and put a gloved hand on hers. "I trust you made the choice that was right for you."

It was then that Judita knew she was capable of anything.

Passenger ship *Agon*, Palestine

January 1945

JUDITA LUDMILLA MAGIDOVICH looked at the distant shoreline of the city of Haifa, a hillside dotted with lights and a dockside ablaze with illumination. She stood amid 160 men, women, and children, many of them elderly and horribly emaciated after their lives in Nazi Europe. Most of them were also rendered seasick during their journey from Trieste, through the Adriatic, into the Mediterranean, and finally, to the shores of Palestine. Judita watched with a focused eye so different from that of her fellow travelers as their ship was dwarfed by a British battle cruiser escorting them through the waters.

The British warship had sailed out of Haifa after a telegraph from Cyprus warning the authorities of the illegal refugee ship headed their way. The battle cruiser had met the small Greek passenger liner some fifty nautical miles off the coast of Palestine and transmitted a radio warning to the Greek captain that they would board and arrest him and his crew and confiscate his ship unless he put himself under British orders and sailed with them into the port.

He had no alternative. There were numerous examples preceding him of ships trying to smuggle Jews from the desolation of Europe into Palestine being boarded and impounded. He had been well paid by rich Jews from England and France, known the risks, and taken them anyway. But he would not risk lives, so he shrugged his apologies to the passengers and followed the directive.

The ship docked at the port, and without delay, the refugees were pushed and shoved down the gangplank onto the dock. They were a ragged group. Wearing old clothes that they hadn't changed in weeks, exhausted, lice-infested, many of them emaciated from hunger, children limp in the arms of mothers, sons supporting their elderly parents, most barely able to stand. They stood in the boiling sun under the dispassionate gaze of the British soldiers, waiting for the arrival of the commanding officer.

Many of the women were sobbing, their hopes and prayers of freedom from the Nazi terror of Europe, and now the hopeless aftermath of starvation and confusion, suddenly dashed by British soldiers. Several had fainted, and others had gone to their aid. When they moved, the British soldiers shouted harsh warnings for them to remain still. But these men and women were used to Nazi soldiers, and despite the raised rifles, the British were no Nazis. So the passengers ignored the orders, knelt down, and gave comfort and water to the weakest of their own.

Eventually, the army commander, a self-important diminutive man called Lieutenant Colonel Pickford, roared up to the dock in a roofless military car. He stood up in the well of the passenger side and turned to address the group. There was a babel of languages among the refugees, but English was rare. To the predominantly German, Hungarian, or Russian speakers, his words were gibberish. Judita, however, understood every word. And in that moment she was torn. Her training told her to remain quiet, unnoticed, unremarkable. To blend in and be nondescript. But her time on the boat with these desperate people compelled her to speak and calm their rising fear and panic. She began to whisper a translation into German for those standing closest to her. Then into Hungarian, then Russian.

"He's saying that we're illegal immigrants who have violated international laws by traveling to British mandate Palestinian waters without approval. Because we're illegal, we'll be taken to an internment camp and processed. From there we may be sent to another country in the Mediterranean, or else sent back where we came from."

The men and women standing around her looked at her in horror. But she continued with her translation as Colonel Pickford, bellowing through a megaphone, continued to shout at the refugees.

"Men and women will be separated and sent to different camps for processing. Children will accompany their mothers. This will happen immediately. This is a naval dockside and needed by the British navy for the war effort . . ."

As she finished the translation, a dozen armed British soldiers walked toward the huddle of refugees, their rifles pointing at them from waist height, and began barking further orders. Judita lowered her gaze and shrank into the crowd, hoping she didn't stand out. She had been carefully prepared for the journey, her NKVD handlers believing the best way to make connection with the Jewish rebel groups would be to arrive as a refugee with a clear backstory validated by fellow passengers. For all her carefully rehearsed story, Judita could not physically hide the fact that she had not suffered through the horrors of Nazi Europe: She was healthy, her skin not drained of color, like all of the other people on board. Conscious of this, she pulled her scarf tighter around her head and shoulders.

From either translation or inference, the refugees now largely understood what they had to do, and most of the men and women began to separate. They picked up their battered suitcases or bundles of possessions tied together in tablecloths or sheets, and followed a soldier away from the dock, forming long lines. Some women, however, screamed in their native language that they wouldn't leave their husbands, and when this happened, the Tommies moved in and forcibly separated them with the barrel of a rifle. The refugees were then marched to waiting trucks, where they were loaded in to be driven inland to a camp that had been created months earlier to deal with the increasing numbers of illegal Jewish immigrants arriving in Palestine.

As the people climbed on the trucks, Judita moved from where she'd been standing outside the group, translating the colonel's instructions, and fell in at the end of the queue of women. In front of Judita, an elderly woman was panicked in confusion and slumped to her knees. Judita knelt beside her and asked where she was from, first in Russian, and when that received only blank looks, she tried German and then Czech. The final language flared recognition in the old woman's eyes, and she clung to Judita's arm as she was helped to her feet. Czech refugees were rare on this boat, and the woman was traveling alone.

Focused as she was on the elderly woman, Judita did not see Colonel Pickford stop and watch her as he surveyed the lines of people. The old woman was quickly moved on by a soldier, and Judita hunched her shoulders and retreated further into her scarf to blend back in.

Suddenly, the officer's clipped British voice called her out. "You! Girl. Come here."

She turned and saw Colonel Pickford, standing next to his car, pointing at her. "Come here." When she delayed, he shouted out, "Immediately, when I give an order!"

Judita walked over to where the colonel was standing. She wanted to stare him in the face, not to flinch or show any sort of deference. But she knew better, knew her mission was too important, so she lowered her eyes as it flashed in her mind that the officer was the same height as Beria. That didn't seem to be the only similarity.

"What's your name, girl?"

Judita told him. He asked questions about her origin, and she told him her story, a story she'd learned by heart in her training in Moscow.

"So, you come from Ruskie Land, do you? And how did you get here?"

She explained that she had managed to escape from Leningrad during the Nazi siege, crossed the border into Finland, and hidden in the woods. She'd made her way into Norway, where she'd been looked after by a family of evangelical Lutherans; then she had been given money for passage to Trieste in Italy now that the Fascists had been defeated. Wanting to emigrate to Palestine, here she was. It seemed an extraordinary story and yet was entirely consistent with any that the people getting on the British army trucks could tell.

"And you speak a number of languages?" said the colonel.

Judita was angry with herself, knowing that helping the old woman had made her stand out; the officer must have heard her speaking in Russian, German, and Czech.

"All these damn refugees from everywhere but Timbuktu! I need a girl like you in my office." With that he turned to his sergeant and said officiously, "See that this girl is fed and washed, then bring her to my quarters."

The sergeant saluted and barked, "Yes, sir."

Colonel Pickford got back into his car, and his driver roared away, leaving the sergeant, Judita, and some soldiers on the dock. Everybody else had been taken away. The sergeant escorted Judita to a small truck. She remained silent, eyes downcast, yet her mind raced through scenarios of what might lie ahead.

As they were walking, much to her surprise, the soldier said to her softly, "Listen, love. I got nothing against you Yids, okay? But—" The soldier stopped, cutting himself off midsentence, and looked around before continuing. "Look . . . just do what he fuckin' says, all right? And then he'll leave you alone and you can go back to your people. Like it never happened."

Judita imagined the confusion such an instruction might have had on any other young girl fresh off the ship. But she understood perfectly what he was saying. Though she did wonder if this soldier had tried to warn or even help others. She considered staying silent but instead, seizing the small chance to understand her enemy better, said, "Why are you telling me this?"

"What?" The soldier was genuinely surprised by the question.

Judita wanted to probe the nervous young man. "He's your commander, so why do you tell me this? Aren't you loyal to him?"

"I don't know. It just ain't right. This army's a fuckin' joke. Just an old boys' club. Them fuckin' officers do what they like and we take the bullets and run their errands." The soldier looked Judita in the eye for the first time. "I got a girl back home. We're gettin' engaged when this palaver's over. It ain't right what he does to the refugees. They're just kids. He shouldn't do it, that's all. I just wanted to warn ya. Just do what he says and then forget about it."

"I understand. And thank you. Your girl in England. She's lucky to have a man like you."

• • •

An hour later, washed and fed, Judita was shown to the top floor of the officers' quarters. The sergeant knocked on the door and nodded to the colonel. He smiled at Judita, pleased that she'd scrubbed up so nicely. She was indeed very pretty. One of the perks of the job, he had convinced himself, especially as he'd been stuck in this disgusting, stinking hellhole of a baking country when he should have been commanding a force of men, beating the living daylights out of the Krauts, or tending his roses back in Wimbledon.

Judita entered his quarters. They were sparsely furnished, no pictures on the walls or photographs on the credenza. It was the archetype of a bachelor's apartment, cold, austere, and friendless. The colonel invited her in, but said hardly a word to her. Instead, he acted like a medieval warlord, nodding at her to take a seat on the distressed lounge, the bottom sagging close to the floor, the cushions looking dusty and unkempt.

He came over and sat next to her. This was no seduction, no smiling gentleman plying her with drinks or soothing her nerves with soft lilting words. To Judita, it felt very far removed from the drunken diplomat in the Moscow bar all those months ago.

He put his arm around her shoulders and pulled her to him. "You know why you're here, don't you, girl?"

Judita said nothing but held his gaze.

"Play your cards right, and I can do a lot for you. If you're a good girl and please me, I can arrange to have you set free, and you can join your other Jew friends in Tel Aviv or wherever you want to go. But act like a little fool, and things will go very poorly for you. Do you understand me? I have the power to send you back to wherever I choose; and if you don't do as I say, you'll be very, very sorry."

Judita's mind was desperately working out what to do next. Her training in Moscow stood her in good stead; the one thing she didn't do was panic.

"Good. Now, get your clothes off, my little Jew, and go inside into the bedroom. I'll be in there shortly. Lie on the bed; don't get in it, because I've just had clean sheets put on."

She stood and walked toward the bedroom. As she crossed the floor, her eyes urgently searched for something she could use to protect herself. She deliberately walked slowly so that in those brief moments, she took in the landscape. As she passed by a simple kitchenette, with little more than a sink, a cupboard, and a gas ring with a kettle, she saw what she wanted.

She turned and asked, "Sir, might I have a glass of water?"

He was reading a report but looked up momentarily, nodded, and went back to his reading.

She turned on the tap, and while the glass was filling, the sound of the running water masked what her hand was doing. She slipped a short and fairly blunt knife from the cutlery drawer and pushed it up into the sleeve of her dress. She was amazed that this nasty little British man could be so arrogant as to give her, a hostage to his power, free run of the place. It was madness, but to her advantage. How could he be so stupid? Had the other girls he'd brought here been so weak-willed, so broken, as to blithely capitulate? Was he so conceited as to think each would simply comply?

After Judita had finished drinking, she put the glass back in the sink and went into the bedroom. She stood behind the door and waited for the colonel to think that she'd done as instructed.

Standing behind the door, she heard him walking across the floor. She saw the handle of the door turning. She waited for him to come through. He entered with his back to her, walking into the bedroom, looked for her on the bed, assuming she'd be naked, her legs open, waiting for him.

She was certainly waiting.

Judita observed his posture and saw a man with no conception of being in any danger, a man accustomed to safety and power. The very opposite of the refugees who had trundled off the boats only hours earlier. If this was the British in Palestine, they would surely lose in the fight ahead.

The colonel walked to the base of the bed, then looked around the room. Judita had been trained in many forms of armed and unarmed combat in Moscow. She had also been schooled in her limitations— she would never have size or strength to overcome a large man, but she would always have speed, and she could manufacture surprise. Although she was diminutive, here and now she had speed, surprise, and a knife.

She sprang forward, whipping her arm around the colonel's chin, her hand over his mouth. With her other hand, she twisted his neck as viciously as she could, not enough to snap the spine but enough to jolt his balance and shock his mind into panic, his body into an agony of pain. Using the weight of her body, she threw herself onto his back, his head at a murderously twisted angle. He was unstable and fell headlong to the floor. Acting quickly, she retrieved the knife from her sleeve.

She grasped it and stabbed it sharply, through the gap between the jacket and trousers of his uniform, underneath his rib cage, tearing apart his diaphragm, and sticking the sharp point of the otherwise dull knife into his heart. She'd chosen a dull blade with a sharp point because she wasn't using it to cut but to pierce. The accuracy with which she drove the blade up through his body overcame its lack of sharpness.

Hand still gripping his mouth tightly, she held his body firmly as she felt it twitch for a couple of moments, as though he was struggling before his heart stopped beating. Then he became a deadweight, and to any observer he could have been asleep on the floor at her feet. She waited for three long minutes for his heart to completely stop before she stabbed him twice more. She sliced his carotid artery and then thrust the knife once again up through his chest into his now still heart. In her training, she'd been taught to ensure that a victim was definitely dead, never to assume that the first strike had killed him. The reason she'd waited for the heart to be completely still was so when she sliced the artery in his neck, it didn't spurt blood over the walls and the floor. The little British bastard was well and truly dead. She dragged his heavy body across the floor, opened the wardrobe, and stuffed him inside, closing the door. Then she straightened the mat in front of the bed and covered the small stain of his blood and urine with some of his clothing from the drawers to make it look like he was just a messy individual. Anybody walking in and casually looking for the colonel would see nothing out of place.

Hopefully, it would take some time for his quarters to be searched. But now Judita had blood on her hands. She returned to the kitchen, where she washed carefully with carbolic soap and water, dried, and then checked herself to ensure that there wasn't any blood on her or that she wasn't unkempt when she left the quarters and met the sergeant, who was under orders to return her to the camp.

She had an hour to wait. She sat down on the dusty couch and read some of the colonel's papers. They appeared to be very low-level stuff, just basic administration, an order from Whitehall about costs, efficiency, and dispersal of troops. He might be a colonel, but outside of the army, he'd probably be some minor office bureaucrat. He was a nonentity, and the power he'd exercised over her and other girls must have been the most exciting part of his day.

Judita rubbed her eyes hard so they turned pink, so the decent sergeant would assume that she'd been crying. She hoped he wouldn't be blamed when the colonel's body was discovered.

Central Israel

161 C.E.

HIS MOUTH WAS full of mud and his lungs were bursting for air, his limbs little more than deadweights desperately trying to crawl up the riverbank. But Abram was alive.

How long had he been beneath the surface of the water? It was so calm on top, yet the undertow had carried him far, far from the village. At first he'd struggled, but then he'd let the strong current carry him away from Abimelech and the others.

How far had he drifted? These things he didn't know. But he knew he was alive. Abimelech's grip, the followers of Jesus on the riverbank, were an event of his immediate past, something that had happened far up the river. Surely they believed him to be dead, as he had believed until the Lord Almighty had caused him to cough and then struggle to the surface for air. The moment he choked, the gasping cough had awakened his senses. Floundering in the river, he'd managed to paddle to the side, and with a final almighty effort, he'd climbed the bank and now felt God's sun on his body.

Abram lay there for a long time, long enough for his shirt to dry on his back and become brittle with caked mud. He forced himself to roll over and, pushing himself up with one hand, felt a short stab of pain. He looked at his arms and saw the mud dark with dried blood. He didn't remember the injury, but from the irregular tear, it looked to be the work of a branch or rock he must have bounced off as the current swept him away. He looked back to the river and continued to wonder why the surface was so smooth and bland, yet the current below was so strong. Was that why Abimelech had held him so tightly?

Abram flopped over onto his back and felt the late-afternoon sun on his face, warm and soaking into his skin. He forced his eyes open, saw the sky, and drank in the air. How far had he come? Which direction had he been carried by the brown water? Abram let these thoughts wash over him, happy just to feel the sensation of breathing.

And then he remembered the stone seal.

. . .

It was a long walk, but the river was his guide, and the stars gave just enough light in the dark for the exhausted boy to find his way back to the road and the Roman milestone. He felt as though he should pray that the seal would be there where he had hidden it, but he didn't. He couldn't face the idea that his prayers wouldn't be answered, which would be a sign of his failure.

Abram stood over the milestone looking down at its foreign markings, marks chiseled into the surface of the stone in clear lines and crosses. The starlight cast just enough illumination to create contrast in the chisel marks, and Abram reached out to find the X that he'd identified earlier that day.

He swept both hands over the dirt at the base of the short stone obelisk, recalling how he'd pretended to stumble and pushed the stone seal into the dirt to hide it.

Finding nothing of the familiar shape, Abram pushed his hands deeper and scraped away handfuls of dirt and rock and sand as he felt his heart pound and his stomach sink. Could the seal be lost? Had he failed? His movements became more frantic as he cleared the ground, feeling for the seal, until his hand closed around a smooth, hard object and a shape his fingers knew so well. He didn't even have to look down to know that he had found it.

Abram collapsed at the base of the milestone, held the seal to his chest, and sobbed in the darkness.

. . .

A week later, even the air felt charged with danger. The closer he came to Jerusalem, the more cautious Abram grew, traveling at night and sleeping in the undergrowth of trees during the day.

As he traveled northeast, ascending the hills on top of which sat the thousand-year-old city of Jerusalem, he was forced to hide more often when he encountered larger and more heavily armed Roman patrols and even the occasional legion marching to their headquarters. When he was growing up, he'd been told the stories of his great-great-grandfather—a gentle doctor named Abraham who'd sacrificed himself by confronting a Roman century, allowing his wife and children to escape. It was told that the synagogue in his village of Peki'in in the northern Galilee had been built in his honor. This story was meant to make Abram feel brave, that such bravery was in his bloodline, but as he drew closer to Jerusalem and his objective, his trepidation grew.

Abram could feel when danger approached and when he should hide, because even from far away, his keen senses could detect the creaking of the soldiers' leather and the clanging of their metal armor. At these times he'd hide in the woods, bury himself underneath leaves and branches and twigs, and wait silently. He often mused that if he were armed with a bow and arrow or even a pilum, the javelin that Roman soldiers carried, he might show the bravery his ancestor had, attack the Roman soldiers, and escape into the forest like the Zealots without being caught.

But for a Jew to be caught with a weapon was death. So he would lie there, peeking out from his hiding place, watching the soldiers march in tight formation behind the horse on which their centurion was riding.

The Romans weren't his only problem as a traveler in Israel. There was also danger from the Zealots who sometimes wandered these hills, hoping to kill members of a small Roman patrol. And they were known to kill Jews who looked as though they were supporters or collaborators with the Roman army. Such Jews, who usually dressed like the Romans in short togas, might be those who were feeding off the fat of the land instead of suffering, like their co-religionists. It was Jewish women who were the targets of the Zealots, women who wore trinkets or jewels, who painted their faces or smelled of perfumes. Any one of these might become a target.

Abram found himself in a valley at the foothills of the city. Exhausted, he lay on the ground, staring up at a city on the hill, the city about which the rabbis in the cave had spoken with such devotion and awe, the city they called Jerusalem.

He looked at it, and even from here, he could feel its mystery, its otherworldliness. Jerusalem seemed built on the side of a hill, and the gleaming white wall surrounding it seemed to be stopping the city from falling down into the valley. Abram stood to get a better view and hid behind a tree, hoping to be out of sight of the men on the wall above. He stared up, wondering how to get past the soldiers who guarded the gates to the city. Perhaps he should wait until it was night and try and climb over the wall and hide himself in the shadows—

"Who are you? Why are you hiding?"

Abram whipped around in shock, his heart pounding, wondering at the failure of his ears to hear someone coming. His eyes darted about to find the source of the voice. In the distance, standing among the trees, he saw a young woman, perhaps a year or two older than he. She wasn't a Roman but a Jewess, dressed in a long gown with a shawl over her head and neck. She was beautiful, and he stared at her.

"I asked who you are. And why are you hiding behind a tree?"

"N-nothing . . ." Abram stammered.

"Nothing? Is that your name or what you're doing?"

Abram had no answer under the scrutiny of the young woman.

"Well, if you're called Nothing and you're doing nothing, then why are you on my father's land? And who are you hiding from?"

"Abram."

"Abram? So that's your name? But I prefer to call you Nothing, and that's what I'll call you until you tell me what you're doing here."

"Nothing."

"Don't start that again. You're Nothing from nowhere, and you're doing nothing. Stop being silly and tell me who you are and why you're here."

The young woman's voice was shrill yet commanding. But Abram's heart began to settle, and he pulled his senses together.

"Who are you?" he asked.

"I'm Ruth. I'm the daughter of Eli and Naomi of the Tribe of Judah who own this land. And one day, when I'm a woman, I'll own it, because I have no brothers. So there." She walked over to him and seemed to be scrutinizing him. "You smell," she said.

"I fell into a river. I've been walking for two weeks. I've been sleeping in the fields. I'm sorry." Though, in that moment, Abram had no idea why he was apologizing.

"The Kedron River runs into this valley. Its water is clean. It comes from Jerusalem. You should wash in there. But you mustn't drink the water because the Romans are in the city, and my father says that the Romans are filthy and may even piss down the wells. When you've washed, come back and talk to me. I'll be here tomorrow."

And with that, she was gone. Abram looked at Ruth's departing back and wondered why she'd spoken to him like that. She was rude and arrogant. But she was very pretty, and despite her offensiveness, he thought it was a good idea to go and wash in the river. He would then come back to this spot, not only to meet the girl again but also to work out which was the best way to enter Jerusalem.

The following day, Abram realized that he wasn't looking up at Jerusalem but peering through the trees in the hope that Ruth would walk toward him. Not only had he washed himself thoroughly in the cold water, he'd also found a private place where the river meandered through fields, and washed his clothes as best he could. He'd spread them out on the bank to dry, lying naked in the warm sun and hoping that nobody passed by.

Dressed and no longer smelling of rotting earth and decaying grasses, Abram sighed, wondering whether it was part of her rudeness to promise to return and then fail to do so. He'd been waiting for quite some time and was beginning to think that his morning had been wasted when a voice behind him said, "You're not much of a spy, are you, Abram Nothing? I've been watching you from behind this tree for a long time, and you didn't know."

Abram spun around, again dismayed that his ears had failed him.

She came out from behind a thicket and walked toward him. Today she was dressed differently. Yesterday she'd been in a plain brown gown and a black shawl; today she was dressed in an iridescent blue dress with what appeared to have different-colored threads running through it. A pure white scarf was pulled over the back of her head, and she wore sandals on her feet. Her hair was black, but her eyes were what fascinated him. They were a deep and rich purple, the color of the dyes made from seashells found on the shores of the Mediterranean. He'd never seen such eyes. He could feel himself staring as she walked purposefully toward him.

She stood just the distance of an outstretched arm from him and sniffed at the air.

"Well, you certainly smell better than you did yesterday. Have you eaten? You look starved. Come with me now."

Ruth turned and walked in a northerly direction away from the hill of Jerusalem. Without a word, Abram followed her.

• • •

"Would you like some water or pomegranate juice?" Ruth's mother, Naomi, asked as Abram finished off his second bowl of lentils, wiping the bowl greedily with a large wedge of bread.

The woman was thin and pale, but her eyes shone the same deep purple as Ruth's. Abram had been welcomed into the home by Naomi with warmth and the taste of real food. His palpable relief showed on his face, and Ruth's mother couldn't help but smile.

It was only when his stomach was full and he leaned back from the table that he remembered his fears and his experiences with the Christian family, who had also shown him kindness at the beginning.

Ruth's father, Eli, sat at the end of the table. Abram glanced at him from time to time, but his manner warned the young man not to trespass on his mood. He appeared to be cloaked in shadow, an expression of indifference lining his face. He had said little since Ruth had pulled a reticent Abram into the home, but his eyes had rarely left Abram's in that time. Even as Abram looked down into his bowl to finish the last of the lentils, he could feel Eli's eyes boring into him.

"Where have you come from, Abram?" asked Naomi as she set down the water jug.

"Peki'in." Abram hoped that his home village was so small that his hosts hadn't heard of it.

"He looked half starved when I found him, but he seems better now," said Ruth.

"Someone must have helped you along your journey, Abram. Surely you didn't travel that far on your own," said Naomi.

"I can look after myself," Abram replied, almost defensively, trying to keep his eyes away from Eli's gaze.

"But you must have seen many things on the roads, many dangers. These days nobody is safe traveling, especially a man as young as you. Romans soldiers and Zealots and caravans and all manner of strange people are throughout the land. And every one of them is a danger to us Israelites."

"Not just them," said Abram. "I encountered madmen and men who called themselves Christian Nazarenes. Strange people who laugh at our laws."

"You met Nazarenes?" asked Eli, his interjection surprising Abram. "You weren't taken in by these Nazarenes and their nonsense, were you, boy? They're heretics who ignore the laws of Moses. They're thieves and madmen. I know these people. A month ago, they were scouring this part of Israel seeking out converts, telling everybody that they could drive the Romans out with love and the word of this Jesus person. Some fools of neighbors went along with their nonsense, but I drove them off my land." Eli burst out laughing. "Wash away sins in a river? What rubbish! That this life has no value but all will be well in the next? That's just an excuse to be lazy! Only fools and the desperate would believe such things."

Abram felt compelled to respond and, in some way, defend himself. "In my village, I served the Rabbi Shimon bar Yochai . . ." The words came out of Abram's mouth as a way to prove his Jewishness and stave away the memories of the baptism by river. Again Eli surprised him.

"Rabbis are little better than these Nazarenes," he said, taking a last drink of water. He looked at Naomi and Ruth, but they'd heard it all before. "Rabbis! What good are rabbis? Have they defended us from the Romans? Have their words eased our suffering? And what good did the temple ever do but take our money and make sacrifices of animals that we might have eaten instead of going hungry? Listen to me, boy. Don't put your trust in anything but the work of your own hands and the family around you. Everything else is empty. God doesn't care about us. Look around; the proof is everywhere. We starve and struggle. Moses gave us a land of milk and honey, but in the time that's passed since he walked these hills, we've had nothing but war and conquest and rape and pillage.

"Land of milk and honey. What a lie! If this is God's land and we're God's chosen people, then it can only have been God who sent the Romans to crush us. That's how much He cares for us!"

"Eli, you're scaring the boy," hissed Naomi, but Eli ignored her and continued.

"The Romans crush us and all we can throw against them are the Zealots. Where's our Jewish army? Where are the soldiers of Solomon and Samson, Gideon and Joshua? How can we defend our land and our people when all we have are rabbis, and now these Nazarenes are telling our people that this life has no value, and the only time they'll be happy is when they're dead?"

Abram wanted to say something, but Ruth looked at him and almost imperceptibly shook her head, so he remained silent.

Ruth's mother tried to change the subject. "Where will you go to from here, Abram? Where are you headed?"

"Jerusalem."

Naomi shook her head and Ruth raised an eyebrow at him.

"I'm going to Jerusalem," said Abram more clearly. "I have something that I must do up there."

There was a long moment of silence before Eli spoke. "You've been in the sun too long, boy."

"You cannot go into the city, Abram. It's forbidden," Naomi said.

Abram was worried by the urgency in her voice. "I know. But there is something I must do."

"What could be so important you would risk death?" asked Eli, his voice softer, more kindly—the first genuine question he'd asked. But Abram realized that he'd said too much and took another sip of water.

"His business is his own, Father. Perhaps he has a sacred quest he's not allowed to tell us." Ruth's voice rose in excitement.

Abram looked at her and was worried that the beautiful young woman was reading his mind. She gave him a wink. But the sweet moment was broken when Eli thundered, "I forbid it! You will not go. Now that you've eaten in my home, I will not have your blood on my hands. I forbid you to go anywhere near the city. Do you understand me? If the Romans catch you up there, and they surely will, they will put you to death without a second thought."

Abram and Ruth remained silent.

"Do you understand me?" Eli said.

Still Ruth and Abram remained silent, simply lowering their eyes from his intense gaze.

• • •

Later, as Abram lay curled up on the floor in a corner of the room, he thought of Rabbi Shimon and touched the stone seal inside his shirt. The high priest had tried to dissuade him and taken the stone from him, declaring that he should abandon his task. Abimelech and the followers of Jesus had scared him with their zeal and their desire to change who he was, telling him that his task was for nothing and what he did in this world did not matter. In this house, he was being blocked again as Eli decried God Himself and forbade him from entering the city. Abram felt as if he'd entered a world of madmen.

The youngster was confused and angry. He'd been brought up to trust the words of men and women older than he was, to respect them. Yet he'd found three people whom he, by rights, should have trusted, who were acting against him and his mission.

Suddenly, he heard a shuffle in the pitch-blackness of the sleeping household. He strained to hear what it could be and nearly cried out when a blanket was dropped unceremoniously on top of his body.

Over him stood Ruth. Before he could say anything, she crouched beside him and lowered her mouth almost to his ear, so close he could feel her moist breath on his cheek.

"I can get you into Jerusalem," said the fiery young woman. "Trust me, it's easy."

Jerusalem, Palestine

May 7, 1945

ALTHOUGH THERE WERE nearly twenty people in the room, there was a sudden silence, broken only by the static from the radio. The ceiling was blue with cigarette smoke, the table was groaning with bottles of wine and black beer, as well as piles of plates, knives, and forks alongside the remnants of hastily eaten food. The young men and women, many red-eyed and exhausted from hours of duty, expeditions, and danger, listened eagerly in case the clipped and very proper voice of the BBC announcer came back on. They and the rest of the world were waiting to hear what was happening in the red-brick schoolhouse that served as the supreme headquarters of the Allied Expeditionary Force in the champagne city of Reims in France.

All of the young Jewish men and women, fighters for the guerrilla force Lehi, had temporarily put down their rifles and sidearms, their grenades and explosives, and gathered in the secret meeting room near Ben Yehuda Street in order to listen to the broadcast. Through a tinny radio speaker, they would soon hear the announcement of the end of World War II. For the first time since Hitler's coming to power in 1933, Deutschland would soon no longer be *über alles, über alles in der Welt.*

The BBC announcer was reading from hastily written notes handed to him by his reporting staff, who were on the telephone to their man in France observing the solemn proceedings. Hitler had killed himself a week earlier. His body, along with that of his new wife Eva Braun, had burned to a cinder. Reichsmarshall Herman Göring decided to take control of the beleaguered nation, hoping that as the new führer, he'd be treated with respect by the British and the Americans; but he'd been peremptorily removed and replaced by Grand Admiral Karl Dönitz.

It was left to the chief of staff of what remained of the German Armed Forces High Command, General Alfred Jodl in France, to sign the instrument of unconditional surrender and hand over power and the government of Germany to the representatives of England and America and the other allies. Soon Field Marshal Wilhelm Keitel would sign a similar instrument in Berlin to the commander of the Soviet forces, General Georgi Zhukov. And then it would all be over—in Europe, at least, because Japan was too far away for the Jews of Palestine to worry about, and it was America's and Australia's problem, anyway.

It had been four months since Judit had arrived by ship into Palestine and escaped from the internment camp. In that short time she had been readily absorbed into the fighting force of Lehi. She was highly valued for her ability with languages that, in many ways, united the linguistically disparate group.

As the radio voice excitedly reported what was happening, Judit translated from English to Hebrew, then quickly paraphrased into Russian and Polish. Many in the room loved to listen to the way she formulated the words, all with her deep and melodic Russian accent, using the idioms of the language that were music to their ears.

The overwrought announcer said breathlessly, "I've just been informed by my colleagues that . . . that . . . yes, General Jodl has just signed . . . and . . . yes, the instrument is being moved across the table to the British and American representatives . . . I'm informed that they've all now signed . . . General Jodl is standing and holding out his hand to shake the British and American generals' . . . they're refusing to touch his hand . . . they won't shake . . . but now they're turning to each other and . . . yes . . . they're shaking each other's hands . . . the Americans and the British . . . Jodl is looking downcast . . . they're saying something to each other, but we can't hear what they're . . . now Jodl is being escorted out of the building . . . it's over. The war in Europe is finished. Ladies and gentlemen, it's over. It's all over . . . grounds for celebration . . . count the dead in days to come . . . rebuild our future . . . His Majesty the King will greet the crowds gathering outside Buckingham Palace even as I speak . . ."

People in the room began laughing, slapping backs, kissing, tousling hair, and drinking whatever alcohol was left in their glasses, shouting "mazel tov" at the tops of their voices. Everybody was hugging and kissing and jumping in the air.

Almost everybody.

A diminutive man sat on a stool in the corner, looking at his young charges, wondering whether or not he should bring them down to earth now or let them have their moment of happiness. Sitting beside him was another man, also short in stature but with a face as hard as granite. Not even the news of Germany's surrender could make him smile. The two men—Nathan Yellin-Mor, head of Lehi's political wing, and Yitzhak Shamir, head of the organization's operational units—sat and watched the party. They looked at each other. They knew what had to be done.

"Chaverim v'chaverot," shouted Yellin-Mor, "brothers and sisters, calm down. Quiet. Brother Yitzhak Shamir has something to say."

It was as though a cold blast of air had entered the room. All the exultant young men and women turned and looked at the two Lehi leaders, their faces impassive, their bodies relaxed. The reputation of these men was undeniable. Just two years earlier, Nathan Yellin-Mor had escaped from a British detention center by digging an underground tunnel almost seventy-five meters long and taking nineteen men to freedom. Yitzhak Shamir may have been barely five feet tall, but he enjoyed a fearsome legacy as a firebrand warrior within Lehi and the mind behind their strategic attacks, bombings, and assassinations.

"Mazel tov to us all. The war with the Nazis is over. Good. Meantime, they've murdered millions of our people in their death factories. This will never be forgiven. This cannot be forgotten. One of the Jews' enemies has been destroyed. Thanks to the sacrifice of the British and their recently engaged allies, the Americans, the greatest evil ever to befall the Jewish people, Adolf Hitler and his gang of thugs, has been destroyed. Excellent. Wonderful! But let us not lose sight of our goal, and that is to make Palestine into Israel so that whichever poor Jewish bastard remains alive in Europe after this holocaust can find a place here, a home of safety and a sanctuary for the rest of his or her life. And that means that we have to persuade the British that their mission here is at an end, and that they have to pack up and go home." Shamir paused for effect.

"While ever they are here, in Palestine, ours is not free air to breathe. How can we create a Jewish state of Israel while there are British in command of our cities and our people? How can there ever be an Israel while we can be stopped in the street by a British Tommy who demands our papers; while we can be arrested just for looking like a Jew?

"When this happens to us on our land, those who perpetrate such crimes against us are our enemy. The Nazis were never the enemy we had to fight here in Palestine. The British were and continue to be our enemy, as are the Arabs who reject our presence. Remember that the mufti of Jerusalem is Hitler's greatest ally; remember that the mufti spent much of the war living in Berlin, being treated like some potentate.

"While the Nazis were destroying our people in Europe, it was the British who refused to let our people flee to Palestine. They are as responsible for the deaths before our brothers and sisters reached our shores as the Nazis. Had they allowed our people to enter Palestine, thousands, perhaps millions, could have been saved.

"Now is the time to send the British this message: that there will be no peace until they are forced out. Now is the time for us to strike, when they're drunk on victory and distracted; now is the time for us to intensify our fight!"

Shalman sat in the back corner of the room watching Shamir make his speech. He knew he should have felt joyous at the news of the end of the war, but for reasons he couldn't quite grasp, he felt a strange melancholy. The people around him were his brothers and sisters, and yet they were not like him.

It had been his guardian, Dov, who had brought Shalman to Lehi. The Stern Gang had become his family. They had trained him and given him purpose when he felt aimless, given his anger a target and a name. But still he felt like an outsider. These people all around him might be his brothers and sisters in the struggle to throw off the British, but he was different from most of them. They were refugees and migrants while Shalman had been born here in the land of Palestine. The childhood memories of jumping off sand dunes at Shabbat beach picnics with his parents were ingrained in his mental landscape. When his comrades fought for the land, it was because of what they wanted it to be, for they had enjoyed no childhood here, no memories of this place. This made Shalman feel different from the others. What he fought for was for the homeland he loved, the landscape of his childhood. He was fighting for what he knew.

So why did he find pulling the trigger so hard?

These were the thoughts on Shalman's mind when, amid the noise of revelry, Shamir had taken him quietly and conspiratorially aside and introduced him to a beautiful young woman whom others called Judita but whom Shamir had renamed Judit after the biblical heroine.

Before Shamir walked away to leave them together, he turned to Shalman and whispered, "Be careful of this one; remember your Bible and what Judith did to Holofernes." And for the first time that he recalled, Shalman heard Shamir laughing.

•   •   •

An hour later, in the early morning, the streets were empty and pitch-black. It was usually warm in May, but tonight in Jerusalem it was unseasonably cool, and they were grateful for the overcoats that concealed the Sten carbines with silencers that they carried beneath.

Earlier, before they left the group celebrating the end of the war, Shamir had given Shalman and Judit a mission. The official armistice in Europe was a night of celebration for the British. With the Nazi menace now over, enlisted men and officers alike would be drunk and disorderly in the streets of the ancient city. Among them would be a specific trio of soldiers whom Shamir had earmarked.

When told of the order, Shalman had questioned it openly. Why these three men? What did they do? Why not bomb a train line, an airfield? Why three ordinary British Tommies?

Shalman had surprised himself with the questions, which seemed to come from nowhere. Judit eyed him quizzically but said nothing as Shamir answered. Bombing train lines and airfields hurt the British military machine, killing officers fractured the British command, but killing regular soldiers was about hurting the British soul. To blow up a train would make headlines, but to kill a conscript from Leeds or Birmingham or Manchester would send a shudder of disgust through the city; everybody in the city would identify with the dead soldier, his widow, his children. And soon the wails of anguish would be heard in London's parliament, where decisions were made. The British, Shamir told them, were exhausted from a six-year war. The idea of more deaths so far from home was more than they would be able to bear.

"On this night, when they are thinking themselves invincible, we need to show them just how personally vulnerable they are. Rot them from the inside," Shamir had told them.

Now Shalman and Judit lay on the low roof of a closed and empty shop, surveying a narrow alley, preparing to cause that rot. It was a precise location where Shamir seemed to know the three men would be heading at this particular time. A direct route from their barracks at the end of the duty shift to the enlisted men's recreation hall at the end of the alley.

Shalman and Judit had gotten here by skirting the shadows of the nighttime streets and avoiding the King David Hotel, the epicenter of British control in Jerusalem.

The spot where they were lying was ideal because the flat roof joined three other roofs in easy stages. When they'd completed their assignment, they could scamper across the rooftops and disappear into a street behind that would take them far away from the shooting. By the time an alarm had been raised, Shalman and Judit would long since be gone.

Shalman glanced at the young woman next to him. The mixture of beauty and focus in her face turned his glance into a stare, which soon drew her attention away from the street below. Shalman quickly stammered a question to explain his gaze. "Have you ever used a rifle before?" It was a stupid question. The look Judit gave him told him that she had. Nervously, Shalman elaborated. "I mean like this. To kill . . ."

In the moonlight, she was quite lovely. She wore no makeup, as was the habit of young Jewish women in Palestine, but her skin, her cheekbones, her deep-set eyes, her lustrous hair pinned beneath the dark brown scarf she wore, almost made the young man forget the reason he was there.

She smiled at Shalman and gave him a reassuring nod. "I'll be okay. Thank you for thinking of me," she said with a liberal hint of sarcasm to which Shalman was oblivious.

He continued to dig his hole deeper. "But if you become frightened or nervous—"

Judit cut him off, more with a look than what she said. "I'll be fine, Shalman."

Shalman retreated, feeling somewhat foolish. Judit sensed this and her voice softened. "They're not innocent, Shalman. I know men like these. Not enlisted men, maybe, but the officers commanding them. You don't know them like I know them. And what they're capable of doing."

"What do you mean?" he asked.

She thought back to the time she'd landed in Haifa, when the awful little British nonentity of an officer had tried to rape her. But she kept quiet. At that moment there was a distant sound of several men laughing and talking loudly. Shalman and Judit heard the men walking nearer, their voices becoming more distinct. One was even singing.

Suddenly, the men stopped moving, even though the sound of voices continued. Judit strained to hear and then turned to Shalman. "I think they're pissing against a wall. Men always grow quiet when their dicks are out. Why can't men piss and talk at the same time?"

Shalman looked at her in astonishment, having absolutely no idea what to say. He turned back to look at the road. The noise of the men started up again and came closer to where they were stationed. Then, around a corner, they saw three men weaving on the pavement. They were carrying bottles of beer, drinking and stumbling and falling and laughing and shouting and singing. Shalman and Judit had been told that the Tommies would be on their way to drink, not drunk and leaving the barracks. Everything was out of kilter because of the end of the war. The news had prompted early celebrations, which would make their task all the easier.

Judit and Shalman readied their Sten guns for when the Tommies were close enough. They peered through the sights and held their breath. The noise of the men, fracturing the silence of the early-morning city under curfew, grew closer and closer. They slowed and swigged from their bottles, threw their arms around one another's shoulders, then continued to walk. They ambled closer until they were opposite the low rooftop where the two young Jews were lying.

Shalman drew in his breath, squeezed his left eye shut, and looked down the barrel of the carbine. At the end of the sight was a British soldier who reminded Shalman of the day his father was taken away, of his mother's grief. He reminded him of Dov and what he had said to him two years ago: "If we're to keep this land, we have to fight for it; we have to take it, Shalman."

The Tommies were close now, the line from his gun sight to their chests clear and steady, and the presence of Judit seemed to slip away, leaving Shalman in his own world. He lifted his finger to the trigger and could feel his hand twitch and shake as it drew close to the thin strip of metal. All he had to do was press it, and it would unleash hell. As he held his breath, Shalman remembered the night when Yitzhak Shamir had shot the British officer after Shalman hesitated. Shamir had been true to his word, telling others that Shalman had done the job. The Pole had given Shalman a wink and never mentioned it again.

Shalman wanted to kill. He had every reason to kill. But something inside weighed him down and slowed his response. And it was in this delay that Shalman heard a series of short, deadened pops in bursts of three. With his eye still down the barrel, he saw the bodies of the men twitch like puppets whose strings were pulled by some monstrous kid, then begin to fall to the ground. First to fall was the one that he had in his gun sights and who he was yet to shoot. His gaze and his rifle sight shifted to one of the other men, but even before his eyes focused, he saw that man, too, stumble forward in the instant of the metallic bullet pops. He shifted his gun sight immediately to the third man and found him already facedown in the alley.

Amazed, he scanned the three bodies again. They were all splayed like animal carcasses on the ground or against a wall; two were twitching, while one lay still. Shalman hadn't even had time to squeeze his trigger, and Judit had shot each and every one.

He turned to face her, but she was looking down the barrel of her gun. She squeezed the trigger once more, firing into the body of a soldier on the ground, then the other two a second time each.

She turned to look at Shalman staring at her, his mouth open. Judit said softly, as though discussing a recipe for a cake, "Always make sure the job is done. A sniper must never be satisfied with the first shot. You can't tell from this distance whether you've wounded somebody or killed him. Best to shoot once or twice more, just to make sure. Now let's get the hell out of here."

• • •

Shalman sat drinking orange juice in a café, waiting for Judit to arrive, and pondering the events of the night before. But it wasn't the bullets or the mission that was exercising his mind; rather, it was the young woman who had been with him and who, truth be known, had surprised him with her attitude toward her job. Since joining Lehi, he'd killed a couple of British soldiers, but each time it had made him feel sick to his stomach. When he killed, it was always with the greatest reluctance; Judit killed with the clinical approach of a surgeon performing an operation.

Shalman still felt guilty about the night Yitzhak Shamir had covered for him, so he had been the first to tell the Lehi operations leader how she'd killed three Tommies before he'd even had a chance to squeeze the trigger.

Shamir simply laughed out loud and slapped him on the back, saying, "She's quite something, isn't she?" Shalman had been expecting a reprimand, but evidently, Shamir saw the news as evidence of Judit's prowess rather than the young man's failure.

The café door opened and a draft of air blew into the room. Judit sauntered over to where he was sitting. He looked at her closely. Her features were fine, her face slender, her eyes deep-set and sparkling and as black as night, and she had a radiant smile.

"Shalom, Shalman. How are you?"

Before he could answer, the waiter appeared and Judit ordered food and drink. Shalman joined her, ordering a plate of dips and pita bread.

"So, what have you been up to?" she asked, as though they were on a date. In fact, they were on a date of sorts. Returning from the mission the night before, they'd settled into an animated and easy discussion about history as they passed under the white stone walls of the old city. It was the history of ancient Jerusalem that had fascinated Shalman ever since he was a boy.

His father had fostered this love in him from an early age, and Shalman had since filled his nights with every book he could scrounge to feed his thirst for knowledge about Israel's past. For her part, Judit was an enthusiastic audience and encouraged him to tell her more as they walked the long way back, steering clear of British soldiers. She was evidently intelligent and understood much of the world, and Shalman found himself wondering how she knew so little of the city's history. Or was she just being polite?

Whatever it was, it filled him with a confidence he rarely had, and before he knew what he was saying, Shalman found himself asking this mysterious young woman to have lunch with him, to continue their discussion.

And now here they were. The excitement of it, entranced by her as he was, made Shalman forget his misgivings about the attack the night before and his own hesitation to pull the trigger. Judit raised the topic nonetheless. "That wasn't easy for you last night, was it?"

Shalman didn't answer the question, though he knew exactly what she was referring to.

"It's okay," she continued. "It shouldn't be easy. We have to remember that we're not killing sons and brothers and fathers but targets. It's never easy, Shalman, but it has to be worth it."

Shalman pondered what that meant. Was the creation of a nation of Israel, a land of history and culture, morals and intellect, worth being rebuilt on the blood of British soldiers? Was the way Lehi performed its goals worth the grief to soldiers' families? Both ideas seemed right, and yet both were hideously flawed in his mind. And these thoughts, at this moment in the restaurant, were a distraction. Enough of war and killing: All he wanted to think about was peace and calm and the beautiful girl in front of him whom he so desperately wanted to know.

Shalman tried to change topics and asked about her family, where she was from, how she came to Palestine. Remembering her training, Judit told him the story that had been created for her. She answered openly and honestly as best she could about her family but of course said nothing about her training, her enlistment into the spy ranks of the Soviet Secret Service. What she told him, and the way she explained things, denied the gravity of her story. Her tone made even horror stories seem bright. Her attitude entranced Shalman further.

"So tell me, do you have a girlfriend?" she asked.

He was stunned by her question. What could have caused her to ask? No, surely . . . but while he knew he should answer, all he could manage was to shake his head.

Judit filled the void left by Shalman's silence. "I don't have a boyfriend. Mind you, that's because I've not been here long. Some of the guys in Lehi are sniffing around, but I'm not interested in them. You fascinate me, Shalman. You're so reluctant as a soldier, I don't understand why you're here."

He told her about the British arresting his father, about his mother's grief, and about Dov enlisting him in the youth group of Lehi. She nodded and reached across to hold his hand. Hers was warm and dry, and he thrilled at her touch.

"Tomorrow night," she said matter-of-factly, "there's a film being shown at the cinema on Ben Yehuda. It's called *Here Comes M. Jordan*, and it's about a boxer who goes to heaven but he's not supposed to be there, and he's sent back. I love romance and comedies, and this is both! We never had films like this in Moscow. Will you take me?"

Shalman looked at her in amazement. She continued talking as if it were the most natural thing.

"Back in Russia, the films were all so serious. And how can you be interested in a two-hour movie about tractors and great leaps forward and Stalin's next five-year plan? But here you have Hollywood films. When shall we go? Shall I tell you where I live? Do you want to go for some food before or after the movie? I don't mind, because I'm used to being hungry, but you might need something to eat before the movie starts."

He looked at her and realized that he hadn't said a word in minutes. He was sitting in a café in Jerusalem with a girl who just the previous night had killed three soldiers, and now she was talking excitedly about going out to see a movie. And Judit wanted Shalman to take her.

Kedron River

161 C.E.

"YOU MUST SWEAR that you'll never ever tell them, even if the end of the world happens and everything around us is destroyed—not even then. Swear it to me, Abram. Swear."

"I swear."

"By the most holy?"

"By the most holy. How do you get past the guards and into Jerusalem?"

It was the morning following the meal he'd eaten at her parents' home, and in the sunshine, their feet were dangling in the Kedron River. Ruth smiled and looked up to the white city gleaming in the sunlight on top of the hill.

"I put on a special dress made of the wings of seraphim, and I fly over the gate at night, and I become one of the teraphim and smite the Roman soldiers and leave many dead."

Abram looked at her, his eyes wide. Everything about her seemed so extraordinary that even the tale might have been true.

Ruth held the moment before bursting out with laughter. "You're silly, Abram Nothing. There's an old disused tunnel that leads from the floor of the valley up into the city. Nobody goes there. It comes out in the middle of Jerusalem, at the foot of where the old temple used to be. I've climbed the tunnel. The Romans don't know about it because the entrance in the valley where the water trickles out is covered with rocks and grass and rubble . . . Why are you looking at me like that?" she asked, suddenly aware of Abram's strange gaze.

"That's the tunnel . . . That's the tunnel the rabbi sent me to look for," he said. "That's . . . that's . . . ." He was speechless.

"You mean you do have a sacred quest? I was right! I thought you were special, Abram Nothing. What is it? What do we have to do?"

The word "we" made Abram recoil and look away.

"It's very simple, Abram Nothing: If you don't tell me, I won't show you the tunnel. You won't complete your quest, and I won't get to go on an adventure. And neither of us will get what we want."

It was all so matter-of-fact that Abram told her before he could stop himself. "I was given something to put back in the tunnel by Rabbi Shimon. The rabbi and his son live in a cave near my home, hiding from the Romans." Despite the caution he'd shown since leaving home, and the injunction from the rabbi not to speak to anybody about the seal, Abram took it out of his special inner pocket and showed it to her.

She held it toward the sun so that it caused shadows to fall across the letters. "I can't read it. What does it say?"

"I don't know," answered Abram honestly. "But I know what it is. The rabbi told me. It was made by the man who built the tunnel for King Solomon of blessed memory, and when the rabbis escaped from Jerusalem, they took the seal to protect it. Now they want me to put it back so that God will know that the tunnel is ours and not the Romans'. The rabbi said it was something to do with our birthright. That Jerusalem and all of Israel is ours and not the Romans'." Abram took the seal back from Ruth and slipped it inside his shirt. "I have to return it."

"But of course God will know. He knows everything," she said.

Abram shrugged. "The rabbis have given me a special mission to put it back."

Ruth seemed to ponder this before saying, "Why?"

It was a very simple question, but Abram found his mind blank for an answer.

Ruth pressed on. "Why do you have to return it?"

"Because it's important . . ." It was all Abram managed to say but the answer was unsatisfying to Ruth. She put a hand on his shoulder and turned him a little to face her more squarely, probing for more.

And then he confessed. Her brilliant purple eyes made him open his heart and tell her the truth. "Because it makes me feel important."

All his life Abram had been a nobody. A small boy in a small village in a tiny outpost of the Roman Empire, a family under the heel of conquerors. But with the seal tucked inside his shirt and the task before him, he didn't need to feel like a nobody. He was a man, and he had a mission for the Children of Israel.

"Because it makes me feel important," he said again, as if saying it twice made it more real, more honest.

Ruth tilted her head and gave him a wicked grin. "And because it's an adventure . . . our adventure!" She thought for a minute and said softly, "You'll still be my Abram Nothing, even when we've put the seal back in its place. But if we succeed, I might let you kiss me."

• • •

After they'd eaten their midday meal, Ruth and Abram wandered off, and now they stood inside the ancient tunnel. Until they'd struck their flints and lit the wicks, producing a thin but welcome light, the tunnel had been as black as pitch and as silent as a grave. The entrance had been almost impossible to see, covered in rocks and scree and vegetation. But weeks earlier, Ruth had traced the source of the water coming from the mountain, and she'd discovered the narrow opening into the mountain.

The only noise they could occasionally hear as they rounded a bend was distant running water and droplets that fell from the roof onto the slippery floor. Sometimes the droplets fell onto their heads or backs, but usually, they fell onto the sodden, moss-covered ground and made ascending the tunnel treacherous.

Ruth had taken two large oil lamps from her home, secreting them inside her cloak so that her father didn't see. She knew she was disobeying him and knew too well the rage that would descend should he learn what she was doing. But this knowledge only quickened her heart and set her skin tingling with excitement.

The oil lamps lit their faces and the walls, floor, and ceiling in their immediate vicinity, but the light was soon overwhelmed by the enveloping blackness. Abram had never been anywhere as dark. In his life, he was blessed with light, either from the sun or from the plethora of stars that illuminated the sky above the Galilee. But the tunnel, stretching upward ahead and falling to the floor of the valley behind, was blacker than anything he'd ever known.

"What happens now?" whispered Abram. "Which way does the tunnel go?"

"I don't know," said Ruth.

"But you said that you've been up and down this passage many times."

She remained silent.

"Ruth?"

She was still silent.

"Ruth!"

He could barely make out what she said next. "I've only been to the entrance in the valley floor. I was too scared to go farther. I didn't have a lamp. I've never been this far. I don't know what happens now."

He should have been angry, but her voice was so soft, so different from the confident and arrogant Ruth of the open air, that the emotion soon dissipated.

"Don't worry," he said, trying to sound confident. "According to the rabbi, this tunnel was used by lots of people for many years. It takes the water from the city, so it must be safe."

They climbed and slipped, rested and continued, climbed and slipped again, until they were hungry. They placed their oil lamps on a rock ledge and sat down to eat the food that Ruth had taken along with the lamps. Simple bread and olives, but they ate them greedily.

Ruth seemed lost in thought as she chewed the bread, and Abram found himself staring at her. When she saw his gaze, she looked him hard in the eye. "Do you like me?" she said.

The question stunned him and seemed loaded like a slingshot, but his answer was given without any thought. "Yes."

"Do you want to kiss me?"

"I don't know."

"Have you ever kissed a girl?" As an afterthought, she added quickly, "Not your mother or your sister."

He didn't reply.

"I've kissed a boy before. His name is Uriel, and he lives half a day's walk from my home. We were in a field and we lay down and I rolled over and kissed him. He enjoyed it and he kissed me back, twice. Then I went home. I haven't seen him since, and that was four months ago. I suppose he's still thinking about me and that kiss."

"Why are you telling me this, Ruth?"

"If you want to kiss me, you can. But only once."

He tried to find a suitable response but grasped nothing except air. He looked away and quickly began to get to his feet and put away what was left of the food.

"We have a tunnel to climb, and I have to find the place for the seal." The response sounded weak, but it was the wrong time and place to be thinking about kissing Ruth. "If we succeed and find our way out, then I'll kiss you," he stammered in an effort not to let the opportunity be lost forever.

"When we're back in my home and we're safe, I might not want you to then," she warned.

They climbed higher and higher into the tunnel, ascending all the while, slipping on ground that was almost totally covered in ugly, spongy black moss, and squeezing through gaps in the rock that were little wider than their slim bodies. At one point, they had to walk sideways and bend almost double because their shoulders were too wide for the gap, and the rock seemed to have fallen in an ancient slide. But after what seemed like an eternity, they ascended to a larger and more open space. They felt like they'd climbed from the bottom to the top of a mountain, but in reality, they had no idea how far up into the city of Jerusalem they had climbed.

After a final steep ascent up steps that had been carved out of the rock and were little more than half the length of their feet, Abram and Ruth rounded what appeared to be a bend in the tunnel. Here, out of the deadened silence, punctuated only by their footfalls and their breathing, they heard a noise.

"Hide your lamp," warned Abram. "Listen. People."

Fear rising in her throat, Ruth hid the lamp inside the folds of her dress, and they were plunged into darkness. They listened, their skin prickling in fear, and held their breath. Their hearts were thumping against their chests.

The more they strained to listen, the more they realized that the noise wasn't coming from the tunnel but from somewhere else. It was the sound of footsteps, but not just one or two pairs of feet. It sounded like a whole army of feet trampling above their heads. And in the mix of the sounds, they clearly heard people talking, laughing, coughing. The language wasn't Hebrew. It was Latin.

"It's the city. It's the streets of Jerusalem. We're almost touching them. They're on top of us," said Abram. He brought out his lamp from inside his cloak and climbed a few more steps in the tunnel and farther around the bend.

As they edged forward, they saw a brilliant thin ray of sunlight piercing the blackness above their heads. The sun was shining through a tiny crack in what must be the pavement above. Inside the roof of the tunnel was a corner of a massive stone block thrown down from the Temple of King Herod when the Romans were taking it apart stone by stone. The block was now embedded for all time in the ground. When the Roman general Titus had destroyed the temple, this block must have been too big to move.

"Ruth, I'm going to find a crack in the rock and put the seal inside it. Can you scoop up some mud and I'll use that to cover and hide the seal so it'll be secure?"

Ruth bent down and picked up mud from the floor of the tunnel. Walking up to where Abram was standing, she waited for him to push the seal into a small crevice in the roof of the tunnel. But before she was able to push mud into the crack, Abram stayed her hand and looked at her.

"What's the matter?" she whispered.

He thought for a moment and looked up as if he could see through to the Roman soldiers marching above. He then looked down into the black depths of the tunnel, where the water was flowing.

It was then that he realized the flaw in what he'd been asked to do by the rabbi.

"What if the Romans find this seal? What if they go to the bottom of the well and open the tunnel to find the source of this water, and they find the seal? They'll destroy it. Then the Almighty One will never know the name of the builder."

Ruth nodded. "What shall we do? Take it back with us?"

Abram shook his head. "No." He sighed and continued to think. Then he saw the mud in Ruth's hand and beamed a smile. "Give me some of that mud," he said. "I have an idea."

She put some of the mud into his hand. He smoothed it into a level surface. Then Abram buried the seal deep inside, pushing it in so the impression of the seal was left in the mud. Satisfied, he removed it, and on another lump of mud that Ruth gave him, he buried the other side of the seal. He carefully removed the engraved stone, rubbed it onto his tunic to clean it of mud, and slotted it into the wall. Abram took more mud from Ruth and caked it over the entrance to the fissure.

"This will dry soon and become hard as rock. Then the seal will be hidden for all time. And now that we have impressions of the front and back of the seal, it'll be easy for a metalworker to make a copy. I'll give one to the rabbi, and I'll keep one myself. Then, Ruth, if the Romans find the seal, we'll have enough copies so we can bring it back."

The logic was clear to Ruth, and she smiled at Abram and nodded. She couldn't bring herself to tell him how clever he was, because that might have made him arrogant. But she knew, and that was enough.

As soon as they were convinced that the mud over the seal was drying hard and protecting it from falling out, they descended the steps, slipping and sliding as they went. Abram carefully nurtured the two pats of mud, which were getting harder and harder in the warmth of his hand.

It took them as long to negotiate their way down the tunnel as it had to ascend, and by the time they emerged, cautiously checking that nobody was near the overgrown vegetation that hid the tunnel's mouth, their oil lamps were almost exhausted. Any delay in descending and they'd have been plunged into the dangers of darkness.

But they walked away from the tunnel entryway to make their way downstream into the Kedron Valley, where the river narrowed and deepened.

Ruth and Abram lay on the northern bank and looked up into the sunlit sky. Sweating, tired from the exertion, still tense from the dangers they'd faced, they remained silent for what seemed a very long time, and sunset came.

Ruth reached over and felt for Abram's hand. She clasped it. "When I first saw you a few days ago, I thought you were a silly little boy. You were filthy, lost, and nervous. You were Abram Nothing. But you were very brave, climbing the tunnel today, and that idea of making a mud copy so the seal will be safe for all time . . . Well, Abram, that was really very clever. Now I think you're Abram Something and no longer Abram Nothing. And I like you, Abram Something."

Abram's tongue searched for words but found only the echo of Ruth's voice in his mind.

"And now you can kiss me. More than once if you like."

PART TWO

PART TWO

Jerusalem
1947

TWO YEARS HAD passed since that day in the café when Shalman had sat entranced by the beautiful, confident young woman before him. Most Jews in Palestine had been fascinated by world events, like the carving up of the old Third Reich and the growing tension between the Soviet Union and the West. But for Shalman, the two years had been a blissful time of falling deeper and deeper in love with Judit.

They were rarely separated. Many times they sat in the theater watching Hollywood stars in epic tales of adventure and romance. At the beginning, he sat very close to her, hoping their shoulders would touch, that he might smell her hair. Then this innocent simplicity gave way to holding hands as they watched the film, and they continued to touch as he walked her home. And from handholding to deep passionate kisses, and from kisses to staying overnight at her place or his. He was besotted. And he knew that she was in love with him.

He'd known young women before, but never one like Judit. The few other girls he'd made love to had been enjoyable, and he'd sought them out until the relationship came to a natural end. But Judit was different. She was superbly intelligent and worldly, knowledgeable and often profound in her understanding of things. Alone, in the privacy of their shared accommodation, she was at once a wife, a companion, and the most passionate lover he could imagine. She would initiate their lovemaking; she would create an environment of lust and longing in their simple apartment. She would invent scenarios that excited both his mind and his body. She was everything he had ever dared hope could happen to him.

He'd fallen in love with a woman who challenged, provoked, and startled him on any given day and yet who was perpetually a mystery to him. For her part, Judit seemed to find something in Shalman that she had never known. Here was a man who was not a target or a victim. A man who was soft-spoken yet determined, generous yet protective. He was superbly intelligent, yet pathetically unworldly.

Judit found in Shalman a man so very far from the father figure she had grown up with in Moscow, a distant cry from the officers and diplomats she'd spied on, manipulated, or even killed. He was nothing like Beria and her Soviet commanders, yet he was nothing like their Lehi comrades—he was no Shamir or Yellin-Mor. Yet neither was he cast from the same mold as their refugee fighter colleagues. For her, he was an enigma, yet there was nothing she didn't know about him. He was the opposite of all the men she'd known, yet he was everything she'd ever sought.

Her Soviet handlers had readily approved her relationship with the young Jewish man, suggesting that it deepened and strengthened her standing in the community and gave weight to her "future objectives." Exactly what they were, she had yet to be told. She knew they had something to do with Soviet designs on Palestine, but she knew none of the details.

The day finally came when Shalman found courage to ask Judit to be his wife. The words "Will you marry me?" tumbled from his lips; they surprised even him, but once out they could not be ignored. They married soon after, and for the first time since he was a boy playing on the beach, Shalman felt utterly happy.

He felt even more exultant when Judit returned from a visit to the doctor and told him that she was pregnant. He was so exultant at the thought of being a father that he could barely control his emotions. Judit had a different slant on the news. She was worried that their baby would affect her ability to build a young and strong Israel, and to carry out the sacred mission given to her by Beria himself.

There was nothing she could do, though, and eight months later, she gave birth to a daughter, Vered. When he first looked upon his daughter, Shalman saw her as the most perfect fusion of the very best of his wife and himself, someone so beautiful, so flawless, that though she was tiny and defenseless, she would hold their love together for all time.

To Judit, Vered was a strange burden. Though he never doubted she loved their daughter, Shalman knew that her affiliation with Lehi took precedence over everything. As soon as she was fit after the birth, she returned to the Lehi command and demanded the tasks she'd done before she was pregnant. A month later, she told Shalman that she was going to express her milk into a bottle so she could leave him with their baby at night, while she was engaged in operations for Yitzhak Shamir.

She planned it like a military operation, and it became part of a parallel logistics plan. Judit would fill a bottle and leave Shalman with Vered while she was away. He raised only small complaints, but she always countered with the importance of what she was doing. In truth, Shalman relished the time alone with Vered and time away from the role of a Lehi soldier. To earn money and pay their rent, when Vered was sleeping, Shalman wrote articles about Israeli archaeology for newspapers around the world, making them like detective stories; or he helped the local greengrocer sell fruit to customers. He didn't mind what he did, so long as he had Vered and Judit as his family. For her part, Judit brought home purses full of Palestinian money and British pound notes, which, she told him, she'd taken from the bodies of Tommies or the officers she'd assassinated. She made fun of him when he told her how amoral such theft was. "What?" she said curtly. "They need to spend money when they get to heaven?"

The world around Shalman and Judit grew steadily darker. The dream of a Jewish homeland now seemed a real possibility, but the realization of the dream brought with it the deadly reality of war. Conflict was a daily occurrence in Jerusalem and other cities in Palestine, filling it with gunfire and flame as Lehi and the other Jewish nationalist movements fought ever more fiercely—fighting that had the British on one side and the continually escalating violence with their Arab neighbors on the other. It seemed to Shalman that everyone around him had a gun pointed at someone else.

Holding a weapon and wanting to fight had started to come naturally to Shalman. His initial reluctance to kill British soldiers or Arab mercenaries slowly disappeared; he'd successfully assassinated several targets that had been selected for him. But unlike Judit and the others, he never celebrated such murders, and even though he'd done it a dozen times, he didn't find pulling the trigger easy. Now that he was a father, his worldview had shifted.

Several weeks had passed since he'd met with his Lehi comrades, and he found that the missions he was tasked with were ever harder to embrace. It had been a hot morning with the sun baking the stones of the old city. Shalman had been out with his tiny daughter snuggled closely in his arms, talking to her of the old city. He was looking for something of interest for an article he could write for an American magazine; they paid the best.

Shalman whispered in her ears about their city, Jerusalem: its history, its peoples, its places, and its stories. He rounded a corner and made his way up toward the Damascus gate, an ancient structure built and rebuilt by each of the occupiers of the ancient city. First a Roman gate under the emperor Hadrian in the second century C.E. and then later remade by the Christian Crusaders in the twelfth century. The gate where Shalman stood had stones dating from 1537; it had been erected by workmen for Sulieman the Magnificent, sultan of the Ottoman Empire. Shalman looked up at the stones and the tower and told his tiny daughter about their history.

It was then that he heard his name. The voice was familiar, and it carried across the square in urgency. It was Yitzhak Shamir, his boss from Lehi, standing at a distance across the throngs of people moving in and out of the gate. Shalman turned to wave, but Shamir didn't wave back. Rather, he beckoned him urgently.

Puzzled, Shalman looked intently at his friend, trying to see why he was so agitated. Yitzhak repeated the gesture and called again. Shalman looked around to see if there was something he had missed; was there something Yitzhak wanted him to see? He looked back to the Pole and saw that Yitzhak was walking backward away from Shalman, away from the gate, still gesturing as if calling him to follow.

Shalman was confused but took a few slow steps toward Yitzhak. Conscious of tiny Vered, who was almost asleep in his arms, Shalman was slow and deliberate, trying to keep his movements smooth. He scanned again for Yitzhak. He saw that the Pole had moved farther away, almost running backward, still looking to Shalman and still drawing him urgently on.

Where is he going? thought Shalman. He quickened his pace but not enough to satisfy Yitzhak, who was about to disappear into the shadow of a building and a street leading away. Just as Yitzhak was about to vanish from view, Shalman could see his face clearly through a gap in the crowd. What Shalman saw was panic looking not at him but past him.

Shalman stopped to look back at the Damascus gate, then to Yitzhak ahead of him, and once more to the gate . . .

Then Shalman started to run. He was an idiot; he was distracted by thoughts of his family; in the old days when he was still fighting with Lehi, he'd have known immediately where the danger lay. Shalman gripped Vered tightly and pushed his way forward as fast as his feet could carry him, hunching his body, drawing Vered close to him, almost enveloping her.

And then came the explosion. It bellowed through the gate and threw Shalman off his feet and onto the ground. Rather than throw his arms out to catch himself, he kept the baby wrapped tight against him and took the full force of the impact on the ground with his shoulder. Pain coursed through his arm, but he didn't let go, and remained curled in a ball around his child as debris rained down over him.

* * *

He now sat opposite his wife in their small home, telling her this story as she bathed his badly bruised shoulder and strapped it with a white linen bandage.

"If Yitzhak hadn't seen me . . . if I hadn't heard him . . ." stammered Shalman as he looked at his hands and saw them still shaking—though whether from fear or anger, he did not know.

"That's a lot of ifs, Shalman" was Judit's curt reply as she pulled the bandage tight and he let out a small yelp.

"How could they be so . . . ?" He didn't finish his thought because he wasn't really expecting an answer.

"The bomb went off prematurely. Nobody knew you'd be there."

Shalman spun around to face his wife. "Prematurely?"

"Yes. It was planted in an Arab taxi. It went off too early."

"Why did it go off at all? Why there?"

Judit looked at him strangely.

"Your child, Judit!" Shalman found himself yelling. "Your child was right there, in my arms, under the gate."

"You shouldn't have been there," she said in a voice so calm it shocked him.

"Did you know about this attack?" demanded Shalman.

"No," replied Judit matter-of-factly before adding, "Very few did. Shamir played it close. But we knew to stay away from the Old City. You would have known, too, had you been at the operations meeting, as ordered. But you were not."

"Why didn't you tell me?" Shalman shot back, but he didn't wait for a reply. "Because you're never here, Judit! Sometimes I barely see you for days. Or when you are here, it's only to sneak off again in the middle of the night."

Judit didn't answer. She picked up the scissors and the remains of the bandage she had used to strap Shalman's shoulder and turned to walk away to the kitchen.

Shalman called after her. "I was there, Judit! It could have been me."

Judit stopped but didn't turn back. "But you're all right, Shalman. Yitzhak warned you, and you're fine. And your shoulder will be fine."

Anger flared in Shalman's eyes. "That's not the point! Goddammit, Judit. Who do we think we're fighting?"

Judit finally turned back, her arms crossed, and responded to Shalman in a voice so controlled it unnerved him. "No one will protect us, Shalman. We are alone in a sea of enemies. Europe, Arabia, we cannot live in these places anymore. So here we stand on this narrow strip of earth, surrounded by people who hate us and the British who control and manipulate us. Only when they are gone can we be free."

"I know this speech," spat Shalman, though hearing his own words, he was shocked by their anger. The image of his daughter in his arms as he ran from the exploding gate was fire in his veins. "Destroying airfields and railways, this I understand. But today our child was almost a victim of our own fight. How many other children were at that gate? How many innocent sons and daughters, mothers and fathers?"

Judit looked at the face of her husband, the man she loved. Shalman had been on a dozen Lehi operations in the past six months, and his mood on returning had grown increasingly dark. But this was something more.

"Don't think I'm not distressed by what happened, Shalman. Vered is my child, too. But she's alive. You're alive. Reflecting on ifs and maybes serves no purpose." This was the voice of Judit's Soviet handlers, always prompting her to see the bigger picture and eschewing personal attachment. But Shalman knew nothing of that part of Judit's life.

Shalman shook his head in bewilderment. He loved her, he'd married her, he'd had a child with her, yet in this moment he felt he hardly knew her. "There has to be a better way."

"No, Shalman. There is no other way. History tells us there is no other way. It's hard for you, I know." She stepped forward and put a hand on his chest. "You didn't come here on the boats. You didn't flee horror to arrive here. You know the stories, but they're not your stories." Judit kissed Shalman on the cheek and said, "The answers aren't easy, but they're clear to anybody who opens his eyes."

Alexandria, Egypt

184 C.E. (fourth year of the reign of Emperor Commodus)

ABRAM THE PHYSICIAN felt no joy as the ship approached the famed harbor of Alexandria. But he did smile when he looked at his fourteen-year-old son, Jonathan, who was enraptured at the sight of the massive tower with its burning light on top of an island on the western shore.

The boy turned to his father and asked what it was. Abram smiled and stroked the boy's head. "It's the lighthouse built by Alexander. The Greeks called it the Pharos. It's said to be seventy times taller than a tall man."

"But why? What's it for?"

"It warns ships at night that the coast is near, and they have to be careful of rocks. As the sun descends into the distant western sea, far beyond the Pillars of Hercules, men climb the many steps with wood and kindling and set alight the pyre. To make the light more intense, when the wind is strong and in danger of blowing ships onto the rocks, they add oil to the wood, and it flares so brightly they say that it can be seen half a day's sail distant. The fire burns all night."

Jonathan was astounded. "Every night? Men climb that tower every night?"

Abram smiled and nodded. He reached across and kissed the tall, muscular boy on the cheek. For the past two years, since the death of his beloved Ruth from the heat caused to her body when her humors were out of alignment, he'd mourned her to the exclusion of their son. From the very first moment he'd seen her in the woods at the base of the mountain that housed the city of Jerusalem, he'd been in love with her. His love had grown as they climbed the tunnel and replaced the precious seal that the original builder in the time of King

Solomon had written. It was confirmed when he first kissed her on the riverbank, and since then, since their marriage, he'd grown to love her every hour of every day.

She had been the most beautiful, exquisite, feisty, annoying, faithful, loving, and challenging woman he'd ever known, and when, after years of trying, Ruth had gotten pregnant fifteen years ago and given birth to Jonathan, he knew that his life was complete.

They'd traveled back to the village of Peki'in, where Abram had been born, and his parents had loved her as much as he. Even the elderly and nearly blind Rabbi Shimon bar Yochai, still hiding from the Romans in a cave above the village with his son, Rabbi Eleazar, had told him how excellent she was. It was Ruth who encouraged Abram to study medicine, and he had happily become a doctor, curing people and being a friend to many.

But even his skills hadn't been able to cure his beloved wife when she'd fallen ill two years earlier and died of the fevers. He'd studied the Greek physicians and knew that her illness was caused by misaligned humors. He'd cooled her body, bled her, fed her the root of the beet and honey, and done everything in his power, all to no avail. And he'd made her a final promise just before she died, emaciated and exhausted from the violent coughing and the blood in her phlegm. She made him promise that he'd take Jonathan to Alexandria in Egypt so that he could be trained as an alchemist by Maria the Jewess, a woman reputed to be able to cure ills and ailments that caused great suffering. Ruth wanted her husband and son to be taught by Maria so that other husbands and sons didn't suffer as Abram and Jonathan were suffering in her sight. Her words, among the last she ever spoke, still resonated in Abram's mind. "My son will be an alchemist . . ."

As their ship docked in the port in the failing light of the evening, Jonathan clung to his father and walked onto the dockside feeling insecure in the crowds of people, all of whom were wearing different styles of clothes, many of whom had different-colored skin and were speaking languages he'd never heard. Abram realized with embarrassment that this was the closest he'd been to Jonathan since Ruth had been buried.

He'd distanced himself from everybody, continuing to treat patients, but his zest for life, his passion for anything other than his memory of Ruth, had evaporated. When he said goodbye to her in the burial cave in the foothills of the Mount of Olives east of Jerusalem, he'd placed her favorite amulet in the folds of her shroud, just above her heart. It was written in both Hebrew and Aramaic script. It said simply: "I am Ruth wife of Abram the doctor. I walk in the footsteps of Yahweh." He'd bought the disc of the amulet from a trader in a caravan that came from Parthia, south of the Black Sea. He had employed a metalworker to carve the inscription, and he'd given it to her when Jonathan was born. She'd worn it ever since, and she would wear it as she lived the rest of her life at the right hand of God in heaven. He was going to place something else in the folds of her gown: the inscribed stone written by King Solomon's tunnel builder, Matanyahu. Instead, he determined to retain it as a fond keepsake of their first days together. He remembered with warmth and aching fondness how they'd climbed the dank slippery tunnel all those years before to place the original at the top of the tunnel. So it was the amulet that would tell Yahweh who Ruth had been, and ensure that she was given pride of place in His heaven.

"Father, look at that," Jonathan said, pointing to three men who were amusing the crowds by eating fire. "How can they do that without being burned?" he asked in amazement, wandering closer to the semicircle of the audience, some of whom were throwing coins onto a blanket spread out in front of the fire-eaters.

Abram smiled and held his son back. "We haven't got time to look at such wonders, my son. There's so much to see in Alexandria, and we must find lodgings before night falls and the curfew is rung out."

"How do they do what they're doing without being burned? They're smiling, not screaming in pain."

Abram looked carefully and saw that the men blew some liquid out of their mouths onto the flaming torch, which then burst into flames, making it look as though they were eating the fire.

He smiled and whispered, "They put something like oil or a strong drink into their mouths and then spit it out, which causes the

. It was the merchant who had suggested a meeting with Maria
ewess and alchemist, and on the basis of the messages he'd re-
d, Abram's wife, Ruth, had suggested that she, Abram, and their
ng son travel to the Egyptian coastal city to meet with Maria and
rn from her. But then Ruth had died of fevers.

But at the end of the previous year, he realized that he'd grown
stant from Jonathan, and the lad was sensitive enough to feel the
etachment. So Abram determined that as there were only two of
them left, he would fulfill Ruth's wishes, and for the past four hours,
he and Maria had been engrossed in discussions concerning alchemy,
the transmutation of base metals into gold, the nature and reality of
the Philosopher's Stone, and the ideas espoused by Aristotle, Plato,
and Pythagoras. When he'd told her that in his younger days he'd become a Christian follower of a self-proclaimed messiah called Jesus
who came from Nazareth in Israel, she nearly jumped out of her seat
in excitement. She told him that although she was a Jewess, she was a
student of the words of this very same Jesus, stories now being
preached by bishops who lived and proselytized in Alexandria.

"One night," she told him, "when I was asleep, this very Jesus
came to me and took me to the top of a mountain. I wasn't afraid, because he held me and I felt secure. His skin was as black as pitch, like
that of an Abyssinian. From the top of the mountain, I could see the
entire world spread out before me. In the distance, I could see the
Greek philosophers arguing in their academy. Then this very Jesus lay
me down and his essence entered my body. I grew very frightened,
but he said to me, "Why are you afraid, oh ye of little faith; if I have
shown you earthly things and you did not trust me, how then will
you believe the heavenly things which I will show you?" Then I returned and woke in the morning. I told this to the bishops, but they
cursed me, telling me that I was spreading heresy. They forbade me
from entering their prayer rooms."

"For me, and for my son, Jonathan, we are more suited to the
faith of Moses and Aaron, of David and Solomon."

But the moment he mentioned his son's name, for the first time
all afternoon, Abram realized that he'd been so absorbed by the conversation that the sun was about to set into the western sea, and Jona-

firebrand to flare. It's a trick, Jonathan. And a
cept things for what they seem, only for what t₁
my son, pick up our bags and we'll find somewh₆

As they walked away from the ship that had b
the past four nights, taking them from the port of
laestina to Alexandria, they didn't know that they
served. She was a tall woman, her head and much of he₁
by a black scarf, her body encased in black robes. The
her to become invisible in the shadows of the dock, allo
see who walked off the boats. Most were sailors or mer₆
some were travelers. Many were too old for her, but so
young men, and they were of great interest.

The youth who'd just walked off the boat from Palestin
the older man was of particular interest. So she followed them, ₁
ing in the shadows of the darkening night, waiting to see where ₁
went.

• • •

Though they had been in the city for several days, Abram was a worried man. Day was becoming night, and he feared that his son, whom
he'd sent on a mission, had become disoriented.

The doctor looked out the window at the position of the sun and
realized that it was approaching dusk. Jonathan had left their lodgings just after the noontime meal; he had been ordered by his father
to go out to buy some bread, olives, peppers, and a roasted haunch of
sheep from one of the many butchers in Alexandria so they could
enjoy their dinner. He was instructed to come straight back. Since
midday, Abram had been entertaining Maria the Jewess, the most famous alchemist in Alexandria—perhaps in the whole world—and
they had been engrossed in the myriad of things that people of science and knowledge talked about.

His introduction to Maria had come through a merchant he'd
treated for fever when the man was passing through Jerusalem on his
way to Babylon. So impressed had he been with the treatment that
Abram had prescribed, and the modest cost compared to that of his
doctors in Alexandria, that he had written to Abram and kept in

than wasn't home. Maria noticed the look of concern on his face and asked why he was worried.

"He is a young man. He doesn't know Alexandria. Many people pass through here, strangers and sailors, merchants and slave traders. I shouldn't have sent him out on his own. I should have gone with him."

"He will come to no harm," said Maria. "He will return soon. He's probably met a pretty girl in the marketplace and lost all sense of the time."

But Jonathan wasn't talking to a girl; nor was he in the marketplace. Since he and his father had arrived some days earlier by boat, they had been carefully watched by a woman in a dark robe, her head covered in a cowl whenever she was outdoors.

The woman, Didia, was a slave trader who purchased Nubian, Abyssinian, Libyan, and Berber boys and girls sold to her by their parents or merchants; she trained them and then sent them off to Greece and Rome to work as servants or prostitutes.

Her captivation with Jonathan began the moment she saw him. It was when he walked from the boat, to the time they purchased room and board in a lodging house near the dock, to this sudden meeting with Maria the Jewess. Not that she was interested in an alchemist, nor in Maria's fame for heating things in a bath of hot water, but because she was monopolizing Abram the doctor. And because the alchemist and the doctor were ensconced in his room all afternoon, he had unwisely allowed his beautiful son, Jonathan, to wander Alexandria alone.

And being a young lad alone in a strange land, he'd left the main merchant streets and was wandering along alleyways to see what sorts of houses and public buildings were in the city. Jonathan's curiosity enabled Didia to do what she most wanted. It was only through the intervention of the gods of Egypt that she had spotted him. Had she not been sending her latest batch of slaves off to the Roman port of Ostia, she wouldn't have been on the dock and wouldn't have seen Jonathan walking alongside his father.

At first she couldn't believe it. She looked and felt her legs turn to water. But on closer scrutiny, even though she kept to the shadows, the resemblance to her own dead son was even more remarkable. His hair, the shape of his face, his broad shoulders, even the way the young lad walked, striding in footsteps that seemed too large for his body, was identical to that of Didia's beautiful son, Kheti. She barely kept up as they walked from the dock into the town. She felt as though a brilliant beam of light had descended from the heavens. Seeing Jonathan brought her beloved son back to life. Over the year he had taken to die, Didia had seen her beautiful son wither away, coughing, weak, and shrunken, incongruous compared to the glowing son she had loved with all her heart. She'd known of the wasting disease in many slaves from the poorer lands south of Egypt but had never thought that her beloved son would become a victim.

As Jonathan walked, she saw not Abram's son but her own beautiful boy. And for the first time since he'd died, she felt her heart beat in excitement. Now he was hers. She sat in her home and looked at him closely. The resemblance was nothing short of remarkable. His hair was slightly darker, and his nose was more Roman than Egyptian, but aside from those differences, they could have been brothers. On her orders, Didia's slave had thrown a sack over the boy as he walked into an alley, bound him with rope, and brought him struggling and shouting to Didia's home.

"You're wondering why you're here, aren't you, boy?" she said.

His mouth was full of cloth, and a bandage was tied tightly around it to stop him from shouting; he was bound hand and foot and couldn't move. But he could nod.

"You are very valuable to me in ways that you could not even begin to understand. If you promise to remain quiet, I will remove the bindings around your mouth and give you food and drink. Do you promise not to shout? Not that it matters, but be assured that it won't help you, because nobody can hear, and if they could, this is the house of slavery, so people of your age shout and scream and beg all the while. But I don't want you to shout. My son, Kheti, never used to shout. So, will you promise?"

Jonathan looked at the woman. She'd removed her cowl, and he could see her graying hair and her face, lined with worry. She was much older than Ruth before she'd died, but there was a resemblance.

The shape of her face, her arched eyebrows, the way her mouth turned up when she smiled.

It was Ruth's smile that had always given him such pleasure when he entered the house. A warm and loving smile, until she became ill. But this woman was not his mother, and he was frightened of her. Still, he was desperate for a drink and hungry, so he nodded.

Didia nodded curtly, and her slave removed the bandage from Jonathan's mouth and pulled out the rag. He licked his dry lips.

"So, boy, what's your name?"

His voice was hoarse, but he tried to sound confident. "Jonathan."

She nodded. "From now on, you will forget what your mother and father called you. From now on, in my house, you will honor a different name. I will call you Kheti."

• • •

Abram and Maria the Jewess searched every street near his lodgings. But when it was pitch-black, with only a few streetlights to pierce the darkness of the moonless night, they met again in the doorway of a baker's shop.

"Nothing," said Maria.

Abram nodded. "I'll pray to the Almighty God that he's safe and unharmed; that he's met with some other lads and is with them; that he's drinking and has fallen asleep. I will pray, because without prayer, I am nothing."

Maria shook her head. "You can pray, Abram, but I have an evil feeling in my bones that prayer won't help you. I've seen your boy. He's tall and beautiful. And in Alexandria, we have dozens of men and women who trade in the lives of slaves. Alexandria is well known as an unsafe port for boys and girls."

Abram looked at her in horror. "A slave?"

"You must face that reality, Abram."

"My son . . . my Jonathan? No!"

"These are evil times, my friend. And Alexandria is an evil place."

"But this is the most enlightened city in the world. Your library, your schools of philosophers, your . . . How can you allow the evils of slavery, the barbarism of—" He couldn't continue.

Maria looked at his disconsolate face in pity. "Alchemy teaches that the three emanations of sentient beings—intellectual, celestial, and corruptible—form a fourth, which is the one machine of the whole world. But the ancients tell us that it is also necessary to have the corruptible to form a fifth essence, the quintessence, in order to have unity. We need evil, like these slave traders, in order to have the quintessence of life. I'm so sorry, my friend."

"I'll go to the authorities," he said. "The Roman procurator and governor of Alexandria. I'll demand that they and their soldiers tear apart every slaver's place of business until my lovely son is returned safe and well."

She shook her head. "Much of the money that runs Alexandria, and which goes into the pockets of the procurator, comes from trade. And the slave trade is one of the sources of this city's wealth. They will laugh at you, Abram. They will tell you that you never should have allowed your Jonathan to wander the streets of the city alone."

Terrified, he asked, "What can I do?"

"Together, we will visit the homes of the major traders. You will offer to buy your son back. Whatever happens, don't tell them he's your son, or their price will double. Don't show them fear or sadness or anger, because these people can smell a person's innermost thoughts, and they will know a desperate father when they see one."

Abram nodded. "Where shall we start?"

Maria thought for a moment. "We'll begin with the slave trader Khnumbaf," she said. "If he doesn't have your son, we'll visit Bocchoris. And then Didia. After her, we'll go to Shebitku. These are the biggest traders in boys and girls, and the most likely to have men watching the ports for lads like your son. Remember, you're not a father searching for his son. You're my husband, and we want to buy a slave to clean our home."

A valley northwest of Jerusalem

1947

THE SCENT OF pine was in the air. Or was it cedar? Perhaps it was a wild olive tree or a sycamore sending out its fragrance to attract pollinating bees or butterflies. Or maybe it was one of the millions of eucalyptus imported from Australia and planted in order to drain the swamps and transform them from malarial death traps into arable farming land.

Whatever it was, in the buoyant air of a Palestine awakening to the warmth of what everybody hoped would be a mild and fruitful spring, it was a refreshing perfume. It was a scent that enlivened Shalman's senses as he trudged over the mountains on the outskirts of Jerusalem before plunging into one of the many deep valleys that dissected the landscape.

He was alone, wandering the ancient time-trodden pathways that crisscrossed the mountains, following thin dusty tracks etched over the millennia into the barren earth by generations of shepherds tending to flocks of goats and sheep. Shalman looked at the landscape carefully, this time not with the eyes of a freedom fighter but with the eyes of a participant in the history of the land.

Though he still loved Judit with all his heart, Shalman was working to ensure the family's future. He would become a professional archaeologist, and when the coming war with Britain or the Arabs was over, now that the universities had became proper institutions of learning, he'd qualify and earn a good living, especially as he now had interesting contacts in the American media. This meant, though, that he had to leave Judit and Vered to be on his own, to wander the landscape and engage in archaeological digs.

Leaving Judit with Vered was also important, in part to enforce the responsibilities of motherhood on his wife, but also it enabled him to journey out into the ancient hills and valleys that were the landscape of the Bible, of his people's history. In no other nation in the world was a document of theology used as a guidepost to a country's history. Yet while most Jews who came to Palestine arrived with little or no religious belief, every child who went to school was taught the Bible as lessons in Israel's culture, geography, history, and society. And the more Shalman learned about and practiced archaeology, the more the accuracy of the way the ancients wrote about the events in the Bible proved true.

For a hundred years, scientists, archaeologists, and adventurers had been scouring the land of the Ottomans and, more lately, the land of Palestine, using the Bible as a tour guide to history. More and more archaeological digs had uncovered what the ancient scribes of David and Solomon, Elijah and Ezra had written thousands of years earlier in stone and priceless artifacts.

Shalman's forays into the biblical landscape were both an enlightenment and an escape. They were also the realization of something latent within him. Shalman had spent so long steeping himself in the history of this land and yet feeling removed from it that he believed it was time he put his hands in the earth and into his history.

He was one of hundreds of students who had enrolled at the Hebrew University in Jerusalem since World War II had come to an end. He joined the many young men and women who wanted to further their education despite the growing tensions with the Arabs and the British. Instead of studying agriculture, politics, or science, as might have been expected by those seeking a career in a growing nation, Shalman had decided to further his love of the ancient world.

Resting after the climb up the mountain, he sat on a rock and surveyed the landscape. It gave him time to catch his breath and ponder the future. Britain had recently announced that it would hand back its mandate over Palestine, allowing the fledgling United Nations to determine the land's future. This had been read by Lehi as a reason to intensify attacks on the British and Arabs alike. The logic expressed by the Lehi leadership was that if the countries that were going to vote in the United Nations saw the region as a powder keg of violence, nobody would want to take up the mandate that Britain wanted to relinquish.

They'll vote for our independence, split the country between Arabs and Jews, and leave us alone, Yellin-Mor told a gathering, his calm voice carrying a weight of rationality that galvanized his fighters. But for Shalman, the logic felt increasingly flawed. All he could feel was despair because of a coming war, which was seeming more and more inevitable as the sides grew further apart.

Shalman took out a flask of water. There would be streams in the valley below, so he wasn't worried about conserving it, and he swallowed deeply. He then stood and began to walk down the steep path toward the bottom of the valley, where he knew there to be a network of caves. The ancient Hebrews had often buried their dead in the caves, and in the time of Jesus, bodies had been laid in shrouds on ledges in caverns and grottoes. After the bodies had decomposed, descendants would reenter the cave and collect the bones, depositing them in boxes. These ossuaries often went untouched for thousands of years; it was an archaeologist's dream to find one that was still sealed. That was what Shalman was hoping to do.

It was these thoughts that filtered through his mind as he descended the steep path. As he walked faster more from the demands of the slope than his own volition, he was forced to steady his feet with his hands on the rocks. Distracted, he imagined himself holding ancient relics in his hands, sifting soil to unearth Roman ruins, dusting away centuries from the objects of antiquity.

And then his foot slipped.

It was a gnarled root of a long-dead tree that had caught the side of his boot, and his ankle twisted over. Pain shot up his leg but was quickly replaced by fear as he fell head over heels, tumbling down uncontrollably. He screamed in pain and terror as his arms flew out to try to catch something solid, but there was nothing except loose stones. Each time his body tumbled over and over, his side crashed down heavily, knocking the air from his lungs and filling his mouth with dirt. He put out his hand to stop himself from falling on the scree, but the weight of his body kept propelling him down the steep hill.

Shalman twisted his body, trying to dig his boots into the ground, to force traction that would stop the fall to the valley below, but he was moving too fast.

In an instant the earth and stones gave way beneath him and he found himself in the air, tumbling over a rock ledge. As he twisted in the void, he saw the hard ground beneath him rise up dramatically, and then everything was dark.

• • •

It was not just the pain but the intense light that hurt him. Shalman squinted and forced his eyes carefully open to see the ground undulating and moving past in a strange rhythmic way. It took him a few moments to understand that he was lying on his stomach across the back of a donkey walking forward over a narrow path. Each lurch made his bones hurt, and the sway of the ground made his stomach turn.

His first words were incoherent, but they caused somebody nearby to say "Whoa" to the donkey, which obeyed and stopped. Shalman was greatly relieved, and the feeling of sickness rapidly disappeared. Then a pair of naked legs and sandaled feet appeared in his field of vision.

"So you're alive," said a young man's voice in Arabic.

"I'm not sure," said Shalman in Hebrew, understanding the Arabic but not yet cognizant enough to answer in the same language.

"You are," said the young man, in awkward but clear Hebrew.

"I think I've died and this is my punishment," said Shalman, speaking in Arabic as his brain caught up with the situation and some comprehension of his circumstances.

The young man laughed and said, reverting to Arabic, "Another hour or so out there, you'd certainly be dead. Or blind. The vultures go first for your eyes, then your lips, then your tongue. That's how I found you. I saw the vultures circling and thought it might be one of my goats."

Shalman tried to push himself off the back of the donkey, but his head was throbbing so much that he couldn't raise the strength. So the young man grabbed him by the shoulders and eased him off the back of the animal and part carried, part maneuvered him into a sitting position. Shalman propped his back up against a large rock and faced his rescuer.

"Mustafa," the man said, sitting beside him and holding out his hand.

"Shalman," he responded, clasping it. The young man had a weak grip, or was it because he knew that Shalman wouldn't be strong enough for a good handshake after his accident?

Mustafa looked at him questioningly. "What kind of a name is Shalman?"

"In your language, I'd be called Salaam. In Hebrew, it means 'peaceable.'"

Mustafa shrugged. "I thought you may be British. But you're a Jew."

Shalman nodded, but a pounding roar reminded him that he had cracked his head on a rock. He put his hand up to his skull and felt a large patch of bloodied and matted hair.

"At first I thought you'd been shot in the head and were dead. I'm taking you to my father's house."

He helped Shalman to his feet, but his legs were still like jelly.

"You'd better ride the donkey. It's only a mile or so to go, but you have no strength to walk."

Sitting on top of the animal, Shalman looked down at the young shepherd. "You're being very kind," he said gratefully.

"Yes," said Mustafa. "I am. Allah demands it."

Even through his haze, Shalman thought this curious and found himself staring at Mustafa walking beside him.

Mustafa added, "Many I know would have left you there to die if they'd known."

"If they'd known I was a Jew?" asked Shalman. Mustafa just shrugged. But Shalman pressed the question as the reality of his situation and his rescue dawned on him. "But not you?"

"Not today," Mustafa replied dryly, and Shalman could not tell if it was meant as a joke.

Shalman put his hand to his head once more and felt for the wound with his fingertips.

"My mother will wash the wound for you, and then you can go on your way. Better you don't touch it," said Mustafa. "Leave it to bleed and you won't become infected."

In that strange moment, Shalman remembered his own mother washing his cuts and bruises when he was a child.

"Where are your family? Where is your father from?" asked Mustafa, his curiosity surprising Shalman.

"He's dead. The British killed him."

Mustafa responded with a silence that spoke of shared tragedies, and then he walked ahead to lead the donkey.

A year ago, Shalman may well have been instructed by Lehi to kill such a man; to bomb a building or street where such a man walked. He knew just as certainly that Mustafa might well have joined an Arab resistance group armed to kill Jewish settlers and attack kibbutz villages. Such groups had been rallied by the mufti of Jerusalem, Amin al-Husseini, who was now exiled in Egypt because of his collaboration with the Nazis. But his influence was still powerful.

Yet at this moment in the story of their peoples, an Arab was walking on an ancient rocky path trodden by countless forgotten men and women of history, while a Jew was riding the Arab's donkey. Shalman looked at his rescuer and saw a young man of his own age who probably had much in common with him; though they lived together as neighbors, they were worlds apart.

Alexandria, Egypt

184 C.E. (fourth year of the reign of Emperor Commodus)

IT WAS ALREADY the middle of the night when a tired, frustrated, and increasingly anxious Abram and his friend Maria the Jewess knocked on the door of Didia's home.

A slave opened the door a fraction to see who was standing there so late; robbers and murderers didn't knock, so the slave wasn't all that wary, especially when he saw a well-dressed middle-aged man and woman, carrying no obvious weapons.

"We wish to see your owner, Didia," the woman said, her voice strident and confident.

"Come back in the morning," the slave said. "The house has retired for the night."

"We will see her now," said the woman, pushing past the slave.

They entered the opulent home, with its marble statuary, its tiled mosaic floor, and walls painted with flying birds and naked men and women. Abram looked around in amazement; he'd seen such a house, a Roman villa in Tiberias on the shores of the lake that was shaped like a harp, but it was the only time he'd been amid such wealth until now.

Standing in a doorway that led off the vestibule was a tall, thin woman wearing a gown edged with lapis lazuli and a collar glistening red with rubies scintillating in the light of the oil lamps.

"Leave us," she said to the slave. She motioned to Abram and Maria. "Please, enter my home and let me offer you some refreshment."

Maria and Abram walked uncertainly from the door into a chamber furnished with carpets and chairs made of wood and the finest animal skins. The table was of a dark brown wood, almost the color of black marble; Abram had never seen such a thing. He felt he was in the home of a king.

A woman slave appeared, carrying a tray with drinks. As Maria and Abram sat, the drinks were placed on the table, and the slave, bowing, presented them, bowed again, and walked out of the room.

"Thank you for allowing us into your home, and our apologies for visiting you so late at night, but our boat leaves for Greece on the morning tide, and we wish to purchase a young lad, a slave, to take back with us. We have particular needs," said Maria. "He must be—"

Didia held up her hand. Smiling, her voice like that of a priestess rather than a merchant, she said, "I know and understand perfectly what are your needs. You are the Jewess Maria, the alchemist; and you are Abram, the doctor from Israel who searches for his son. I have your boy. He is perfectly safe and well."

Abram looked at her in astonishment. Until now, in the two slave houses he'd visited, he'd remained silent, letting Maria do all the talking. Now he was about to say something, but Didia continued. "You want the return of your son, Jonathan. Of course you do. And you shall have him."

She smiled and looked at their faces. Maria's became hard and uncompromising. Abram looked stunned, as though he'd just been hit on the head. "How much?" Maria asked.

"Nothing. No money. You can have him back without payment."

Maria frowned. "I don't understand."

"Surely one favor deserves another," said Didia softly.

Warily, Abram said, "You stole my son. You're a thief. You'll give him back without any favors or conditions. If not, I'll—"

Maria didn't allow him to finish, interrupting him. "What favor?"

"I want you to steal something for me. Something that belongs to me. Something of no value to anybody except me."

Abram was about to speak, growing more and more furious, but Maria quickly cut in again. "What is it you want back? And who has this thing?"

Didia sipped her drink and fixed Abram with a stare that made him feel wary. "Let me tell you about my son, Kheti. My beautiful boy. He died last year of the wasting sickness. For a year, he grew weaker and weaker, coughing blood, until he was so weak, he took to his bed. I watched him die. Every day I fed him, washed him, prayed to the gods of Egypt, of Greece, of Rome, and even of Israel. But he slipped further and further away from me, until one day he breathed no more. His four brothers and three sisters and I mourned for him for seven days and seven nights, until the priests had finished with his body and it was time for him to be entombed. And it was they who supported me through my grief, because even though I have children who will carry my name into the future, my Kheti was my youngest and most beautiful of sons.

"I buried him in the way of our Egyptian deities, so that in the afterlife, he would be ready to be presented to Osiris. He was mummified, and as he was being wrapped by the priests and embalmed, I placed his favorite amulet of the four sons of Horus inside the linen.

"But while I was watching him being wrapped, the Roman procurator, Gaius Lucius Septimus, happened to come along to watch the process. He was fascinated by Kheti's amulet and ordered the priests to remove it so that he could keep it. I remonstrated with him, forbade him, and eventually begged him. But he's an arrogant man, and he treated me as though I were some insect biting his arm. So he now has the amulet in his home on the hill, and without it, my beautiful son will be unhappy in the afterlife, and Osiris will not find pleasure with him. I have been to the procurator's home, but he will not let me in. I am forbidden to tread on his land, and his men have orders to strike me down if I come near Gaius Lucius while he is being carried on his litter through town."

She looked at Abram and Maria, and her face became that of a grieving mother rather than a slave trader.

"You want me to enter the procurator's home and take back your son's amulet?" said Abram.

Didia nodded.

"Why shouldn't I go to the procurator, tell him that you've stolen my son, and have you arrested?"

"Because, Abram, if you do that, you will never see your son again. I will die, but my death will be instantaneous. For the rest of your life, you'll never know whether Jonathan is dead and buried in some stinking rubbish pit, or alive and toiling away his life as a slave to some Greek or Roman overlord."

"You would do that to a father? You! A mother who's just lost her son? What evil thoughts must pass through your mind," Maria said.

Didia turned and glared at her. "Don't think that you know what passes through my mind, you sorceress. You and Abram are Jews. I, too, was born a Jewess. My mother was a Jewess, as was her mother before her."

Abram was shocked. "I don't understand. Your son was buried as an Egyptian."

"My family came to Egypt hundreds of years ago. When King Cyrus was overlord of Persia, during the rule of King Manasseh of Judah, my ancestors were paid to come to the island of Elephantine in the upper Nile to help the pharaoh in his battles with the Nubians. They stayed there until Alexander came to Egypt three hundred years later and founded this city. And here they've been ever since, remaining even after the massacre of the Jews by the emperor Trajan. That was when my grandmother changed her religion to become a worshipper of Egyptian gods. But in our hearts, we've always been Jews. And my family can trace its ancestry back to the Temple of King Solomon."

Abram laughed. "That was a thousand years ago. How can you?"

Didia wasn't amused at being disbelieved. "My family passes its heritage from father to son, mother to daughter. From the time we're children, as one generation succeeds the next, our mothers and fathers have taught us about the great men and women of our family. When we have learned to read and write, our parents consider that we're ready to learn the history of our family. We're told that in the Temple of Solomon in Jerusalem, our greatest ancestor, Gamaliel, son of Terah, was the man who constructed the house of the god Adon, stone by stone. So do not doubt me, Maria the Jewess, or you, Abram the Israelite, when I say that I, too, am a Jew."

"Yet," Abram said softly, as though to himself, "you trade in children. You take young boys and girls away from their parents and sell them into slavery."

"Abraham of the Bible owned slaves, as did many of the ancients. I am just continuing a tradition."

"But Jews no longer own slaves. Yes, those of us who are wealthy have servants, but the servant can leave his master's employment and is free to wander. Yet the children you trade . . . they have no life other than a living death of servitude."

Didia sighed. "It's the parents who sell me their unwanted children. Egyptian, Nubian, those from Sudan and Punt and far south, where the natives are as black as mahogany. These unwanted children, who eat and take up living space, would be murdered or drowned; I give the parents money, take them off their hands, and for the rest of their lives the children grow into adults with a place to sleep, a good meal in their bellies, and a master and mistress to tend to them if they fall sick. If not for me and my slavery, these boys and girls would be dead."

She shrugged, knowing that Abraham could not refute her argument. The three fell into silence, looking at one another, until Abram said, "So for you to return my son, I have to go to the home of the procurator and steal back the amulet that once belonged to Kheti and which you want to return to his shroud."

Didia nodded.

"And then you will return my son, Jonathan, to me."

Again she nodded.

"If I steal it back for you and give it to you, how do I know that you'll keep your word?"

Didia looked at him and shrugged. "You don't know that, Abram. But what choice do you have?"

For the rest of the night, until they were too exhausted to continue, they discussed ways of Abram getting into the procurator's home and treating him for the disease for which he was well known— the falling sickness. During his first meeting of the city elders in the week he arrived as the new Roman procurator and senatorial overlord of Egypt, he had stood from his throne, clutched his head, and called to his servant to help him leave the chamber. Before his servant could get the rod to put in his mouth, Gaius Lucius Septimus fell on the floor and looked like he was having a fit. His legs, arms, and body shook, and foam flowed out of his mouth.

Those who understood these things said that he had the same falling sickness as the greatest of all philosophers, Socrates, and as Alexander the Great and Julius Caesar. For days after his malady, Gaius Lucius hadn't been seen outside of his palace; it was unwise for anybody to mention his illness.

"I have an idea," said Abram. "Didia, you spread the word to all you know that a great doctor has arrived from Jerusalem who has cured men of the falling sickness. To ensure that he knows I am a friend of Rome, you must say that I am from the city of Aelia Capitolina in the country of Syria Palaestina. Only then will he feel trust in me. Perhaps the gossip will come to the ears of his servants and administrators; perhaps they will whisper my name into his ear. But even when I'm inside his palace, how will I find the amulet?"

The two women looked at each other. Neither had the answer.

• • •

Even Abram, doubtful of whether the scheme would work, was surprised by the swiftness of the response. It had been two days since his meeting with Didia the slave trader. Though he was anxious about the welfare of Jonathan, his fears had receded because he knew that his son was alive and being cared for. The fears he'd suffered when Jonathan hadn't returned to their lodgings had been replaced by his very real concerns about being able to cure the incurable disease of the falling sickness, and of finding some small amulet in a short time in the vastness of the procurator's palace.

So when somebody knocked aggressively on his door in the middle of the night and shouted out in a language he barely understood, "Open, in the name of the procurator," he was quite unprepared.

Abram jumped out of bed and opened the door to find a huge, burly centurion standing there, dressed in the regalia of the Roman army, his breast badge showing that he was a member of the Legion XVII Alexandrianus.

Without any introduction, the centurion commanded, "You're the doctor from Syria Palaestina. You will come with me immediately."

Not wanting to indicate that he was aware such a command might be made, Abram spluttered, "What . . . why . . . I'm a doctor . . . who demands I come . . . who are you?"

The centurion eyed him coldly. "Don't ask me any questions. Just get dressed, bring any instruments you use to cure people, and come with me. Now!"

Within a minute, Abram was marching in the middle of a phalanx of men toward the upper part of the city. They were the only people on the road, as the curfew forbade anybody to be on the streets late at night, after the city bells had been rung. When they reached the residence of the procurator, Abram was overwhelmed by its size, grandeur, and opulence. His whole life had been spent in villages and large towns; he had been forbidden, like all Jews, to enter Jerusalem except on the one day, the ninth day of the month of Ab, when Jews were allowed to grieve for their history. His only view of Jerusalem had been from deep in its bowels, when as a boy he and his beloved Ruth had burrowed to the top of the tunnel to return the seal.

He'd never allowed himself to enter Jerusalem, so the first truly major city he'd entered had been Alexandria, and in the few days he'd been there, he'd explored little more than the port area. As he was marched through the streets, he was amazed by the city's size and complexity, no more so than when they ascended a hill and the procurator's palace came into view. Abram looked at the enormity of the home where Gaius Lucius Septimus lived in a manner beyond the Israelite's belief.

They entered through a fortified and guarded stone-and-iron gate. The walls of the vast villa were painted in reds and yellows, blues and greens, and adorned by parrots and lions and tigers and elephants. Columns held up balustrades and walkways built seemingly in the air, where servants sauntered into and out of rooms. Fountains played the music of waterfalls, and when he looked inside the enormous basins, he saw fish swimming in them.

And the floor. This was no rush matting or earth floor; this floor was a mosaic pattern of the faces of men and women, of courtesans and governors. He felt uncomfortable walking across such graven images, but he was forced to follow the patrol who had escorted him from his lodgings.

A servant led him upstairs to a series of corridors and rooms, where he entered a sumptuously furnished antechamber. A man was seated at a desk, writing on a vellum scroll. He looked up as Abram was escorted into the room. The middle-aged man, gray, gaunt, suspicious, eyed him up and down; it was obvious that Abram's attire didn't suit his new surroundings.

"Have you searched him?" the man asked.

The centurion shook his head and apologized. "He's a doctor. I didn't think it necessary."

"Fool! He's about to enter the private chambers of the procurator. Search him for any weapons in the folds of his . . . his . . . whatever that thing is that he's wearing."

The centurion crudely felt every part of Abram's body for knives, swords, or any other weapon he might have been concealing. It upset and angered Abram, who winced when the centurion felt his private parts.

"Might I remind you, whoever you are, that I've been dragged from my bed for reasons that haven't been explained to me. Now, why am I here, and what do you want with me?"

"You're here," said the man, who still hadn't told him who he was, "because His Excellency, Gaius Lucius Septimus, has commanded you to be here. That's all you need to know. In a moment, I'll take you into the procurator's quarters. You'll address him as 'Your Excellency.' You'll answer his questions simply and explicitly. You'll ask no questions of him unless given permission by him. And you'll initiate no conversation or engage in any unnecessary talk. Is that understood?"

Abram nodded. The seated man stood and almost apologetically knocked on an interconnecting door. A muffled response was heard, and the door was opened. If Abram had been surprised by the opulence of the public parts of the palace, when he entered Gaius Lucius Septimus's personal apartments, he was breathless. Deep reds, blues, and yellows were the dominant colors. The huge room was full of a type of furniture Abram had never seen: armchairs made of beautifully carved wood and leather; divans of deep crimson plush; intricate wooden chests of the blackest wood, inlaid with ivory and alabaster; tables large and small covered in sophisticated marquetry where the craftsman had used wood and gold leaf to create sculptures of birds and bears, foxes and lions. And in the middle of the room was a huge bed with some sort of translucent curtain around it, joined to the ceiling by a canopy.

Seated at his desk, reading from scrolls, was Gaius Lucius Septimus, the procurator and governor of all Egypt, one of the most important men in the world.

The man who'd brought him into the private quarters saluted, his arm rigidly outstretched, his palm facing down, and said, "Excellency, the doctor, Abram the Jew from Syria Palaestina."

He retreated and closed the door behind him, leaving Abram standing there while Gaius Lucius continued to read his scrolls, ignoring the doctor. Abram felt increasingly uncomfortable. Eventually, the procurator glanced up and spoke to him.

"Do you know why you've been commanded here?"

"No, Excellency."

"A century ago, one of the greatest of all of the Romans suffered from the same malady as that which causes me to be ill from time to time. But because he was the leader of all the Roman Empire, he tried to keep it secret, to hide it from the world, for fear that it would show him to be weak. I have no such fear. I've been informed by the doctors in Rome that my malady is not uncommon and tends to strike powerful men of great intelligence. It is called the falling sickness. Have you heard of it?"

"Yes, Excellency."

"It is an inconvenience for me. It strikes, often without warning, and it lays me in my bed, sometimes for days. I feel weak and listless afterward. So I want to be cured. But the Roman doctors have not been able to prevent it from happening, despite the foul medicines they've prescribed. And word has reached my ear that you have had success in Syria Palaestina in curing this disease. Is that true?"

"No, Excellency."

Gaius Lucius looked at him sharply. "No?"

"No and yes. I have no proof that the falling disease can be cured. But I have prevented its recurrence for years in some people, such that since I treated them, it has not made its return.

"I might have cured some people, but others have merely had their disease made less frequent. Those who had the falling sickness every week found after my treatment that the incidents occurred only after months, sometimes six or more. But I was unable to prevent their malady from recurring altogether. While many of my patients who have not had any fits or episodes claim they're cured, I can make no such claim. Their fits, Excellency, may recur in them at some stage."

He stopped talking. It was a risk to admit such a doubt, but the moment he saw him, Abram realized that such a man would prefer truth to the sycophancy to which he would normally be subjected.

The procurator nodded. "If you can delay the onset of these fits for weeks, or better, months, then I will be satisfied."

"And my fee?"

The procurator looked at Abram in astonishment. "I do not discuss such things. You'll talk about that with my amanuensis."

But the doctor shook his head. "No, Excellency. I don't like your man, and I don't think he likes me. I'd rather we discussed my fee between us. I have to live, and I'm not prepared to—"

"You dare say these things to me?" Gaius Lucius said in astonishment. Nobody had spoken to him in this way for years.

"You want me to cure you?"

Another risk, but like the first, this one paid off. The procurator smiled. "You'll be well paid for your skills. Now, what medicines do I have to take?"

"None," said the doctor. He remained silent, looking at the procurator.

"None?"

"None. You have to understand that what ails you is an agency of your body being out of alignment. The disease from which you suffer is called by the Greeks 'epilepsia,' from their word *epi*, which in Latin means 'from' and *lepsis*, which in your language, Excellency, means 'seizure.' The great Hippocrates examined it carefully. Before him, it was called the sacred disease because it was thought to have been sent to us by the gods, so people sacrificed animals and sought expiation.

"But Hippocrates said that its cause was that the humors of the body were out of orientation, and the remedy I dispense is to put the humors back in order."

"Humors?" asked the procurator.

Abram nodded. "Hippocrates taught that our bodies have four humors: blood, phlegm, black bile, and yellow bile. Each has its own complexion. Blood is hot and dry; phlegm is cold and wet; black bile is cold and dry; and yellow bile is hot and dry. In a person who isn't sick, each of these humors keeps the others under control, but no one is the master of all. In your language, none would be considered *primus inter pares*. Each is the equal of the others, and all act in harmony. But if illness causes one or more to take prominence, then the body loses its orientation, and the disease takes hold.

"In your case, Excellency, the black bile, which is usually cold, becomes heated when its normal dry condition becomes clogged with bodily fluids. Perhaps you've eaten something unusual or drunk too much wine; or something that you've eaten or drunk was afflicted by rot. Whatever it was, it has adversely affected your black bile, which heats and causes the foam to come out of your mouth when you fall to the floor."

The procurator was staring at him in amazement. "Where did you acquire this knowledge?" he asked. "Why didn't my Roman doctors tell me such things? How do you know so much, Jew?"

"I am a student of the great Hippocrates. And also of the physician to your own emperor Commodus, one Aelius Claudius Galenus, who is known for his writings on anatomy as Galen of Pergamon. It is these men, and great doctors like them, from whom I have acquired my knowledge. And, of course, by practice and observation of medicines on my own patients."

"I've heard of this Galen," the procurator said softly. "Wasn't he banished from Rome?"

"Yes, Excellency, but only because of the jealousy of the other doctors who saw him undermining their faith in the curative powers of their gods. But when the Great Plague broke out in Rome, killing two thousand people a day, your emperor's predecessor, Marcus Aurelius, summoned him back, and today he is the greatest physician after Hippocrates."

"So you have learned much from these men," said Gaius Lucius. "Now what do they suggest to cure me of this epi . . . whatever you call it."

"Epilepsia. We have to get your humors back into alignment. As I said, the normally cold black bile in your body is now hot, and the heat must be taken out of it. We do that by removing from your body some of the heat that is causing your black bile to become warm. This new and unaccustomed warmth causes an excess of saliva in your mouth and throat, and because there is a surfeit of it, the saliva heats, which is why it bubbles out of the mouth when you have a fit. The fit itself is caused by black bile flooding the cavities in your brain. You lose consciousness after the fit, until the black bile slowly ebbs away and you recover.

"So to drain some of the heat out of your body, we have to cool you by plunging your naked body into cold water, or drain some of the heat by bleeding you. I prefer bleeding. I do it by putting leeches on your wrists and neck, or by making an incision in your leg and letting the blood drain out. I usually take a bottle full. You will need complete bed rest for two or three days afterward."

"And that's all?" said the procurator. "The doctors in Rome prescribed wild mushrooms from caverns in the hill, and insisted that I put the flesh of a weasel on my leg until it rotted and stank. I did as they suggested, and the stench caused me to lose some friends. But when I took it off, I had maggots in my skin where the meat had been, and a week afterward I suffered an attack of the epi . . . whatever you call it. I had the doctors flogged for being liars and thieves."

"So, Excellency, do you want me to proceed with this treatment?"

"Certainly," he said abruptly.

"Then may I suggest that before we bleed you, we begin with a cold bath. I'd prefer to watch your signs and assess the success of cooling the body before I take blood away from you. Can you arrange a body of cold water?" Abram already knew what the answer would be.

"There are fountains downstairs. I don't mind bathing with the fish. Is that suitable?"

"Ah, but is the water cold? This is Alexandria, and the temperature might have heated the water."

The procurator smiled. "For the fish not to die from overheating in the little lake, I've created the fountains to keep the water cool. And I have a man whose job it is to feed the water regularly, day and night, from the deep wells beneath the city. This ensures that the water is always cool. But is it cool enough for me to reverse the heating of these humors?"

"Oh yes, Procurator. Certainly. You go downstairs and bathe for as long as you can stand the cold temperature. When you can't stand it any longer, continue to stay in for the same amount of time. It will not be pleasant, but the longer you can bear it, the more effective the treatment. Then return here, and I'll examine your signs and, if necessary, bleed you. With your permission, I'll remain here and look at the room to ensure that nothing here is causing your humors to be aroused."

The procurator left his office; Abram was completely alone. His heart thumping, he walked cautiously around the huge room, looking at the tops of tables, of desks, on the arms of the chairs, on the floor, behind some wall hangings. He looked everywhere, and he knew that time was his enemy. He had no idea how long the procurator would be downstairs in the atrium of the building.

Then he looked on the procurator's desk. Hidden under a pile of scrolls, pushed to the back of the surface, was a disc made of silver. He picked it up and saw that it had Egyptian hieroglyphics on it. He had no idea what they meant, but it fitted the description that Didia had given him two days earlier. Was it too easy? No, it must be the amulet. It was of momentary interest to the procurator, so it was just another object on his desk in which he'd lost interest, but to Didia, it was the life and death of her beautiful son. And he doubted that the procurator would miss it.

He prayed to Yahweh to forgive his theft and to keep him safe until his son had been returned to him. He slipped the disc into his bag of instruments and concoctions and waited for the return of the procurator. He realized that his face was flushed and his heart pounding. A man of Gaius Lucius's skill at judging people would immediately realize that he was looking at a man with guilt written all over his face. Abram dried his brow on his tunic, took deep breaths, and forced himself to think about his beloved wife, Ruth.

By the time Gaius Lucius returned, wet and blue with cold, and looked anxiously at Abram, the Israelite doctor had calmed down. He smiled at the procurator and felt confident that he and his beloved Jonathan would live long enough to leave the city of Alexandria and return to the country of their birth.

Palestine
1947

MUSTAFA'S VILLAGE APPEARED nestled in the fold of one of the hills as they rounded a bend in the track. It was a small village, and Mustafa told Shalman that it was called Ras Abu Yussuf. Shalman knew that he'd journeyed only about ten or twelve miles northeast of Jerusalem, yet from the looks of it, the village appeared hardly changed since medieval times.

"Tell me about your village," said Shalman.

"What's to tell? It's a village. My father's father's father was here and many more before that."

They rode on until they reached the edge of the village. Shalman's head was thumping mercilessly, and he was seeing double. He prayed that he didn't have some form of clot under his skull, putting pressure on his brain.

As they entered Ras Abu Yussuf, one, then three, and then a few dozen villagers came out of their houses to look at Mustafa leading Shalman astride his donkey. Shalman attempted a smile at the villagers, but they didn't smile back. They just looked at him in silence, recognizing from his clothes, his features, and the cut of his hair that he was either British or a Jew. Either way, he was unwelcome. Shalman felt the hostility rising in their gaze.

An aging woman emerged from a modest home at the northern end of the main street and stood in the front doorway. As Mustafa approached, leading the donkey, the woman called out loudly so that everybody could hear her disapproval, "Mustafa, who's this man? Is he one of us? If not, why have you brought an enemy to your father's door?"

Mustafa answered equally loudly, "Mother, the man has fallen and injured his head. I couldn't leave him out there. The vultures were circling."

The woman looked at Shalman suspiciously. "He's not Arab. What is he? Jew? English? Are you so stupid that you bring this into our village, to our house?"

Shalman lifted his head, deciding he needed to try to explain himself, but the simple action left him with extreme vertigo. Shalman looked at the woman, whom he assumed was Mustafa's mother, and blinked because there were two of her standing side by side. Then three. Then . . .

Shalman fainted and pitched headfirst off the donkey and into the dust.

● ● ●

For the second time in recent days, a blinding pain shot from his left to his right temple the moment he struggled to open his eyes. He closed his eyes again, but the pain stayed with him.

He tried to lift his head above the pillow, but his neck was too stiff. Then he tried to feel the rest of his body, moving his fingers, his toes, flexing his knees, lifting his arms above the blanket. When he'd finished, he realized that not only was he still alive, but he was safe and secure, despite his nightmares about a flock of huge black vultures tearing his flesh with their beaks.

Shalman opened his eyes slowly and looked around the room. He didn't recognize the furniture, the bedding, or the walls or ceiling. He tried to glance out the window, but the glare from the daylight hurt too much.

Cautiously, he maneuvered his body out of bed and saw that he was wearing only his underpants. He stood on shaky legs and looked around for his clothes, but they were nowhere to be seen. Sliding his hands along the wall for support, he walked cautiously to the door. His legs were barely responsive, and he teetered like a ninety-year-old man.

When he opened the door, he saw that it certainly wasn't a Jewish home. It had cushions against walls instead of chairs, and the table, made of some sort of dark wood, was still laden with food from a previous meal. In the corner, at a bare kitchen sink, stood a woman dressed in traditional Arab clothes, her head covered in a scarf, her back to him. Desperately, he tried to place himself within this landscape and recall how he got here, but it was too foreign. He was on the verge of panic. Why couldn't he remember?

The woman heard him enter the room and turned. In Arabic, she said curtly, "So, you're awake. Well, now you can get dressed and leave my house. Enough."

His voice rasping, Shalman asked in Hebrew, "Who are you? Where am I? What's happened?"

The woman put down the cabbage she was washing under the single tap, dried her hands on a towel, and walked over to him. There was no warmth in her face, no empathy. She continued to speak to him in Arabic. "My son found you nearly dead. Now you're alive, so it's time to leave."

Switching to his less than articulate Arabic, Shalman mumbled, "My head hurts."

The woman went back to her work in the kitchen but continued to talk to the room. "I didn't want you in my home, but Awad doesn't allow you to be sent away. My husband has the mind of a goat. He insisted that we put you into our bed. Awad and I have been sleeping here," she said angrily, pointing at the cushions on the floor. "Our mullah came to see you and looked at your wound. I cleaned it, and you have a big bump on your head. But your skull isn't broken. So now you can walk and you can leave, and that will be that."

Shalman waited for a pause in the woman's monologue. "Might I have a drink of water? I'm very thirsty . . ." Aware that he was standing in his underwear, he added, "And my clothes?"

She handed him a glass of water. "Your clothes are washed," she said. She wiped her hands, went outside, and returned with them. "Now you get dressed and go. Before my husband returns."

"I'm sorry that you and your husband had to sleep elsewhere."

He took the clothes and walked slowly and painfully back to the bedroom. He was desperate to wash and brush his teeth, but as he was struggling to put on his trousers, he felt faint again. The room spun, and he sat heavily on the bed.

He may have blacked out. He didn't know. But a disturbance outside woke him. He had half put on his trousers and was sprawled out over the bed.

The door opened and Mustafa was standing there beside an older, diminutive man with a week's growth of beard, who was obviously Mustafa's father. They looked at him and said nothing but turned, and the older man said to his wife, "You will not send him away, Rabiyah. The man can barely dress himself. What's wrong with you, woman?" Awad said softly to Shalman, "You speak Arabic?"

"A little," answered Shalman.

"Then understand, until you are recovered, my home is your home. This is the way of my people." The man touched his hand to his heart. Raising his voice so that his wife could hear him clearly in the next room, he added, "Our Prophet, peace and blessings be upon him, said, 'Feed with food the needy wretch, the orphan, and the prisoner.'"

Then he walked out of the room.

Memory was returning. Shalman remembered Mustafa as the young man with the donkey who'd rescued him.

"Which one am I?" asked Shalman, putting his hand to his aching head once more.

"Maybe all three," came Mustafa's dry reply. "You feel like shit, don't you?"

Shalman nodded, lightning flaring up behind his eyes, and he lay back on the bed.

"Do you remember anything?"

"You're Mustafa. You stopped me from being eaten alive by vultures. You have a donkey that stinks."

Mustafa grinned. "I'll have him washed next time I rescue a Jew from certain death."

"Your mother really doesn't want me to stay here. I'll dress and go. I need to get home to my wife and daughter."

"And how will you walk the ten miles to Jerusalem? You can't even walk to the kitchen. Don't worry about my mother. She's not prejudiced; she hates the Jews and the British equally."

This brought a smile to Shalman's face despite the pain in his head.

"There's a car in the village that belongs to the headman," continued Mustafa. "I can drive it. When you're feeling better, maybe in a couple of days, I'll drive you back to the outskirts of Jerusalem. Until then, rest. Go out in the garden. It'll do you good."

"How long have I been here, unconscious?" Shalman asked weakly.

Mustafa shrugged. "Three days."

Shalman thought immediately of Judit and Vered and how his wife must be worrying. "I have to get a message to my wife. She'll be—"

"I've already sent her a note. I told her you'd banged your head and we were looking after you."

Shalman frowned. "But how—"

"Your wallet. It has your address. One of the men from our village was going to Jerusalem to buy from the market, and he took the message. Your wife insisted that she come to see you, take you back to Jerusalem, but my friend insisted that you couldn't be moved and you had to stay. She said she'd send a doctor, but he assured her that you were all right, except for needing to rest. Look, Shalman, everything's all right. Just lie down, shut up, and get better. Then we can get rid of you."

• • •

An hour later, Shalman, his head still pounding, was dressed and sitting on a rough wooden seat in the garden of the house, feeling the sun on his face. Mustafa came up and sat down beside him, holding in his hands a Lee-Enfield rifle. The weapon was aged and worn, poorly maintained, and had taken more than a few bumps and scratches. It was a British military standard issue.

"The sun heals better than any medicine," Shalman said.

Mustafa worked the bolt action of the rifle with his hand, attempting to loosen a jam in the mechanism, and swore under his breath.

"Can I help?" asked Shalman. He knew the rifle well, having stolen many of them. In fact, it was these types of rifles and pistols, stolen by Dov on the kibbutz, that had led to his father being taken away, never to return.

"You know something about guns?" asked Mustafa.

"A little," said Shalman. "May I?" He held out his hands for the rifle. Mustafa hesitated but then quickly unclipped the magazine from beneath the barrel and disarmed the rifle before letting Shalman take it. His moment of uncertainty didn't go unnoticed. Mustafa held Shalman's gaze.

Shalman set to work on the rifle, stripping the bolt action out and dislodging the debris that clogged it.

"Where did you get a British rifle?" asked Shalman, knowing full well the question was a loaded one.

"How did you learn how to fix one?" asked Mustafa.

The young men looked at each other. There was something in Mustafa's face that demanded complete honesty from Shalman.

"Fighting the British," he said.

Mustafa simply nodded, taking the rifle back from Shalman's hands. "And what of Arabs?"

Shalman didn't answer. Mustafa looked at the strange Jew and then shifted subjects. "There are many who fight the British. Not just here. Everywhere the British have gone. You have to wonder how many British weapons have shot bullets back at British soldiers over the years."

Shalman smiled. "Many."

"Yes . . . They fight the British in India, too. And in Africa. I hate the British. What right do they have to be on my land and tell me what to do?"

Shalman looked at Mustafa curiously. "That's how I feel. Funny you should talk about India. It looks as if the natives have beaten the British. A man called Gandhi. He's led an entire nation in fighting the British, but he didn't use guns or anything like that. He invented a method of fighting without violence called peaceful non-cooperation. He got the people to just sit down in the streets and refuse to cooperate. And the British army doesn't know how to stop them."

Mustafa stood and slung the rifle over his shoulder. "You Jews are killing the British to drive them out. Maybe if you just sat down in the streets, they'd leave sooner."

Mustafa turned to depart. Shalman caught his arm.

"I never thanked you," said Shalman. "I want to thank you."

Mustafa just shrugged again. He hesitated and then asked, "When the British are gone, will you fight us?"

"We don't want to. But if we have to . . ." replied Shalman.

"Perhaps we should just lie down in the streets and refuse to move. How will your terrorists in the Irgun and your army, your Haganah, deal with millions of Arabs who won't move?" asked Mustafa. He didn't wait for an answer. He changed the topic. "What were you doing out there, anyway? In the hills. Alone."

Shalman let out a small laugh. "I was looking for something."

"What?"

"History," he said, and Mustafa looked at him more closely, evidently concerned that the blow to Shalman's head may have affected his brain. "It's a science called archaeology," added Shalman. "Archaeology is when you study—"

Mustafa cut him off. "I know what archaeology is."

Shalman apologized. "Of course. I'm sorry."

"Not all Arabs are unread and ignorant, you know." Mustafa grinned and both men smiled. He sat back down next to Shalman. "My father cannot read. Nor my mother. But I want to go to Lebanon, to university there."

"Why don't you?" asked Shalman.

Mustafa simply cast his arms wide to encompass the modest house and the impoverished village beyond. "There is no money here. To go to a university, you need money."

A moment of silence passed between the two young men, who in that moment seemed so alike yet so far apart. The silence was broken when Mustafa turned to Shalman. "Archaeology, you say? Let me show you something."

Minutes later, after leaving Shalman to go inside the house, Mustafa came back out and dropped three coins into Shalman's open hand, a smile of pride on his face. The coins were Roman, ancient and worn but unmistakable.

Shalman recognized one of the coins immediately and told Mustafa that he believed it was exceptionally rare. It was the Iudaea Capta coin, minted by the Romans after they had put down the Great Jewish Revolt in 70 C.E. With growing excitement, Shalman pointed out to Mustafa the figure of a woman in mourning sitting beneath a palm tree, and a man standing behind her with his hands bound behind his back.

"Where did you find these?" he asked.

Mustafa smiled. Shalman looked into the man's eyes and saw a shadow of doubt and mistrust. Would he tell him?

And then Mustafa said softly, "One thing at a time, Shalman. One thing at a time."

The House of Wisdom, Baghdad

820 C.E. (188 years after the death of the prophet Mohammed)

HIS ARRIVAL IN Bayt al Hikma, the House of Wisdom, caused not an eyebrow to be raised, not a glance to be directed his way. Zakki ben Jacob had traveled with his wife and four children from Jerusalem to the new city of Baghdad and expected some recognition, some welcome, perhaps even some excitement at his arrival. But as he stood at the doorway of the central library and surveyed the vast room, full of noise and argument, discord and debate, there wasn't a murmur of interest in the new face standing at the threshold.

Instead, the room resembled a huge cage of parrots, men crawling over the floor looking at unfurled scrolls, or sitting on cushions at low tables shouting at one another as they pointed at texts. Younger scholars rushed up and down ladders at their masters' bidding, finding scrolls or codices or books or drawings that would disprove or validate a particular point of view.

There was a rainbow of colors in their dress, clothes that showed the scholars came from Africa and Arabia and India and China. Amid the cacophony of noise and the kaleidoscope of color were some men who stood out because they were dressed in the earthen dark and dull cloaks and cowls of Christian monks. These men, Zakki guessed, had come from the countries far to the west and north of Baghdad—lands full of impassable forests still mired in the darkness of ignorance and chilled by the frosts of winter.

Zakki ben Jacob was used to silence when he thought and read and studied in his own library in Jerusalem. But as he stood on the threshold of this monumental room, the rabid scholarship terrified him.

Had he made a terrible mistake, accepting the invitation of Caliph Ja'far al-Ma'mun? Was he wrong to leave his comfortable home in Jerusalem to come to Baghdad?

His wife, Dorit, had been vehemently against it. Their life had been comfortable and rewarding in Jerusalem, and they had been able to visit the monuments built for their ancient ancestors who were said to have been priests in King Solomon's great temple. Similarly, his children had been against going; the world they knew was in Jerusalem, not far from there, to the southeast within the Islamic caliphate.

But the emissary had been so seductive, offering Zakki so much, that he'd felt compelled to agree almost on the spot. Dorit had been furious, telling him that he could earn a good living in Jerusalem, so why would he want to leave? Dorit didn't understand that the offer from the caliph had been far more than material; it was a chance to be a part of unfathomable intellectual stimulation among the greatest scholars of the age.

And now here he was, one of Jerusalem's most revered doctors and philosophers, a mathematician and astrologer, a man recognized in all of the streets of his homeland, standing at the gateway to the greatest institute of learning in the world, and being completely ignored.

For the first time since he'd become a doctor, Zakki ben Jacob felt uncomfortable among his peers. Here it was as though he were a void, a phantasm, a djinn without form or substance. Ill at ease, he reached up to his throat and gripped the pendant hanging around his neck. It was a glorious pendant hanging by a thick golden chain. Made of ancient metal, it was a copy of a seal created by the tunnel builder Matanyahu of the time of King Solomon. It was his good-luck charm, a link to Zakki's ancient lineage, so it was his strength in times of uncertainty.

Grasping the seal in his left hand, Zakki coughed. Nobody looked up; all were too busy with the particular tasks they had set themselves. He coughed louder, and several men finally turned their eyes to him, frowned, and returned to their texts.

Resigned that he couldn't turn back to Jerusalem, Zakki picked up his traveling bag and walked into the room, peering over the shoulders of the scholars hunched at tables, looking down at the floor where elderly men were stretched out comparing the text of one scroll against another, or translating from Greek into Arabic and Latin. He continued to walk around the hall until he came to a table where three men were seated. It was as though he were standing in the middle of a howling desert wind, unable to think, to make out any coherence in all the cacophony.

Then he heard words that stimulated his ears, words in a language native to him.

He stood for a moment at the table and listened to the men speaking in heated voices, their hands animated as they pointed at the texts in front of them. The words they used were desperate attempts to pronounce the Hebrew language from a scroll. But they were using the language so wrongly.

"Brothers, may I be of assistance?" he asked in a loud voice, summoning confidence.

One of the elderly men looked up at him. "Is the language of the Jews your native tongue?" he asked in Arabic.

Zakki smiled and showed the man the ancient seal hanging around his neck. All could see that though the Hebrew was from an ancient era, it was clearly the language they were trying to translate.

"I speak Hebrew, and it's my native tongue. I also speak Latin and Greek and Aramaic. My name is—"

All of the scholars put their fingers to their lips, demanding his silence. Zakki was confused but cut off his words at the gestures.

"Brother, we are all here scholars of many different disciplines. Those who have been summoned have come in response to the *hadith* of their holy book, the Koran, which says that the ink of the scholar is more holy than the blood of a martyr. That, brother, is why you have no name in this House of Wisdom. We are known only by our relationship of brother.

"Some of us are students of medicine, some of optics, some of astronomy, some mathematics and *al chemica*, and so on and so forth. In our homes, we are well known and respected. And we are all revered here for our knowledge. But in this place, brother, we are all of the same height; only our books are elevated onto a table. None of us is greater, better, or more than the other. Only knowledge and scholarship are elevated, not the scholar. That is why, in the House of Wisdom, we keep our names to ourselves."

To Zakki, the words were like poetry: noble, powerful, and intoxicating.

"What is your field of study, brother? Is it language? Can you help us translate these ancient writings of the Greek philosophers Thales and Anaxamander into Hebrew?"

"Perhaps," Zakki said, "but my work is that of a doctor and philosopher. I've trained in Rome and Alexandria, like my father before me, and his father before him unto the hundredth generation when, it is told, we were priests and healers in the Temple of Solomon."

"Then," said the elderly scholar, rummaging among the texts on his table until he pulled out a thick and dusty tome, "you can assist us with the medical and anatomical terms used by the great Hippocrates of Kos, which we scholars of language have found difficult to translate into languages from his archaic Greek. He uses terms for the human body and its ailments with which we are unfamiliar."

Zakki found a cushion and sat among his peers. "Gladly . . . brothers."

• • •

It was his second week in the House of Wisdom when Zakki's intellectual life was turned on its head. He had come to Baghdad at the invitation of the caliph to share his knowledge with other scholars. He also hoped that he would learn greater things from them.

Neither a proud nor hubristic man, Zakki was wise enough to know that there was much he didn't know; he was always open to learn more. Like his forefathers, he came from a long and honorable line of priests, scholars, and healers. And like them, he had always gone in search of knowledge.

He had spent a lifetime acquiring the knowledge of his professions of medicine, healing, and alchemy. His rubric was that the facts he collected were just that, facts and information, often disparate and disconnected. Yet in his mind, he somehow transformed them into knowledge of the world, and through that knowledge, he could determine the right treatment for his patients.

But Zakki wasn't satisfied. Knowledge wasn't enough. Facts weren't sufficient fuel to give him the wisdom on how his knowledge fit into a universal landscape. When he was with philosophers, discussing the deepest of subjects—such as why mankind had been ordained by the Almighty One to be above the animals—he felt himself a supplicant at their feet.

When he sat and thought as a philosopher, his knowledge was insufficient. For knowledge to metamorphose into the wisdom of philosophy, what was required was the company of other minds, discussion and argument, challenge and intellectual conflict, which would, in time, lead him to deeper and deeper thoughts. And this was what he had found for the first time in his life at the House of Wisdom.

None, though, neither the Muslims nor the other Jews nor the men who had traveled from the farthest reaches of the world, challenged him, or transmuted his knowledge into the wisdom of philosophy, more than Osric the Monk, who came to Baghdad from an abbey in a township called Glastonbury in a country called Anglia, which was north of Gallic France.

Invited like other scholars, to the House of Wisdom by the caliph, Osric of Leicester was a small and wiry man, balding yet with a face that defied all but the crudest indication of age. Osric was a monkish scholar who had brought with him to Baghdad twenty volumes of a Codex he called the *Etymologiae*, written a hundred years earlier by the greatest scholar of his age, Bishop Isidor of Seville. This bishop had written what Osric called "a summation of all the knowledge of the world." The works contained 450 chapters of densely packed facts concerning the earth itself, the life of men who lived in the past, religion, science, and much more.

"Not since the time of Homer, Pliny, and Thucydides has a man known everything that there was to know, here on earth and in the heavens above," Osric had told Zakki when they first sat on low cushions, legs folded, to discuss the intersection between the books of Moses and those written by the disciples of Jesus of Nazareth.

But when Osric explained to Zakki what the long-dead bishop had written about Zakki's own city of Jerusalem, he argued that much of the information was simply incorrect. Bishop Isidor had written that King Solomon had left a great and incalculable treasure for the benefit of mankind, yet the Romans didn't realize that it was in the treasure house of his temple when they pulled it down to punish the Jews. So the treasure of gold, silver, and precious gems was, to this day, buried under a massive heap of stones.

Zakki told Osric that, yes, there was stone upon stone in massive piles of rubble, far too heavy for the citizens to lift and clear away. It was so much, Zakki told him, that successive governments of the city, the Romans, Jews, and now Muslims, had left it as it was for hundreds of years, and it was true that nobody knew what was beneath the massive stones. But to think that the Romans, the greatest scavengers the world had ever known, would have left even a single precious stone or the smallest golden object was nonsense.

Yet day after day, Osric argued that the treasure was there to be found, and that when it was, it would herald the return of Jesus Christ as Messiah in the second coming, to save the world from its misery.

"When it is found, Solomon's wealth will be distributed to all the poor of the earth and raise them above the status of serfs and villains. It is even said that the noble emperor Constantine himself, first great Roman to convert to my faith, sent his very mother, the blessed Saint Helena, to find the treasure of Solomon. Wherefore, then, should we doubt or fail to seek this treasure?"

Zakki turned on the monk. "What nonsense you Christians talk," he said sharply. "Helena made a pilgrimage to Jerusalem to recover the cross on which your messiah was crucified. And it has been told that when they found out the emperor's mother was in Jerusalem, there were a thousand scoundrels who picked up branches from their gardens and made them into splinters, telling her that they were fragments of the true cross, and sold them to her for a fortune. Stories abound in Jerusalem of a man who lived there and owed a great debt, so when Helena visited the city, he convinced her that the ground he owned where stood a pagan temple was the very land upon which Abraham almost sacrificed Isaac, and upon which your Jesus of Nazareth was crucified, and where his sepulcher was laid to rest. She wasn't looking for any treasure of Solomon, Osric, but for the remnants of the life of your Jesus."

The monk looked at him disbelievingly and cited chapter and verse from Saint Isidor's works to prove his case. To pacify the distressed Christian mystic, Zakki promised him that when he returned to Jerusalem, he would search diligently for such a treasure, though he knew in his heart that it had been dissipated when the Jews were sent on their first exile into Babylonia and then dispersed around the world.

On this point and others concerning science, ethics, theology, and philosophy, Zakki and Osric argued every day. They would also read from and debate Bishop Isidor's other chapters in the *Etymologiae*. Zakki found it so amazing to read that he begged Osric to allow him to buy the set of books so he could spend the rest of his life studying them, but the monk had just received an urgent note from his monastery to return to Anglia. Zakki regretted his leaving, but Osric assured him that whenever Zakki was in Baghdad, he would always have access to St. Isidor because the monk would leave the volumes of the *Etymologiae* in the great library of the House of Wisdom, where they would be available to him and every other scholar.

Zakki spent his days either disputing with other sages, reading in the library, or translating ancient works, except those days dedicated to prayer. Several weeks passed before he decided to take some time to himself and explore the wonders of the city.

The construction of Baghdad had begun sixty years earlier by the Abbasid Caliph Al-Mansur when he transferred his capital from Damascus. It was in the fertile valley between the two great rivers Tigris and Euphrates and hence called by the Greeks Mesopotamia. The city was replete with palms and gardens, cool spots for contemplation, and roof gardens for the growing of vegetables such as carrots, herbs such as bananas, and fruits and flowers of every color and description.

Despite being in existence for such a short time, Baghdad was already greater and more prosperous than Jerusalem, which had never fully recovered from the devastation wreaked by the Romans seven hundred years earlier.

Meandering through the wide city streets, Zakki found that the epicenter of the city was a huge mosque. Around it were Islamic study houses and instruction centers for pupils from all over the world who had come to study at the feet of the great Abbasid Koranic teachers. These buildings were surrounded by a ring road, and beyond them were churches for Christian worshippers and synagogues for the many Jews who lived in Baghdad. Surmounting these were shops that sold meats and cloth, copies of holy books, jewelry from Asia and farther east, ivory and the incredible skins of animals from Africa, and much more.

Tired from wandering in the heat of the day, Zakki walked beneath a cloth canopy attached to buildings on the side of the street and sat on a low stool at a wooden table in a market stall. The owner came over and asked what he wanted to eat or drink.

"Just a drink, please," Zakki said.

The owner looked at the scholar's clothes and sneered. "I suppose you're a Jew! Why won't you people eat my food? Isn't it good enough for you?"

Zakki smiled. "It's probably very good, my friend," he said. "But our holy book prohibits us to eat that which hasn't been prepared according to our ways, just as you Muslims are forbidden to drink spirits that intoxicate the mind or, like us, eat of the flesh of the pig."

"I'm not a Muslim, friend," the owner scoffed. "I'm a Christian, and I'll starve in this city trying to feed people like you."

Zakki took pity on him. "Then tell me, follower of Jesus, when you make bread, do you use the fat of a pig or the milk and butter of goats or sheep?"

"I use the milk and butter of cows."

"Good," said Zakki. "Then kindly bring me slices of your bread, and I'll have some olives and seeds with it."

The owner showed the rudiments of a smile. "And what about some beef? I've slices from the haunch of a cow, if you'd like that."

Zakki shook his head. "No, friend, just the bread."

He sat alone, reveling in the silence of the street. Silence? It was full of the sounds of people and commerce. Yet compared to the perpetual din, the never-ending discord and shouting and arguments in the House of Wisdom, this was like being in the Fields of Elysium.

When he'd finished his bread and olives, he decided it was time for him to move on, but as he sat, he wondered where he should go. To another stall selling pomegranate juice? To look at more mosques, minarets, churches, synagogues, shops, houses and schools of learning? Or should he just sit here in the heat of the day, reveling in the freedom his mind had been given to think.

His cascading thoughts were broken when a shadow was cast over the table. Zakki looked up and saw a man about to walk underneath the canopy of the café. He was tall, dressed in fine clothes, and Zakki saw standing in the roadway a dozen of the caliph's guards as escort.

Instead of sitting at one of the other three benches, the man sat on the remaining wooden stool at Zakki's table, much to the doctor's surprise.

The man looked at Zakki and nodded without smiling. "Greetings to you, Zaccharius, son of Jacob, son of Abraham of the tribe of Levi. Welcome to Baghdad. I hope you like my city after your life in Jerusalem. How does the day greet you?"

"It greets me well, thank you, sir. But you have the advantage, for I do not know you."

The tall man waved his hand as if his identity was of no consequence. "Yet I know you. And why you're here by request of our caliph, Ja'far al-Ma'mun, at his pleasure and munificence."

Zakki studied the face of the tall man. He was obviously wealthy, and his skin had been softened with oils and unguents to protect him from the fierce heat of the desert. His clothes, unlike those of the scholars with whom Zakki worked, weren't just colorful but richly endowed with jewels and made of the finest silks from distant Asia. The man's movements, even sitting, showed that he was a person of position in the city, comfortable in himself and apparently used to the respect of others.

"How do you know me, Your Excellency?"

"Ah, it is a strange tale. The world is indeed getting smaller." The man left an elongated pause, seemingly for dramatic effect, before continuing. "Many years ago, your great-grandfather of blessed memory cured my great-grandmother of a sickly yellow disease that caused her to faint all the while. Your grandfather called the disease 'chlorosis,' and she recovered when your grandfather forced her to eat the leaves of vegetables."

Zakki nodded at the simple cure.

"This is something that my family has done ever since and which I believe has kept us well and healthy. So when I heard that your reputation in Jerusalem had grown sufficiently, I suggested to my caliph that he send for you to join other scholars in our House of Wisdom."

"Then I owe you thanks. And I gather from what you've said that you're a Jew."

The tall man nodded. "It seems that our paths have crossed before. In the distant past. Isn't it told that your ancestors were priests in Solomon's temple?"

Zakki smiled. "I'm told by my father and his father before him that our family line can be traced back to Zadok the Priest. That's why I was given my name. But how does that relate us?"

"I come from a long line of builders and traders. King Solomon's temple came into existence and was fashioned by the money of my ancestors. So there is perhaps much, Doctor, that we have in common."

"Except that I still don't know your name," retorted Zakki, his curiosity and suspicion growing.

"I am Hadir ibn Yussuf ibn Gibreel. I am the vizier to the caliph of the Abbasid ruling family, the ineffable and all-powerful Ja'far al-Ma'mun, may Allah and Mohammed His Prophet, Moses, and Jesus all smile upon him and bring him wisdom and great fortune."

"You say these words of blessings to Mohammed and to Jesus? Yet you are a Jew? And you've taken an Arabic name. Why is this?"

Hadir shrugged. "We are a practical people. We are flexible. We adapt. To survive, we've had to; we've been exiled many times since Father Moses brought us out of the land of Egypt with a mighty hand and an outstretched arm. So we Jews prosper wherever we find ourselves."

"Perhaps, Hadir, but we have always retained our faith," said Zakki.

"Indeed, my friend. I am as much a Jew as you, but to look and sound part of this great city, I dress like them and speak like them. And I have prospered—greatly. Many Jews have risen to power and status in the reign of the Abbasids. We are recognized for our skills as merchants, our knowledge of the laws that govern this and other lands, and our learning. And because of our lines of families and friendships scattered throughout the world since the Romans expelled our people from Israel, we have a great advantage over others in trade."

"True, but many of our people have returned to Israel."

"As did my ancestors. But the growth and spread of Islam has given us boundless opportunities. Where once Islam was warlike, today it is calm and peaceful, and men like my caliph are striving to uncover all that this world has to offer. That's why the House of Wisdom was built. It is the golden center of Islamic learning, and that's why I wanted you to be part of it, Zakki ben Jacob."

Zakki looked at the other man and saw beyond the smile, the visage. There was something more, something deeper, that the man was hiding.

"Is that the only reason you've invited me to Baghdad, Hadir ibn Yussuf?"

Hadir smiled and turned to the owner of the stall, standing in the corner. The shopkeeper was at a loss to understand why such an important man as the caliph's vizier would have visited.

"Your finest juice, my friend, and I'll also have some bread and olives."

Bowing, the shopkeeper returned to his counter. Never had his stall been full of such eminent men. He couldn't wait to regale his wife and children with the story later that night.

Hadir turned back to Zakki. "You have a suspicious mind, Doctor."

Zakki shrugged. "I'm told many things, but I'm trained to see beyond the words, into the minds and thoughts of those who seek me out. There are many eminent scholars in our world. Many far more knowledgeable than I. Yet you selected me. I'd like to know why."

The café owner reappeared and set down a glass of pomegranate juice before Hadir, as well as a plate of bread, olives, oil, and a paste of pulverized lentils. He stood there, smiling at the important man and waiting for a word of thanks.

Hadir looked up at him. "This looks delicious. Thank you, my friend." He took some coins out of his pocket, far more than the owner normally charged, and put them in the man's palm. The shop owner backed away, bowing.

The two men ate in silence until, at last, Hadir leaned forward to close the gap between them. He lowered his voice to a near whisper. "There is something you must do for me."

"Must?" said Zakki incredulously. "Is there some debt I owe you for having me summoned here?"

Hadir smiled, but it was insincere and cold. "There is no debt. But you may feel . . ." He paused as if looking for the right word. "Compelled."

The word made Zakki's muscles tense.

"Be at ease, my friend. Let me explain. How much do you know about the great schism in the religion practiced by my caliph: the division between those who are calling themselves Sunni, who believe that Abu Bakr, Mohammed's father-in-law and close companion, is the rightful heir and the first caliph, and those who call themselves Shi'ite and believe that Mohammed's son-in-law and cousin, Ali, was his rightful heir?"

The scholar in Zakki pushed ahead of his more nervous self. "I know a little . . . I know that when their Prophet Mohammed was nearing death, his followers were confused as to whom he had named as his successor to be caliph. As you say, some thought it was Abu Bakr, while others thought that it was Ali."

Hadir leaned closer before replying. "And this disputation has gone on now for nearly two hundred years. It gets worse as the years go by. Deaths, murders, wars. I fear that even the great house of the Abbasids will be brought low by the internecine conflicts. Yes, my friend, there is going to be a war between those who are devotees of the Sunni tradition and those who believe with all their hearts in the Shi'ite lineage of the Prophet Mohammed. My caliph's brother, Abu Ishaq al-Mu'tasim, is a devout Sunni, but he hasn't the intellect or culture of my beloved employer and is driven by demons in his mind. He has sworn to murder a young boy, aged only nine, who claims to be the ninth imam of the Shi'ites, a boy called Muhammad al-Jawad. He declares that by killing the child, he will put an end to the Shi'ite heresy."

Zakki's mind was intrigued by the politics but confused about what this had to do with him.

"If the boy-imam dies, then this city, and I fear much of the empire of the Abbasids, will be torn apart by civil warfare, and all will be lost. This must be prevented."

"Then warn the boy and his family," said Zakki matter-of-factly. "Go to him and tell him to leave."

Hadir sat back on his stool. "I cannot. Al-Mu'tasim has ears everywhere in the palace. I am too visible. Were I to warn the boy, then I and others will be killed, and the boy will die regardless."

Zakki thought for a moment. "Send another, then."

Hadir shook his head. "I cannot be seen to be sending a Muslim. The hatred between the factions is unfathomable. Somebody would betray us."

"Then send a Christian." Zakki half turned and looked at the café owner.

"The Shi'ites would never listen to a Christian. Muslims accept Jesus as a prophet, but the Christians go much beyond that and teach that Jesus was the son of Adonai Elohim, and that's a heresy in the eyes of Islam. No, I need a different messenger." Hadir looked intently into Zakki's eyes.

The Jerusalem doctor understood. "No," he said simply. Involuntarily, he reached to his throat and touched the seal around his neck.

Hadir did not flinch or balk at the flat refusal. "It must be a Jew who delivers the warning. And that man must be credible and free of all connections. A man who is clean."

Zakki was a man who lived inside of books and scrolls and his own thoughts, but he was not naive. The House of Wisdom was the most wondrous place he had ever been, and he felt more at home there than anywhere, but he was still a stranger in a strange land. Politics was a desert of shifting sands and deep rifts, and Zakki knew nothing of those involved. To align himself, to become a part of intrigues he did not understand, could be disastrous.

"I want no part of this," he said, even as he looked around the flanking bodyguards of the vizier standing at watch around the square.

Hadir seemed to consider the response. His eyes remained fixed on Zakki's. "You have so much to gain here, Doctor. So much this city, this land, can offer you. There is no center of learning in the world to rival Baghdad. And yet you also have very much to lose."

Zakki found himself leaning back on his stool and wishing he might stand and leave. But the eyes of Hadir held him rooted to the spot. All he could do was repeat his answer to the question Hadir never asked. "I want no part of this."

"I'm afraid, Zaccharius, son of Jacob, of Jerusalem, that you are already a part of this."

"You have no power over me. I will not be compelled."

Hadir smiled insincerely once more. "You have a family, yes? A beautiful family. Dorit and the children . . ."

Zakki's eyes widened.

"Anyone can be compelled, my dear doctor. And it is a simple thing I ask."

Jerusalem

1947

JUDIT SAT LISTENING to Lehi leader Israel Eldad address the members of the larger and more moderate Jewish freedom-fighting force, the Irgun. The year before, Yitzhak Shamir had been captured by the British and exiled to Africa. He had escaped and sought asylum in France. In his place, Israel Eldad had become one of the major figures in Lehi. Where he once was focused on ideological determination for the group, he was now actively leading the struggle.

As Judit listened, she was reminded of the old saying: "Two Jews, three opinions." Lehi was one of a number of militant groups formed under the British mandate of Palestine, and they were often far from united. While the ultimate goal might have been shared, the methods and opinions on how to achieve that goal were varied and, at times, contradictory. Beria and Judit's Soviet commanders had selected Lehi as the best vehicle for Judit, as the group of freedom fighters represented the most hard-line, the most determined, and the most willing to do what needed to be done. No doubt Beria had placed other agents in other groups, but Judit likely would never know their names or who they were.

As she listened to Eldad, she tried to reconcile the dichotomy within her. On the one hand, Lehi as a militant Zionist organization had moved toward Moscow as a way of ridding Palestine of the British and their mandate; at the same time, she was working secretly to rid Palestine of those militant Zionists and more mainstream politicians who would oppose such a union. Only through knowing that her secret goals for Soviet Russia were both aligned with and yet divergent from those around her was she able to reconcile the need for unity. And this was why the two groups, Lehi and Irgun, were coming together.

The leader of the Irgun, Menachem Begin, kept looking at Judit, and she wondered whether he was more interested in her as a woman than in the discussion taking place about the two organizations working hand in hand to fight the British.

Menachem Begin reminded her strangely of the NKVD captain who'd come for her that day at the schoolhouse. She realized that he was neither looking at her nor through her but working out where she fit into his scheme of things. She could almost see the cogs of his mind figuring out whether she could be used as a seductress, or as a killer, or as a decoy.

Judit turned her eyes from him and looked intently at the wiry Eldad. He was talking about the importance of increasing the assaults against the British, and the atmosphere in the room lay heavily on the shoulders of the thirteen men and two women. None underestimated the importance of the decisions they would soon make. If they increased their violence against the British army, public hostility on the streets of London might force their parliament to pull them out of the land; it could also oblige the British government to dramatically increase the numbers of soldiers stationed in Palestine. The imposition of martial law was a real possibility, which would have negative effects on their operations.

"We're at the turning point, my comrades," said Israel Eldad. "We always knew we would be surrounded by enemies, Arab and British. But it is the British who have the most to lose. Here they are occupiers, so their will is weak. The world's media is on our side. There are stories in the American and European newspapers about British soldiers assaulting Jewish refugees. This we can leverage, and from this the British can be broken and sent back to their homeland. Now is the time to strike harder and not diminish our struggle."

There were nods and murmurs of agreement around the table. Menachem Begin surveyed the faces of his Irgun colleagues and the young Lehi men and women. He was a shrewd politician who could smell the winds of change. He knew that if he didn't agree to a joint assault, then Lehi would walk away from the Irgun, and both organizations would be diminished.

Judit cast her eyes across the room from Menachem to Eldad and back. These two men were very important to her goals. If a future Israel would be an effective communist client of Soviet Russia, then future political power may rest with these men; and if that was the case, then perhaps Begin would have to be dealt with.

• • •

A week after the meeting, late at night and well beyond the hour of curfew that the British army had imposed on the nation because of the killings, fifteen people, alone and in small groups, made their way through the streets to a designated point. There were thirteen men and two women. One of the women was Judit. The other was a Tunisian Jewish girl named Ashira, new to Lehi but so bristling with gritted determination that Judit could not help but wonder what events marred her past.

The group converged on the quiet and dark of the Alliance Girls' School, a modest but well-constructed building set back from the street. The caretaker of the school was a covert member of Lehi who had cleared the building and waited for the group in the dark.

The caretaker ushered them in quickly and led them to the school's hall. With just a small oil lamp casting a dim orange glow, the group found a long table where British army uniforms were laid out. The men put on the uniforms, while Judit and Ashira ensured that their weapons were loaded with ammunition.

When they were ready, Israel Eldad inspected each man as though on a parade ground. Satisfied that they would pass muster if an officer happened to demand an inspection, he nodded and ordered them to prepare to move out. He then turned to Judit and put a hand on her shoulder, drawing her away from the group and lowering his voice.

"I know you, Judit. I know you would like to put on one of those uniforms and fire the first shot into the building."

Judit raised a corner of her mouth in a wry smile.

"But your task is more important. The British will respond quickly. They are prepared, and they're scared. The rear access is too narrow; when help comes, it will come to the front door. This is where you will be, machine gun at the ready. You understand? No one enters that building while our boys are inside."

Judit gave a curt nod, and Eldad squeezed her shoulder once more. "Good. Now go. And take care of Ashira."

Judit often wondered about her Lehi comrades and whether they, like her, were agents for the Soviet Union. Was Eldad under the wing of the NKVD? Would he be part of the push for a great communist state in Palestine? Was this why he was pushing Lehi so strongly toward Comrade Stalin, or was it only because of his hatred of Britain?

Judit nodded again and turned to Ashira, standing behind her. They picked up their bulky weapons and followed the men out of the door. It was two in the morning, but none of the men or women was tired. They were alive with the task ahead.

The two women climbed into the back of a truck that had been painted the previous day in the colors of the British army. It was not a perfect imitation, but in the dark of night, to a casual observer it would pass.

Judit, and Ashira, along with ten men, sat silently on wooden benches on either side of the truck's cargo area. The other three men had stepped into a waiting taxi. The plan was that the taxi would drive past the Officers' Club, and if there were no vehicles parked in front of the building, they'd stop and pretend to pay the driver while the truck pulled up behind them.

One of the men was Dov; she'd once met him with Shalman, but now that her husband was no longer intimately part of the group, more father to their child than freedom fighter, she and Dov had developed their own friendship. She enjoyed her infrequent moments with Dov, listening to the kind of boy Shalman had been on his kibbutz.

Theirs were among the very few vehicles on the road that night due to the curfew. Judit wasn't frightened as they drove at a normal Jerusalem speed toward King David Street. She had reconciled herself years ago to the fragility of her existence and had come to terms with the possibility of being killed during one of these operations. It was for this reason alone that she had deliberately distanced herself from her daughter, Vered. It pained her; she could not deny who she was as a mother. But she had been trained to remain focused on larger objectives; if the future for her daughter was to live within a safe and unified communist state under the protection of the Soviet motherland, then it would take people like Judit to make such sacrifices.

Her solace for both her private and political lives was that, on the one hand, she was not the only agent of Beria and the NKVD in Palestine and, on the other, the way Shalman doted on their daughter, she knew deep down that if her existence were snuffed out by a British bullet, Vered would be safe and loved with her father.

It was these recognitions that steadied her resolve as she rode in the truck toward the British Officers' Club in Goldschmidt House.

Judit glanced over at Ashira and saw that the young woman was nervous. She leaned forward and smiled at her. "Don't worry. It'll go like clockwork. We're taking them by surprise."

Ashira nodded, and while the nervousness didn't dissolve, the fierce determination to see it through was evident in her eyes.

Ashira had escaped anti-Semitic gangs murdering the ancient Jewish communities in Tunisia and had been gang-raped on her journey on foot across the top of Africa by Bedouin, who'd left her for dead. Somehow, she'd survived and managed to cross from the west to the east of Egypt to reach Palestine. Once she arrived, she was quickly taken into the bosom of Lehi and her hatred was given focus. But her reasons for the fight differed from those in the truck. She'd joined Lehi to fight Arabs, not the British. She would follow orders; she had no other choice, no other family. But to Ashira at the moment, Sten gun in hand, she felt like her real enemy was still waiting.

The two vehicles reached the intersection with King George Street, checked that there was no traffic, and turned right. They drove slowly north toward the Officers' Club. But the taxi drove past when he saw three Jeeps parked outside. The truck trundled past. One of the officers standing on the pavement looked at the truck, full of servicemen in British uniform. Instantly, Dov stood and shouted out "tenshun" and saluted. It was a gesture returned by the officer, who gave a desultory salute, little more than a wave of his hand, as he walked into the grounds, past the guard post and barbed wire.

The vehicles drove three streets away and turned left, then left again. The taxi stopped for ten minutes and the truck pulled up behind it in the small side street, all of the expectant occupants nervously waiting for the agreed-upon time to elapse before they could try again.

With a nod from Dov, the taxi driver started the engine, and the convoy drove to the end of the street, then turned left twice until they were back on King George. This time the road ahead was clear; the vehicles outside the Officers' Club had driven away. The taxi drove up to the entrance and three Jewish men dressed in British officers' uniforms got out, carrying fully laden cases. The truck pulled over to the other side of the street, and as the uniformed NCOs jumped down, Judit and Ashira carefully positioned their machine guns on the left side of the vehicle.

The three disguised officers pretended to pay the driver, and the taxi drove off. They walked across the pavement toward the guard post. One of them appeared to take out his identity papers, and after the two guards had saluted, they waited without any concerns for the men to prove their identity before going back inside.

Suddenly, two dull cracks fractured the silence of the night, the pistols' silencers preventing any but those closest from hearing anything. Both of the British soldiers guarding the club fell down dead, and Judit watched anxiously as the three Irgun and Lehi men crossed the large external courtyard. The other men followed quickly, rifles and machine guns poised for immediate firing.

As they burst through the doors of the club, the sound of gunfire echoed off the buildings in the street. Judit looked carefully and saw flashes of light illuminate the interior of the darkened lobby. She looked up to the higher levels where the officers' bedrooms were located; no lights had been turned on. Bullets were a common sound in the Jerusalem night.

Judit and Ashira scanned the road to the north and south, their machine guns placed on tripods as they made ready to blast any approaching British army vehicle with round after round of fire. But it was the early hours of a Jerusalem morning, and there was no traffic on the roads.

The gunfire inside the building became more intense as night staff realized that they were under attack and came running toward the vestibule of the club to defend the building.

Inside, Dov and three of his compatriots were taking the bombs out of the cases and standing them against pillars that supported the upper floors. Dov made sure the first of the bombs, one planted by him, was primed and ready and that the timer clock was counting down the 120 seconds before exploding. Quickly, he placed a mattress around the pillar, completely covering the bomb, then secured it with wire so when the bomb exploded, most of its force would be directed into the structure instead of out into the air.

He then ran, risking being shot in the cross fire, to the other three pillars, making sure all of the timers were working properly before he placed mattresses around them. Then he barked at his colleagues, "Let's go. Now!"

With that, they all turned and ran crouching toward the door, their exit covered by a merciless barrage of rifle fire from the men dressed as privates and corporals to provide armed support so the bomb planters could set their devices.

As Dov and his three companions ran past, he shouted, "Follow us—forty-five seconds."

They emerged into the night air, straightened up, and ran across the courtyard for the barbed-wire entry. For the first time, Dov felt secure enough to turn and ensure that his men were safe. The three bomb planters were by his side, and he looked anxiously for the rest of the team of ten to escape. Thirty seconds before the bombs were due to explode, they came scampering out of the building and into the courtyard.

Judit looked up and saw several lights on in the rooms above. More men had been wakened by the hellish commotion in the lobby. She saw a couple of men in pajamas going to the windows and looking down on the street. Then the men in her troop came running across the road toward her truck. She and Ashira jumped down, leaving the machine guns. Dov shouted to the truck driver to go. He started the engine and drove as quickly as he could to a wadi three miles west of Jerusalem. Once there, the plan was to push the vehicle down the cliff, along with the machine guns. After a night of such devastation, the last thing the freedom fighters wanted was to be caught at a road block wearing British uniforms and in possession of such weaponry.

Judit watched the truck drive off and turned to look at the building. It seemed as though somebody had turned on a massive arc light inside the darkened lobby of the club. From all of the lower windows, a brilliant light burst out, illuminating the trees and shrubs in the gardens. And then the windows blew out, releasing most of the hellish fury as flame, smoke, and a blast of ear-shattering din. The other three bombs went off within seconds. And above the nightmare tumult of the explosions came the screams of men who were thrown out of windows, of NCOs whose bodies were aflame in the conflagration, of kitchen staff trying to escape the inferno.

Dov pulled at her sleeve and shouted, "C'mon, we've gotta get out of here. Now!"

But Judit continued to stare at the site. It looked as though the normally sedate building had given birth to a monstrous being—a brilliant, fiery, stinking denizen of some alien world within. It expanded out of the confines of the lower walls, out of the windows, the doorway, the cellar, its broiling arms reaching out of every opening and enveloping everything nearby.

Then she heard a series of further explosions on the upper floors as gas fittings detonated and radiators burst and flames leaped out bedroom windows. Men continued to scream, and as she watched in horror and fascination, she saw figures on the upper floors attempting to open windows, but the moment they did, the air intensified the flames and the blast grew into an all-consuming Gorgon.

That was only the beginning. The violence of the bombs had caused the supporting pillars on the ground floor to buckle, fracture, and bow. The weight of the upper floors made the building sag in the middle, and then it collapsed onto itself, hurling men in burning pajamas out of windows to be dashed to death on the ground. The building looked as though some huge mischievous child had brought down his fist on the roof, pushing the upper floors into the ground.

"For fuck's sake, Judit, c'mon. Now!" said Dov, grabbing her arm and pulling her backward into a laneway so they would escape the arrival of soldiers and security guards from other barracks.

She ran, separated from her colleagues, fleeing down predetermined routes, finding the safe houses they'd been allocated. She lost sight of the other, but quickly found her way to where she was spending the night. As she ran toward the house, the door opened, and she rushed inside and was enveloped in silence.

Jerusalem

1947

JUDIT FELT A degree of trepidation as she walked toward the apartment in North Jerusalem. It was five in the evening, an hour before the British imposed their curfew. If the meeting lasted longer, then it would be sensible for her to stay the night, but that would cause difficulties for the woman looking after little Vered.

"Damn Shalman and his stupid archaeology. Damn him for falling over," she said to herself, then immediately felt guilt for her unworthy thoughts. It had been days since he'd had his accident, but she'd been so busy with her work for Lehi that she hadn't had time to go to the Arab village and see him. Every other day, he sent her a note telling her of his progress, and with each note, she felt guiltier and guiltier. She just hoped that he would understand.

If only he hadn't fallen down that hillside. Shalman had said he'd be gone for two nights, three at the most, yet two days after he'd gone on his expedition, some Arab had thrust a note into her hand when she opened her front door. Perhaps if things calmed down a bit, she'd ask a friend if she could borrow a car and go and visit him.

In the meantime, things were heating up on the international stage. The United Nations had sent a commission of inquiry to examine the partition of the land into separate nations of Israel and Palestine. Now was the time to exert maximum pressure.

And in the middle of washing the feeding bottles for Vered that morning, somebody else had knocked on her door, and another note had been thrust into her hands. She asked who had sent the note, but the little girl just shrugged and showed some money in her hands, then ran off.

Judit read it immediately. It was from somebody who called himself "A Friend," reminding her of how "beautiful everything was in the summer before last."

Just looking at it, rereading it, came as a shock and an unwelcome surprise. For months and months, she had not been contacted by Moscow. In the beginning, she'd expected new instructions every day; then every week; but as the months rolled past and the year changed from one to the next, Judit grew more and more into her role as a freedom fighter with Lehi. She was still a passionate communist, but amid her daily life-and-death environment, Moscow's geopolitics seemed something of the distant past.

Now, it was present again, front and center. As she read the note, her training in Leningrad and Moscow, her drilling in spycraft, her education as a covert operative, came flooding back. She had to sit down on a chair and brace herself. It felt like she'd seen a ghost. Not even Vered's whimpering broke through the images whirling around her head.

The code was simple enough. It was an instruction for her to go to a safe house to meet with the handler she'd been assigned by Moscow Central. She'd never met her handler, never been contacted since she'd arrived in Palestine. She'd been told that she wouldn't be contacted until Comrade Beria's plans were ready to be put into place. Yet just reading the *Palestine Post*, she knew that some militant Zionists had met with terrible accidents or had been assassinated by unknown assailants such as Arab snipers. She had put two and two together and realized that other covert operatives were in action in the country, but only now had she been tapped on the shoulder. She was about to fulfill the mission for which she'd been trained. She read again the code that called her to a meeting with her unknown Russian handler.

Judit looked at the numbers of the houses and apartment blocks as she walked down the road later that night. Her spycraft came to the fore—long in the recesses of her mind during her time with Lehi, when spying wasn't an issue, but guns and bullets and explosives and timers and trip wires were. Judit knew not to look directly at a number on a door as though searching, because that might alert a passerby that she was a stranger. Instead, she walked at a normal pace down the road, keeping away from the curb, and casually glancing at the numbers of the houses one or two in front of her.

When she found she was approaching the nominated house in Rehov Jabotinsky, she turned into the path that led to the front door as though she'd lived in the house forever. She knocked casually, not looking around to see if anyone was watching. That was another giveaway that she was a stranger, and she'd been taught that strangers are always remembered by inquisitive neighbors.

The door opened almost immediately, and it was all she could do not to gasp. She hadn't known who or what to expect, but before her was Anastasia Bistrzhitska.

Anastasia beamed and almost pulled Judit inside into the hallway. She closed the door quickly so that nobody in the street could see inside the house. Then she held both of Judit's hands, took a step back, and admired her.

"You left Russia a girl, and now you're a woman. My God, but you've grown into a beauty. What's happened? Is it motherhood? Is it this husband of yours? Is it the sun in this hot land?" Anastasia threw her arms around Judit and kissed her. Not on the cheek but full on the lips. Just as quickly, she said, "But come inside and meet your comrades. Some you may have seen around the place; others you won't have because they're operating a long way away. Now that the United Nations idiots are here, it's time to push our plans forward, Judita."

She opened the door, and then entered the room.

Judit smiled at the ten men and two other women, some of whom she recognized from her training time in Leningrad and Moscow. Others were new faces. Her mind was flooded with thoughts of Shamir and Begin. She was no longer a Lehi comrade but a spy for the Soviet Union. Would she be ordered to kill them or any other of the freedom fighters?

She knew two of the men in the room were working with the Haganah—a Jewish resistance group from which the more radical Irgun and Lehi had split. Though she recognized them from Moscow, she didn't know where the other men and women worked. Judit whispered to Anastasia, "I don't know most of these people. They were not in Moscow."

"My little dove, some we trained have been killed fighting in this country; some turned out to be duds and have been liquidated; and some have been enlisted by us since you left Mother Russia. This is a much bigger operation than you know."

Anastasia smiled at Judit's reaction and said to the group in Russian, a language Judit had barely heard in recent years: "Now our group is complete. Good. For those who don't know her, may I introduce Judita. She's just made the observation that she doesn't know some of you. This is true. Some of you trained together, some of you separately in different places. It was vital that this first time you meet as agents of the Soviet Socialist Republic, you begin to know one another. The reason this is your first meeting was determined two years ago in the Kremlin by Comrade Stalin himself; he was concerned that if you worked together before Moscow Central's plans were in place, Zionists could have been warned in advance of a cabal. Secrecy and subterfuge are paramount.

"Friends, comrades, or, as you say in this country, *chaverim*, in the next few weeks the United Nations commission will have completed its task and will recommend that Britain hand back its mandate. The chance that any nation in the world will want to pick up the mess that the government in London has made of its relationships with Arabs and Jews is very doubtful.

"That means, comrades, that when the last British soldier gets on to a troop transport ship and sails down the Mediterranean, there will be open warfare between the Arabs who live here and the Jews who will soon call themselves Israelis. So we can anticipate war between the Arabs of six nations and the Jews of one, and a divided one at that. This presents the opportunity for us. All of you know that Mother Russia has clear need of a warm-water port for our glorious navy. It is this new land that must be open to us to create that port. It is this nation, when formed from the ashes of the war that is to come, that will be Mother Russia's closest and most dependent ally."

A tall, thin, and handsome man named Mikhail spoke up. "But that depends on who wins this coming war when the British leave? Are we, as they say, hedging our bets? Or are we to be more proactive?"

"If we support the Arabs who live here in British Palestine but the Jews win, then we may find ourselves without influence or power because of the strength of Zionism," said another man. "If we support the Israelis but the Arab armies attack and allow the Palestinians to win, then Russia's influence in the Middle East will be lost forever."

A woman named Rebekah, who had been stationed for two years in Syria, spoke up in a shrill voice that cut across the murmur of her comrades. "When two sides are at war, the only questions that concern them are those of supply and logistics. The moment the British withdraw, Arab armies will roll across the borders toward Jerusalem and Tel Aviv. I'm in Syria, and pushing the Jews into the sea is the topic of conversation in all the coffee shops. Israel will be one of the world's smallest countries. A warplane, even those antiques flown by the Arabs, can cross from east to west in a matter of minutes. The Jews know this. The Jews have no standing army. They have at best a ragtag group of armed militia. Six Arab nations can field an army of a hundred thousand men in tanks, troop carriers, artillery, and infantry. The Jews cannot win. We must throw our support behind the Arabs."

People in the room nodded and spoke in agreement. It was all so obvious. But Judit noticed that Anastasia was observing and watching. Though Anastasia had instructions from the Kremlin, and especially Comrade Beria, on how Russia should approach the coming war, she was clearly waiting for her operatives to draw their own conclusions, to test their understanding of the situation.

One of the men, a thirty-year-old Jew named Boris whose family had been exiled to Siberia by Dzerzhinsky, the head of the revolution's secret police, said, "Then it's obvious! We'll be supplying and supporting the Arabs."

All the others nodded, some sadly, because they were Jews. Anastasia looked at Judit. "What do you think, Judita?"

Judit took a moment to consider her answer, though she knew full well what she would say. "When the Arabs attack, the Jews will win," she said coldly.

Anastasia was surprised by the way her protégée had said "the Jews" as if referring to people other than her own.

Every last person in the group smiled. Many shook their heads at her naïveté.

Judit was unperturbed and continued. "The Arabs don't need our help. They've already had enough help from the British, and the Trans-Jordanian army is British-trained anyway. So if we side with the Arabs, we'll get almost nothing in return."

"Gaining little is better than supporting the losing army that has nothing," Boris said curtly.

"No," Judit said firmly, more confident now that she'd had time to reflect. "The Jews have nowhere to go. They'll be fighting for their lives. The Palestinians are small in number and without resources. The Arab army will be foreigners fighting only for something they've been told by their leaders. Their cause will be the removal of the Jews from what they've been told is Islamic land. This is their weakness. Once they start suffering casualties, they'll consider this a foreign battlefield; they won't view it as Islamic or Jewish or Christian land, but as a place where they don't want to die so far from their homes. Their hearts won't be in it. The Jews are fighting for a homeland with no retreat available. The Arab armies come from Damascus and Cairo and Amman. When the bombs fall and their limbs are blown off, they'll want to crawl home. For the Jews, this is their home. They can't go back to Europe, so this is the land they'll defend with their lives. When war comes, the Jews will win. This I believe."

Judit looked at Anastasia to see whether her words had struck a chord. While all the others looked at her in surprise, bemusement, and ridicule, Anastasia was grinning from ear to ear.

The older woman nodded. "There is great wisdom in this young woman, and you would all do well to take heed. Comrades, our consideration of the coming political situation and the advantage it will bring Mother Russia is that we will be approaching the leadership of the Haganah and their fighting force, the Palmach, with an offer of tanks, vehicles, arms, supplies, and any other weaponry they require. And with these gifts, we shall be the muscle and the power of the world's newest nation. Any resistance we meet from Zionists who distrust us will be dealt with by you."

The Home of the Ninth
Imam, Baghdad
820 C.E.

UNLIKE THAT OF the caliph, the home of Muhammad al-Jawad, the person identified by Hadir and known as the ninth imam in the Shi'ite faith, was unassuming and humble. As Zakki stood outside the house, his stomach in knots of hesitation, he reminded himself what was at stake. There was no mistake in Hadir's threat to Zakki's family. Equally, Zakki was aware how precarious it was to be a stranger in this city, even an invited one, if he was caught up in political infighting. It was an unwritten rule of the people that guests were welcomed and accorded respect, provided they remained guests and didn't interfere in the activities of the land.

Zakki had told himself that he was simply a messenger and the purpose of preventing civil war was a noble one. The murder of the imam would be an assassination that might trigger untold deaths, deaths he might now prevent with a warning.

The imam he had come to visit had quite a reputation, though he was only nine years of age. The young theologian's brilliance at answering even the most searching questions demanded of him by other spiritual leaders had been impressive. He had been interrogated in an effort to disprove his claim to be the next imam, and his responses had shown his followers that he was worthy of the role placed on his young shoulders by the death of his predecessor, the imam Ali al-Reza.

It was these thoughts that overcame his fears as Zakki walked toward the porch of the home and knocked on the ornately carved latticed front door. Islamic architecture and carvings were a wonder to behold, strong but light as a feather, and the scholar in Zakki had him examining the design with his fingertips as he waited.

The door was soon opened by a middle-aged woman who looked searchingly at Zakki, quickly asking who he was and what he wanted.

"I am a scholar of the House of Wisdom. I wish to speak with he who is called the imam, Muhammad al-Jawad. My name is Zakki, son of Jacob, a family of doctors from Jerusalem."

"I am Sabika, the imam's mother. Why do you seek my son?"

"I have things of great importance that I am compelled to discuss with him."

"My son is with the caliph. You cannot speak to him. But you may speak to the imam's uncle. His name is Da'oud."

Zakki agreed. So long as he could talk to just one member of the family and give the warning he was charged to deliver by Hadir, he might yet see his task complete and the threat to his family lifted.

Sabika invited him inside the home. It was comfortably furnished but far from ostentatious. Yet he had been told by Hadir that the imam received the most important visitors from throughout the world, who came to seek guidance and hoped to make treaties and agreements. To Zakki, this home did not seem suitable for such important meetings.

Seeing the Jewish doctor looking around her home, Sabika repeated what she had said to many important visitors who appeared surprised that the imam didn't live in a palace. "My family lives modestly, in sympathy with the poor of our world as commanded by our Prophet Mohammed, peace be upon him. My son, the holy imam, spends most of his time in the palace of the caliph, where they determine great things. Though others may look upon him as a child, he has the heart of a lion and mind of a man. He is touched by Allah the All Merciful."

As she was speaking, a gaunt man entered the room. He bowed to Zakki, who returned the gesture. Sabika introduced Da'oud, the imam's uncle, and retired to another part of the house, leaving the two men alone. They sat on divans, and then, without warning or introduction, two young women, their faces completely covered except for slits in the cloth for their eyes, appeared and placed carafes of juice, sliced apples and oranges, as well as a plate of nuts, olives, and seeds on the table between them. Bowing, they left the room as quickly as they had entered.

"Why do you wish to see the holy imam? Important matters are normally discussed at the palace of the caliph."

"The walls of the caliph's palace have many ears. The things I have to say to the imam are for his ears only."

"I am his ears," said Da'oud. "You will speak with me. You are a stranger here and unknown to us."

Zakki took a sip of juice, buying time as he pondered the dilemma. He was under strict instructions from Hadir not to talk to any other person about these matters, but if he could not see the imam, what choice did he have?

At last Zakki nodded. "There are people within the caliph's palace who would see the imam dead," he whispered. "Friends of mine, friends in very high places, have bade me to come here to warn him and advise him to leave Baghdad immediately, for the sake of his life and the lives of those who serve him."

Da'oud leaned back on his divan and stared at Zakki.

The silence impelled Zakki to continue. "This threat is real. Men very close to the caliph's throne, though not the caliph himself, are bent on eliminating the imam so that those of you who are Shi'ites will become leaderless. They want to go to war against you. I am here to prevent this war."

Da'oud nodded. He, too, took a sip of his drink and slowly, deliberately, ate a sliver of fruit. He chewed it as though calculating his response. "Who are these friends of yours who have given you this information?"

"I cannot say." As the words left his lips, Zakki knew how vulnerable he was.

"You are as nothing in my eyes. You say you're a scholar yet you dress in the clothes of a street vendor." Da'oud looked at Zakki, and the doctor was aware of how inferior and plain he looked by comparison with Da'oud's immaculate silks.

"What stock should I put in the words of a poor Jew far from home? How do we know that you're not one of those who wants to get close to the imam and then do the deed yourself?"

Zakki had no answer. What could he offer that would satisfy the question? He spoke anyway. "I am at your mercy, and I have nothing to gain by being here. You are right, though: I am a stranger, one of the many unknown people of Baghdad. I know little of your politics and your struggles. But I have this message and am compelled to deliver it, knowing that I am at your mercy. And having delivered it, I have done my duty. What you do with my information is your decision."

It was all that he could say. It was the truth, and Zakki hoped that it might just be enough to have Da'oud send him on his way, back to his family.

Da'oud considered Zakki's words for a long moment. "And what makes you think, Doctor, that we did not know of the things you tell us?"

At this, Da'oud stood and left the room. The interview was over.

Once outside and on the busy street, Zakki found himself caught up in a stream of people funneling toward the marketplace. Lost in the crowd, he pondered what Da'oud had said and thought of the way in which Hadir ibn Yussuf ibn Gibreel, vizier to the Abbasid caliph, had sought him out. There were many Jews in Baghdad. So why had he been given the task? Was it to stop a war and save the life of a holy boy, or was there something else behind Hadir ibn Yussuf's words?

• • •

Two days passed before Hadir sought out Zakki again. He was walking from the House of Wisdom after another frenetic day of trying to understand the minds of Greek doctors long dead. Zakki was lost in thought when he felt a tap on his shoulder. Startled, he turned and saw Hadir behind him. This time was different; this time the vizier was alone.

His voice came as a whisper. "Did you see the imam? Did you give him my words?"

Zakki swallowed hard. "No."

Hadir's eyes narrowed.

Zakki explained, "I saw the imam's uncle. I spoke to him. I gave him the warning."

Anger flared in Hadir's face. "Da'oud? But you were to speak only to the boy! I gave you clear instruction that you were to speak only with the imam. Why did you disobey?"

Zakki cowered. He was many different people—a man of learning, of thought, of medicine—but he was not a man of conflict. "I did what I could," he stammered. "They would not let me see him."

"Fool of a man! You have no idea how much damage you've done."

Zakki closed his eyes, almost as if expecting a blow. But Hadir had turned on his heels and paced away. On impulse, Zakki reached to his throat and grasped the ancient seal at his neck to steady his nerves.

• • •

The following day, even though the hall at the House of Wisdom was full of scholarly shouts and groans and moans and the occasional laughter of discovery, Zakki found time to sit with Hussain of Damascus, a scholar in the theology of the Koran.

Zakki's mind had been swirling since the encounter with Hadir, and the threat to his family drew his thoughts away from his work. Ultimately, Zakki found the words to ask Hussain what he knew about the vizier to the caliph of Baghdad.

Hussain shrugged. "Little is known about him, but he is not the sort of man you should befriend or whose enemy you should become. He's the sort who will not see you as he walks past, yet is your best friend when he is in need of your services. It's said of him that he came here to Baghdad twenty or so years ago, as a merchant with trading connections deep into Asia, as far as China along the Silk Road. He sought out the caliph's father, Muhammad ibn Harun al-Amin, who was beset by problems. There was war with the Byzantines in Syria and Anatolia, and many of the governors of the provinces were breaking away and forming their own caliphates.

"The caliph's coffers were being drained, so when Hadir came and told the caliph's vizier how he could provide a stream of great wealth because of his connections with the caravanserai and the traders he could persuade to pass through this city instead of Damascus, he was elevated to advise the caliph. And that's when the whispers began."

Hussain looked around the hall as if to check that no one was listening, but the act seemed superfluous, given the din of debate all around them.

"They say Hadir quickly undermined the vizier and took his place within the year. Since then, he has sat at the left hand of the caliph." Hussain opened his hands, palms out. "And again we have become a wealthy and prosperous city. So it would seem Hadir knows what he's doing, even if he had to destroy the wealth and happiness of some people along the way."

Zakki listened carefully and asked his next question softly, so he couldn't be overheard. "You say the left hand of the Caliph. Who sits at his right hand?"

"The imam, leader of those who follow the way of the Shi'ites."

"And if the vizier, Hadir ibn Yussuf, asked a favor of me, in order to do some good in the city, what would you think of that?"

The scholar thought for a moment before speaking. "I would ponder his words. I would reflect on his request. I would look at the city of Baghdad and all that is within its walls. I would look at the wealth that the vizier has acquired in a few short years, and then I would wonder not what good it would do for the city but what good the favor would do for Hadir."

One hour west of Ras Abu Yussuf
1947

ALTHOUGH HIS HEAD was no longer aching, he still didn't have the strength to keep up with Mustafa. Yet his excitement threatened to overwhelm his common sense, and he half ran, half walked down the steep gorges.

Shalman had intended to return home the previous day, but then Mustafa decided to trust him sufficiently to tell him about the caves in a secluded valley, far away from roads or tracks taken by goatherds or shepherds, where he had found the Roman coins. Shalman wasn't well enough for an archaeological expedition, but he had been so excited that Mustafa decided to take the risk. The caves were not far from where Shalman had fallen.

As they made their way there, Mustafa told Shalman of the other things he had seen in the area—stones of ancient houses and shards of pottery—and these thoughts made his head feel even better.

They had reached the remote gorge within an hour of setting off from the village, and from the top of the rise they could see the towering buildings of Jerusalem far in the distance. Because of the folds of the hills in between the gorge and the mountains on which Jerusalem was built, the valley was invisible unless one was standing on its very edge, looking down. It was so narrow, little more than a deep scar on the landscape, that it was easy to miss.

Even from the top of the rise, Shalman could see the entrances to a number of caves. There was little disturbance of the vegetation around them and no sign of tracks or footpaths leading in their direction. This place hadn't been explored recently—perhaps hundreds, if not thousands, of years—and Shalman doubted that many people ever had reason to come to the area.

Though it was difficult terrain and Shalman kept slipping and sliding on the scree, he and Mustafa quickly reached the bottom of the valley and stood in the gorge looking up at the steep sides; from the bottom where they stood, only a strip of sky was visible. Mustafa was correct: Even a cursory glance showed him there were once buildings standing here. It was perfect protection for the ancient inhabitants: far enough from major roads to be ignored by the Romans, yet close enough to Jerusalem to enable them to purchase supplies and trade with only a day's journey. Shalman looked closely at the layouts of the buildings, and it soon became apparent that they were too small to have been dwelling places.

Pointing out the circumference and possible internal structures, Shalman told Mustafa, "I think these are temples."

"Temples? They're too small. They're tiny."

Shalman shook his head and said, "The whole area might have been a necropolis, a burial site from ancient times. I've read about such places in Greece and Egypt and Turkey, but I didn't think they existed in ancient Israel."

"But the caves in the foothills of the mountains north of Jerusalem were the burial places of the ancient Jews. Not here."

Mustafa was right. The burial locations had been decreed by kings Solomon and David and, like so much in ancient Israel, were a ritual born of pragmatism—the southerly wind blew the smell of decay away from the city.

Shalman looked at Mustafa curiously. "How do you know these things?"

Mustafa shrugged. "A man must know the land on which he lives."

Shalman had little time to consider the words of his companion before a sound caught his attention. Mustafa shaded his eyes with his hand as he lifted his head toward the sound coming from the sky.

"It's a plane," said Shalman, and grabbed Mustafa's wrist, pulling him out of the open space of the gorge and toward the caves and small temple ruins.

The sound grew louder until a British Spitfire roared into the gorge. Shalman pulled Mustafa to the ground beside him and watched as the aircraft thundered past at very low altitude.

"British air patrol. They're looking for weapons smugglers."

Mustafa pulled back from Shalman, whose hand was still on his arm, and Shalman could not help but feel that his companion looked at him with an edge of distrust.

"They are looking for your people," said Mustafa, and it was true. The manufacture and flow of ammunition and arms to Lehi through underground networks and secret factories in remote kibbutzim were key to their struggle against the British. And in the wake of bombings and attacks on their major command structures, the British army had stepped up the patrols, road blocks, and searches.

Shalman saw the plane disappear as it rose sharply into the air and away from the valley, the sound of its engines receding and bringing a semblance of peace back to the landscape. But then he saw it bank to the right, its wings curving up toward the sun and arching around to sweep down the valley once more.

"Do you think they saw us?" asked Mustafa.

"Let's not find out." He stood to a low crouch and put a hand out to help Mustafa to his feet. "A Jew and an Arab together out here? They'll think we're conspiring."

There was no time to laugh as the Spitfire wheeled and dived back down the valley. Mustafa and Shalman dashed toward the open recess of a small cave and slipped inside to the cool, dry dark.

Their hearts pounding, they waited for the roar of the plane to grow as it passed overhead, then diminish as it found the valley empty of life.

The cave seemed bare save where the roof had collapsed, probably through earth movement, and debris had accumulated floor to ceiling. They sat there looking out at the narrow space of sky they could see through the cave entrance and listening for the plane.

They waited a couple of minutes. They could still hear the plane but could not gauge how near or far it was. But then silence, a biblical silence of the eons, returned.

As though the Spitfire had been an irritant rather than a deadly weapon of war, Shalman reverted to a previous conversation. "You said you wanted to go to university in Lebanon. Why not Jerusalem?"

Mustafa raised an eyebrow. "A Jewish university?"

"There's nothing to say you couldn't."

Mustafa just laughed.

"I could tutor you," countered Shalman, and in the moment he was unsure why he'd said it or even thought it was possible. Was it guilt? Was it a debt he felt needed to be paid to the enemy who had saved him from the vultures?

"I will," Shalman insisted. "I'll tutor you. People say that I'm the best student. When I learn things, then I'll teach them to you."

Mustafa burst out laughing. "You're a crazy Jew. You know that, don't you?"

"You have to be a little crazy to be Jewish."

Mustafa's mirth faded, and he asked in a voice full of earnestness, "Why? Why would a Jew do that for an Arab?"

It was a simple question and an obvious one, but Shalman was struck by it. "I don't know. Why did an Arab save a Jew's life? I could have died out there: the vultures, the sun, the crack on the head. You saved me."

"So you owe me? This is to repay a debt?"

"Perhaps," said Shalman, feeling the intensity of the young Arab man's gaze. "Or perhaps it's because I like you. We're the same age, and if you lived next door, we'd be friends."

"How could an Arab live next door to a Jew?"

"With that attitude, we'll never be able to share this land of ours."

Mustafa looked at him in amazement. "Ours? Our land? The Jews want all of this land for themselves."

"And what do the Arab leaders say? They want us gone so this land is only for the Arabs. Why is your philosophy better than ours?"

Mustafa sighed. He didn't answer. Then he said softly, "You're right. I was reading about that man you told me about: Gandhi in India. Maybe cooperation is the best way."

Shalman said, "Unfortunately, he was talking about non-cooperation."

"Yes, I know, but I'm only an ignorant Arab. How do you expect me to know the difference?"

Shalman looked across the cave mouth at Mustafa. The young Arab's face was a mask of innocence. They both burst out laughing.

They devolved into silence, but when they were confident that the Spitfire had gone away for good, Mustafa looked deeply into the cave and said, "The roof has collapsed. Nothing here." He turned to leave, but something held Shalman back. He looked closely and saw a gap between the pile of rocks and the roof of the cave. Instead of leaving, he climbed to the top of the pile, where the rocks had fallen from the ceiling, and began pulling the upper rocks away.

Mustafa turned and saw what Shalman was doing. "Why are you doing that?"

"I don't know. I'd just like to see if there's anything beyond this rockfall. It might only have blocked this part of what could be a bigger tunnel."

Mustafa returned, climbed to where Shalman was, and joined in.

It took them half an hour to make a large enough space for them to shine their flashlights inside the depth of the cave. The rockfall had prevented men and animals from entering. As they peered in, they saw that the depths had been undisturbed from time immemorial. They pulled more and more rocks down, until natural light from the cave mouth was able to penetrate and shine a dim glow into the chamber.

The young men climbed over the lowered top of the pile, then half fell and half scampered down to the rock-strewn floor until they were able to enter the rest of the cave.

As he shone his torch around the interior, Shalman's heart leaped. On ledges carved out of the rock wall were three mummified bodies, wrapped in shrouds, as well as two caskets of white sandstone, still sealed with pitch, once jet black but now gray with age.

"My God," Shalman said softly to himself.

"*Allahu Akbah,*" whispered Mustafa as he shone the torch deeper into the cave. He walked gingerly up to one of the shrouded bodies.

"We really shouldn't disturb anything here, Mustafa. This is untouched," warned Shalman.

Mustafa nodded. "These shrouds, they've gone as thin as paper. You can see that they started off white, but they've turned brown with age. There's something here, Shalman." He pointed to what looked like an object tucked inside a fold in the linen covering one of the skeletons. "Look, you can see something sticking up above the material."

Shalman walked over and shone his torch at the skeleton. An object of some sort had been placed inside the folds of the ancient linen. Mustafa began to reach between the sheets of cloth.

"No, Mustafa. You shouldn't touch it. This is amazing. We need professional archaeologists."

Mustafa paid no attention and slid his long fingers delicately between the sheets, grasping what appeared to be a stone or metal disc. He maneuvered it out delicately and held it in the light of his torch as Shalman drew closer, transfixed.

Mustafa turned it from front to back. It was distinct, saved by the cloth from degradation by eons of dust and debris. The folds of linen had insulated it.

Shalman took it carefully and held it between his thumb and forefinger. He read out what was written, first on the front and then on the back. " 'I am Ruth, wife of Abram the doctor. I walk in the footsteps of Yahweh.'"

He looked at Mustafa. "It's written in Hebrew on the front and Aramaic on the back. It must be from one of the early centuries, around the time of Christ. This is . . . this is . . ." Shalman had no words for his amazement.

Mustafa gazed at the shroud and wondered at the skeleton inside the folds. "What sort of a woman was this Ruth? Who was this Abram?" The young Arab man's face glowed in the light of the torch, though his beaming smile seemed to reflect more light than the torch globe. "Was this Ruth tall or short, beautiful or ugly? Did she live to an old age or die young? Where did she come from? What did she do? How did she die?"

Shalman smiled and laughed. "Very good questions, my friend . . . and that's why I'm going to help make you an archaeologist."

Jerusalem
1947

JUDIT SAT WITH Anastasia in a small one-room apartment that was a designated safe house for NKVD operatives. Anastasia sipped at a small tumbler of vodka as she sat on the edge of the bed. The room had only one chair, and Judit was seated in it.

She had been summoned to the meeting by the usual dead-drop note and had expected to see the same gathering of operatives. But when she arrived, Judit found only Anastasia.

As she sipped her own vodka, Judit could not help but take in the figure of the woman before her. The years she had known her had been short, yet Anastasia had seen Judit grow from schoolgirl to woman and spy. Judit remembered the instruction and the motherly hand of Anastasia, always on her back, pushing her forward. The memory of her own mother seemed by contrast as indistinct as a faded photograph.

When Vered was born, Judit unwillingly found herself reflecting on her own childhood—a childhood she had long since pushed aside—and her mother, whom she'd come to think of as weak and broken. But her imagination often confused the beautiful face of Anastasia with the reality of what she was, a master spy, a woman who had ordered a rifle to be put in her hands and for her to assassinate her own mother or father. Sure, it was nothing more than a test with an empty rifle, but Anastasia's hand on her back was a touch that brought back sharp memories, not all of them good.

The test hadn't broken her; it had made her strong. As she looked at Anastasia, Judit felt that the woman was proud of her, and somehow this mattered. Anastasia stood and walked over to the table to refill her vodka glass.

"You've now met all of your colleagues, the men and women who will bring our plan to fruition. And I have to make a choice."

"What's that?" asked Judit, having no inkling where Anastasia was going with this or why she had been summoned.

"Which of them should lead? Who should carry responsibility? Who is capable enough?"

Judit thought back to the group. According to Anastasia, they'd gone their separate ways, some to Tel Aviv, some to Haifa or Jerusalem or Bethlehem or Nablus or Nahariah, some to Cairo and Damascus. Each had a role to play, and Judit might never encounter them again.

Some had been given the names and biographies of politicians, governors, newspaper editors, journalists, and political advisers whom they'd been instructed to befriend and influence, to sleep with and seduce, so that when the crucial time came, they could be blackmailed. It was all in an effort to swing allegiances away from America and the United Kingdom in favor of the USSR. Others had been given a list of future Israeli politicians and influentials who were not well disposed to Mother Russia and would need to be exterminated.

Judit knew that this had been going on in Palestine from time to time. The newspapers carried occasional stories about prominent people being killed or dying in strange circumstances. She knew that this was communist Russians in place. But the real task in the months ahead would be handed over to Judit and the group.

But who should be the leader? Judit looked at Anastasia, who was waiting for a considered answer. The young woman didn't answer immediately but quickly went through all of the men and women in her mind. Eventually, she came up with two names, at which Anastasia nodded and smiled.

"Goshia is a brilliant woman. Viktor is highly resourceful and reliable. Hmmm . . ." said Anastasia.

"So who will it be?" asked Judit.

Anastasia smiled and sat back down on the edge of the bed closest to the younger woman. Her knees touched Judit's.

"Not all situations require the same leaders. Leaders are not all the same. What we need is someone who can and will do what needs to be done. Someone who can see the past and present and judge the right action for the future."

Judit frowned.

"You, my little dove. It's you," Anastasia said softly.

Judit said nothing but placed the glass on the table and looked at her handler quizzically.

"It's you I need. It's you I want." She let the last word linger in the air before she continued. "Goshia and Viktor are capable, but they're not leaders. It's you who is so very special, my dear."

"But I'm too young," protested Judit.

Anastasia reached over and put her hand on Judit's knee and smiled sweetly. "I recommended you to Comrade Beria himself. Long ago, after your group's training in Moscow finished. He agreed but ordered me to wait a year or two, until you'd had field experience as an assassin. That's why we encouraged you to join Lehi. And now you're ready, my dove. You're bloodied and sharp and wonderful. You have an innate ability to command. You will be the leader, but I will be here every minute of the day. You will answer only to me. I will be here in Jerusalem as an attaché to the Russian Mission."

Too stunned to speak, Judit just nodded.

"This is not an easy burden, I know," she said, and Judit was only vaguely aware of Anastasia's hand absently stroking the top of her thigh. "You are married. A wonderful and loyal man. And you have a child. A beautiful child. Yet you sleep with other men."

Judit twitched in reaction, but Anastasia continued.

"At least two other men in two different groups. David Law and Yossi Schwartz. This is right, my darling. We know everything."

Trained not to show emotion in times of trauma, Judit simply said, "Yes," though she felt her pulse quickening.

"How would Shalman feel about this?" asked Anastasia.

Was this another test? thought Judit. What was her handler looking for? What answer did she seek?

Judit had slept with David to elevate her position in Lehi, and with Yossi in case she decided to move over to the Palmach, the elite strike force of the Haganah. Both were strategic maneuvers. She could and did rationalize them. But the question of how such news would affect Shalman pained Judit more than she wanted. She hated cheating on him, but having done so, she had come to the notice of the most senior men in the two forces, not as a woman of easy virtue but as a much discussed fearless and potent fighter for the cause. Making love to them was little more for her than a calling card that empowered her to serve the objectives of her homeland, Mother Russia.

"I did what I had to do."

"Of course you did, my darling." Anastasia's hand stroked Judit's thigh once more. "Just one of many things you will have to do. Are you prepared to do them?"

"Yes," answered Judit as straight and as coldly as she could.

"And what of the Jews? The hardships they have suffered, the faith and traditions they cling to? The things they believe?"

Judit was acutely aware of the word "they."

"What are these things to you?" asked Anastasia.

"I am Jewish," said Judit, though even as the words slipped from her lips, she knew that they were the wrong thing to say. She expected Anastasia to pull away, get to her feet. She expected a change of gear in the test. Perhaps anger. But there wasn't. Instead, the beautiful, elegant woman who had shaped Judit's life leaned closer still.

"No, my child. Jewish is how the world sees you. But it cannot be who you are."

Anastasia left one hand on Judit's thigh and raised the other to Judit's chest, placing an open palm at the base of her throat, her long fingers spread to touch the tops of her breasts beneath the thin cotton of her blouse.

"In here, leave the Jewish girl behind. Be what you must be: a daughter of Russia."

Outskirts of Jerusalem
1947

DOV SPLASHED VODKA into his glass unceremoniously. It was thrown back and refilled before Shalman had even raised his own to his lips.

The two men stood in the dark on the outskirts of Jerusalem. There were no streetlights and no houses nearby, only the lights of the ancient city in the distance and the sounds of crickets in the night air. They were alone.

Shalman had received word that Lehi command wanted to meet with him. He had been back several weeks after the trip into the gorge with Mustafa where they'd made their extraordinary discovery. His every waking thought was to return, and he had promised Mustafa that he would. A strange and unlikely bond had formed between the two young men, and yet when he had said goodbye, promising to return soon, Shalman could not help feeling that Mustafa did not wholly believe or trust that he would.

The note summoning Shalman to the meeting concerned him. He hadn't been in touch with Lehi, nor they with him, for some months, and as he wondered whether the organization would have orders for him—a target, a mission, an objective in the fight for an independent Israel—the cave and its ancient treasures seemed a world away.

A truck had picked up Shalman at a designated time and place and driven him here. It was over that truck's wheel arch that he and Dov were now drinking vodka.

"To victory!" said Dov, and knocked back another shot.

Shalman waved his hand to prevent Dov from pouring another for him.

"What? You're getting soft," said Dov.

"It's late. It's the middle of the night. And we're in the middle of nowhere."

"You *are* getting soft," repeated Dov, and this time it seemed more an observation than a jibe. "There are orders for you," he continued, closing the bottle and plonking it down on the hood.

"For me?" asked Shalman.

"Yes. Just for you."

"Dov, I d-d-don't think . . ." stammered Shalman, his chest clenching at the thought of another order, another mission, another killing.

"You know people are talking. We're both from the kibbutz, so you know how people talk—" Dov cut himself off and put a fatherly hand on Shalman's shoulder. It was a familiar hand, one that reminded Shalman of being a boy and especially of the day Dov had handed him the pistol, leading to his father being taken away from him forever.

"I know you have doubts. We all have doubts. When will it end, you're thinking. It ends when it's over," said Dov with a strange melancholy that Shalman had never heard.

"Is it getting better?" asked Shalman. "We've done so much, but is it getting any better?"

"Soon." Dov drew out a roll of paper from his coat and spread it on the truck panel. "The target is an airfield," he said, stabbing a finger into the map. "It's crucial to the British for their planes that spot refugee ships bringing our people here from Cyprus."

Shalman wasn't listening. He turned away from Dov and the truck. "I don't want to kill anymore, Dov. It's not in me."

"It's just an airfield. No civilians. Just hardware," replied Dov.

Shalman turned back to face the man who had been his guardian at his father's request. "Why me? I'm not a good shot, I'm not good with bombs."

"Because we're spread thin and there are other targets that night. Your attack will be the diversion that keeps others safe," Dov said softly.

Shalman turned away again with a sigh.

"And because I need to know you are committed," Dov continued.

Dov's words stung. Shalman turned around again. "Committed? I've done everything I was asked to do!"

"And yet we don't see you anymore. I hear you're in the hills dig-ging up ruins with an Arab!"

Shalman had made no secret of where he went and what he in-tended to do, but he had made no mention of Mustafa and his rescue. So to hear these words from Dov made him aware that he was being watched by his comrades. There was nothing he could say, nothing that would change the order or the expectation that he would carry out the mission.

"Your daughter is beautiful, Shalman. Little Vered . . ." Dov's voice dropped in pitch and turned cold before he went on, "One day your daughter may watch you taken away by the British who took your fa-ther, or shot by an Arab, one just like your friend with whom you're digging. Is this the legacy you want to leave your child?"

"They took my father because of you!" The accusation had been a long time coming. But Dov seemed to be expecting it and didn't flinch.

"Yes. They took him because of me. He sacrificed his life because I have six children, all of whom are fighting the British and the Arabs. Is this how you want your father to look down on you from heaven? I live with your father's sacrifice every day. And you know what it does, Shalman? It makes me want to fight. It reminds me that we need to fight. Without the fight we can never protect ourselves or the ones we love. Your abba's death has to have meaning. We have to make it meaningful. There will be time enough for peace, time to dig up the past, when the fighting is over, when Israel is ours."

Shalman had no answer. He'd been a Lehi fighter for so long that he was finding it difficult to fight against the other part of him that was growing day by day. And yet right now, with the dirt from the an-cient burial site still on his clothes and under his fingernails, he felt like a different man.

Finally, Shalman lifted his head to Dov. "So, it's just an airfield?"

The House of Wisdom, Baghdad

820 C.E.

ZAKKI BEN JACOB wore his history and his fate on his troubled brow. Today the Jewish doctor needed to gain access to the palace of the caliph Ja'far al-Ma'mun so that he could reveal the trickery being perpetrated by his vizier. Aside from gaining the ear and confidence of the caliph, Zakki could see no other way of freeing himself from the threats that Hadir was making against him and his family.

And the threats were real. He was entangled in a spiderweb of deceit and contrivance that could lead easily to the murder of his wife and children and himself. He had to extricate himself, but he knew that even if he were to escape in the black of night with his family and steal away over the desert, he'd be chased by the vizier's men and slaughtered. Baghdad was full of the stories of murders, of men found in their beds with their throats cut, of sudden and inexplicable disappearances.

Zakki could see only one way out. And if not that, then to do as the vizier asked and hope that the efforts would satisfy him.

Zakki knew what was at stake if the vizier's plans came to fruition; murder that might lead this caliphate into civil war. But it was the preservation of himself and his beloved family that motivated Zakki to overcome his natural caution and approach the caliph.

While the Sunni leader of the empire and the spiritual leader of the Shi'ites seemed to be living beside each other in harmony—one concerned with administration, law and trade, and the other the spiritual well-being of the people—Zakki believed that neither had any conception of the nest of snakes that inhabited the lower levels of officialdom.

He had discussed his situation with the man who had become a close friend during the many days and many nights he spent studying and translating in the House of Wisdom. Hussain of Damascus, one of the most perceptive scholars of the Koran, had listened carefully to what Zakki had to say about his dilemma, about the pressure he was under from the vizier, and continued to caution him. But, as was the way of the House of Wisdom, personal advice became scholarly debate, and the men had spoken at length about the origins of their peoples and their shared God: Yahweh and Allah.

Hussain, apparently transported to another time and place, looked at Zakki. "Times have changed since the death of our Prophet, peace and blessings be upon him. And so, my friend, while you as a Jew are welcome here as a scholar, I don't know whether our caliph will listen to your words. Vizier Hadir bought favor with business acumen. But the caliph would need some token of your worth and trust."

What Zakki needed was a way in. And the answer came from what he knew best: the diseases of the body and maintenance of health.

Through his network of scholars at the House of Wisdom, Zakki spread the information that he had discovered a cure for effluvium of the bowels: a disease causing epidemics that struck down huge numbers of people and made them incapable of work for days as their bodies purged the contents of their bowels as liquid. In some cases, especially the young and elderly, it caused death.

This illness was well known to Zakki. It was so commonplace that members of the royal family had been struck down in the past. Knowing how scholars loved to talk, Zakki was certain that the news of his discovery would come to the notice of the palace. He prayed for the summons that would surely come for him.

In the end it was one of the caliph's wives who sent for the Jewish doctor; her son had nearly died from the disease, and the doctors of Baghdad had been unable to do anything for the boy. The child had recovered and was now healthy, but it had been a battle to save him from death, and they had been advised to burn a cat's entrails in wood from the olive tree and bury an idol to the god Marduk in the sands of the desert. The family feared the illness's return.

Zakki set out for the palace and was admitted into the first vestibule. He looked around and was amazed by the lightness of the building. His own home in Jerusalem was a typical dark structure of walls and rooms and a roof where he and his family ate and slept during the hot summer nights. This palace seemed to have a permanent cool breeze blowing through the corridors and chambers, rustling the delicate fabric of the shimmering white curtains and even sifting through the intricately carved marble and latticework of the upper chambers of the house. It was a miracle of grace, lightness, and color.

The floor was of polished marble, and some of the walls were painted in delicate pastel shades. On other walls were exquisite paintings of birds and animals languishing beside streams with bushes in full bud, fruit and berry trees overhanging the water. Zakki had never seen such delicacy, such splendor. It made the Roman mosaics in Jerusalem seem like the crude scrawls of a child.

His thoughts were interrupted by a palace guard, a retinue for the caliph's first wife, entering the room. In the middle of the guard formation, as though protected on all sides, was the woman who'd commanded his attendance.

She smiled at him—at least he thought she smiled; she was wearing a yashmak and he couldn't see her face. She beckoned him to sit down on one of the many divans in the room.

"They tell me that you're a Jew, a doctor from Jerusalem."

He nodded, his mind working through the next steps of what he must do.

"I am told you can cure that which nearly killed my son. Is this correct?"

"Only in part. Once the disease has ahold on a person's body, there is little that a physician can do other than give the patient clean water and offer prayers." As he often did when he was explaining complex ideas, Zakki used his hands as much as his words. "It was said in past times that the body's health is governed by four humors; fluids of the body. These humors, revealed by the great Hippocrates, are associated with body colors, seasons of the year, and temperature of the air."

Unable to see the woman's face, Zakki had no way of reading her response or judging if the woman understood what he was saying. "Shall I continue?" he asked.

The woman nodded keenly, and he imagined he spied a keen intelligence in her eyes, hungry for understanding. Zakki explained the four body humors, their colors, origins, and effects on the body.

"It has been thought that when these humors are out of alignment, the body falls ill. When they are in balance, we are well. For example, too much blood makes the body overheated and we suffer fever. To cure this, the ancient Greeks cut the skin and let the blood of the patient fall into a bowl. We Jews don't believe this to be a cure. We think it weakens the body."

"Then what is to be done to restore the balance of the body?" the woman asked.

"This is the question. It is my view, based on the experience of my people and the learning I have uncovered in my experiments and from my travels to other cities, that when water is boiled, its complexion changes. Water that comes from a well or a jug might look safe but could be unsafe to drink. Yet when that same water is boiled and cooled, provided it is covered with a cloth, then it becomes safe to drink. Also, we add lemon juice to water, and sometimes other sour substances, but not enough to materially alter the taste, nor to make it poison."

"Boiled water can save my family?"

"By boiling the water, you may no longer suffer the effluvium of the bowels. It is important that the water from your river, the Tigris, isn't drunk without first being boiled. Especially in the months of the summer, and most especially when it is given to young girls and boys or old men and women."

She looked at him in surprise. "But in the summer, when the water we drink is warm, it is then that the effluvium becomes rampant and people fall down in the streets from illness. The exudations from the body cause the air in the city to stink. But I don't understand how boiling water can make it different. It's the same water, isn't it?"

He nodded and appreciated her logic. She had a mind for scientific inquiry.

"Warm and boiling are not the same. We don't know for certain, but there is a theory, first considered by the ancient Greeks, that there might be tiny and invisible animalcules in the water, smaller than the eye can see, which can live in warm water yet cannot survive in boiling water. Even the curved glass that you Arabs have created, and that causes objects to appear larger than they are, seems to be of little use when looking at water because the animalcules are too small to be seen."

She looked at him in wonder. "And that is all that is needed to stop this wasting disease? Just boiling water?"

Zakki nodded.

A servant, covered from head to toe in shimmering gossamer veils, brought in sweetmeats and sugary cakes. Zakki and the caliph's wife ate morsels, and each drank a glass of juice. Instead of retiring, the girl stood close to the divan where the caliph's wife sat, her head bowed in reverence.

"And what payment do you require for your advice and services, Doctor? Would you like money, or perhaps you'd prefer to spend a night with Raniah?" She nodded to the girl, who bowed slightly in Zakki's direction. "She is a slave purchased last year from Persia. She's just thirteen and has known only one man in her life, my husband, and from what he's told me, I am able to assure you that taking Raniah into your bed is worth ten thousand times more than any money you will ask for."

Zakki smiled. "I don't want money for the advice I've given you, Great Lady. And as to Raniah, I'm afraid my wife would be very angry if she knew that I'd spent even a brief moment thinking about her, let alone lying with her."

The caliph's wife nodded and then, with a flick of her fingers, dismissed the girl, who scurried away.

"Is this the way with you Jews? You have one wife and none other?"

"That is our way, Lady," he said. "I want no reward save one request."

Through the gap in the veil, Zakki could see an eyebrow raise.

"I beg your indulgence so that I am allowed to speak with the caliph. That is all the recompense I require. A word with the Caliph."

The raised eyebrow turned into a frown. "You wish to speak . . . to the Caliph? Why?"

Zakki had known this question would come. "There is a danger to him. People within his household who wish for the peace that the mighty caliph has brought to Baghdad to be ended and replaced by war."

Zakki wondered what she was thinking. He'd taken a great risk, one that might see him and his family die at the hand of Hadir, or else here by the hand of the caliph. Yet his family was his greatest concern, and there was no turning back.

The woman remained staring at him for a long moment, until she finally stood. "Remain here," she said in a commanding voice.

She left the chamber, and Zakki sat for what seemed an age. He looked at the corpus of guardsmen. All twenty soldiers were dressed in impressive turbans with light body armor. Their waists were weighed down with swords and deadly daggers in scabbards positioned at strategic points on their arms, legs, and chests. They were the fiercest-looking men he'd ever seen. And each, as a badge of honor, looked identical, having grown a bushy black mustache as though it were another deterrent in their aggressive armory. None looked at him, but he knew that were he to move a muscle without permission, or try to escape, he wouldn't even reach the door.

Eventually, a servant entered the chamber and told him that the caliph would give him an audience. Zakki followed the man and realized that without being ordered or instructed, the guards had pivoted on their heels and were surrounding him in perfect formation.

He walked down seemingly endless corridors, glancing into rooms where important people were meeting and discussing matters of consequence. Yet unlike the arguments and discussions conducted at the House of Wisdom, these conversations were hushed, almost reverential, so that none could overhear what was being said. Nobody even glanced up from their deliberations as Zakki and his guards walked past.

They entered a huge hall, the caliph's official office, whose open windows faced a garden somehow built within the structure of the house. Zakki, knowing only Jerusalem before coming to Baghdad, had never seen such a construction. It appeared to be outdoors and yet was within the building; it was open to the skies but constrained within the walls of the palace.

What was even more remarkable was that the garden contained a wondrous fountain, its water lapping over a series of statues and rocks until it fell from the height of a tall man onto a large blue pond.

Walking around the garden were the most remarkable birds Zakki had ever seen. Birds that seemed to be wearing crowns on their heads, birds whose feathers were blue and gold, green and yellow. Some stood with their heads bowed to the ground, their massive colored tails in a huge fan that looked like a painting containing a hundred eyes. Then Zakki looked up into the trees and saw monkeys jumping from branch to branch. It seemed to him like the Garden of Eden.

The servant leading him came to a stop at the far end of the hall and Zakki stood there, surrounded by the guardsmen, the vast room before him.

Zakki's amazement turned to acute focus as he fixed his gaze on the far end of the room where the caliph sat on a throne. The slender man looked resplendent in his multicolored gowns and his turban emblazoned with enormous white and blue feathers. Of all the color in the room, and outside in the garden, it was the caliph whose clothes were the most vivid.

Beside him sat a young boy not more than nine or ten years of age, dressed in the pure white of a Muslim holy man giving way to a cloak of deepest crimson.

Beside the thrones were the important men of the court, advisers to the caliph, men who would listen to any nuance or gossip if it would advance their wealth or position.

It was these men, in this moment, whom Zakki feared. These men were closest to the Caliph and to his vizier, Hadir ibn Yussuf ibn Gibreel, the man Zakki had come to denounce.

Nervously, Zakki surveyed the assembly. Though they were dressed almost identically, he couldn't discern Hadir's face among the others gathered at the feet of the caliph. The absence of Hadir gave him confidence.

The guard allowed Zakki to walk up to the raised dais where the caliph sat with the young imam. Zakki looked from right to left, and the closer he came to the advisers, the more certain he was that the vizier wasn't there. Was it just luck?

As Zakki bowed, the caliph spoke in a voice of authority. "You are the doctor my wife has spoken of? The one who can prevent assaults of the effluvium of the body?"

"Yes, Great One."

"You wish to speak with me?"

"Yes, Great One."

"Well?"

"Great One, I wish to speak with you about a matter that is for your ears and the ears of none other."

There was silence, but with his eyes still lowered to the ground, Zakki could not read the silence and pushed on. "It concerns a person within your court, close to your throne, who wishes to do harm to this great city, and the empire you and your father have built. To say these things, however, I need to speak with you and you alone."

"Who is this man of whom you speak?" asked the caliph.

"Great One, I cannot—"

Zakki raised his eyes for the first time to look at the caliph. There was silence for what seemed to Zakki the longest time, until the caliph held up his hand.

"I will accede to your request and grant you a private audience. All will leave my court until I command your return. All except his holiness the imam and the captain of my guard."

The guard captain looked sternly at Zakki, a gaze that could melt stone, and Zakki knew it was a warning. If he moved too fast or in the wrong way, Zakki would die there on the steps at the feet of the caliph without another word.

Zakki bowed in respect and then waited for the others to leave. When the room was empty, the caliph beckoned him forward until he stood close enough to speak in a voice that could not be overheard in the galleries above.

But before Zakki could speak, the caliph whispered to him, "I know why you are here this day. You have a friend in the House of Wisdom who is also a friend of somebody close to me. He has made your concerns known to my ears."

The words stole the air from Zakki's lungs and with it the words he had to say to the caliph.

"Your fellow Jew is not here. I have sent him away. You have nothing to fear."

Zakki felt dizzy and struggled to comprehend his position. Was he about to be killed, or did the caliph really already know what Zakki had to say?

The caliph smiled as if reading the doctor's mind. "Do you see the vizier in court today? No. I have ordered him to go to the eastern deserts to collect tributes from the tribes. What you tell me is not new to my ears, Doctor. There is nothing you can tell me that is not already known to me. Do you think I have no knowledge of what is happening in my court?"

"No. No, Great One. I came to warn . . . I came because I was afraid . . . I came because . . ."

The caliph waved his hand for silence. "The vizier has done well for me, and my city is richer now than at any time. As I have grown wealthy, so, too, has he grown wealthier. But I know my people. And I know my faith."

His eyes drifted to the nine-year-old boy-imam at his side, who sat silent, listening carefully, judging Zakki.

"You are aware of the Silk Road, which brings great things from far in the east to our city. At the far end of the Silk Road is a land called China. We have brought many books and scrolls from that land, and they have been translated by our scholars, by ones such as you. One of the books, written over a thousand years ago, was by a great warrior called Sun Tzu. His advice was to keep friends close but enemies closer. This is wise counsel, Doctor. For knowing where the vizier is and what he is planning makes me safer. Aiding him in his plots is someone even closer to me, someone who wishes to sit on my throne, to usurp me. No doubt you will know of whom I speak."

Zakki nodded.

"Then you will also know that my brother has a large following. Were I to move against him, the bloodshed would be great. And the risk to the imam"—he turned and reached over to hold the arm of the young lad—"would be immense. Things will happen in my court, Doctor, but at a time of my choosing and my discretion."

Zakki drew in a deep breath.

"That is why I have not moved against the vizier, because it would precipitate bloodshed at the very doorstep of my palace, and my forces are not strong enough to ensure my victory against the militants my brother could call upon, forces that are interested only in their own wealth and not the good of the empire."

The caliph smiled. "I placed great trust in you, Doctor. I know much about you. I knew from the imam's uncle that you'd been to see him; and I knew from your friend Hussain of your concerns. I trusted that when you came to see me, you would ask to see me alone. I was right to trust you, for had you told me of your conversation with the vizier in the presence of my court, then all would have been exposed. Those who are not loyal to me among my advisers—and I know who they are—would have scurried to inform the vizier. But in the coming months, perhaps years, my brother's base of power will be diluted. Then I shall deal with him and all who try to bring discord to the House of Allah."

Zakki knew then that conflict and destruction would come. The divisions were too deep and the layers of power struggle too complex. The greatest of learning and everything the House of Wisdom represented might be brought low when Sunni and Shi'ite were set against each other for the inheritance of Mohammed.

Did the caliph know this? Or was he too caught up in the machinations of his own power to see the future of his people with clear eyes?

"I'm sorry to say that your presence here in Baghdad is likely to cause trouble for me. You will become an object of division, which is why I am commanding you and your family to return to Jerusalem and to have no further contact with my court. You have nothing more to fear from the vizier, but your time in the House of Wisdom, Doctor, has come to an end."

RAF Station, Lydda Airfield
between Tel Aviv and Jerusalem
1947

SHALMAN MADE CERTAIN that the rope tying the hands of the British Tommy was secure enough for him not to escape but loose enough for proper blood circulation. The ball of fabric in his mouth would prevent him from shouting for help, and the ropes that tethered him to the wall heater would keep him warm in the cold night air.

Satisfied that until he was discovered the man would be safe, Shalman stood and found himself speaking when he knew that he probably shouldn't. "I'm sorry to do this to you . . ."

Shalman thought he heard the British conscript mumble, "Fuck you." It was the least Shalman deserved for the crack on the head he'd been forced to wield. But it gave him access to the fuel truck, which was what he needed.

The massive Avro York military transporter was sitting out on the No. 3 runway of the airfield like a giant bird of prey at rest, waiting to be fueled so that it could carry its cargo of supplies to British forces stationed in Egypt. The mission Shalman had been given by Dov was to take command of the refueling vehicle, initiate the timing mechanism of the bomb, drive it to the underbelly of the aircraft, and then crawl away unnoticed.

Wearing a stolen British uniform, Shalman climbed into the cabin of the fuel truck and turned the key. It roared into life, making a terrible rumbling noise in the confines of the hangar, and Shalman said a quick prayer. Odd, because he otherwise thought of himself as an atheist. But what did the American soldiers say—"There are no atheists in foxholes"? If there wasn't a God, then at least the prayer made him feel better; if there was a God, maybe the Almighty would help Shalman survive. Either way, he felt he'd covered his bases.

He drove the truck away from the hangar, along the periphery of the airport until he came to the end of Runway 3. Then he turned hard left and traveled down the runway toward the aircraft. He checked carefully through the windshield and saw there were only three or four men standing nearby. Earlier, there had been at least twenty.

Shalman put the truck into second gear so that it was trundling along slowly. Slow enough to be thought of as casual and ordinary, not so slow that anybody might easily see Shalman's face and wonder who he was. He pressed his knee up under the steering wheel to hold it on course and free his hands. Beside him was a small satchel; he removed a heavy brick. He placed it on the floor near his feet. With his eyes flicking regularly up to check his slow, trundling trajectory, he reached deeper into the bag. His fingers found the mechanical mass of explosive and wire that was the bomb.

Something so small, yet inside a fuel truck it would radiate out to cause immense damage. These thoughts stayed with him as he thought about what would happen on the tarmac of the airfield.

His fingers slowly and dexterously felt around the explosive for the switch. It was rudimentary, just a break connector that would join two wires and begin a clock countdown. He'd always been told the best bombs were simple. He pressed his finger against the switch, felt its resistance, then pushed and felt a distinct click.

Two minutes. Not long, but enough.

From around his neck, Shalman loosened a thin wool scarf and, looping it around the steering wheel, tied the other end to the thick door handle and pulled it tight so the wheel would not turn either way. Satisfied the truck would hold its course, he eased his foot off the accelerator and leaned down awkwardly to feel the brick on the floor. He maneuvered the brick into position to lean against the pedal, maintaining the pressure to keep the truck moving forward, inexorably, slowly, and aimed squarely at the aircraft.

Shalman had no idea whether the bomb would explode before or after the truck crashed into the plane, but that didn't matter. It was full of fuel, and there was no way the British could stop it. Double-checking that the truck was driving itself on the right course, Shalman opened the driver's door and jumped out on the tarmac. The driver's door faced away from the soldiers on the airstrip, and he was reasonably certain nobody would see him or the truck until it entered the umbra of the lights surrounding the aircraft.

His feet hit the ground and he rolled as he'd been trained, taking the impact and momentum in the tumble. The truck was moving slowly, but still the force of the jump blew the air from his lungs, and as he came to a crouch in the thin, long grass by the side of the airstrip, he struggled to find his breath.

Shalman flattened himself further and lay stationary, watching. He took a small pair of binoculars from a pouch at his waist and adjusted the screw until he could see the underside of the plane clearly. There were four British soldiers standing underneath the plane, smoking and chatting. He couldn't quite see who and shifted the lens to find the other figure. The truck rolled closer. Any minute now one of the soldiers would see the truck and become concerned that it was not slowing. Shalman continued to look through the binoculars, taking in each of the men. He remembered Dov's words, "No civilians, just hardware." In that moment he realized Dov's play on words. Shalman had accepted blowing up a plane but not four soldiers, and his heart sank as he breathed out slowly. Soldiers, not civilians.

And then he saw the boy.

A short boy, his distinctly Arab clothes and dark skin visible through the binoculars under the lights of the airfield. Shalman was overcome with dread as he watched the boy hold up a jerry can. One of the soldiers seemed to be laughing with him and patted him on the head. The boy was asking for fuel.

Shalman had no idea who the boy was, no sense of where he came from, but the simple act forced his mind to race through a narrative—the son of a local farmer, sent to the airfield to scrounge for scarce fuel, a boy known to the soldiers, a familiar face.

Shalman wanted to scream to the boy to run. He never intended for anyone to get hurt, just for the plane to be destroyed, as the orders stated. But because the soldiers were laughing and joking with the boy, they hadn't noticed the truck moving quietly toward them, shrouded in the darkness of the airfield, its cabin empty, the bomb's mechanism slowly moving forward in time and space, on a collision course with the plane.

Shalman watched in horror. The only way for them to escape would be for Shalman to shout a warning. But he couldn't bring the cry to his lips. He half stood in a crouch and moved to run away from the tarmac. But he felt compelled to turn back and watch. He raised the binoculars once more. The idiots still hadn't heard the truck. It was now so close, they surely must—

But it was all too late.

Shalman turned and ran toward the outskirts of the airfield. There was only a rudimentary barrier, and it was easy for him to climb over. As he slipped to the other side of the fence, Shalman looked up once more to the distant aircraft. The truck had almost arrived at the target. It had veered slightly to the left but would still collide with the right-hand wheel of the massive undercarriage. It was then that the British Tommies noticed the truck coming toward them without lights, and they began to shout.

The soldiers scattered away from the plane to protect themselves. The Arab boy was just staring, transfixed, rooted to the spot. Shalman screamed out, "Move!" in Arabic, though he knew he couldn't be heard from such a distance.

The British soldier farthest away raised his rifle and began firing into the cabin of the truck. It must have been an instinctive reaction, because all he accomplished was to shatter the windshield and side windows. And then the truck careened into the wheels of the undercarriage, at the same time as the timing mechanism of the bomb counted down to zero. A massive ball of flame erupted out of the truck's cabin. The momentary inferno spread to the cargo of fuel, exploding with an almighty boom, lighting up the entire airfield, the hangars, the control buildings, and the periphery where Shalman was standing.

He couldn't see, but he knew that the fireball had engulfed not just the plane and the truck but the young Arab boy and almost certainly some of the soldiers. He screamed, "NO!" at the top of his voice, but nobody was listening.

The heat from the explosion hit him and he smelled the heavy, greasy stench of the kerosene. The plane was on fire, and the remaining fuel in its tanks exploded, adding a second fireball to the sky.

His only thought now was escape, so he turned and ran.

With the explosion and flame behind him, Shalman's feet carried him across the grass to where he'd left his bicycle, his only means of escape. As he pedaled furiously away, he saw in his mind's eye the body of a young Arab child, alight in a pyre of aircraft fuel.

Jerusalem
1947

SHALMAN NOW COUNTED the times of happiness in the house in terms of hours rather than days. He looked at his wife, Judit—beautiful, confident, and calm—and knew that things had changed for them both.

Since he had come back from the archaeological site with Mustafa, the change in Judit had been subtle yet noticeable. Something had happened to her, and the more she brushed aside his concerns, the deeper they grew. What he had always seen as a deep calm in her now struck him as a certain coldness. She seemed driven and focused in a way he couldn't understand. And at night she disappeared, returning sometimes by dawn and at other times not for days.

He loved her still with all his heart and ached for the Judit he'd married only a couple of years ago. Yet he knew that they were growing apart. For he had changed, too. They no longer spoke of Lehi and their objectives. Shalman assumed Judit knew about the mission to destroy the airfield, but she never asked about it, and he never spoke to her of the young Arab boy engulfed in flame. And he never asked where she went or what she did in the dark hours of night. When she first disappeared in the evenings, or for a few days, he'd asked, indeed demanded, to know, but she was evasive and told him that these matters went to Lehi's secrecy. So he stopped asking and bore resentment at their growing isolation. The house was filled with silence broken only by the occasional tears and tantrums of their daughter, Vered.

It was this that hurt Shalman the most. Was whatever grand objective or cause she was undertaking more important than being a mother?

Their beautiful Vered's attachment was almost exclusively to Shalman. He was mother and father and entire family to their daughter. He fed her, read to her, dressed her, nurtured her. When Judit was in the apartment, she would play with Vered, but even the little girl clearly sensed that her mother's mind was elsewhere and would seek her father instead. Shalman would watch as Judit asked Vered what she'd like to do, and the child would look at her father for permission. It was heartbreaking.

He confronted his wife one night in their bed. "Something has changed in you, Judit."

She scoffed and rolled away from him to face the wall.

"Is the fight so great that it's more important than your family?"

"The world is bigger than just this apartment, Shalman. Bigger than just this family," she said in a detached voice.

"What does that mean? Where do you go at night? What do you do?"

At this, Judit fiercely rolled back to face Shalman. "What must be done, Shalman. I do what must be done."

"What you need to do is be here, with us, with Vered!"

Shalman's voice had strengthened in volume, and as the walls were thin, Judit replied with a harsh whisper. "And what of you and your expeditions into the past? Digging in the dirt—for what? What happened to you out there? The Arabs want you dead, and the British grind you under their heels, and yet you're scrounging around caves with an Arab!"

"He saved my life," said Shalman flatly.

Judit tilted her head and raised an eyebrow. It was a look that once upon a time he found so alluring. Now it just seemed jaded.

"If it wasn't for him, I'd be dead."

"So it's guilt. You spend time with this Arab because you feel guilty?"

"No!" Shalman had raised his voice again but quickly lowered it. "No. It's feeling indebted. It's a debt I can repay."

"How?"

"I'm teaching him. What I've learned at the university. I'm teaching him."

"So he can be an archaeologist like you? You have to be kidding me, Shalman! If there is to be a nation of Israel, it will need builders, workers, engineers, not people who play in the dirt looking at an irrelevant past."

At other times there would have been so much to say, so much to argue, but Shalman had not the words or strength.

"You're more interested in the fight than you are in your family. We're almost there, Judit. Israel will soon be declared a new nation. Can't you come back home and be a wife and a mother again?"

"And when Israel is declared, you think there'll be doves of peace flying through rainbows in the sky? Don't be naive, Shalman. When Israel is declared, war will follow. Your Arab friend will quickly be your enemy. Where will you stand then?"

"And what of you, Judit?" Shalman shot back. "Where will you stand? You fight for Lehi, but I know your heart. I know there is something else in you. Who do you really fight for? I've seen you when you're with people from Russia and the way you speak of Moscow and Stalin with nostalgia. Sometimes I think you'd prefer to be back there than here."

Judit suddenly sat up. "How could you say that? Have you any idea what those Russian bastards—"

"What else can I say? It's like I don't even know who you are anymore. I'm not sure I ever did."

Judit's face showed no emotion. But inside, she trembled. She looked at her husband, a man who lived his life with a transparency she didn't have and never would. He said what was on his mind; she said what she had been taught to say to avoid telling the truth.

She remembered her mother, brutalized by a drunken and violent husband; her own life as a child, always in fear; then Beria and Anastasia and the power they had given her over her life. They made her capable of anything, and the fear of being that girl under the table again had hardened her.

"There's so much I want to tell you, Shalman. But I can't."

Peterhof, the Palace of Peter the Great
Leningrad, Russia
October 1947

RUBBLE-STREWN, DILAPIDATED, LITERALLY a shell of its former self, Peterhof, the once proud summer palace of Tsar Peter the Great, somehow remained standing. Despite the attempts by the Nazis to destroy all that wasn't German, and despite the cost of tens of millions dead, Mother Russia had triumphed over the Germans.

Since his incarceration as a rabble-rouser in Landsberg Castle, since his rise to chancellor, and since his Nuremberg speeches spitting hatred, Adolf Hitler had defined any race east of Germany as subhuman: the Slavs, the Russians, the Asiatics. Not the Japanese, who were useful allies in the war; but Stalin often speculated how long it would have been before the madman Hitler tried to exterminate them, had he won.

It was only during the relative equanimity of the opening months of the war, when the pact between Germany and Russia held fast, that the Nazi leader refrained from defining the Russians as subhumans. But since he'd instigated Operation Barbarossa and invaded Russia, laying a murderous siege to Leningrad and a scorched-earth policy in the rest of the western territory of the nation, his visceral hatred of everything that wasn't Hunnish and German had been evident to all.

It had taken years and the bodies of more than twenty million Russians, but the invading German armies had been repelled. From that time, the might of the Soviet army had slowly ground down Nazi Germany. Despite the victory, the pride of Russia's greatness had been badly damaged, and Stalin had promised himself that the palaces that once belonged to the privileged classes would be rebuilt and used as Soviet offices and for museums. One of the most pressing was the palace that Peter the Great had built for himself, over the water from Leningrad on the shores of the Gulf of Finland.

For two hundred and fifty years, Peterhof had been the honored sentinel of Russian magnificence, positioned as the entryway to Leningrad and from there to the rest of the nation. Its restoration would be a symbol of Russia's reestablished place in the world.

Yesterday a thousand workers had been feverishly hammering and sawing and screwing and building and repairing, clambering over the walls and gardens like a frenetic nest of ants. Today only two men stood in the long garden, viewing the damage from the seawall, slowly walking up the vast lawns, lakes, and canals toward the distant bombed- and burned-out palace that stood sorrowfully on the high hill. A hundred guards were strategically placed out of sight in the woods, ensuring the safety of the two most important people in Russia—comrades Stalin and Beria.

The two men inspected the rebuilding work, taking in the devastation. They walked from the sea to the remnants of the palace as though they were the only people on the land.

Stalin spat a globule of phlegm on the ground as if that were all that needed to be said of Hitler and the destruction he had wrought.

The two men continued to walk along the long gardens toward the wreck of the palace.

"When will this be ready?" Stalin asked quietly.

"We hope in a year or two. It will be restored, and then we'll use it as an administrative center for Leningrad."

"And the other matter?"

Always wary, Beria didn't want to ask what particular matter, but searched his mind for recent conversations so that he didn't give the wrong answer. "It's going according to plan," he said, stretching out the conversation so that a clue might reveal what was in Stalin's mind.

"And is the group achieving its aim?"

Beria still had no specific clue. Of all the myriad plans they had in place, not least the growing difficulty of tensions with the Americans in Berlin, he had no idea what Stalin was talking about.

The Supreme Leader of all of Russia turned and looked at his second in command. "It has been some years now since they left for Palestine."

At last, the clue he needed. Beria's agile mind slipped into gear. "The natural leader is the Jewess Judita Ludmilla. She's about to take command."

"Is it wise for a Jew to take over a leadership position?"

Beria thought for a moment, so that it appeared he was considering the great man's question with utmost precision. "In this one isolated case, comrade, it is wise. This will be the land of the Jew, and to have a non-Jew in control would look and feel wrong. It would raise suspicions."

Stalin nodded. They continued toward the palace. "This girl. Will she achieve the objectives of Operation Outgrowth? Much depends on it. The discussion about the future of Palestine will soon be taken up at the United Nations. She and the other agents must be ready. When it comes to a decision, we will vote for the partition of Palestine into an Arab state and a Jewish state. And she and the other agents will be our puppets, yes?"

"Yes, Secretary General. But there are those in Palestine—Jews, of course—who are showing some signs of resistance and leaning toward British and American interests. So strategic targets are currently being selected for extermination. Once their voices are silenced, then the road will be clear."

"And do you think this girl is capable of turning the Jewish population in our direction?"

"Alone, no, Comrade Secretary General. But she has a number of highly trained agents under her, and we are keeping our eye very carefully trained on her. Her handler, Anastasia Bistrzhitska, has been moved to our mission in Jerusalem in order to coordinate the operation. She was one of our top people in Washington, and I ordered her back to be in charge of training the Jews for this mission. She's done an excellent job."

They reached the hill that rose toward the shell of Peterhof Palace. "Good," said Stalin. "Very good. And who knows, maybe I can get the Jews and the Muslims to love each other. They once did, you know, Lavrentiy Pavlovich. A thousand years ago, in Baghdad. Now let's see what damage those Nazi bastards did to my building."

Acre, north of Haifa

1947

THEY ARRIVED AT different times and on different days. They stayed in different boardinghouses, some in cheap dockside hotels, some with sympathetic supporters, and some in lodgings as though they were students here to visit the antiquities of the city. By design, some spoke Hebrew, some French, some Russian, some Yiddish, and some German. They went unnoticed by British security.

Also by design, thirty-four freedom fighters from the combined Irgun and Lehi forces gathered in order to break their comrades out of one of the most impregnable citadels in the Middle East.

The date of the assault had been advanced by over a week, in order to cause maximum embarrassment to the British. It was decided by the Irgun leader, Menachem Begin, that the assault on the prison, and the release of a hundred freedom fighters, should coincide with the meeting of the General Assembly of the United Nations that had been specially convened to discuss the British mandate and the entire Palestinian issue.

There were many nations among the fifty-seven member states who would vote against the partition of Palestine into Jewish and Arab nations, but Menachem Begin and other leaders were certain that if enough damage was done to the reputation of the British army, then votes could be swayed away from a further mandate.

The mood of the men and women who met late in the evening at the home of an Irgun supporter in the upper reaches of the Neve Sha'anan region of Haifa was one of restrained fury. Only two or three weeks earlier, four Irgun freedom fighters had been hanged in the prison. The death of the men was the spark that ignited the decision to bring forward the operation to free the other people incarcerated.

To prepare for this mission, it had taken days and days of intense study of the fortress, the roads around it, and the most vulnerable access points.

It was Judit who had been instrumental in sourcing much of the information. She'd seduced a sergeant major in the British army in order to acquire plans of the Acre Fortress so that the Irgun's bomb makers could estimate the type and quantities of explosives necessary. The sergeant major subsequently died in a road accident.

Judit was also put in charge of stealing British uniforms, buying Jeeps, trucks, and ordinary motor vehicles, and then arranging their painting in British army colors and insignia.

To her comrades, she was a fierce strategist for the cause of Lehi who'd do anything necessary to achieve their ultimate goal of a free Jewish Israel. But to herself, she was a servant of Soviet Russia who at this moment saw a clear alignment of both ideals.

In the past month, she'd caused accidents—road, boating, and gunshot—that had led to the deaths of five prominent people on the list she'd been given by Anastasia, people whose right-wing and ultra-nationalist ideas would put them at odds with the ambitions of Moscow in a future Israel, a friend of the USSR. People who said publicly that they saw no point in replacing Britain with Russia; people who would have stood in the way.

In a week's time, she'd have to find an excuse to travel to Tel Aviv to meet with Anastasia and the Russian team of which she was now leader, to receive their reports and mete out punishments to those who had failed in their missions. But in the meantime, she had an Irgun mission in which to participate, helping her colleagues to blow a British prison to hell, and free dozens of imprisoned Irgun soldiers. And by coincidence, one of the men still on her list was participating in tomorrow's assault on the fortress at Acre.

• • •

Dov was dressed in the uniform of a lieutenant in the Engineering Corps of the British army in Palestine. He was supervising five NCOs laying telephone and electricity cables close to the southern wall of the citadel above an old underground Turkish bath. Dov stood and pondered why he so favored the operational name he'd chosen.

All Lehi and Irgun fighters adopted operational names, partly out of security and partly out of bravado. He'd chosen as his nickname "Shimshon," known as Samson to the British he fought. Samson had been the character from childhood stories in Riga who had embedded himself in Dov's imagination. In bed at night, beneath the covers, he'd fantasize about being Samson—a great judge, brave, daring, and relentless against his enemies, slaying a lion with his bare hands, killing an entire army with the jawbone of an ass, and destroying a pagan temple using his strength alone; then appearing before the people and lauded as a hero.

Dov's life hadn't been so heroic. He'd stolen weapons, bombed rail lines, shot British soldiers, and fought off Arab attacks, but always in the dark and the quiet. Something in him longed to be a hero.

He glanced over at his colleague, Ariel Waxman, a right-wing firebrand journalist whose articles in the *Palestine Post* were becoming increasingly militant, calling for the British to withdraw immediately and allow Arabs and Jews to decide the fate of the new nation. Waxman's membership in the Irgun was something he hinted at in his articles, and he'd only just been released from imprisonment in this fortress for inciting revolt.

Dov looked at his watch and hoped that the other Irgun troops under his command, stationed at the other sides of the walls of the prison, weren't meeting resistance or scrutiny. They each knew precisely how to perform their roles, as did the prisoners. It had been planned to begin at precisely 4:22 P.M., when the day guards were tired and distracted, thinking about what they'd do during the night, and the evening shift workers were not yet in place.

The first explosion would be in the one weak spot of the prison in Acre, where he and his men were pretending to lay cables. When the Ottomans had conquered Acre, they'd built a Turkish bath in the basement of the citadel and had significantly weakened the structure above. It was the only point in the walls of the vast fortress that was vulnerable, a weakness discovered by Judit.

The minutes ticked on, and at 4:10 P.M., in the most British voice he could muster, he said, "All right, chaps, that's enough. Clear up. Our work's done here."

It took them three minutes to pick up their tools, leaving the explosive they'd planted inside the hole they'd made in the wall covered with rocks and debris. They'd buried it in a cavity that would ensure the explosive forces expanded up, down, and into the building, and would not dissipate uselessly into the street.

Bundled into the British Army Engineering Corps truck, they trundled north and then onto a side road near the market to wait. Dov peered steely-eyed through the windshield. Around him, the men were silent. No longer naive boys driven by anger and ambition, they were now veterans; experienced guerrilla fighters. It hadn't been easy, and they'd lost many along the way—imprisoned or dead. But those who were here were reliable.

He glanced at his watch, then back through the windshield. His mind ticked away the remaining moments. And then he heard a massive explosion. The sound was deep and resonant, though there was almost nothing visual to show for its scale. The damage was contained and focused and a signal to those inside.

* * *

The moment the explosion in the walls above the Turkish bath was heard and felt throughout the prison, the inmates who knew of the raid—members of Irgun—went into action. For days, TNT had been smuggled inside by Jewish cooks; it had been fashioned into hand grenades and bombs, and as the external bomb was detonated, bombs inside the prison were set off, blasting off doors and breaching the internal structures adjacent to where Shimshon and his men had fractured the external walls.

Though a carefully guarded secret operation, the moment the explosions ripped through the prison, hundreds of Arab and Jewish inmates knew there was a jailbreak happening. They rushed to the sound of the explosions while Irgun and Lehi prisoners, armed with the grenades, blew open iron grilles and doors and held the stunned British guards at bay.

Within minutes, the inside of the prison became a smoke-filled, ear-splitting maelstrom of explosions, gunfire, screams from wounded and dying men, orders yelled, feet running, and yelps of panic. But the prisoners of the Irgun and Lehi knew precisely what they should be doing, and which exit point in the wall they should be heading for. Some Jews knew that their task wasn't to escape but to form a vanguard to hold the British soldiers in position so their colleagues could climb out of the breach; it was a suicide mission for four of the men, knowing they'd be either killed by the guards or hanged for their participation in the escape.

The corridors of the prison became a nightmare of flashes of light and detonations as bullets erupted from the barrels of guns tracing arcs through the dense smoke. The screams of pain and hatred from wounded men blended into a discordant babble of languages. Those who had learned Hebrew when they arrived in Palestine reverted to their native German or Hungarian or Polish as they fell to the floor wounded in the arms or legs or back; those British soldiers screamed bloodcurdling curses against the Jews; those Arabs who used the opportunity to escape begged for the help of their Prophet or screamed out *"Allahu Akbah"* as they ran toward the hole in the wall, hoping to escape from the prison into the ancient alleyways of the city.

Outside the walls, close to where the men under Dov's command had blown the external hole, he and his second in command, Ariel Waxman, waited until the first men had climbed through the breach. Dov turned to Waxman and quipped, "Not a word about this in the *Palestine Post* . . . got it?"

Waxman had already composed in his mind the first three paragraphs of the article he'd be writing later that night, a satirical condemnation of the Irgun for preventing the British from doing their job of murdering Jewish soldiers. "Try and stop me, Shimshon," he said. "This is going to make headlines around the world. Wait till those bastards in the United Nations read it. I can't wait for the reaction of the British ambassador."

Both men looked around to see whether any genuine British troops were appearing on the periphery. They hoped that when the real troops saw the Irgun men in British uniforms, holding rifles to kill escapees, they'd move on to other locations. If not, then there would be a gun battle, which would give cover to the men escaping from the prison.

The smoke billowing out of the massive hole quickly dissipated into the air, and Shimshon and Ariel saw the first man's head appear. He looked right and left, and Dov barked a command in Hebrew: "Move, don't look . . . move!"

He jumped out of the hole, followed by one, then three. Altogether, twenty-eight freedom fighters from Lehi and the Irgun emerged and scrambled into trucks emblazoned with the insignia of the Engineering Corps of the British army.

But more and more men started to appear, men whose faces were unrecognized by either Dov or Ariel. They were Arab prisoners, clearly benefiting from the meticulously planned incursion. Dozens and dozens of Arab men hurled themselves out of the hole in the wall and onto the pavement and ran across the road into the shuks and alleyways of the ancient city.

Suddenly, a British army truck screeched around a corner and accelerated toward Dov and Ariel. It screamed to a halt twenty yards from where they were standing, and a dozen men jumped off the back. They shouldered their rifles and began firing at the Jews who stood on the pavement. Dov screamed in pain, clutching his chest as he fell to the floor. The Jews hid behind their truck in order to return fire, and in the melee, some British soldiers were shot dead or severely wounded. Ariel stood to get a better shot and suddenly yelped, spun around, and fell to the floor, wounded in the shoulder. He had enough strength to shout, "Move out, quick. Go!"

The men knew what to do. They had to save themselves and leave the dying and wounded where they'd fallen. This was the Irgun way. As the truck roared off, the British jumped back into their truck and took off in hot pursuit.

And a place that moments ago had been a vortex of smoke and flames, of gunshots and noise, of joy and agony, was silent. Apart from the sound of distant gunfire, of the occasional barked order, the street where the explosion had taken place was quiet.

Ariel looked around and saw Dov, his eyes staring into the eternal void, close by him. Another Jew was also dead. Ariel raised his head to see the place where the British had been shooting: two Tommies were lying in the roadway. He realized that he'd been spared. He would use this opportunity to crawl across the road and somehow find a place where a doctor could remove the bullet that had torn his shoulder apart. It was throbbing mercilessly, but he was alive, and though an atheist, he thanked God for saving him. And he started to compose the rest of the article he'd write against the British tomorrow.

He was halfway across the road when he sensed somebody walking up to him. A British soldier? It was agony, but he turned his head and saw the legs of a woman in a skirt, a European skirt. Relief overcame him.

He raised his head more to see who it was, flashes of pain radiating from his torn shoulder. And he recognized her immediately. He smiled in gratitude at his good fortune. "Judit. Thank God you're here. I've been—"

She raised a pistol, shook her head, and said softly, "I'm sorry, Ariel."

"I don't . . . what . . . ?"

"I'm afraid you're part of my problem," she said, just a second before she pulled the trigger. The bullet blew his face away from his skull.

West of the village of Ras Abu Yussuf

1947

SHALMAN USED A small trowel to carefully scrape away the dirt from the short, shallow trench over which he huddled. In the cave, the air was cool and dry, while the bright sun from the entrance filled it with light. He teased the soil away and, in looking for remnants of the ancient past, found he was able to temporarily escape the troubling present.

His argument with Judit echoed in his mind and was confused with the images of the truck rolling slowly toward the aircraft on the runway. Judit's cold stare and the determination that put her cause above her family was overlaid in his mind with the body of an Arab boy engulfed in flame in an explosion. But here and now, with his hands in the ancient dirt, such thoughts seemed very far away. This was where he belonged. This was where his head was clear.

He had arranged to come here with Mustafa as often as he could, which in truth was rare between caring for his daughter and the demanding routine of Mustafa having to work on his father's meager plot of land. But here they were, side by side, toiling in the earth for ancient treasures at the burial site of a woman named Ruth.

Despite the calm that Shalman found in the cave, Mustafa sensed something was worrying the strange friend working silently beside him.

"You are very quiet today," said Mustafa.

Shalman just shrugged, the sort of response typically associated with Mustafa.

"That's unusual for a Jew," he said dryly.

Shalman let out a small laugh, then sat back and put down his trowel.

For the past months they'd been together, and true to his word, Shalman had been teaching Mustafa. Shalman had taken pleasure in showing the sharply intelligent and attentive young Arab man the university books he had been studying, and they talked not just of history and archaeology but of mathematics and geography and cartography. It was maps that Mustafa took to most readily, and he would eagerly pore over any that Shalman was able to beg, borrow, or steal away to bring to him. The two men compared maps showing ancient borders and conquests of the Romans and the Egyptians and the Crusaders with modern maps showing contemporary towns, cities, and roads. And they would fantasize about what they might discover if able to dig under some of Jerusalem's most ancient sites.

A map had been published recently in the newspaper showing the UN-proposed partition of Palestine, and Shalman had brought this with him to discuss with Mustafa. His mind was so focused on the map as a reference for where they might explore in the future that he was blinkered to its contemporary implications. Mustafa looked it over with thoughtful eyes.

"Where will you live when they carve up the land?" he asked.

"Stay in Jerusalem, I should think," Shalman answered.

"It is to be a . . ." Mustafa searched with his finger on the map for the term. "Corpus Separatum?"

"That's right. Jerusalem will belong to nobody," said Shalman.

"Nobody?"

"Well, it'll belong to everyone. And be run by the United Nations. Jerusalem is our birthright, yet it's being taken from us by the governments of the world."

"We have as much right to Jerusalem as you do, Shalman," said Mustafa softly.

Shalman didn't want to begin one of the perennial arguments over who had a greater claim to the city, so he mumbled an apology.

"But you could still live there?" Mustafa asked.

"Yes. And so could you if you wanted."

Mustafa gave a snort. "I can't grow olive trees in the city."

The two men sat in silence for a moment before Mustafa spoke again. "Many Arabs won't accept this partition. Syrian, Jordanian,

Egyptian, and especially the Saudis—they'll never accept Jerusalem as a Jewish capital. Funny how the people who don't actually live here have the strongest opinions."

"Not so different for us. The fate of my people rests with the United States, Russia, Britain."

"And in between are you and me. Two men with nowhere else to go."

Shalman smiled. "We could always live together in a cave."

Mustafa grinned back and took a swig from his canteen before tossing it to Shalman.

"You think there will be war, don't you?" said Shalman.

"You Jews have enemies on all sides, my friend. To the north, to the east . . . ." His hand traced the map on the ground. "To the south. Only the sea is your friend." He looked up from the map. "And Arab armies from all sides will drive you into it. And we will be in the middle. If you asked me where I will live when they carve up the land, I want to say the best place for me to be is far away from here."

"There's not going to be a war, Mustafa. People will come to their senses. No one wants to die or fight if they don't have to. After the pounding the British have taken, after the millions and millions who died because of Hitler, nobody wants another war. Not your people, not my people."

Mustafa shook his head sadly. "Yet I think underneath your archaeologist's clothes, you've been a freedom fighter. You haven't said so, but I can tell. You're much more than an archaeologist; the way you handle yourself, the way you're always checking what's around you. You're as much soldier as academic. And Shalman, my friend, if you think there's going to be no war, then you have more faith in people than I do. Which is strange, since it's you who's the fighter and me who's just a farmer."

The words stung Shalman, reminding him of the airfield and the truck and the explosion and the little Arab boy.

Mustafa continued, "I'm more of a rationalist. As you teach me about mathematics, I can do the calculation. There are a hundred million Arabs and only eleven million Jews in the whole world. And how many of your people are here? Three, four hundred thousand

Jews in Palestine the newspaper tells me." Mustafa shook his head again. "The numbers don't add up, my friend. If I were you, I would leave this place."

Shalman detected a strange hint of sadness and resignation in Mustafa's voice that troubled him much more than the weight of numbers.

Jerusalem

November 29, 1947

JUDIT SAT IN the crowded room along with two dozen people around a table on which were coffee cups, dirty plates, dried fruits, hummus, fried eggplant, and ashtrays overflowing with long-dead cigarettes. She'd left Shalman at home with their daughter. Nobody in Jerusalem was willing to babysit, as the whole of the Jewish community was at home or with neighbors, glued to radios. Only Shalman, it seemed, was distant and uninterested in the imminent news. Judit didn't question this strange behavior, as she knew she needed to be present for the announcement.

She looked into the faces of her colleagues in the Irgun, those who had begun this battle with her in Lehi, some members of the Haganah, and others who were associated with Israel's fledgling civilian army. What was happening at this moment was a reminder of the time two years earlier, crowding around a similar radio, listening to the plummy voice of a BBC announcer telling the world that the Instrument of Surrender had been signed and World War II was at an end. In the last two intense years, Judit had honed her skills in what she'd trained to be: a killer fighting the British, but also preparing the way for a communist state and a part of the empire of the Soviet Union.

Judit looked at the faces gathered in the room. Her eyes fell on a young woman she'd known since the attack on the British officers at Goldschmidt House: Ashira from Tunisia.

After that night, Ashira had sought her out with a closeness that made Judit uncomfortable. Ashira was driven by anger; to Judit, that was plain to see. Her brutal treatment at the hands of a group of Bedouin men on her journey to Palestine hadn't broken her but had made her fiercely determined. Not fearless—Judit had seen how

Ashira's hands had trembled on her weapon at times—but the way she gritted her teeth and willed herself to be strong impressed Judit.

As she looked at the crowd gathered around the radio, Judit could not help but think of those who were absent, those who had died or disappeared or were locked up in British jails. And as she thought of the missing faces, her mind also turned to those she was responsible for, the lives she had snuffed out—British, Arab, and Jewish. How many more lay ahead of her? She had killed eight militant right-wing ultra-Zionists in the past year. Between them, her Russian secret group had killed five times that number—nearly fifty leading politicians, journalists, and scholars whose views and potential place in a future government would be counter to socialist ideals.

It was, in simple terms, a strategy based on the fact that decisions would be made by those who were still standing—with Palestine in a frenetic state, with everybody hating everybody else, with bullets flying and even children taking up arms, nobody had yet put together the disconnected deaths of these fifty right-wing Jews among the hundreds of Jews who had died since the end of the war, so nobody had perceived a pattern. That was what Moscow Central had counted on. Palestine was so full of murder and death and trauma that the loss of an individual was no longer noticed.

Judit's attention returned to the present when one young man at the table asked, "Are they really going to do it?"

"They have to," another young man said. "Look at the shit the Indians and the Pakistanis are in since Britain withdrew. The last thing the UN wants is the forced march of hundreds of thousands of Palestinians into Syria or Lebanon like the Muslims from India into Pakistan. They're bound to vote for partition. It's the only solution."

"They might still give the mandate to some other country, and they'd just replace the British," said Ashira.

"No," said Judit, gently moving so that she was sitting next to Ashira. "There's not another country in the world who'll take the mandate from the British. We've created too much chaos, so it's partition or nothing." Judit gave Ashira a wink.

Yossi Dagan, an Irgun leader from Galilee, held up his hand. "Shush!" he snapped. "Quiet! I think it's time!"

He reached over and turned up the volume. At the same time, people cleared the table of plates, so the map of the Plan of Partition could be laid out. As it was unrolled, everybody looked at the reality of what Israel would become should the vote go ahead. While there would be exultation and celebration, the truth told in the map was more somber. The land allocated to the Jews was, in places, so thin that it could be walked from east to west in hours. An army could cut off the north from the south with ease, and a plane could cover the distance in minutes. To look at the map with a critical eye was to realize the reality of being scattered and surrounded everywhere by the enemy, with the nation's back to the wall: in this case, the sea.

"The speeches for and against have finished," said Yossi, listening carefully to the commentator above the crackle and hiss of the static. "They're now calling the vote in alphabetical order."

"So when the vote is passed, we can call ourselves Israelis?" Ashira whispered into Judit's ear.

"No, it's just the beginning," Judit whispered back. "A lot of politicians still have a lot of talking to do. But it means the British will withdraw, and within a year the UN will vote to declare Israel and Palestine the world's newest nations."

Yossi looked at a sheet of paper, a long list of countries divided into columns. The first was the name of the country, then a second, thinner column was headed "Yes" and another column, equally thin, was headed "No." A fourth column was headed "Abstain." He was ready with his pen.

"First is going to be Argentina; there're so many fucking Nazis there that they'll probably vote no. Australia will say yes, then Belgium . . . that's going to be a yes. But as to Bolivia and Brazil, you can bet they'll be a no. Byelorussia, God knows. Canada will be positive, I'm sure, but Chile, China, Colombia . . ."

"Yossi," said Judit, "how about we let Trygve Lie go through the list. He's secretary general of the United Nations, not you, so don't try to do his job for him."

They all burst out laughing, including Yossi.

Judit knew that the simple voting of yes or no belied the complexity of the undertaking and the process ahead. Even if the UN voted for partition, there would have to be an agreement on an economic union between the two states, and then a seemingly endless series of commissions and advisory groups and inspections. Then the General Assembly of the United Nations would have to vote in twelve months on the recommendation to give independence to the two new nations. For their part, the Jewish leadership had agreed to accept the findings of the UN and the borders the General Assembly agreed upon. But the Arab people had not. If the vote was for partition, then the moment it was declared, the Arabs would prepare for war. So as she sat, listened, and looked over the map, Judit knew that the battle against the British would become a war against the Arabs. And she was the only one in the room who knew for certain which way the ambassador from the Soviet Union would vote.

Her reality was that she and her fellow Russians were instructed to use the national excitement and the mayhem that would erupt onto the streets the moment the vote was taken as a time to seek out the twenty remaining targets on the list that Anastasia Bistrzhitska had given them. They were to become collateral damage in the attacks that the Arab forces would undoubtedly launch.

• • •

Two hours later, immediately after partition had been voted for, and when the cheering and backslapping and shouts of "Mazel tov!" and "L'chaim" had quieted down, the celebration was replaced by explosions of gunfire. They began in the distance, just one or two sporadic events separated by minutes, but they grew closer and increasingly rapid until they were a staccato orchestrated throughout the Arab areas of Jerusalem.

Though the sounds of rifles and pistol shots were far from uncommon in Jerusalem these days, the volume and aggression of the screams and anger that erupted, as word spread to cafés and mosques, was far beyond the usual.

The role of the Irgun and Lehi that night was not strategic attacks on British targets but defense of Jewish homes and people as the city fell into chaos. Judit looked down to Ashira beside her, holding a short-barreled Sten gun. Gripping tight to the stock, Ashira's hands were steady as stone. Tonight Ashira felt she would be firing bullets at Arabs, and this felt much more natural to her than British targets. Because now, only now, could she exercise restitution against the race who had raped her in the desert.

Judit slipped from the group into the streets of Jerusalem. When she was clear of the building and confident that she wasn't being followed, she snaked from street to street into an area she knew well.

Her target for assassination was Professor Emile Durace, head of the Department of Political Studies at Jerusalem University, by all accounts an eloquent, incisive speaker and a highly influential man.

Though he was not an orthodox Jew, having migrated to Palestine from Paris, where his family members were scions of the secular movement, his philosophy for the creation of the State of Israel was based in right-wing Zionism. His father, also an academic, had been an early supporter of the founder of modern Zionism, Theodore Herzl, who had witnessed the degradation of Alfred Dreyfus, a Jewish French army officer wrongly imprisoned for treason when it was obviously a show trial. Like his father, Professor Durace was a militant Zionist, and this made him Judit's target.

It took her half an hour on foot to reach the street where the professor lived with his wife and three children. She saw lights blazing in a number of the rooms of his house. She studied the pattern of lights in the house and could see that the family had been listening keenly to the radio announcement, as was much of the city. Durace and his wife, Colette, along with their two daughters and son, were downstairs drinking champagne and celebrating.

Hidden by the shadows of trees and bushes at the bottom of the garden, Judit drew out the sniper rifle that she'd concealed in her long overcoat and moved into a position where the front room of the house was clearly visible. Through the scope, she could see the aging professor and his wife sitting at a table. From moment to moment, his head was obscured as his children moved into and out of her field of view, but because of the way the family was relaxing, she knew she had a good amount of time to frame the target for the kill.

Judit studied the geography of the room through the telescopic sights. French paintings on the wall, menorah candlestick on a chimney breast, photographs of the family group in the foreground of the Eiffel Tower. Judit moved the scope slowly over the people in the room.

The professor seemed grandfatherly, with his tufts of unruly white hair above his ears and his exultant face as they lived and relived the moment of success in the UN vote. Colette must have been a beauty in her early years and was still a handsome woman, with salt-and-pepper hair and eyes that were luminous even through the rifle scope. The eldest of the children, a young woman about Judit's age, was stunningly attractive, with raven hair and deep-set seductive black eyes. Judit couldn't see the rest of her body, but she seemed to be tall and slender. In Paris she might have been a model for one of the fashion houses, but Judit thought that in tomorrow's Israel, she'd more likely be an engineer or driving a tractor on a kibbutz. For a brief moment, Judit pondered the extraordinary nature of the place in which she lived.

She studied the younger children, both of whom had faces that were interesting, arresting, and full of lively character. It was a lovely, warm, close family group.

Regret descended on her. All of her training in Moscow had taught her to be removed from her target, to consider them as nothing more than a step toward a grand vision to the benefit of everyone. She once was an alienated Jewish child and the daughter of a violent and aggressive father. And now she was an instrument of the communist state. It was a role she had accepted. It had given her solace, a place, and power.

But now Judit looked through the rifle scope, through the windows, to a family bathed in warm light and felt regret. In the years she'd been in Palestine, Judit had been a willing assassin for the cause. But confronted by the reality of destroying a family at the moment of its triumph, in order to prevent nothing more than a political possibility, she hesitated.

And in that hesitation, she became the family's other daughter—a sister to the young man and the two beautiful young women seated at the table. The professor and his wife could have been—should have been—her father and mother. She should have been in this family, talking about politics and philosophy, history and religion, listened to, respected, admired, and loved. This should have been the family in which she had grown and been nurtured.

Judit saw in that house everything she would never have. Tears began to well up in her eyes, clouding her vision. Years of hiding secrets, of frustration and of pent-up anger, of lying to Shalman, the man she truly loved, and missing her daughter, Vered, who was growing up without a mother, absent for whole days at a time. Judit breathed deeply, trying to steady her emotions. She blinked away a tear as if trying to blink away years of a childhood filled with fear. Her mind floundered and stumbled, but her body remained committed, her hands mechanical. She held her breath, fixed the crosshairs on Professor Durace's head, and slowly squeezed the trigger.

She heard the shattering of the window, but for once she did not look at the scene to check her work. Tears cascaded down her cheeks at the awful reality of what she'd done. Who she was suddenly struck her in the gut. So much killing, so many lies, so manifold the deceptions. She felt that she was drowning in a pool of quicksand. She could barely breathe.

Judit turned on her heel before the screams of the family inside the house reached her ears. She walked quickly away from the garden into the street, buttoning up her overcoat to conceal the weapon.

Judit's rapid escape, however, didn't go unnoticed. Ashira watched her retreat up the road and then into the main street where men and women had, until the shooting started, been dancing and singing at the recent news.

Ashira had followed Judit when she left the meeting. She hoped to accompany her, to learn from her, to be near the woman she so admired in a world dominated by men. But what she saw had shattered her confidence, and she found her hands shaking with nervousness once more.

What in God's name had Judit just done? Why had she fired a bullet into that house, a Jewish house? No, it couldn't be a Jewish house. Surely! Yet on the post at the front door, quite clearly displayed for all in the street to see, was a large mezuzah, the box that carried part of the Jewish prayer, the identity of a house where Jews lived.

The village of Ras Abu Yussuf

First week of December 1947

SHALMAN STOOD IN front of the crowd of Arab men gathered in the center of the small village and felt his hands shake. The sun was not hot, the air had a crisp edge, yet he sweated. Many of the men knew him, some even seemed to like him from his time spent in the village with Mustafa, but most were attuned to the direction the political wind was blowing and looked upon him as the enemy. But he had been brought to the village as a guest of Mustafa, and for now they watched him coldly but respectfully.

Just a few short days ago Shalman had been home alone with baby Vered in their small apartment in Jerusalem. With the child asleep in the other room, he had sat alone and listened to the radio, as all the peoples of Palestine did that day, while the votes from the United Nations were announced over the radio. Where others had gathered in hotels and restaurants and on street corners, in groups and crowds, Shalman sat alone and in silence.

He had felt his life was lived on quicksand. Where once his footing had been on solid earth, it was now insecure. Faith in the cause and the fight of Lehi, revenge for his father's disappearance, haunted by the stories of those who had fled Europe and had nowhere else to go but a land under oppression and beset by enemies—these were the things that had made his world clear and solid. Falling in love with Judit had only cemented that footing further . . . until now.

He had sat by the radio, listening to the count of countries and their votes, and wondered where his wife was. Other families were together on such a momentous night for the nation, but where was she on this night? What cause did she serve? How many lives would

she take? Shalman thought again, as he had so often, of the Arab boy
on the airfield runway.

He turned to Mustafa standing beside him and whispered, "I
think this was a mistake."

"Probably," said Mustafa with a shrug.

The village headman was speaking to the group, but his words
were clearly for Shalman, saying nothing that the crowd didn't already know—that Arabic radio from Cairo, Amman, and Damascus
was calling for Arab unity in the face of United States and Zionist aggression; that the armies of the Arabs were ready to invade Palestine
and push the Jews into the sea so that all of the Middle East remained
under the shield of Islam.

The headman was no firebrand but spoke in calm, deliberate
tones, and Shalman could see the genuine worry that creased his
brow. The village was close to Jerusalem and, should war come,
would be clearly boxed between Arab and Jewish armies.

When the headman finished speaking, Shalman was about to
rise, but he stopped as Mustafa's father, Awad, got to his feet and ascended the platform. For such a mild and gentle man, his voice was
surprisingly strong.

"This is our home, as it was home to my parents, their parents,
and those generations who came before us. It is small and it is poor,
but it is ours. There have always been occupiers. Before the British, it
was the Ottoman Turk; before the Turk, many others. And then the
Jews arrived in large numbers, and today our land is still our land, but
our neighbors have changed once more.

"I know that many of you hate the Jews, but perhaps that is because you don't know them. My son Mustafa brought home a young
man, badly injured and perhaps about to die. A man born a Jew. But
the Koran demanded that we give him comfort, and by the grace of
Allah, he recovered and prospered.

"Allah is great and merciful. So when this young Jew stands before
you to say what he has to say, I ask you to listen to his words. Because
more than any other Jew, he has proved himself a man of good faith.
He made a promise to my Mustafa that he would help him in his education, and he has been true to that promise. He is a man of trust."

Awad nodded to Shalman that it was his time. He stepped forward to face the congregation of Muslims. He cleared his throat, hoping he wouldn't sound too nervous, hoping that his knowledge of idiomatic Arabic would prevent him from making a linguistic mistake.

"I come here in peace. I come here on my own. Nobody has asked or told me to come. I am here because much is being said about what's happening in Palestine. Some of it is true, but much of it is false and causing trouble between our two people, between Muslims and Jews . . ."

In truth, Shalman had not prepared what he was going to say. There was no plan, just a need to speak. A conscience within that compelled him.

"This should not be a question of blame. There's enough blame for everyone. Too much blood has been spilled already. But if war comes, there will be much more. Too many tears and too much suffering.

"The land is to be divided, a homeland for each of our peoples. The Jews have not had a home in two thousand years. This," he said, pointing down, "is the homeland of Abraham, forefather of both our peoples. It is where Moses and Aaron stood. It is where the armies of Mohammed, peace and blessings be upon him, were sent to spread the light of Islam. It is a home rooted in the past but belonging to the present. Our present. When the United Nations votes to create Israel next door, then your people, too, will finally have a home that is not controlled by an overlord from far away but governed for yourselves.

"But there are those who would tell us to hate. We are both the children of Abraham, and if we listen to those voices, the hatred will become louder and louder until nobody can think clearly.

"I've come here today to ask you to shut your ears to those who will drive you to destruction. If your village of Ras Abu Yussuf, and a hundred villages like it, will shut their ears to the hysteria that surrounds them, if you'll see the opportunity for both of our peoples to live side by side and share the wonders of this land, then there's hope that there will be no more bloodshed.

"The United Nations will send people to inspect the land, to see how we live together, to decide how the land should be divided. And when they do, there will be those on both sides who push for violence and killing and chaos. Why? Because each side will try to prove they are entitled to all the land. This is the case for both of us, Jews and Arabs. The madmen on both sides will try to prevail.

"If we don't participate, if we don't listen to the voices of hatred, if we don't take up arms, then there can be peace upon us all."

They were all the words he had. There was nothing left for Shalman to say. He looked at the audience. Some were listening, others were showing signs of growing anger, still others were drifting back to their homes. It was what he had thought would happen, but he had to take the risk.

•   •   •

Later, when everyone had dispersed, Shalman sat on the ground under an olive tree with Mustafa.

"Well, at least they didn't stone you." Mustafa's desert-dry humor carried not even a hint of a joke.

"Do you think they were listening?"

Mustafa gave his trademark shrug. "Perhaps."

"I know so little of your people. All I hear is the anger and rhetoric and hatred. But that's not here. It's not in you or Awad."

"We're a tribal people. Family binds and defines us—brothers and cousins. The things that make us angry are personal, not political." Mustafa stopped and reached up to pull a leaf from a low branch, seeming to take time to ponder what he might say next. "A boy was at a British airfield begging fuel from the soldiers. His name was Munir. There was an attack by the Jews, an explosion, a bomb, and the boy burned alive. This was in the mind of the village when you spoke . . . Not war, not the United Nations. They were thinking of a boy who should not be dead. And now they are angry because that boy was a cousin to one of the men who was listening to what you were saying, Shalman. You were talking about the United Nations; we were thinking about one of our cousins; everyone hates the Jews because his murder has come home to our village."

The words cut Shalman like a surgeon's blade.

"I know you fight the British, Shalman. Did you know about this?"

Shalman lifted his gaze to meet Mustafa's. "No," he lied.

Ten miles away from the village, Shalman's daughter was being minded by a young student who lived in the apartment block three doors away. The girl's arrival had enabled Judit to go to a meeting in a house that was a twenty-minute walk away.

Judit hadn't been to the house before; it was a safe house, probably owned by a Russian who harbored empathy for the motherland, and who had taken his family out to a meal in a good restaurant, paid for by Anastasia Bistrzhitska.

When Judit arrived at the house, she knocked on the door. It was opened by Anastasia. Dressed in a tight sweater, pencil-slim skirt, sheer stockings, and high heels, she looked like she was going to the theater.

Anastasia quickly closed the door after Judit and reached for her hand as she led her down the hallway into the living room, where the curtains were tightly closed. The two women sat down on opposite chairs, a table full of coffee and cakes between them.

"A celebration?" said Judit.

"Judit, my dearest, the first part of your mission is at an end. It has been conducted faultlessly. We couldn't have asked for more. Many potential obstacles eliminated. And all without raising any eyebrows." Anastasia gave Judit a sly and flirtatious wink. "You and your comrades are to be congratulated, my dear. Your leadership, your inspiration of the agents under your command, your control of their activities, has been extraordinary for a woman so young. And it has been noted at the very highest levels of the Kremlin."

There was a time when such praise would have made Judit proud; they were words she had lived for and silently dedicated every action to achieving. But now, as Anastasia looked at her and sat so close, Judit felt empty. The image of the professor through the window, his head in her gun sight, was seared into her mind. All Judit did was nod.

"Darling! Is something wrong?"

Judit shook her head.

"I've known you since you were little more than a child. In many ways, I made you. And so you cannot pretend with me." Anastasia leaned across and put a gentle hand on Judit's knee.

"I'm fine. I'm just tired."

"Of course you are, my dear. You are leading many lives at once."

"I'm one person for my husband and daughter, one for the fighters in Lehi and the Irgun, and another for you. Sometimes I can't remember which face I'm wearing."

Anastasia smiled. "Your true face is here. With me. A Russian face. Loyal. Strong. Resolute. This is who you are. Who you have always been." Anastasia leaned back and sipped her coffee. "I remember the day I took you to meet Comrade Beria. I've seen grown men faint at the thought of meeting him. But not you. No, no. You squared your shoulders, stood up straight, and faced him. It was at that moment, my little dove, that I knew you would go to great heights. And it's those heights that I've asked you here to discuss."

Anastasia took another sip of coffee while observing Judit carefully. Her years of training in the manipulation of people told her that something had happened in the weeks since they'd met last, and her protégée was at a turning point. Handled poorly, Anastasia knew, this valuable woman might be lost.

"But there's more, isn't there? Tell me, darling Judita, what's the matter?"

Judit was no longer staring at her Russian controller but at the table; then at the window, through the curtains, and beyond at an unseen vista of bloodied bodies and hatred in the streets. "Just tired," she repeated.

But Anastasia was not so easily dissuaded. Putting down her coffee, she leaned closer, elbows on her knees, to take one of Judit's hands.

"Is it the killing? Or the lies you have to tell?"

Judit knew they were the words of someone who once felt as she did, someone who knew and understood, someone who had also looked down the barrel of a rifle to kill a man she never knew.

Judit's body deflated, as though all the life had drained out of her. "I don't know. I truly don't. I know what I'm doing is for the good of our future, but the cost is so great. I wasn't born a killer; that's what I had to become. And I wasn't born a liar, but I no longer know when I'm telling the truth."

And then the dam broke. It started softly, with a catch of breath. Then a gasp of air, and the tears began to flow, and Judit was sobbing, burying her face in her hands, crying like a baby. Anastasia held her tightly, like Judit's mother used to hold her when her father came home in one of his drunken rages.

Through her sobs, Judit said, "I miss my baby. I hardly know Vered."

"You are not alone," Anastasia whispered. "And you are not weak. It happens to all of us." And then she hit on a brilliant idea. "Darling little dove, we're going to take a trip: you, me, and Vered. We're going to get out of here."

"A trip? Where?"

"To Moscow. It is time your little one saw the motherland. It's time your parents saw their granddaughter. In this way, you'll feel like the mother you deserve to be."

Anastasia paused, letting the idea settle in. Then she said softly, "And when you're there, my dove, when you're removed from the fighting and the murder, when you walk in Gorky Park and along the Moskva River and look at the domes of St. Basil's, and when we're sitting in a café sipping coffee and there's no gunfire, just happy Russians enjoying life, then you'll begin to feel like the old Judita, the young woman who is going to run for the Knesset, and who, one day, will become prime minister of Israel. Yes?"

Judit looked at her in amazement. "Prime minister?" She burst out laughing, but Anastasia's face was serious. "You're joking, aren't you?"

Anastasia smiled slyly. "I'm Russian. I have no sense of humor. You're destined to be prime minister of Israel. It's part of our long-term planning. And Comrade Stalin himself is looking forward to meeting you and discussing your political path."

PART THREE

PART THREE

Cathedral of Clermont, Auvergne region of central France

November 27, 1095

HIS KNEES ACHED from three hours of prayer on a freezing stone floor. When Otho de Lagery, revered by much of the Catholic world as Pope Urban II, rose to his feet, his sacristan and his confessor rushed over to grasp him under the arms and aid his standing.

Pope Urban was successor to Pope Victor III. His predecessor, who had spent most of his time hiding from the papacy in a Benedictine monastery in Monte Cassino, had been faced with many of the same problems that now beset Urban: troublesome monarchs such as Henry IV and their contesting of Rome's control, wars with Germany and France, and even rival false, self-declared popes.

Had his thoughts been confined to these problems, Urban might have been more composed. But recently, his worries had been compounded by a letter from the Byzantine emperor in Constantinople, Alexios the First Komnenos.

Komnenos was the successor to the Caesars of the Eastern Roman Empire and, in his correspondence, had begged Urban to send help in repelling the invading Seljuk Muslim Turks.

It was his role as pope to hear the will of God. And when no voice was forthcoming from the heavens, it was his role to decide the will of God. But divine directives could have practical and political outcomes, and in the letter from Constantinople, Urban saw an opportunity to galvanize the warring and fractious children of Europe into something more coherent.

What was required was a common cause. The defense of Constantinople would be the beginning, but Urban saw a larger prize that could empower the Church to levels it had never known. Once their mission had been successfully completed in Constantinople, the armies motivated by the Church would march on to Jerusalem and free the holy city from the contemptible grasp of the Muslim heathen.

• • •

For two months past, Urban had let it be known through the complex but highly effective communication system that was the Church hierarchy, that when the Great Council met in session, he would make a pronouncement that would change the course of the world.

People had come, in hundreds and thousands, to hear his words. Knights and barons, ladies in their finery, and peasants from the fields. So vast was the crowd assembled in Clermont that fitting them into the cathedral would be impossible. Instead, Urban ordered the construction of a huge platform in the fields behind the church from which he would make the proclamation that he had spent so many hours on his knees formulating.

As the sun began to climb to its zenith above the wintry horizon, Pope Urban II left the home of Bishop Guillaume de Baffie, where he'd been staying, and walked the short distance toward the field and the platform through the massive crowd that had formed.

Urban was surrounded by his ecclesiastical servants, carrying his shepherd's crook, with his chaplain carrying before him an open illuminated manuscript of the Gospel according to St. John. Surrounded by the trappings of his station, Urban knew that he was an impressive figure. His vestments were of the very finest silk from China, gold thread made by Italian craftsmen and sewn into the chasuble by the sisters of the Nunnery of the Virgin of Madrid, a miter in the form of a triple crown. To all who saw him, he was, on earth, the representative of the Father, the Son, and the Holy Spirit.

Urban climbed the steps of the platform, his gown dragging on the wood in soft folds hiding his feet so that he appeared to float upward. Spread before him were representatives of the greatest of all the kings and rulers of Europe and their retinues, surrounded by swaths of loyal peasant Christians. The crowd slipped into a hush, and people fell to their knees and crossed themselves.

A huge illustrated Bible had been placed on a lectern upon the platform, open at the page of the prophet Micah, which Urban would take as his text. Elevated far above even the tallest peasant, Urban could see how huge the crowd was, and hoped that his voice would carry to the back.

He'd made notes about his speech but instead trusted God and his memory that he wouldn't need to read what he was about to say. As a man who sought out the pleasant company of actors when he was appointed the papal legate in Germany a decade ago, he'd learned how to hold the attention of an audience, how to pause to make them concentrate, and how to stress his words.

And so he began, reading from the great book before him.

"For behold, the Lord comes forth from His place, and He shall descend and tread upon the high places of the earth. And the mountains shall melt under Him, and the valleys shall split, as wax before fire, as water poured down a steep place. All this is because of the transgressions of the Jews and the Arabs, and because of the sins of those who do not worship Jesus as the Son of God."

He looked up from the text and shouted, "Brothers in Christ, I speak to you today of a grave matter. Not a matter of the flesh, of kings, or of governance of our Holy Roman Congregation. But today I must address you all, even the most lowly among you, the congregation of the faithful, concerning the very survival of our mother Church itself."

When his words settled on the multitude, he heard gasps and even some cries from deep within the audience. It was a good reaction. The weather was freezing cold, yet there were no murmurs of dissent. All had come from far and wide to hear his voice, and like an actor delivering rehearsed lines from a morality play at Easter, he waited for a reaction.

"The Muslim is now at our door; the very Saracen himself, with his vicious scimitar and his leering countenance, killing and maiming in the name of a false god, spreading like the very plague through the lands of the East. And how long, brothers and sisters, will it be before he is here—in Rome or Paris, Hungary or Bavaria, even Clermont it-

self, raping and killing and forcing your children to bow to his prophet
in his mosque? To turn aside from the true cross of Christ and instead
worship the evil crescent of Islam, a pointed thing like the horns of a
devilish goat."

There were screams of fear. Had he gone too far? He looked at
the three hundred clericals who had accompanied him and saw that
they were looking at him in horror. Good. He had their attention. He
looked beyond them, into the crowd of thousands, and was pleased
to see that they were terrified.

"The Muslim is knocking on our door in his wild and unruly
haste, and he desires to take our house, our chattels, our very God
and Almighty Jesus himself. So now, today, you must apply the
strength of your righteousness to issues that involve both yourselves
and Almighty God directly. For your brethren who live in the East are
in urgent need of your help, and you must hasten to give them the aid
that has often been promised them. For the Turks and Arabs, the Saracens and the Seljuks, have attacked them and conquered much
Christian land. They have killed and captured many and have destroyed the churches and devastated the empire. If you permit them
to continue in their pagan brutishness with impunity, then they will
take this as a sign of our weakness, and they will be heartened and attack even more of the faithful of God.

"Because of this, the Lord beseeches you as Christ's heralds to
publish this everywhere and to persuade all people of Christ to raise
up their arms, sharpen their swords, carry aid promptly to those
Christians living under the threat of the Muslim invaders, and destroy that vile race who has stolen the lands of our Lord."

The air seemed to be heating up before him as the fanatics who
inhabit every group of sane men began to whip up their brothers.
Urban saw before him the beginnings of a frenzy. This was good, but
he would need the dukes and the earls, the kings and their knights, to
galvanize the forces of the Church.

"We must raise an army and create a new pilgrimage to go to
Constantinople and then on to Jerusalem and rid our lands, our holy
lands, of this plague among mankind. I will call this pilgrimage a

Crusade, named after the very cross on which our Christ suffered for our sins."

Ever the strategist, Urban knew that war needed to make promises to those who partook in it; war needed to speak to both greed and aspiration.

"Let those who have been accustomed unjustly to wage private warfare against the faithful now go against the infidels and end with victory this war that should have been started long ago. Let those who for a long time have been robbers now become knights. Let those who have been fighting against their brothers now fight in a proper way against the barbarians. Let those who have been serving as mercenaries for pay now obtain the eternal reward. Let those who have been wearing themselves out in both body and soul now work for a double honor. For all who join in my Crusade and wear the cross of a fighting pilgrim, for those who take up sword and lance, bow and arrow, and fight against the heathen, you will be absolved of all your sins, and when you die, you will pass through the golden gates of heaven and live an eternal life."

And now the crowd was his. The ruling class saw in the Crusade power and profit; the masses saw advancement and absolution.

"Some of you may ask by what authority I call you and your congregants to arms. To those who dare to question me, I say that it is I, Urban, by the Grace of God Almighty, pope and pontiff and vicar of Christ, who commands this. For in my prayers I heard the voice of God demanding the cleansing of His house in Jerusalem. And so I say to you *Deus Vult!* God wills it."

As one, the three hundred clerics, scores of dukes and kings' envoys, and thousands of laymen and -women fell to their knees on the frozen ground, their voices reaching to heaven, and shouted aloud, *"Deus Vult!"*

• • •

Deep in the crowd were two white-haired men, bent from a lifetime of service. They fell to their knees with the crowd, but they were not Christians. Jacob and Nimrod were Jews in the service of the duke of

Champagne, Meaux, and Blois. They were listening to the pope at the duke's request and were to report back to him.

As they knelt on the ground with the echoes of *"Deus Vult"* around them, they looked at each other, fear for the future clear on their faces.

Moscow, USSR
1947

WHEN SHE WAS dragged out of her class in the basement Hebrew school, she was Judita Ludmilla Magidovich, daughter of Abel Abramovich Magidovich and his wife, Ekaterina Davidovna Magidovich. Six months of training in Moscow and Leningrad transformed her into another person, one called Judita Magid, daughter of Muscovites who had escaped the Stalin regime and who was making her way out of Russia, south to Palestine and a new life.

It had been no direct route. To ensure that her travel documents held up to scrutiny, Judita traveled from Leningrad to Moscow so that her passport and other papers were properly stamped, then by train to the Ukraine before a boat from Odessa, through the Black Sea, to Istanbul. From there, she'd traveled by train north through Bulgaria to the most northerly part of the Adriatic Sea and the international port of Trieste, where she presented herself as a Jew fleeing the aggressions of totalitarianism and the privations of a Russia bruised and battered by a murderous war against the Nazis.

In Trieste, she had joined hundreds of German, Austrian, and Polish Jews, and a menagerie of other nationalities trying to board a boat bound for Palestine. It had taken her three weeks of queuing, negotiating, demanding, and begging, but eventually, she managed to find passage with dozens of other refugees fleeing the remnants of war-ravaged Europe.

During that journey, Judit's intense training as a spy transformed her. She metamorphosed slowly and cautiously from an angry young Jewish girl, demeaned by a society that hated her, to a woman of stature, potent and commanding.

But since then, her identity had changed again. Today she was

Judit Etzion, a married woman, a mother, and a citizen of a Palestine that would soon become Israel.

As she pondered her reconstructions, Judit was struck that even her mode of transport had changed and seemed to embody the heights of her renovation. From cattle cars and leaky ships and waiting in long and interminable lines of people, to how she was traveling today, returning to Russia not by train or boat or car but in an airplane. The Russian Lisunov Li-2 was once fitted out as a light bomber, with explosives and machine guns. But the one Anastasia and Judit traveled in was made for passengers and felt like futuristic luxury to Judit. Nor was she concerned by leaving Shalman. When she'd told him of her decision to visit her parents and take Vered, he'd welcomed the idea. Having no parents of his own, he wanted Vered's only grandparents to enjoy the delights of the little girl. Silently, Shalman prayed that when she was in Russia, Judit would think back on her relationship with him and the joys that being in a family could bring her. He kissed her tenderly at the airport and wished her a wonderful visit to Moscow.

The journey took them by plane from the Tel Aviv airport to Cyprus, then to Ankara in Turkey. From there they'd flown to Sochi on the shores of the Black Sea, where they stopped for the night and had been given a very private conducted tour of Stalin's favorite dacha.

The following day, they'd flown directly north onto a concrete landing strip in a field near the village of Domodedovo, twenty-five miles south of Moscow. Here a ZIS limousine was waiting to pick them up. Traffic along the route was cleared for them by motorcycle outriders as they entered Moscow central. Their car skirted the wall of the Kremlin, drove to the right of the Bolshoi Theater, and came to a halt outside the entry to the Metropol Hotel.

Holding Vered, who was fast asleep in her arms, while porters scurried to take their bags, Judit looked around the marble columns and the grand ceilings of the famous and exclusive Metropol, then at Anastasia. "We're staying here?"

Anastasia smiled and nodded, whispering, "Yes, my lamb. And there are many other surprises for you."

Fifteen miles north of Jerusalem
1947

AS JUDIT AND Anastasia were being shown around the Metropol Hotel by sycophantic staff, sixteen hundred miles to the south of Moscow, Ashira sat on a low wooden bench outside a café in a western suburb of Jerusalem and waited, holding her breath because she was so nervous.

Weeks had gone by since the UN vote; it had also been weeks since Ashira had followed the woman she idolized, Judit Etzion, out into the streets of Jerusalem. The city had been infused that night with a mix of celebration and rage, yet what Ashira had seen made the city feel deathly quiet save for a single piercing gunshot.

The young woman, so eager and yet so naive, had spent the weeks wrestling with her conscience, wondering what to do with the knowledge she held, the thing she had seen Judit Etzion do. She'd been back to the house and confirmed it was a Jewish home. A home in mourning because, according to the British police, some Arab madman, furious at the UN vote, had gone on a rampage that night and shot the scion of the family.

Whom should she tell? What would she say? And the more she asked the questions, the more she felt doubt creeping in. What had she seen? Was it really what she thought? Perhaps there was a reason, a plan, that she was not privy to and could not understand.

Yet in the end it was the great weight on her conscience that she could no longer carry. It was then that Ashira had contacted the leadership of the Irgun and asked to meet with Immanuel Berin, head of the North Jerusalem division of the Irgun.

Ashira had been told to wait at the café until somebody came to collect her. The situation in Jerusalem had escalated into open violence between Arabs and Jews; shootings into cafés, roadside bombs, and cold, brutal attacks on the streets. As the British planned their withdrawal, the chaos was expanding. Attacking the British never sat well with Ashira, but fighting the Arabs with whom she associated all her hatred felt right. And it was this, perhaps more than anything, that had compelled the girl to speak up about what she'd seen that night. When the bullets of the Irgun should have been spent on Arabs, why had Judit Etzion killed a Jewish man from a Jewish family in a Jewish home?

The door to the café opened and Ashira was summoned to enter by a tall thin man who told her to follow him.

He pushed open a door at the far end of the café, and they exited to a laneway. He beckoned her into a car, which drove only two streets before depositing her in the garage of a nondescript house. The garage doors were closed immediately, and she was told to get out and follow two men holding guns.

Inside the heavily guarded house, she found Immanuel Berin seated behind a small and cluttered desk. In the corner was a fan panning slowly but achieving little more than dispersing the thick cigarette smoke more evenly about the space.

Ashira coughed.

"I'm told you have something important you wanted to tell me," said Immanuel. He was known as a direct man but also a cautious and deliberate one. Less the freedom fighter and more the methodical strategist than many of his counterparts. "I'm afraid that I can only give you a few minutes. Sit down." He gestured to a stool.

How should she begin? She'd been practicing what to say all morning, not wanting to sound stupid or hysterical. But now that she was confronted by one of the Irgun leaders, she was lost for words.

"I . . . I mean . . . I don't know whether I should . . . I saw a . . ." She devolved into silence.

Berin looked at her and forced a smile, trying to put her at ease. "You're pregnant?"

She looked at him in shock. "What? No!"

"You want to convert to Islam?"

Her eyes widened as she stared at him.

"Well, if it's neither of these, then you won't shock me. Just tell me what's on your mind."

She smiled. "I'm sorry. I must seem very stupid to you."

"Not at all. You seem nervous. So just start at the beginning, one word in front of the other."

She nodded. "It's about Judit Etzion."

Now he was surprised, but he remained silent, nodding and encouraging her to continue.

"I joined the Irgun in part because of Judit. She's such a hero in the movement. She's so brave . . . I . . ." Ashira stumbled again.

"Go on. What about Judit?"

Ashira swallowed and continued. "The night of the UN vote, I followed her. I just wanted to . . . I don't know. I followed her hoping that I could be with her, learn from her."

Ashira looked down at the table, unable to continue. Immanuel knew from the look on her face that the young girl was wrestling with a dilemma she desperately wanted to be free of. Before the Nazis and his arrival in Palestine, Berin had been a psychiatrist in Vienna. While far from a practical skill in times of war, it had nonetheless proved a valuable asset for a leader in understanding the minds of his people. He knew this was a moment when he had to remain silent, putting gentle pressure on Ashira to continue.

"She . . . I don't know why . . . I followed her. I was going to catch up, just to talk with her, be with her . . . but something made me hold back. I don't know what. She walked quickly, as though on a mission, but there was no mission for her that night. She was hiding in the shadows. Then she turned down smaller and smaller streets. And soon she came to a street with houses, Jewish houses. People had been celebrating. You could see people through the windows. They were all so happy with the partition news. And then I saw her go into a garden. She took out a sniper rifle from inside her overcoat, and then she . . ."

"She what, Ashira?" asked Berin, his voice barely above a whisper.

"She fired a shot into the house. In front of his entire family. She just stood there hidden by a tree and fired. She murdered the man. He was a Jew. A professor. Then she walked away. She didn't see me.

I just stayed in the shadows. I was stunned. I didn't know what to do. I could hear screaming from inside the house. The window into the front room was shattered. I could see his wife and children screaming. I walked toward the house and knew immediately that it was a Jewish house. There was a mezuzah on the doorpost."

Unable to continue, Ashira began to cry. She buried her head in her hands and sobbed. Immanuel looked at her and could understand her inner demons. The child was hideously conflicted. But he knew of the incident. Everybody knew of the murder of Professor Durace in front of his entire family on the night of the UN vote. And like so many, Berin had assumed it was an Arab attack. Or at best a stray bullet with no deliberate target.

Berin's mind began to spin. Judit? Judit Etzion? How could this be? Was Ashira mistaken? It didn't make sense. What was the motive? Why would Judit kill a Jewish professor?

"Ashira, you've done well to bring this to my attention."

Ashira verbalized the questions in his mind. "Why? Why would Judit do this thing?"

"I am a methodical man and we are a methodical people," said Berin, standing and putting a hand on Ashira's shoulder. "We shall not jump to conclusions."

"But I know what I saw." Her worst fear of not being believed rose up inside her.

"I don't doubt you. But we shall be methodical, and I will need your eyes for that, Ashira."

The young woman looked up at Berin, uncertain what he meant.

"I need you to be my eyes so we might learn the whole truth. And part of that learning is this must remain between us until we understand what happened. You mustn't discuss this with anybody—I mean anybody at all."

Ashira nodded, feeling a weight lifted from her shoulders now that she'd unburdened herself.

Metropol Hotel, Moscow, USSR

1947

JUDIT AND ANASTASIA sat in the dining room of the Metropol
Hotel in Moscow, with Vered in a pram. They were eating breakfast
on their second day in the city and marveling at the sophistication of
their surroundings. A harpist on the stage was playing for them. A
marble fountain cooled the middle of the room. Both women looked
up at the stained-glass ceiling high above them, painted with motifs.

To Anastasia, Judit looked like a country girl visiting the city for
the first time. "You know," Anastasia said, "Fyodor Shalyapin sang
here . . . right here. And Lenin himself made speeches here. And the
Englishman George Bernard Shaw stayed here and extolled the vir-
tues of the Soviet people."

"He was Irish," Judit said.

Anastasia frowned. "Irish. English. What does it matter? This is a
place for special people."

Judit looked around the room, examining the other diners. Many
of the older, more overweight men had young women at their tables.
Others had wives and children.

Anastasia lowered her voice. "They're party officials; some from
the provinces—they're the ones with their fat wives and snivelly kids.
The wives insist on coming to Moscow so that they can show off to
their friends back home how important their husband is. The others
are here with their 'nieces.'"

Judit turned to her handler quizzically.

There were times when Anastasia was reminded of how young
Judit was, despite the role she played and the things she had done in
Palestine.

"Prostitutes, my dear, although some of them, the taller, thinner ones, are ballerinas from the Bolshoi just over the road. The ballet is the zoo where our leaders go to find their next pet."

Judit looked shocked. "But prostitution is illegal."

At this Anastasia laughed out loud. "Yes, it is, my dear. But this is Moscow, and for some women, working on your back is better than standing in poverty."

"But the system should provide. For everyone." Judit's concern was genuine. Her memories of childhood poverty were always sharp, but now that she was back in Moscow, they were particularly focused.

"The system should provide. It can. But sometimes . . . not so much. There have been hard times since the war."

"Are people starving?" Judit asked.

"Not like in the winters after the Revolution. You were too young, but I remember the winter of 1932, when I was in the Ukraine. Seven million people were deliberately starved to death by Kaganovich, just so he could provide his Moscow masters with grain. They were dark times. I'm ashamed to say that we can't be proud of all the things the Soviet has done in its past, but things are no longer like that." Anastasia leaned closer almost conspiratorially. "But you and I are women, Judit. We're not like men. We're far more pragmatic and strong. So if it was the difference between hunger and cold and dining here in the warmth on caviar . . ." She sat back and cast her arms wide at the magnificence of the hotel. "I know what I'd do. If I were starving, then for a good meal, I'd let them have me."

Listening to these words, Judit found herself doing something she rarely did any longer: She thought of her family. Not Shalman and Vered but her parents and her siblings and the life she had left behind. She looked to the "nieces" laughing and smiling at the tables of privileged fat men and wondered if that might have been her fate. Was she as pragmatic as Anastasia was suggesting? If her father had died and left the family alone, what choice might they have had? In that moment Judit was struck by how sentimental she felt.

"This will be an exciting time for you, Judit. You are now in the bosom of Mother Russia; you are intrinsic to her success. And Russia intends to show you her love."

Anastasia went on to tell Judit of the important people she would need to meet with and the places she would need to visit. Lenin's tomb, the Alexandrovsky Gardens, the Kremlin.

"Why will I be going to all these places?"

Softly, Anastasia answered, "We have an enduring problem with our agents in faraway places. When they're training, surrounded by the symbols of their country, they understand the bigger picture. But holding on to that when they're operatives abroad is not so easy. This you know yourself, Judit. Agents in a foreign land sometimes become too integrated. You, my dear Judit, are too important for that. We have to ensure that you're not blinkered by the relationships you form in Israel. Not blinkered by your Jewish friends."

As though on cue, Vered began to whimper in the pram.

"Are you saying I'm blinkered by the love of my daughter and my husband?"

"No, of course you must love Vered and Shalman. But you must love your mother more. Not the poor woman who gave birth to you but failed to protect you from a drunken father. I'm talking about your real mother, Judita, the mother who loves you more than life itself, Mother Russia."

It had been two days since the reception in the palaces of the Kremlin. Judit had never seen such opulence and ceremony, and her former life in Moscow as well as her current life in Palestine both seemed alien that night. She had been made a Heroine of the State by Comrade Beria, and for the briefest of moments General Secretary Stalin had shaken her hand. In that moment, Judit felt more tiny yet more powerful than she had felt in her whole life. As the great leader's hand slid away from hers, she knew who she was, what she was—what her purpose was—without doubt or hesitation.

But it had been two days since the reception, and the power she had felt was receding. She was also, for the first time since arriving in Moscow, alone. Anastasia had left her to attend meetings, and Judit had time to walk the streets of the city she once called home.

As she pushed Vered in her pram along Vysheslavtsev Street, within sight of the synagogue, Judit's heart beat faster. These streets were so familiar yet so strange. Her life was now in Jerusalem. Her home, the roads where she walked, had their names in Hebrew, Arabic, and English. The Cyrillic Russian letters that she could read perfectly now looked strangely foreign. These potholed and filthy streets from another era seemed to belong to another person's life.

Then she looked at the men and women in the street. Post-war years of privation and austerity had been cruel to most of them. Their hollow-eyed and gaunt faces studied her as a stranger, a potential threat. Had she changed so much? Or maybe it was because she was well fed, tanned, and walking with upright square shoulders, while they were gaunt, dour, and bent in stature.

Judit walked without any conscious direction or decision about where she wanted to go, but her feet seemed to carry her until she found herself standing on the street of her old family home.

The building where she had been born was a house divided into seven apartments, each of one or two rooms where upward of four or five members of the same family eked out existence. Judit was struck by the irony: Moscow was ten times bigger than Jerusalem— Russia was a thousand times bigger than Palestine—yet here, everybody was squeezed into a living space the size of a cupboard.

Judit stood in front of the building, Vered cooing softly and wide-eyed from the pram, and looked up at the building and all its memories. She had no idea how long she stood there, but the trance was broken by a face. Judit did not remember the woman appearing and wondered in that moment if she had been standing in front of her all along.

"Judita."

Judit blinked at the sound of her name. The woman stepped forward.

"Judita."

Closer still she came, age and incredulity worn into her face.

"Judita?" No longer a name but a question.

Judit's mother, Ekaterina, stumbled as she walked toward her daughter, and Judit instinctively threw out her strong arms to catch her. The woman's body was bony and light as a feather. Ekaterina looked up at her daughter and said her name again with disbelief in her eyes. "Judita . . ."

• • •

A short time later Judit found herself seated at the tiny living room table of the cramped apartment with her mother standing before her. Judit couldn't help but remember her child self hiding under that very table all those years ago.

Her mother wept. Ekaterina knew, as did the whole community, that Judita had been taken away by the NKVD—taken from school when she was only fourteen—and never seen again until now. No one ever would have expected to see her again, so to her mother, Judit was a walking ghost, bringing as much fear as joy.

Judit expected to be asked where she had been, what had happened, but her mother managed no such words between sobs, so Judit instead asked after her siblings.

"Maxim works at the factory. He works so hard . . . Your sister, Galina . . ." Ekaterina didn't finish the sentence, and Judit wondered if her sister had been forced to sell herself to support the family, like the women in the hotel where she and Anastasia were staying. Judit left the question hanging and scanned the room for signs of her father.

Why had she returned? Was it to show her vicious, violent papa that, despite the fear she had lived through, she had grown powerful and strong? Was it to show her mother that there was a better way than weakness and appeasement? Was she here to prove something?

Ekaterina reached into the cradle to lift out the softly stirring Vered, and her tears ran anew.

"Her name is Vered," said Judit. "In Hebrew, it means 'rose.' When she was born, the roses were in bloom, and the air smelled like perfume."

"And her father?" asked Ekaterina in an apprehensive voice.

"Shalman," she answered, then added, "He's a good man," as if to allay her mother's unspoken fears. "Training to be an academic. A good Jew."

Ekaterina held the child close and sobbed. Judit found she had nothing to say. What did she hope to accomplish by coming here? Judit's mind was flung back to the day in the park when Anastasia had handed her a rifle and given her an order. The choice had been hers and she had made it.

Without thought or intention, Judit asked another question. "Where's Father?"

Ekaterina lifted her head from baby Vered's and stared with a great weight of sadness at her daughter. When she spoke, it was in broken sentences. "He is sick. These past years. Since you were taken away. Can no longer walk. He dribbles and can barely speak. In the hospital. The drink and the stroke . . ." She paused and swallowed. "He will die soon."

And the anger toward her father, her desire to confront him for the beast he'd been when she was a child, the very essence that had filled her mind and body in her adult life, and which had grown and grown and become the epicenter of Judit's persona, suddenly drained away.

Castle of Henri Guillaume
Duke of Champagne, Meaux, and Blois
1095

"*DEUS VULT*? THIS was the pope's decree! A Crusade and *Deus Vult*? God wills it! And this milk-livered pribbling hedgepig of a priest wants us to believe that he knows the mind of God!"

Henri Guillaume, duke of Champagne and count palatin of Meaux and Blois, bellowed as his servant dressed him in clothes for hunting. The duke wasn't angry, but he was aroused, and his barrel chest was more than capable of filling a cathedral with sound.

Nimrod took bombast in stride. The Jew was dressed in a fine doublet of blue and scarlet cloth embroidered with red and yellow stones to emulate precious jewels. On his head was his scholar's cap of wisdom, which failed to hide his plume of white hair, and he stood in the middle of the baronial hall holding the proclamation from the pope, his eyes scanning the text as he half quoted, half paraphrased, the text.

"His Holiness says that God spoke to him and told him to raise a pilgrimage, which he is calling a Holy Crusade. And that all men of Christian lands should gather and ride across the land east through Germany, then south to the Middle Sea, and then on to the Eastern Empire. There they will free Constantinople from the Seljuk and continue on to Jerusalem, where they will rid the holy city of the Muslim. He calls on all men to join him in this Crusade."

Nimrod looked up from the parchment and added from his memory of that day in the field: "A commandment from God demanding the cleansing of His house in Jerusalem. This is the pope's edict, my lord."

"And what do you make of this? What would a Hebrew make of such proclamations?"

"We're a naturally skeptical people. We've had many prophets but we tended to ignore them . . . or stone them . . . or banish them to the desert . . ." said Nimrod dryly.

The duke was not a man of intellect, but he was no fool, and smart enough to have kept the services of Nimrod and Jacob in his employ for many years, one as doctor, philosopher, and adviser, the other as treasurer, tax collector, and receiver of estate revenues.

Nimrod advised the duke on many matters but had learned to be succinct. This edict from the pope troubled him, and he found himself in the rare position of being unsure how to advise his master without lengthy debate.

Henri Guillaume, duke of Champagne, who hated priests more than he hated the king's tax collectors, shuffled on his stool beside the roaring fire and looked up in bemusement at his adviser as his servants struggled to put on the nobleman's left boot. Seeing the man in difficulty, the duke's liegeman pushed him roughly aside, picked up the boot, and slid it on his leg. The duke nodded his appreciation of his liegeman's skill as a dresser.

He turned to his Jewish philosopher. "I cannot refuse the order of the pope, or the king will have my bollocks for his dinner. But as a Jew outside the grace of our Lord, how would you counsel me, Nimrod? Should I gather my soldiers, draw my peasants from the field, and march on Jerusalem?"

Nimrod considered the words. Deep down he wanted to yell that the Crusade was folly, an absurd distraction that would reap destruction on so many. But this would never do. He needed a more delicate response that might steer the duke away from war.

"It will be expensive." Nimrod hoped this simple answer would speak to the material rather than the spiritual in his master.

"That cannot be a consideration when I'm commanded by the pope."

In truth, Nimrod was terrible with money. He was a seeker after wisdom, not a treasurer. He kept the duke's political alliances intact and treated him with mercury for venereal diseases acquired from the countless whores who shared the duke's bed. It was Jacob who handled the duke's finances and who had, through his consummate skill, made Henri Guillaume very rich indeed. Jacob, however, was old, and at times Nimrod wondered what might happen when the old man passed away.

"Jacob will give you a full account, but it is fair to say that this Crusade will be exceedingly costly. You'll have to equip your army, pay their wages, and feed them while they're away, and that could be for several years. And of course you'll have to employ itinerants to work the land while they're in the Holy Land. You must weigh the benefits against that cost."

"And there will be the benefit of plunder, but spiritual benefit is what is promised by the pope, is it not?" asked the duke as he pulled on his gloves.

"It is, my lord. The absolution of all sin for those who take up the Crusade. For what that's worth."

"It is worth a great deal!" bellowed the duke. "With all the whoring and sinning I've done, it's worth an eternity of sunshine!"

Feeling the comfort of the ancient seal, an heirloom passed down in his family from generation to generation, Nimrod gained sufficient strength to continue making his concerns apparent. He hoped that the duke was well humored before his Christmas hunt, so much that the philosopher risked a comment on the papacy. It was one thing for the duke to excoriate the pope but quite another for a Jew. "My lord, any Christian who obeys the dictate of a pope may find himself following the Holy Father through the gates of hell. Do you have to be reminded of the evil of previous popes to know that those whose arses warm the seat of St. Peter are members of a reprobate and execrable concatenation who follow in a line of mendacious, perfidious, and deceitful thieves and murderers, simonists, and miscreants. I need only mention the names of previous popes who have shat on the throne of Peter for you to understand how evil the papacy has become."

Without a pause, Nimrod continued, "John XII, who turned the Lateran Palace into a brothel and raped women pilgrims in St. Peters; or what about Pope Sergius III, who murdered Pope Leo V and the anti-pope Christopher and fathered a future pope? And let us never forget Pope Benedict IX, who actually sold the papacy itself. So if you're a true Christian, you would refuse to obey the dictates of this or any pope."

"Of course I'm a true Christian. And while there have been many Satanic arses and warty pricks who've followed the blessed St. Peter, this pope seems to be a good man, and he's probably quite correct. I'll certainly roast in the eternal fires of hell for the life I've led because of my whoring and hunting. Apart from those sins, I've lived a good life. I invite Bishop Fulk here every Easter and Christmas to enjoy my table. And I've extended my beneficence to you, a Jew."

"True," said Nimrod, "but look at the benefits that my presence has brought you. Scholars from across France and Italy and Germany come here to debate and discuss matters of the greatest import. Would they have come to the castle of Duke Henri Guillaume, even if he has the best wine in the world, without me being here? Think what my presence has brought to you, my lord. *Gloria in Excelcis.*"

Duke Henri laughed. "You know, there are times, Jew, when I truly believe that you should be burned at the stake. Yes, I think I'll have you roasted tomorrow, along with the pig I slaughter." The duke laughed again.

It wasn't the first time Henri Guillaume had made such statements, and Nimrod felt the license to counter. "Roast me if that is your wish, but not with a pig, I beg you. Think of the tenets of my faith!"

"But if I burn you, you'll be a light unto other nations." The duke laughed. He enjoyed making biblical jokes.

"And when I'm fully burned, my lord, my flame will wither and you'll be cast into the same darkness which surrounded you before I arrived."

Henri laughed again. "Enough of this banter, Nimrod. I'm off to the hunt. Walk with me to the bailey and help me mount my horse. And while we're walking, you can explain some things to me. Your people come from Jerusalem; tell me about them. If I am to take the city from Muslims and Jews then I should know something of them, should I not?"

"Indeed," answered Nimrod.

"And perhaps you can explain why you Jews don't hunt or ride horses or take part in tournaments. Why do you just study scrolls and manuscripts and books all day long? Why don't you ever seem to enjoy yourselves? You're a miserable lot. You know that?"

It was in such moments that the duke revealed traces of an intellectual curiosity that defied his gruff demeanor. As they walked out of the baronial dining hall toward the castle courtyard, Nimrod took some relief that the decision to go on the Crusade would leave behind him and Jacob to manage the estates. It would be a sign of trust and Nimrod found himself silently pleased at the prospect.

Nimrod spoke even as he quickened his pace to keep up with the long strides of the duke. "My family is reputed to have come from Jerusalem, in the ancient times of King David. It is said that my ancestry can be traced back to the time of King Solomon the Wise. My name in Hebrew is Nimrod, son of Isaac the Cohen. The significance of the term 'Cohen' means that the ancestors of my family were originally derived from the family of Zadok the Priest, who himself was descended from Eleazar, the son of Aaron, the brother of Moses. If this is true, and I have no reason to doubt my ancestry, then my forebears would have been priests in the holy temple built in Jerusalem by King Solomon of blessed memory. And that would have been two thousand years ago."

Nimrod absently touched the medallion under his shirt. It was an ancient piece of metal that had come down to him from his father and his father's father before him. It was said to have been cast by the stonemason of King Solomon. But how much of that was myth and how much truth, it was impossible to say. Yet the words on the seal around Nimrod's neck spoke volumes. An ancient Israelite named Matanyahu had cast a seal, which later had been copied. God only knew where Matanyahu's original seal was today.

Duke Henri looked at the Jew with skepticism. "Two thousand years? You can trace your lineage back two thousand years? God's blood, I can't trace my family back beyond my great-grandfather, winemakers who planted vines! As far as I know, they could have been peasants in the fields. Certainly, the bishop thinks I'm a peasant, the way he treats me."

"I've studied your family line, and I can assure you that what you think of your forebears is not so, my lord. When Hugh Capet was crowned as the king of France a century ago in the cathedral at Reims, your ancestors were already famous as vignerons and wealthy property owners. Soon after the Capet monarch visited, your family was ennobled. In this blessed region, they had been known for centuries by their trade as champenois. And though the line is indistinct, I have traced some of your family back to the time of the Romans, for it was they who planted these vineyards. So you have a long and proud ancestry."

And turning his head away from his employer, Nimrod whispered to himself, "Nearly half as old as mine."

"I heard that!" bellowed Duke Henri. Nimrod smiled to himself, but his mirth was snatched away as the thin and wiry shadow of Chevalier Michel Roux fell between him and the duke.

Roux's hair was copper-red, framing a ruddy complexion, pockmarked and deeply etched in lines. He was a bitter man, and his diminutive stature did nothing to dilute the cold menace in his eyes. Michel Roux was chevalier commander of the field to the duke and, in the coming Crusade, would no doubt lead Henri Guillaume's troops.

Roux looked Nimrod the Jew up and down as if appraising cattle for slaughter. Nimrod quickly looked down at his feet.

"Be away, Jew; the duke's hunt is to begin, and only men are required," sneered Roux.

Hearing the joke, the duke let out a small laugh. "Back to your books, Nimrod," he said. "And consult with Jacob. I shall need his full account of my assets before we set off on this Crusade."

Jerusalem
1947

SHALMAN WAS ALONE.

Judit was away with his child, traveling to Russia to visit family, and Shalman had accepted the lie with resignation. Alone, he wondered what other lies she'd told him; or what truth had ever passed between them. Suddenly, she had the money to travel by airplane back to Moscow! Did she seriously expect him to believe that? Why hadn't she just told him the truth? He'd accept anything, provided it was the truth.

He had a loaf of bread tucked under his arm as he walked toward his home. Where once he would have had his eyes perpetually raised to the golden dome of Islam, the crosses of the Holy Sepulcher, and the Magen Davids of the synagogues that watched over the city and the souls of its inhabitants, now his gaze was downcast. Shalman stared at his feet and heard little of the buzz of the city around him. He'd willingly agreed to her going to Moscow because he hoped it would save their marriage; but after she had left, her lies grew and grew in his mind.

He had not been back to the dig site, had not seen Mustafa, since the disastrous village meeting. Without Judit, without Vered, he was adrift, so Shalman walked the streets of Jerusalem feeling utterly alone.

His life had shaped his senses. Growing up under the dominating, suspicious, and armed glare of the British, he was ever alert to being watched. Years more of training under the tutelage of Dov and his indoctrination into Lehi had sharpened his awareness of people and events around him. And yet today Shalman walked with none of the muscular memory, the alertness, of the freedom fighter. He was alone and his senses were all trained inward. He did not see the man following him.

A thickset man in dirty overalls paced some five meters behind Shalman and maintained that distance precisely. His eyes occasionally shifted from side to side, but his focus never strayed from the target.

At a farther distance, a dark car, a British Austin 14, so dirty its black paint looked gray, trundled along the rough and pothole-riddled street. In the front seat sat the Irgun commander Immanuel Berin and, beside him, Ashira.

"That's him," said Ashira in a nervous voice. Berin didn't reply but brought the car to a slow stop. Berin didn't normally come into contact with lower-level operatives, but in this case, because it could involve Judit, one of the stars of Lehi, he'd decided to handle it himself.

"We'll take it from here, Ashira. You be on your way home."

"You're not going to hurt him, are you?" Her voice was hard.

"No. Of course not. We need to ask him some questions. We need the truth. And you have done well, my dear. You have done the right thing."

Ashira quickly stepped out of the car. Berin slid the car away from the curb again and quickly caught sight of his operative up ahead, still a precise five meters behind the unsuspecting Shalman. Berin waited for the cue.

The man in the overalls, who went by the name of Raffe, quickened his pace and slowly drew his left hand from his deep pocket. He held no weapon but would need his hands free. The gap closed to three meters and Raffe turned his head to the right to catch the dusty Austin 14 in his peripheral vision. He then drew his right hand out of his pocket and, with it, a small red kerchief, which he then stuffed, half protruding, into his back pocket.

Berin saw the movement and knew the signal. The car had been little more than idly rolling, but now he picked up the pace. Berin knew that Shalman was no ordinary citizen; he had been trained well and raised to fight, so he was not to be underestimated.

In ordinary circumstances Berin simply would have summoned

Shalman—sent a message to meet and fully expect that he would come. But with what Ashira had told him about Shalman's wife, and from what he had learned himself of Shalman's strange dealings with the Arabs, Berin did not believe his actions would be easily predicted.

Whose side was this man on? Where did his loyalties lie? There were too many variables, too many unknowns, not least the motives of his wife and the apparent murder of a Jewish professor. For all Berin knew at that point, Shalman was just as likely to disappear as cooperate, and he was taking no chances.

Raffe looked over his shoulder once more and then, with a small movement of his hand, flicked the kerchief from his pocket and transferred it to his trousers. This was the signal. Raffe took two quickened paces to pull up behind and to the left side of Shalman. Berin accelerated past, then reached over and flung open the door to the car while Raffe seized Shalman's arm in a tight grip and, with his shoulder, pushed Shalman bodily into the car through the open door and into the front seat.

So smooth and fluid were the actions that, before Shalman even knew what had happened, the car door slammed shut and the car had accelerated sharply forward. Raffe in the backseat behind him snapped a Hessian bag over Shalman's head and thrust the barrel of a pistol at the base of his skull.

"Don't move and don't make a sound and you'll be just fine."

* * *

When the bag was snatched from Shalman's head, he thought for a moment he was staring at the sun. The room was small and dark, but a bright lamp on the table where he sat burned into his eyes.

The violence in the air of Palestine, the killings and explosions, maiming and torture, kidnapping and murders, made all its citizens cautious. Whoever had pulled him off the street struck fear into Shalman's heart. In the landscape of Palestine today, his kidnappers easily could have been Jewish or Arab or British.

As his eyes adjusted, he found himself looking across the simple wooden table at Immanuel Berin. He quickly turned to see who else was in the room and any clues as to what or where the room was.

There was only one door; it was behind him, and in front of it stood a thickset man in dirty overalls.

All the obvious questions filled Shalman's mouth: Where am I? What do you want? But his tongue felt like rubber and he said nothing.

"Don't be afraid, Shalman. You'll have to forgive the means by which I brought you here. These are dangerous times, and I am an overly cautious man. You know who I am?"

"Yes. Of course," said Shalman. And then, finding a steadier voice: "I want no part anymore. I've left Lehi. My fight is over."

"Is it?"

After the airport explosion, Shalman had told Dov that he wanted no more and since then he'd had no contact with any of the Jewish resistance groups. But deep down Shalman had known it was never going to be that easy or simple.

"I have questions for you," said Berin.

Shalman found his strength in a rising anger. "It was the bombing I did at the airfield. I'm not coming back. I have a daughter. You could have called upon me, sent me a message. You didn't have to snatch me off the street! I would have come."

Berin pondered this for a moment. "This has nothing to do with you or your past, my friend. Maybe you would have come. Maybe not. But you say you're no longer one of us. So I have no guarantees, do I? A man in my position needs to be sure of things or else mistakes are made. And right now I am not sure of you, Shalman. You have left the fight, you consort with Arabs, and your wife—"

At this, Shalman's eyes flashed angrily. "What of her?"

"Have you heard from Judit, Shalman? Do you know where she is?"

Shalman was suddenly nervous and shook his head unconvincingly.

"We realize how much pressure the Resistance can be on a family," said Berin, looking sincere. "Young men with no attachments make the best soldiers. But married men with children and responsibilities—for them it is much harder. Not to mention mothers . . ." Berin leaned in closer over the table. "The loyalty of a mother can never be greater than to her child, no matter how noble the cause she fights for. Is this not true?"

"What do you want from me?"

"Your daughter, Vered, I believe. She is with your wife?"

Shalman nodded.

"And where are they, Shalman?"

"She's in Russia to see her family. It's where she is from. Surely you know this. Why are you asking these questions?"

"We're only concerned about her welfare. Have you noticed anything unusual or different about her recently? Her behavior? Where she goes? Who she sees?"

"What's this about?" Shalman demanded. "You don't kidnap me off the street to ask personal questions about my wife! What's happened?"

"Nothing's happened. Can you tell us a little bit about your wife and where she comes from? We know she's Russian, but we know nothing about her family. Who did your wife associate with here in Jerusalem? Outside of Lehi, what people was she friends with?" Berin turned a small paper pad around to face Shalman and placed a pencil on the paper with his other hand. "If you can write down their names . . ."

Shalman involuntarily picked up the pencil. "I don't know."

"Really? Think hard, Shalman," replied Immanuel Berin.

"I don't know!" Shalman's voice rose in frustration and he tossed the pencil across the table. It was not a lie; Shalman didn't know. "I never know where she goes. I assume it's missions for Lehi, working for the Resistance. But . . . I don't know."

Berin nodded as if he understood.

"Believe me, Berin, I don't know where she goes. I don't know what she does. I don't know who she sees," said Shalman, the words tumbling out of him.

Immanuel Berin found himself believing the young man. By all appearances, he was thoroughly decent and likable. He changed tack. "Shalman, we have great hopes for Judit's future. She is a woman of great courage and intelligence and very valuable to our cause. She's going to be a prominent woman in the new Israel when it is created. But in truth we know very little about her. And, well, if she is to play this important role, we need to know who she really is."

Shalman lifted his eyes to meet Berin's.

"You can help us with this. I don't want to doubt your loyalty. I want to trust you. Can I trust you, Shalman?"

Castle of Henri Guillaume
Duke of Champagne, Meaux, and Blois
November 1095

"HE HAS TO be stopped!"

Jacob rubbed at his forehead hard in desperation.

"Going on this pilgrimage will ruin us all. It's madness. And imagine the slaughter. Once roused, these armed peasants will crush everything in their path. I've seen it happen, Nimrod. I've seen marauders on a rampage!"

Nimrod looked at the old man and rolled his eyes at the hyperbole, though deep down he believed Jacob's words.

Jacob continued unabated. "Mark me, Nimrod. Innocent villagers will be murdered and their crops stolen to feed this multitude. They will begin their journey full of faith and prayers, and as soon as they run low on food and drink, as soon as they're tired and blistered, they'll turn their aggression on the innocents. They'll turn on us—"

"Don't be ridiculous!" snapped Nimrod. "The only ones who should be fearful are the Saracen."

"Fool of a man! Muslims and Jews are the children of Abraham. Do you think that Christians will see such a fine distinction when they're wielding swords and axes in a Crusade? And we will bleed just the same for their bloodlust. Does Jerusalem, home of our ancestors, really need an invading force of chevaliers and infantry? An army of madmen charging into the city? There is no peace at the end of such an invasion. By the bones of Moses, this is a bad idea."

For nearly five hundred years, Jerusalem had found a prosperity it had rarely known in the centuries before. Islam had exploded out of Arabia and conquered the northern lands of Africa, but under the rule of the Muslims, Jews, provided they paid a tax, could worship freely, as could those Christian pilgrims who could afford to do so. They had long been granted safe passage, and the walls of Jerusalem enclosed a harmony where the three faiths of the Book rested side by side.

But now, because of the declaration of a pope, a massive force was to be unleashed, and that harmony of common but separate belief was to be sundered apart.

Nimrod waved away the concerns of the old man. "In any case, you and I will not be going. What use are two old Jews on a campaign? No. The duke will leave us here to manage his estate, and this will be good for us."

"Do not be so sure!"

Nimrod was confused for a moment and looked at Jacob.

"The duke employs us, protects us; he finds us useful and productive for our knowledge and our skills. And our families, our children, are happy here. But don't be mistaken, my friend. The duke does not trust us."

• • •

Jacob felt that his fears were well founded when, late that afternoon, the duke returned from his hunt. With the boar that he had speared with his third arrow being prepared by the cooks, Henri Guillaume made his way through the halls of his castle, calling for Nimrod and Jacob at the top of his lungs.

The two Jewish men quickly made their way through the stone passageways to meet their lord and found him in an energized mood.

"I have hunted the boar and I have made my decision!" yelled the duke of Champagne, as if the two acts of hunting and decision-making were directly related, one dictating the other. He flung his gloves across the room, paying no heed to where they landed. "In the forest, with a bow and arrow in my hand, I felt a presence . . ."

The duke was not a pious man, and such language from their lord made Nimrod and Jacob uneasy.

"As I unleashed the arrow that slew the boar, I knew that this hand"—the duke held up his ungloved fist—"must wield a weapon against more than pigs and game." He lowered his fist and stepped toward the two Jewish scholars, his face beaming. "For my soul and my estate, we shall go on this Crusade!"

Nimrod made to protest but was cut short by the duke. "And you, both of you, will come with me!"

Moscow, USSR
Christmas Day, 1947

AS THEIR LIMOUSINE'S heating warmed the cabin so that it was comfortable for the journey to the airfield, Judit stood close to one of the tall stone pillars in the marble lobby of the Metropol Hotel and studied the important guests as they walked toward the elevator or sat in the deep armchairs.

It was a side of Moscow, of Russian society, that as a young girl she never thought she'd see, let alone be a part of. Often she'd stood in Red Square, in the shadow of the walls of the Kremlin, and gazed over at the Metropol Hotel, the epicenter of Moscow life, and watched as huge cars pulled up and the expensively dressed party apparatchiks and their wives emerged from the darkened maw, stood momentarily on the pavement as if they were American film stars parading to be admired, and then sauntered toward the brilliantly lit lobby as a uniformed flunky saluted and opened the doors to admit them.

She'd always viewed such pretension with distaste, but secretly, she'd envisaged herself doing the same thing. Then she'd take the trolley bus back home and walk through the potholed and muddy streets, the air redolent with the smells of cabbage and beets boiling away in a thousand begrimed kitchens, and all thoughts of how the elite of the classless society lived their pampered lives would evaporate. Yet only a dozen years later, here she was.

And the expensively dressed men and women who treated the lobby of one of the best hotels in Moscow as though it were their second home, draping themselves over the furniture, didn't look at her the same way they looked at Jews in the street. When she was a girl, venturing into the center of Moscow and walking along Tverskaya

Ulitsa or Varvarka or Bolshaya Nikitskaya Ulitsa, people had looked upon her with contempt. She didn't wear a yellow star as Jews did in medieval times, or more recently in Nazi Europe, but her Semitic looks branded her as a Jew. Even though Stalin had condemned Russian anti-Semitism, it was still the most prevalent and widespread prejudice of the Soviet Union.

How different things were now.

She glanced down at Vered, fast asleep on the floor in her little traveling cot, rugged up against the fiercely evil weather of a Moscow winter. She looked so innocent, so peaceful. What sort of a life would she have? Surely not like that of Judit herself, a living contradiction, one moment part of a warm Jewish family and the very model of a modern Israeli woman; the next aiming a sniper's rifle at some hapless Arab or Zionist or British soldier. No, Vered would grow up in a very different place.

Just a few days ago Judit had stood and looked down at the near comatose body of her father when she visited him in the hospital. She had felt all the anger and hatred evaporate. But she had also walked away, knowing that the door was closed and that her new life was free from that concoction of anger, guilt, and regret. She saw her father before her, powerless, and knew that she would never be powerless again.

There was a sudden movement behind her; Judit turned and saw Anastasia walking hurriedly from the elevators. Judit's smile disappeared when she saw how serious her controller looked.

"What's wrong?"

"We've been summoned."

"Summoned where?"

Anastasia smiled wryly. "The Kremlin."

Judit scooped up Vered, and together she and Anastasia hurried out the front door of the Metropol Hotel into the freezing, snow-filled, Moscow air. The limousine was outside, its exhaust creating a cloud of vapor behind the car.

Judit looked to the right, where the Bolshoi Theater stood proudly, white against the dark winter sky. They climbed into the car, and Anastasia barked an order to the driver.

It took them under two minutes to drive from the hotel, past Red Square, through the wall in the Alexander Gardens, to the private gates of the Kremlin Palace.

Once out of the car, they climbed the steps into the armory where they were met by an unsmiling minion dressed in a dark conservative suit. They were shown to an outer office on the second floor and instructed to sit and wait.

Minutes later, the door to the inner office slowly began to open. Judit's heart was beating fast in a way she couldn't explain. The presence of Anastasia should have quelled all anxiety, but in this monstrous building, it had little effect.

They watched the door open wider and wider, and out stepped a middle-aged woman whose gray hair was fixed in a bun at the back, and whose dark blue cardigan, long black skirt, and thick wool stockings spoke of a life devoted to being a secretary.

"You may go in now," she said.

Judit and Anastasia stood on shaky legs. Judit picked up her baby's cot, and together they walked through the door. Behind a huge mahogany desk sat a short, balding, bespectacled man, writing a note on a pad of paper. As they entered his office, he looked up and beamed.

Judit stopped in her tracks. The man stood when he saw them enter, came around his desk, his arms outstretched, and hugged each woman in turn, kissing each of them on both cheeks.

Vyacheslav Mikhailovich Molotov, foreign secretary of the USSR and second only in importance to Stalin, said, "It is a privilege to meet you both, especially you, Judita Ludmilla, our heroine of the Soviet Union."

Where Beria was a name to be feared by those who knew of him and the power of the NKVD, Molotov was a huge public figure. The man was on the front pages of newspapers everywhere, one of the most famous people in the world. His avuncular smile and genial manner belied a razor-sharp intelligence, a Machiavellian way of manipulating people, and an iron will to make the Soviet Union into the greatest superpower the world had ever known. He was regularly seen with British Prime Minister Clement Attlee and with Harry S.

Truman, president of the United States of America. And now he was calling Judit a heroine. Her head was swimming.

He led them to a couch opposite the window, which looked out on the multicolored onion domes of St. Basil's Cathedral. But no matter how extraordinary the site within a stone's throw of where she was sitting, she had no eyes for the view; her gaze was upon the man who sat in an armchair opposite.

"Let me first of all apologize to you for delaying your return to Palestine by asking you to come here. I know you were on the way to the airfield at Domodedovo village, but I wanted to meet you before you returned to the vital work you are both doing for us in the Middle East."

At the sound of his voice, tiny Vered began to whimper in her cot. Molotov looked down and smiled. "Do you need to feed her, my dear? There's a private office next door."

Judit smiled. "No, thank you, Excellency. I fed her just before I left the hotel. She will soon settle." Judit reached down, picked up her daughter, and gently rocked her on her shoulder.

Molotov smiled tenderly. "I have two grandchildren, you know. One of my great pleasures, something which I love and do far too infrequently, is to return to my hometown of Kukarka and cuddle my daughter's babies."

Anastasia, still dumbstruck at meeting the foreign minister, sat and listened, almost shaking her head as if this moment, indeed this entire occasion, were a dream.

"Fear not; the pilot will wait for you under my orders. I have for you a very specific instruction that comes direct from Comrade Stalin himself."

Anastasia was impassive, and Judit had no idea if what Molotov was about to say was known to her.

Molotov continued, "The removal of important and influential Jews who would oppose our plan can soon be brought to an end." He sat back in his chair, shifted his gaze, and seemed to change the topic.

"There are many people we have been watching in Palestine over recent years. Many of them will be well known to you. David Ben-Gurion, Yitzhak Shamir, Golda Meir, Menachem Begin . . .

"Shamir is currently in France after his exile in Africa, but be assured that he will return soon to Jerusalem, and we believe that when we put the proposition to him, he will support our plans. Even though he hates the Poles, he has shown a certain warmth toward Mother Russia.

"Menachem Begin is a different matter. I have my doubts. Before the war with the Nazis, our NKVD stupidly arrested him as a British spy and sent him to the gulags. He wasn't there long, but I think his internment may steer him away from us." Molotov's voice contained not a hint of sarcasm.

"But we have many candles burning brightly now in Palestine and none more brilliantly than you, Judita. I call you all candles, as it is you who will be a beacon of Soviet glorification in that troublesome and benighted region. And as you know, with warm and fraternal relationships such as we hope to have with a new government in Israel, our fleet of ships will be offered a permanent port in the Mediterranean, and will be an everlasting deterrent to the imperialism, expansionism, and colonialist hegemony implicit in the empire building of the United States of America."

Judit couldn't help but think Molotov was reciting some sort of prerehearsed speech. Surely she had not been asked here to meet with Molotov simply to be told what she already knew.

She could not help herself and spoke up. "Mother Russia is supplying both the Jews and the Arabs with guns and armaments. Aren't we in danger of alienating both groups by playing one side against the other?"

Molotov smiled. He'd been told of her sharp tongue and fierce intelligence. "It is in our interests for there to be war between Arabs and Jews, both before and after the British withdrawal. There are great advantages in this for us. Egypt, Syria, Jordan, Iraq, and Lebanon will inevitably launch armed assaults against the Jews, though we're assured by our man there that Lebanon will not participate other than to show Arab brethren that she's done something. Of course, this is all predicated on the United Nations voting to create Israel."

"But how does that benefit us?" Judit was genuinely puzzled.

"If there is full-scale war and Arab invasion after Israel is created, then the UN will be—how shall I put this?—encouraged . . . to ask us to place our troops between the two forces. America may be asked, but they will refuse because they've seen the mess that Britain made of it.

"By having our troops in Palestine, we'll outflank the Americans in Greece, Iran, Turkey, and control the entire eastern Mediterranean. It's what the Americans fear most, even though neither their feeble president nor their weary people have the stomach for another war. But Russia is not so weak-willed. And in the long term, there is always the treasure beneath the sand."

Judit did not have to ask to know that Molotov was speaking of oil. There was no oil in Palestine, but Russian influence there could shape the pipelines from the oil-rich nations of Arabia.

"You may wonder, Judita, why I am telling you these things now—surely things you already know."

Judit nodded.

The foreign minister leaned forward in his chair. "You will bring about the moment of triumph that we require . . ." Molotov shifted in his chair, almost for dramatic pause. "The most capable army in the region that can set itself against Israel is that of Trans-Jordan. However, we know that various Jewish leaders have been in discussions with King Abdullah and there is the distinct possibility that the Jordanians may withhold from any invasion. This is not to our advantage. We need insurance that such an agreement cannot be accomplished by the Jews."

Judit was aware that Molotov used the words "the Jews" as if she were not one, and she remembered what Anastasia once said to her: "Leave the Jewish girl behind. Be what you must be: a daughter of Russia."

Molotov continued, well used to speaking at length without interruption. "King Abdullah must be put under intense pressure from his people to go to war. Blood will bring about that pressure."

"Who, then, is the target?" asked Judit, racing through her mental files as she thought of prominent Arab fighters who might be targeted. Quietly, she found herself relieved by the idea that she would not be asked to kill another Jew or a civilian.

"In this case it is as much about how the target is removed as who the target is," Molotov said. "We need you to kill a man in a particular way. And not to be invisible but to be seen to kill."

Judit knew her confusion was clear on her face. "You want me to be exposed as the killer?"

Molotov smiled and shook his head. "No, you'll arrange everything; we want the killers to be visible and immediately known." He stood and paced the room as he spoke. "I assume you know Immanuel Berin? Regional commander of the Irgun?"

Judit was stunned but finally found her voice. "A Jew? But I thought you wanted an Arab target to bring the Jordanians into the coming war."

Molotov shook his head. "No, we want Immanuel Berin to die and the Jordanians to be blamed. We want the investigation of his death to show that it was a Jordanian army commander who did the killing. Because Lehi and the Irgun are tinderboxes, it will be the spark that will make them retaliate. They will commit an atrocity across the border, and it is this retaliation that will leave King Abdullah with no room to maneuver. He will have to go to war."

A field outside Paris

August 15, 1096

THIRTY THOUSAND FOOT soldiers, all wearing tunics with the cross of Christ emblazoned on their breasts, as well as ten thousand noblemen and chevaliers on horseback, had gathered in a vast army and now waited in fields outside the walls of Paris. They had walked there from all parts of northern France, from the lands of the Dutch, from Britain, Germany, and the cantons of Switzerland. As each group arrived, it was directed into the fields of assembly south of the River Seine. The gathering grew until the last cohort of soldiers, who came from a distant part of Bavaria, arrived.

On the day of their departure for the great adventure, they were blessed by Pope Urban, sprinkled with holy water by dozens of priests, provisioned with food and drink. They gathered, and despite different languages, dress, and foods, there was bonhomie in the fields. Their commanders, Raymond of Normandy, Godfrey of Bouillon, Raymond of Toulouse, Stephen of Blois, Baldwin of Boulogne, Robert of Flanders, and many others, sat in their separate tents with their priests and confessors, their treasurers and advisers, and talked at length about the campaign ahead, what rewards they could expect from participation.

Pope Urban had originally determined that the Crusade would leave for Muslim lands on August 15. It was to begin on the Feast of the Assumption, but holy madness had spread like a wildfire throughout the Christian lands, and the official Crusade of soldiers for Christ was preempted by a ragtag collection of some forty thousand men and some women, and many lesser noblemen and third sons of barons, intent on making a fortune denied to them by their birth. Inflamed with the divine mission of freeing Jerusalem, this rustic crowd of peasants, armed with pitchforks and clubs, set off in April from the city of Cologne, completely unprepared for the rigors of the journey or the reality of the armies they would face on the way. They were led by Peter the Hermit, who had whipped the mob into a religious frenzy. Anyone experienced in war believed few, if any, would return alive. Sadly, it was the cause of much laughter and joking in the fields outside Paris.

In the early morning, when their tents had been folded and packed alongside provisions and arms onto wagons, it took the entire army over three hours to file out of the fields and onto the road that led to the southeast. First to leave were the dukes, earls, barons, and attendant squires, who rode on wagons; then chavaliers on horseback, followed by foot soldiers slipping and sliding through the increasingly muddy grass, walking two by two in a line stretching as far as the eye could see. Citizens from Paris had come out to stand beside the road and cheer on the army of heroes of the Catholic Church. Girls dressed up in pretty dresses handed flowers to the soldiers.

In the first days of the march, while they were still close to Paris, the men would burst spontaneously into song at night. But as the weeks wore on, singing was replaced with shouting and fighting and then bronchial coughs and, at times, debilitating silence. Paris and their homes became a distant memory.

For their part, Nimrod and Jacob were well separated from the foot soldiers, but the stench the troops generated wafted on the wind. The two Jews slept together in a tent, erected by the duke's squires, and had comfortable straw rolls on which to rest from the exhaustion of the day's horse ride. The ancient seal, which Nimrod always put under his pillow, remained securely around his neck. Theft and assaults were commonplace. Being away from his chambers, he wouldn't risk some stranger creeping into his tent in the blackness of the night and stealing it. And so he went to sleep, his hand grasping the replica of Matanyahu's seal, made in the time of the Romans by a young boy named Abram, Nimrod's distant ancestor.

The village of Ras Abu Yussuf,
nine miles west of Jerusalem

THE STEEL WRENCH felt like it might snap in his hand before the bolt would loosen. Lying flat on his back in the dirt underneath the old truck, Mustafa pushed with all his might, but the nut was rusted tight. Exasperated, he tossed the spanner aside and laid his head back down on the dirt. For too many years he'd been able to keep the truck running, knowing the village was too poor to buy another. But as he lay under the vehicle in the shade cast by its rusted body, he resigned himself to the idea that her engine may never splutter again.

"Are you working under there or just hiding from your mother?"

Mustafa could just make out a pair of sandaled feet and slid out from under the truck.

Shamil was short and pudgy, with the scraggliest beard of any man in the village. He reached down and helped haul Mustafa to his feet.

"I think the truck's gone this time. Rusted through, and we don't have the parts."

"Allah will provide," said Shamil, but both men laughed at the unlikely idea that God had even noticed.

Shamil handed Mustafa a water bottle. "From your mother," he said grimly. Mustafa took the bottle and swigged deeply. "I'm surprised you're around to try and fix the old truck," Shamil added.

"Why do you say that?"

"So often you are out digging in the dirt with your Jew friend."

Mustafa shrugged. He had spent a lot of time with Shalman at the caves and had reveled in both the discovery and the learning that his friend shared with him. He also knew that the people of his village were talking, and the one thing nobody wanted to be in an Arab village was the center of gossip.

"Where is he? The Jew? Not seen you with him for some time."

Mustafa shrugged again. "Who knows?"

Shamil picked up the wrench and twirled it absently in the air. Mustafa sensed there was something unsaid and waited for Shamil to continue.

Finally, Shamil spoke. "Don't think the Jew is your friend, Mustafa."

Mustafa caught the wrench midair as Shamil tossed it up, and lowered himself to crawl under the truck once more.

"This is Palestine. I'm happy to call anyone a friend who isn't aiming a gun at me."

Shamil caught Mustafa's shoulder with his broad hand. "What about one who points bombs, not bullets?"

Mustafa pushed the man's hand away in annoyance. "What are you talking about?"

"I was there, Mustafa." Shamil hesitated, but looked Mustafa dead in the eye. "I was there that night on the airfield. I stayed outside. The British don't like Arab men, but they like our children. That's why I took little Munir with me. I sent him inside while I stayed outside on the edges of the airfield. I saw everything.

"I wasn't sure until he came to our village and spoke to us, telling us not to be full of anger when our land is carved up. But when I saw him, I knew. I knew it was him. I remembered his face."

"What are you saying?" asked Mustafa.

"Your friend the Jew . . . He was the one at the airfield. I saw him with my own eyes. He was the one who drove the truck."

Mustafa brushed away the half-formed accusation with a wave of his hand and pushed himself to the ground to continue his work. But Shamil stood over him, silhouetted against the sun.

"He was the one who set off the bomb that burned my cousin alive!"

"You're mistaken. You must be," said Mustafa angrily.

"Ask him. Ask your friend."

"I did!"

"And what did he say, Mustafa?"

Mustafa said nothing.

"War is coming. Our Arab brothers will be arriving soon with guns and tanks and planes, and your Jew friend and all the others will be driven out. Friends tell the truth. And Jews are liars . . . And soon they will be gone!"

Lydda RAF Base

December 27, 1947

SHALMAN DROVE THE borrowed car along the dusty road heading west, down the steep and winding road away from Jerusalem toward Tel Aviv and the sea.

He drove toward the RAF air base outside the Palestinian town of Lydda, where international airplanes had just begun to fly passengers into and out of the region. He was heading there to meet his family.

Soon after arriving and parking the car on an open field, he was searched by British soldiers. They went over every inch of his car, made him remove his jacket, and patted down his trousers. Almost begrudgingly, they moved him on. He and a dozen other people then waited in the Customs and Excise Hall, an unused aircraft hangar, for the transport plane from Turkey to land.

Shalman watched as the plane drew closer, transforming from a distant smudge in the brilliant blue sky to a giant metallic bird, feet outstretched, landing with a bump and a bounce. The propellers roared and spluttered as the plane wheeled in a wide arc before coming to a halt. Ground crew strode out to place large chocks under the wheels to hold the aircraft in place as the propellers slowed down.

Judit was one of the first to appear at the top of the stairs, which had been wheeled up to the fuselage. Shalman watched as she stepped into the sun. She raised one hand to shield her eyes while her other hand held Vered close to her body. Shalman walked out onto the grass and watched his family descend. His mind was fraught with mixed emotions. Love for his child, longing for his wife, yet fear, mystery, worry, and questions, always questions.

When Judit arrived at the bottom of the stairs, Shalman extended his arms and wrapped them around both her and Vered. They embraced without speaking. But it was a cold embrace and relinquished quickly. They hardly spoke to each other. Shalman's attention shifted straight to his daughter, and he scooped her out of her mother's arms and kissed her warmly. He turned to face Judit, but she had already turned to where the baggage was being removed from the plane.

• • •

Shalman reversed the car out of the grass field and steered it toward the road that linked Tel Aviv with Jerusalem and would return them home. Vered was in the backseat, resting in a cot. Judit sat next to Shalman in the front bench seat, staring out the window; the landscape seemed so foreign because of where she'd been, yet so familiar.

They said nothing for some time, each alone in thought, until Shalman broke the strained silence. "Did you see your family?"

In truth, he knew almost nothing about his wife's family and had no idea what to expect in her answer. But he knew that family had been her pretext for traveling to Moscow, so it was an obvious question to ask.

"Are they well?" he continued when Judit did not answer straight away.

"They're dead," Judit said, and the cold obliqueness of the answer surprised him. "They passed away."

"I'm . . . I'm sorry . . ." stammered Shalman. "I don't know what to say." He reached out his hand to take hers. "I'm still here . . ."

Judit was desperate to tell Shalman the truth. She wanted to tell him all she had done, all that had happened, all she must do. Of her meetings with Beria, with Molotov, her moment with Stalin when he'd walked into the room, smiled, shaken her hand, and walked out without speaking; of receiving Russia's highest civilian award; that she was being groomed for high office in the new nation, and with that came a past she must hide.

Judit's silence compelled Shalman to say something he'd been holding back until now. "Immanuel Berin asked about you."

The statement rattled Judit, but she held her gaze out the window, and when she spoke, she fought to keep concern out of her voice. "I thought you were having nothing more to do with Lehi and the Irgun and the fight. I thought you wanted to put that behind you."

"I do. I have . . . It's nothing."

At any other time, the mention of Berin's name would have been ordinary, but at this moment the name was more than ordinary—a senior leader of the Irgun and the final target for Judit under orders direct from Molotov himself.

"What did he want?" she asked.

"He just . . . He just asked how you were, where you had been . . ."

"And did you tell him?"

"I said you had traveled to see your family. That was the truth." The final word hung in the air.

Judit's mind raced over the things that she had done and said before she had left for Moscow. Why the hell was Berin asking about her?

"That was the truth, wasn't it?"

"Of course," she said, but her response was delayed a fraction too long.

"Why the hell are you lying to me, Judit? I'm your husband. Tell me the truth. Why were you in Moscow? What's going on in your life that you have to lie to me?"

He fell silent, praying that she'd answer with the truth and put an end to all his doubts. But after a long and painful moment of silence, she said softly, "I was visiting my family. Believe me, Shalman. Please believe me. But to find both my parents dead, without a word from my brother or sister . . . it was heartbreaking. I'm sorry if I don't meet your expectations, Shalman, but . . ."

They drove for ten or fifteen minutes up the hill toward Jerusalem in complete silence. Instead of thinking about how she was endangering the love between them, she thought only about Berin.

She thought back to conversations and meetings. But she was always so careful. She had been meticulously trained in how to separate her normal life from her clandestine life. She'd been taught to divide her personas into distinct compartments in her mind, to allow those thoughts and events to rise to the surface only when she was in control of her situation.

Even when she met one of her agents incidentally in the street, their eyes would never meet; they never faltered in their gait; they never turned after they'd passed each other. And yet they would completely recognize each other.

No, she thought, there was nothing that could have given anybody in the Irgun the remotest clue about her role. She had been so careful. Hadn't she?

Shalman knew he couldn't take the issue further without causing a catastrophe in his marriage. He had seen his parents' lives ruined by his father's arrest by the British. The people on the kibbutz had told him repeatedly that his dad was a hero who'd sacrificed himself for the lives of others. But Shalman had still lost his father, and the loneliness and yearning never left him. He had then watched his mother slowly sink and almost will herself to death from grief. Family dissolved around him, and he knew with utter certainty that if he pushed Judit too far, she'd walk out on him and Vered. And that was a lifelong trauma that he had no desire to ever cause for his beloved daughter.

Jerusalem
January 7, 1948

"I NEED TO be absolutely plain to you about the coming war."

Immanuel Berin spoke to the men and women of the North Jerusalem forces of the Irgun gathered before him.

"Our best advice is that when the UN vote for partition is passed, the Arab armies will not hesitate. They are gathered and well armed and have made their intentions clear. Their target will be Jerusalem. Jerusalem is a symbol, and it's been easy for Arab leaders to motivate fighters from abroad—from Egypt, Jordan, Syria, and Lebanon—to fight with that one target in mind.

"Should we fail to defend Jerusalem, then Israel will fall, no matter what other territory we manage to keep. If we lose Jerusalem, we've lost the war."

Berin knew he was giving a speech, but the men and women were listening intently. Nobody needed to be reminded why they were fighting.

"For the past six months, Palestinian Arabs have been conducting a guerrilla war against us, hoping they will frighten us away. Small targets: homes, businesses, kibbutzim. But this is not the real war and will not prepare us for what is to come. You've seen the map a thousand times. We are surrounded. North, east, and south, with our backs to the sea. When they come, it will be a massive pincer movement.

"The two armies that most concern us are the Jordanians and the Egyptians—the other Arab armies are not nearly as dangerous. The more medals the generals wear, the less professional they are. Not so the Jordanian army. It was trained by General Sir John Glubb, a highly regarded British military strategist who rose to fame as

commander of the Bedouin Desert Patrol. He has done much to galvanize Arab fighters, who are often more focused on internal tribal
fighting than external enemies. He's now commander of the Arab
Legion and effectively the Trans-Jordanian army, and we have to be
very wary of him.

"The Arab Legion is a serious force to be reckoned with. They've
got modern equipment and are well trained. They'll be a problem for
us and the Palmach. The other force that concerns us is Egypt. Egyptian soldiers are poorly trained and known to be cowards on the field,
but they've been whipped into an Islamic jihad frenzy by crazy members of the Muslim Brotherhood, and into nationalistic fervor by the
Arab Higher Committee. In case you don't know that one, it's led by
Mohammad Amin al-Husayni, Adolf Hitler's best friend. And one of
their best field officers, Gamal Abdul Nasser, is under his sway."

The young men and women looked incredulous at the mention
of Husayni's name.

"Let me just remind you of the real enemy we're facing. This bastard, the former mufti of Jerusalem, is a vicious piece of work. He
aligned himself closely with Hitler and led a vitriolic anti-Semitic political campaign before the war. He was expelled by the British, and
now that he's in Egypt under the protection of King Farouk, he's had
ample time to instill a religious as well as a nationalistic Islamic fervor
into the armed forces. They're being impelled to fight because they're
told that they have to free Jerusalem from Jewish hands, since Jerusalem is the third holiest site in Islam. Not so. Jerusalem isn't mentioned
once, not one time, in the Koran. Jerusalem becomes important to
the Muslim only when it's used as a political weapon. Remember
that when you hear Islamic war cries."

As he spoke, Berin knew he had yet to tell his men and women
about the biggest problem: that of logistics, which might well eclipse
any religious or strategic issues. The British had embargoed the im-
portation of more sophisticated weaponry to the fledgling armed
forces of the soon-to-be-created nation. Against British- and Russian-
supplied tanks, artillery, and aircraft, the Israeli forces would be
equipped with small arms. Or as Berin had dryly observed to his
other commanders, "kitchen knives and pitchforks."

Berin held nothing back. This would be a life-and-death struggle. Sadly, this was nothing new; many of these soldiers, two years earlier, had been refugees from the genocide of the Nazis.

• • • •

As the fighters were departing, Berin noticed Judit seated at the back of the room. He watched her stand and turn to leave with her comrades, but their eyes met for the briefest of moments. It was her look that Immanuel Berin pondered now as he sat at his desk and watched Ashira walk toward him and sit down. They were sitting in a schoolroom on the western side of the city, abandoned because of the fighting, but a convenient and usually overlooked part of the city where British troops or Palestinian gunmen rarely ventured.

The trepidation she once displayed so prominently now seemed gone. She had changed. The tasks he had set her had instilled confidence. And yet he felt profoundly saddened as she sat down because she reminded him of his wife now long dead in the Nazi concentration camp of Maidenek. Some women did remind him of his wife. He had long resigned himself to this burden.

"Well?" he asked.

"Since she returned, she's not put a foot out of step."

"She's met nobody?"

Ashira shook her head.

"Not in Tel Aviv when she went there? She didn't meet up with anybody?"

Again Ashira shook her head.

"Phone calls?"

The young woman shrugged. "Maybe from her apartment; I wouldn't know. She goes to Irgun meetings."

Berin nodded. "Of course." He paused. There had been many deaths in recent weeks but no one important, no one extraordinary. Perhaps his suspicions were misplaced. Perhaps Ashira was wrong.

"Why don't we just deal with her? We need to act," said Ashira, and her confidence and coldness worried him. Immanuel shook his head. When she'd come to him a few weeks ago, she'd been an ingénue, an innocent, an impassioned but naive kid. Now she was suggesting murder as though it were an extension of the life she led, a part of her normality.

"We do not yet have facts."

"I have facts, Immanuel. I saw her shoot that man in his home. In front of his family. I saw what she did. I know what I know."

Berin put a calming hand on Ashira's. "I understand. But I must be certain. Another agency could have instructed her; there might have been something about the professor that we don't know . . ."

She nodded, but her anger didn't subside.

• • •

Later, Immanuel Berin drove toward Tel Aviv to meet with someone he believed might provide insight. Though questions raised about Judit were pointing in a dark direction, one that terrified him, there was little proof.

He'd done his own investigations of recent violent Jewish deaths. Why had so many prominent Jewish leaders, intellectuals, militant politicians, and journalists suddenly died, many violently? Their murders had been blamed on the British army's extra-judicial way of removing troublemakers, or else rogue Arab gunmen targeting those who spoke out publicly. Even in a world of violence and a cacophony of gunfire, those who had been killed had not been gun-wielding members of the Jewish paramilitary but civilian firebrands, speaking to crowds, their only ammunition microphones and typewriters.

Berin had examined all the cases he could find, all those that stood out. And he had begun to see a pattern in the information. He'd managed to confirm at least six instances that put Judit in the vicinity or at least where her whereabouts could not be verified.

Before too long, Berin was sitting in the smoke-filled apartment of Avraham T'homi, an old mentor. T'homi was once a senior commander in the Haganah but now had little to do with the Jewish paramilitaries, angered as he was at their politics. He was nonetheless a man who understood the subterranean world of spies and spying.

T'homi believed in direct and immediate action and was called a wildcat by his colleagues. Some years earlier, he'd murdered the Jewish Dutch poet Jacob Israel de Haan because the man spoke out against violence and wanted a negotiated settlement between Arabs and Jews. Berin rarely agreed with T'homi's hard-line approach but respected his insight and experience enough to ask what might motivate such a woman as Judit and whether he was right in thinking that she was behind the murders.

T'homi's initial question was: "Where does she come from, where was she born?"

Immanuel told him she was Russian. T'homi laughed. "Then she's working for the NKVD, or the MGB, as they call themselves now. Put a bullet in her head," he said bluntly.

Immanuel was shocked. "But—"

T'homi waved away his protests. "I'm not being irrational, Immanuel. And I'm not leaping to wild conclusions. You're just not asking the right questions. No one does. It's why everything has turned to shit! How did she get to Palestine? Who did she come with? Was she alone, or did her family accompany her? When she arrived, did anybody on the ship know her previously? Was she invited to join Lehi or the Irgun, or did she just turn up one day and volunteer out of the blue? Has she been suddenly absent for any amount of time without her colleagues knowing where she was? Has she had meetings with people you don't know and recognize? Have you been following her and seeing with whom she associates? If the answer to these questions is that you don't know, find out. If the answer is yes, then put a bullet in her head."

The village of Ras Abu Yussuf

January 17, 1948

BLEAK-FACED, FRIGHTENED, BREATHLESS from walking eight miles through valleys and scrubland to avoid being seen by British patrols or Arab insurgents, Shalman Etzion finally crested a hill and saw the village ahead of him. He stood there for a few moments, drinking from the canvas-covered flask he'd stolen from a dead British Tommy in the days when he was in Lehi, and tried to see who was moving in the valley below.

It was the height of the day, and although the air was cold for January, the sun had a radiating heat. He took off his kova tembel hat and wiped his brow. It was such a stupid shape for a hat, like a pointed cone, yet it had become the national symbol of Israeli farmers, and now everybody wore one.

A few days earlier, not far from the village he now surveyed, a massacre had occurred.

Arab fighters besieged the kibbutzim at Gush Etzion, blocking all food and supplies in and out of the settlement. The remaining British forces were under orders not to intervene and so sat and watched. The settlements were on land that was due to be ceded into the Palestinian–Arab state after the UN vote. And this created a ripe target for Arab anger.

In truth, Shalman knew, it was one of many such places—communities of Jews on land that was soon to be Arab, and Arab villages soon to be deemed on Israeli land. A complex patchwork of people deeply and irreversibly intertwined, now politically divided by invisible map lines.

The Israeli paramilitary group Haganah sent a troop of thirty-five men and women with supplies of food and water to relieve the kibbutzim. These men and women walked on tracks through the night so they weren't observed by British or Arab patrols. But the path was more difficult than they'd thought, and they were delayed. They were still on open land when the sun came up, and they were spotted by Arab patrols, who raised the alarm. Residents from the local Arab villages, men and women, poured out to block their path.

And that was when the fighting started.

Hundreds of Arab fighters from a militant training base arrived in trucks and cars. The Haganah fought until they ran out of ammunition, and then they were hacked to pieces.

Shalman had convinced himself that he'd come to try and stop the fighting, to speak to the people of the village once more and urge them not to participate. But this seemed an entirely futile, even childish notion.

The truth was that Shalman had come to see Mustafa. It had been some time since he'd seen his friend. Now that war was surely upon them, he knew they would soon be viewed as enemies. This was perhaps his last chance.

It took Shalman just ten minutes to descend the hillside and walk into the middle of the village. Arab men and women came out of their houses to see who the stranger was. None smiled. He had been tolerated before—some even liked him or respected the hospitality offered by Mustafa's father—but things were different now.

Shalman stopped and waited. He knew word traveled fast in villages. Mustafa soon appeared down the road and walked up to him. The two young men stood and looked at each other for what seemed a long time. Finally, Mustafa spoke. "Why have you come here, Shalman?"

Shalman didn't have an answer. Not one that was easily expressed.

"There is no place for you here." The words were blunt and cold, and they hurt.

"I heard what happened . . . at Gush Etzion . . . It wasn't you, was it?" said Shalman calmly.

Anger flashed across Mustafa's face, an anger Shalman had never seen in the young man.

"And what if it was? What if it had been my rifle? How would that change anything now?"

"It doesn't have to be like this. I came to beg you not to be a part of this bloodshed. The talk in Jerusalem is of reprisals. If you make yourself a target, they will come for you . . ."

"And are we not a target now? Have we not always been a target? Your target!"

"What are you talking about? You're my friend," insisted Shalman.

"You lied to me!"

Shalman did not have to ask what Mustafa meant. He knew it in his bones.

"You lied to me," Mustafa repeated, his voice lower, resigned, and filled with a strange sadness. "You lied. It was you. On the airfield. It was you . . ."

Shalman's mind scrambled for words. "You have to understand—"

"I understand very well."

Shalman pressed on desperately. "When you first brought me here, I spoke to you of Gandhi, the Indian man who said that an eye for an eye will leave the whole world blind."

"Gandhi is not an Arab. Nor a Jew. We don't think in this way. Our way is to fight. An eye for an eye . . . And we all have to take sides. We all have to be true to our blood."

"But Mustafa, our blood is the same! Isn't that what we were learning in the cave, digging treasures from the earth? My blood is the same as your blood. Can't you see that?"

"It doesn't matter. You have your people. I have mine. There can only be trust, and how can I trust you when you murdered one of our children and lied to me?"

Antioch

1098

THE PUS OOZED from the infected boils on the duke's penis, and though he took great pride in its enormity, it seemed to shrivel and retreat from Nimrod's probing before he put on the bandage.

The doctor had long been treating the duke's afflictions, but now, on the Crusade, on open roads where hygiene was unknown, Nimrod's skills were insufficient. The duke let out a bellowing cry, though the Jewish doctor's hands were steady as he cleaned the infection and applied an unguent to the wounds.

"Dear God! This suffering had better be at an end when we take Jerusalem or so help me!" the duke yelled.

Nimrod ignored his master. It was no longer the physical health of the duke that worried Nimrod so much as the state of his mind. The itching from the disease he'd caught from the prostitutes was causing him madness at night. In France, Nimrod ensured that the prostitutes took a vaginal lavage before they were introduced to the duke, and that he used a specially concocted oil before he entered the women. This had kept him relatively pox-free. But since the duke had been in the company of all the other nobles, sharing God knew how many camp whores, and because of the lack of water to wash adequately on the road, hygiene had deteriorated and his health was suffering. The consequences of the whores he'd lain with after they crossed the Alpine Mountains into the lowlands of the Italian people were evident. And God only knew what fresh diseases he'd picked up since they'd entered the land of the Turk and raped all of the women who prayed to Mohammed for help. Nimrod had no idea what diseases such women would carry in their bodies, and daily he prayed that he could make the itching in the duke's penis disappear.

"Give me wine!" roared the duke.

Nimrod handed Henri the wineskin from beside the bed and watched as the big man greedily swallowed, partly out of thirst and partly out of pain.

The campaign had, as Jacob predicted, started with great excitement and song. Enthusiasm quickly dissipated once thirst, hunger, and blistered feet took hold. Some of the soldiers and camp followers had lasted barely a few weeks before drifting off in the night, presumably to return to their homes, or to settle into a village where they'd met some wench.

The duke tried to keep his men enthused with declarations of riches and glories of battle, even rehashing the Church's proclamation of the cleansing of sins for those who would see the campaign through. He was a man of considerable motivating force, but Nimrod could see that the inspiration would be unlikely to last should they not find victory and plunder soon.

As the Crusade progressed south and east toward Jerusalem, the cities and towns leading to Constantinople had come and gone, the heathen Mohammedans driven out, and the pressure on King Alexios the First Komnenos relieved.

Now the great city of Antioch loomed before the diminished throng and became a much-needed beacon of hope for the Crusade as a place that would fulfill the promise. But the walls of Antioch were so wide and high and long that it was impossible for the Crusader army, far smaller than that which had set out from Paris and led by quarreling commanders, to stem the flow of supplies into the city. The siege seemed destined to last indefinitely, as the Turks threatened to send reinforcements.

And Nimrod was fearful of what he had seen. War was brutal and the casualties had been grave; more so on the citizens of the towns and cities they ravaged than the soldiers at arms, but the Crusaders were suffering nonetheless.

Nimrod had seen barbarism he could not wipe from his memory.

He had seen heathen men boiled to death in the great camp caul-
drons and children impaled on spits to be roasted and devoured by
Crusaders driven mad by hunger. And Nimrod had seen his own people caught up in the conflict between Christians and Muslims as Jacob's prophecy came to pass—the Crusaders saw little that
differentiated Jews and the followers of Mohammed. As he tried to
sleep at night, Nimrod often found himself wondering why he could
not speak up against such atrocities—all these men, Christians, Muslims, and Jews, were children of Abraham; all died with their faith in
the same God. The guilt of his silence weighed upon him.

As he finished his task and drew the bedsheet over the duke's legs,
Nimrod knew he was being watched. He did not need to turn to
know that Michel Roux stood behind him.

"Leave us, Jew," said Roux, but Nimrod was already collecting his
medicinal tools and salves and shuffling toward the door, averting his
eyes.

Chevalier Roux filled Nimrod with fear. He represented everything that darkened men's hearts. The duke kept him close as a brutal
warrior and leader of his cavalry, but Nimrod feared the power that
Roux craved. He was not of significant noble birth and could never
hope to claim the duke's title or estates save by sword and cunning,
and Nimrod felt in his heart that he was quite capable of succeeding,
especially as the duke's health was failing. Before the Crusade, Nimrod had attempted to delicately counsel the duke on the dangers of
such men as Roux, but war made them more valuable than in peace-
time, so Nimrod had stifled his concerns.

Nimrod made his way through the torchlight and drunkenness
that was the camp after dark to the small tent that he shared with
Jacob. He made this walk with a heavy heart as he knew that this
night would likely be Jacob's last. The old man was suffering greatly,
and there was no medicine that Nimrod possessed that could alter
the passage of age.

"Slaughter is coming," said Jacob, whispering as he struggled to
breathe. "You must leave, Nimrod. Be away from here before the
slaughter comes."

"I cannot. I serve the duke," said Nimrod as he wiped Jacob's brow. The Crusade had taken its toll on the duke's treasurer. He had performed his duty carefully, managed the duke's accounts, paid the soldiers, and maintained the most meticulous records of any in the campaign. When they had left France, the duke had made clear his orders concerning the treasury that Jacob was to oversee.

"All that is plunder will be given immediately to you as my treasurer. And in God's good time, a fifth part of what we take from the heathen will be divided among the men. Earls, barons, and chevaliers will be allotted a fifth part of that fifth part. The Church will be allotted another fifth part, and two fifth parts will be retained by me in recompense for my service to the Holy See."

Jacob had followed these orders perfectly. The duke had made it clear to his Crusaders that there would be a price to pay for failing to be honest in the account of what they had taken.

Nimrod recalled well the words delivered by the duke from the back of his horse before they set out. "Any Crusader who steals plunder for himself will suffer the most horrible of deaths for all eternity. Your headless body will be left in a ditch, and you will not be buried in consecrated ground. You will never go to heaven but instead will be consigned to the hottest flames of hell, where your flesh will burn for ten thousand years. For I will not tolerate any crimes during this Crusade. You are soldiers of the cross; you are soldiers for Jesus; yours is a holy and God-ordained mission. So what you steal from us, you steal from God Himself, and for that blasphemy you will die."

It had been Nimrod who advised the duke on the phrasing. Nimrod had a way with words. Yet now, after he'd seen the carnage of what such men of God had reaped, the words tasted as bitter as bile.

Nimrod had kept the duke's health and Jacob had kept the duke's accounts. But the strain of the journey had stolen Jacob's health and threatened to leave Nimrod on his own.

"You have not seen what I've seen . . ." Nimrod feared the old man's words would slip into incoherence and delusion, but they maintained clarity even as Jacob closed his eyes for a memory. "The terrible massacre that went before this Crusade. They came for us, for our people. This fate will come again . . ." The cough returned, stealing any further words from Jacob's lips.

Nimrod knew the stories of the expulsion and massacre of the Jews from the cities of Europe. Since he had found his place and purpose in the court of the duke of Champagne, such stories had felt far away. And yet now, as he himself was a part of the destruction being wreaked upon the East, as he had watched what men could do to other men, as Christians slaughtered Arabs in the name of a peace-loving God, the stories felt very close to home. And Nimrod was without anyone to trust.

Jacob's words softened and slid into a soft babble. Nimrod held the old man's hand and waited, listening softly to his breath as it became a hiss and then a rattle and then nothing.

• • •

Soon after Jacob died, the great walls of Antioch were finally breached. It wasn't might of arms that allowed the Crusader army to flood into the massive city in the height of summer but, rather, simple bribery. The commander of the south tower had been paid a massive sum of silver to open his gates, and the siege that had appeared to be unending was now over in an orgy of looting and killing, the walls of the city intact. Yet the revelry was short-lived as the former besiegers became the besieged and a fresh Muslim army arrived, preparing to take back the city so recently captured.

The armies met in the open field outside the city and clashed like two mighty mailed fists. The army that would win would not be the strongest or best armed but the force that could be held coherent in the chaos. In the end it was the Muslims who broke ranks as internal power struggles drove whole cohorts to quit the field and return to their tribal lands.

The Crusaders were left holding the bloodstained ground as stories circulated among the men of the Holy Lance having been found in the city as a sign from God, or even that a host of saints had been deployed on to the battlefield to drive back the heathens.

To Nimrod, observing the carnage, it was nothing more than the winds of war that, on this day, had blown in the favor of the Crusaders but tomorrow may well blow back in their faces.

Since the death of Jacob, the duties of the duke's treasury had fallen to Nimrod. But he had no head for numbers, and the scope of the task, now that Antioch had been conquered and the Muslim army broken, was beyond him. He attempted to follow Jacob's accounts, tried in vain to understand the conflicting reports of the duke's men as to what amounts had been taken and what must be recorded, and all the while he listened to the screams of the city as it cried out in pain.

Nimrod bundled the day's scrolls of accounts under his arm and shuffled off toward the rooms the duke had taken up in the wreckage of the city's palatial buildings. He kept his face down, his eyes on the ground, and tried to block out the world around him. The last remaining prisoners were being rounded up; Saracens were herded together like cattle and put to the sword. Yet it was impossible to tell if they were soldiers, stripped of their scimitars and clothes, or innocents collected up in the fever of fighting.

As Nimrod walked, he heard words in a language none of the soldiers around him spoke, causing him to lift his head in surprise.

The words were a mix of English and Hebrew. Nimrod found himself looking across the flagstone courtyard to see a roughly bearded and wiry man pulling with all his feeble might at the grip of two Crusader soldiers who held him fast. "I am not a Saracen! I am not a Turk! I am not a soldier. I am just a merchant."

The soldiers continued to pull the man, and he changed his language from English and Hebrew into German, then Arabic. Nimrod, without consciously choosing to change direction, turned toward the man and the knights. It was only when he came close enough that Nimrod saw the pockmarked face and flame-red hair of Michel Roux.

Then the man spoke in faltering French. "I am Jewish, not Muslim. I am a friend to the Crusader. I want only to trade. I have wealth and I can—"

Roux lashed out with a mailed fist straight into the merchant's chest, forcing the wind from his lungs and causing him to cough and then fall painfully silent.

"Jew or Muslim, you are a godless heathen, and you'll die like the rest. Take him away!" he ordered, and the knights on either side of the man heaved him around with his feet dangling above the flagstones.

Nimrod involuntarily raised a hand to stop the knights, and the scrolls fell to the ground with a clatter. The movement caught the attention of the soldiers and Roux, and all three turned to Nimrod. Caught in their glare, the doctor was compelled to speak.

"This man . . . what has this man done?"

Roux looked at Nimrod, baffled by his audacity. But Roux remained silent.

"This man . . . he is a m-merchant?" Nimrod stammered.

"Jew? Merchant? What of it?" sneered Roux.

"He may have—" Nimrod's words caught in his throat as he crouched to gather up the scrolls, which threatened to blow away in the wind. "He may have skills that the duke . . ."

By now Roux was upon Nimrod, so close that the doctor could smell the man's putrid breath. He felt Roux's metal-clad hands grab at his shirt and all but heave him off the ground.

"By what right do you question me?" Roux said, his voice menacing.

"I am tasked by the duke . . . this man might be . . . we should speak first with Duke Henri and—"

Roux hefted Nimrod backward, throwing him flailing through the air and crashing to the ground. His head collided with the flagstones and his sight flooded with swirling colors. He put his hands to the ground to push himself up just in time to see Roux stand over him with his sword ready to end his life.

But the blow didn't come. Nimrod heard the thundering voice of the duke.

"What in God's name is going on here?"

Nimrod opened his eyes to see Roux still clutching the sword and, behind him, the Jewish merchant staring with panicked eyes at the scene.

"Roux, what is the meaning of this?" demanded the duke.

"Just a prisoner, my lord," said Roux, his gaze turning to the merchant still held by the soldiers.

"And why is my doctor on the ground? Why are my accounts scattered in the dirt?"

Nimrod scrambled to his feet and, snatching up what parchments he could, said, "A merchant, my lord, this man is a merchant."

"And what is that to me, old fool!" said the duke.

"He is a collaborator, working with the Saracen, and he will be put to the sword," Roux shouted, not wishing to be outflanked by the old Jew.

"I am not. I am a merchant, I have money, and I—"

"Silence!" shouted the duke. "Nimrod, why is this man of concern to you?"

"Since the death of your treasurer, Jacob, my lord, I have been unable to do my work. I am not skilled at figures. This man, though, is a merchant, and were we to spare his life, he could be useful." Nimrod walked over to the side of the man. "This man is clearly not a Turk nor an Arab. He may be of value to you, my lord."

"Value?" The duke pointed a gloved finger at the merchant. "Value to me?"

Nimrod quickly spoke before Roux had a chance to speak. "This man will ensure that the Church and your estate are paid their due from the plunder. This man has value, my lord."

The duke pondered Nimrod's words and paced forward to put a hand on the Jewish doctor's shoulder. To Nimrod's surprise, the duke leaned down and whispered in his ear, "Yes. I need a treasurer. And I also have great need of a doctor. He may sleep in your tent." He turned to Roux. "This Jew belongs to Nimrod the doctor. He shall be entrusted with my accounts."

And without looking back, the duke strode away. The soldiers let the merchant go, and he quickly drew himself away from them and toward Nimrod.

Roux eyed them both coldly. "Mark my words, Jew," he spat at Nimrod. "You are in the duke's sight for now, but you had better pray you die before he does, Christ killer, for once he's gone, you and your new merchant will be mine, to dispose of as I wish. And on that day, you'll have wished you'd died here, in Antioch, with my sword piercing your godless heart."

And with that, Roux spun on his heel and stormed away, followed by his guards.

The man whose life he had just saved turned to Nimrod. "Simeon. My name is Simeon, son of Abel. And I thank you."

Nimrod looked the man up and down with weary eyes. "I sincerely hope you are good with numbers, Simeon. For both our sakes."

Moscow, USSR
January 19, 1948

GOLDA MEIR LOOKED the very archetype of the Jewish grand-mother. Her elegant dark blue twinset, white top, pearls, and gray hair tied in a matronly bun gave her a nonthreatening air that defied her determination and political savvy. Like a mountain lion, she looked benign as she walked along the street, but anybody who crossed her risked the worst mauling imaginable.

Formally, she was head of the Jewish Agency for Israel and charged with political negotiation with the British. More pragmatically, she was a fund-raiser, building networks of donors to fund the soon-to-be-established Jewish nation of Israel. Nobody could extract vast sums of money from American and European Jews like Golda. When she spoke, people felt guilty if they didn't give, especially when she reminded the comfortable and assimilated Jews that Israel was their birthright. In a more subtle reality, Golda was a deft diplomat, weaving international alliances. Of all her roles and motivations, it was this that brought her to Moscow.

Golda walked down the gentle slope on Teatralnyy Prospekt and turned back to gaze up the hill toward the offices of the terrifying Lubyanka headquarters of the MGB. She knew that anybody who entered there as a prisoner was never seen again. The lucky ones died in interrogation; the less fortunate were sent to Siberia and worked, sometimes for years, until they dropped dead from the biting cold or their bodies gave up from the aching exhaustion of slave labor and inadequate food.

She'd never been inside the Lubyanka, but from all the reports that came to her, Golda knew more than most Russians about the torture, the murders, and the disappearances concealed by the building's four walls.

Golda walked smartly past the Bolshoi Theater as she left the Metropol Hotel, crossed the street, and entered the massively guarded complex of red walls, multicolored onion domes, and grim towers that was the Kremlin.

She showed the guard at the fortress gates the slip of paper and the official stamp of office and, without any words, was escorted through the courtyards to the inner sanctum.

Within minutes, she was shown into the offices of the Soviet Union's minister for foreign affairs, Vyacheslav Mikhailovich Molotov. The dapper man rose from his desk as his secretary ushered Israel's most prominent woman into his office. He walked around, extending his hand and smiling in a gesture of friendship.

"Mrs. Meir," he said. "I've been looking forward to meeting one of Mother Russia's most engaging and important women."

"And it's a pleasure to meet you, Comrade Vyacheslav Mikhailovich."

"How does it feel to be back in Moscow after so many years absence? What is it? Forty years?"

She smiled. "This is my first time in Moscow, comrade. I was born in the Ukraine and left when I was but a child to join my father in America."

"But your Russian is excellent."

"Then thank Gogol, Tolstoy, and Pushkin. I've a facility for languages."

They sat in the armchairs and waited until Molotov's secretary had laid out the tray of black tea and cakes before continuing.

"I was somewhat surprised to receive your note, madam. When it arrived from Jerusalem, I was concerned about meeting with somebody, even someone as important as you, at a nongovernment level. As foreign minister, I have to be careful to meet with my counterparts and not people who are, in effect, private citizens, albeit ones as important as—"

"And I appreciate your giving me this time, Comrade Foreign Minister. But I think that as this meeting is top secret and nobody in

Palestine knows of my visit other than my prime minister and the head of our secret service, this will not leak out. Unless, of course, the plumbing in the Kremlin has degraded since the time of the Revolution."

Molotov let out a small laugh but looked more closely at her. Her face was lined from living for so many years in a hot country, but the eyes were what held his attention. Golda Meir had the eyes of an ancient mother of Israel, burning with intensity and sharp intelligence. Molotov loved trying to analyze people through their eyes.

"You said in your note that this meeting was of great importance to the future of relationships between our two countries, when your Israel is established by the United Nations. Of course, that's an assumption that may or may not be——"

"It will come to pass, comrade. Believe me when I say that Israel will be the world's youngest country in a handful of months. With a voice and a vote at the United Nations, we will enjoy the same stature as the Soviet Union and the United States of America."

Molotov suppressed a smile. "My dear lady, while what you say may be true, it doesn't behoove us to exaggerate our importance in the world. When Comrade Chairman Stalin was told how Russian Catholics could help us win the Vatican's approval, he said, 'The pope! How many divisions has the pope got?' You may have one voice among many, but Mother Russia has many army divisions, ships, aircraft, and guns."

"I'm not exaggerating the importance of Israel, comrade," Golda said. "Merely pointing out to you that we live on a lump of rock floating on a sea of petroleum oil. And your tanks, planes, cars, and factories need oil to turn."

Molotov raised an eyebrow. "But Palestine has no oil. Your Moses turned left toward the sea when he brought your people out of Egypt. He should have turned right and settled in Iraq or Persia, Saudi Arabia or the Gulf. I can't see what point you're making, madam."

Like a grandmother dealing with an intransigent grandchild, Golda Meir spoke softly and patiently. "Comrade, who has the oil today may not have it tomorrow. You, more than I, know the geopolitics of the region. The Arabs sold themselves to the highest bidder in World War I, vacillating between the Turks and the British. In World War II, they stayed out of the fray, having learned their painful lesson, except for the mufti of Jerusalem, who became Hitler's best friend, but he's in exile and no longer counts. But the Arabs are not nations, even though they have national borders. They are tribes, and there is as much dispute between tribes within their country's borders as there is between warring nations."

Molotov frowned. "And?"

"And soon there will be war. Egypt, Iraq, Syria, Trans-Jordan, and Lebanon. Some Palestinians will participate, but we anticipate no true opposition."

"This we already know, madam. But what army does Israel have to mount? Our estimates are that the Arab armies will number sixty thousand. They have planes, tanks, modern weaponry. How can a small nation without an army match this might?" Molotov asked.

Golda knew that this was a rhetorical question, and he already knew what her answer would be. "Comrade, in the Yishuv, we have four experienced fighting forces: the Haganah, the Palmach, the Irgun, and Lehi. Together, we can mount an initial repulse consisting of thirty thousand men and women. And if the battle lasts longer than a month, we'll call up more than a hundred thousand of our best and brightest. Remember, comrade, that the Arabs are fighting to push the Jews into the sea. When they get tired or wounded, they'll just go back to their homes. But we Jews are fighting for our lives, because we have nowhere else to go."

Molotov remained silent and sipped his tea.

Golda continued. "But you already know this. Your people in Jerusalem have informed you of everything I've told you. Tomorrow I travel from here to the United States to raise money to buy arms, ammunition, tanks, and planes. I have speaking engagements in dozens of cities throughout America. I'm told that I might be lucky to raise a couple of million dollars because everybody is tired of wars and just wants peace. But I will return with fifty million dollars or I will not return."

Molotov considered her words. "You are aware, of course, that Russia's official stance is to oppose Zionism."

"Let us also never forget, my friend," said Golda, "that since Catherine the Great, Russia has been the most pragmatic diplomat in the world. You may be officially anti-Zionist, but your reality is that you need influence in the Middle East, and not just to accelerate the decline of British influence but also to ensure that America doesn't become strong in our arena. You need us, Comrade Foreign Minister. You need Israel as a friend. Because you know who's going to win this war, and you know which nation will become the key player on your southern border."

Molotov found himself intrigued that Golda Meir's thinking was so closely aligned with his. He was nothing if not a pragmatist; flexible adaptation was always the key to survival, whether in evolution, politics, or war. Might Golda Meir make some of his work with his agents on the ground, with people such as Judit and Anastasia, redundant?

"You and I are frank people, madam. You asked for this meeting. It has been my pleasure to entertain you. But what is the real purpose of your being here?"

"Two reasons. The first is to ask for a gift of fifty million dollars' worth of gold so that we can buy more munitions and planes on the open market."

Molotov remained silent.

"And the second is to ask for the names of the death squad you currently have in Palestine murdering our best and brightest Zionists."

His face was a mask of indifference, but Golda detected surprise in his eyes. She drove the point home by saying, "I do hope, comrade, that we can come to some agreement before I leave here and begin my talks with the Americans. And it would really assist our future friendship if your assassins could stop killing my people."

• • •

The following morning, as Golda Meir was packing her bags to prepare for her trip to the United States, there was a knock on her door at the Metropol Hotel. She opened it and found a tall, gaunt young man standing there. Nobody other than a handful of people in Moscow and in Jerusalem knew that Golda was in the Soviet Union, so she was immediately suspicious.

The young man, dressed in a charcoal gray suit, nodded in greeting. "You left a document on the desk when you finished your meeting yesterday. The gentleman with whom you met has asked me to return it." He handed over a brown manila envelope and walked back to the stairs. Golda closed the door and ripped open the envelope. In it, she found a list of names. Many were Russian, such as Anastasia Bistrzhitska, and were listed with their known aliases. Some were clearly Jewish, the name of Judit Etzion standing out. Golda had heard of the girl's bravery, but while she felt some distress, the boil had to be cauterized.

Asking for the list of Soviet agents in Palestine had been risky but carefully calculated. The gamble was that the Kremlin might hand over their agents as a peace offering for future cooperation with Jerusalem if they believed it was a more secure bet. Having twenty minutes before her car took her to the airfield, Golda opened the lid of her suitcase and took a small code book from a hidden pocket in the lining. She sat with a pencil and piece of paper, cross-referencing the names on the list with the codes she had to use to transmit them to Jerusalem.

• • •

Judit and Anastasia sat in deep armchairs in a luxurious safe house. It had been purchased by a Russian Jew who had managed to emigrate to America but was still covertly a communist. While he lived in America waiting for the State of Israel to be created, the Soviet intelligence agencies used his abode.

The windows were barred, the curtains closed, and they'd entered the house by a side door. For additional security, one had entered the house an hour after the other, and they'd leave at different times.

The women appeared relaxed but in truth were pondering carefully the next steps they would need to take.

Anastasia's spies had confirmed what Judit had suspected since she had been picked up from the airport by Shalman. Immanuel

Berin was suspicious, though neither could say how much he knew. It was Anastasia who worked out the source.

"The truth is that you were careless, Judita."

The rebuke from her handler, a woman so much a mother to Judit, stung her almost physically.

"You must have been careless, and you were seen."

"By whom?" demanded Judit, wanting so much to deny the charge, yet knowing that Anastasia would not have made the statement had she been anything other than certain.

"A young Irgun woman named Ashira. I assume you know her?"

Judit remembered back to the Lehi raid on Goldschmidt House, the British officers' club. The girl had been so young, naive, but darkly determined. Ashira had also been there on the night of the vote, listening to the radio. That was the night Judit had killed the Jewish professor in front of his family. Anastasia vocalized the next thought in Judit's mind. "That was the night she must have followed you. You were careless." Anastasia leaned over and put a hand on Judit's knee. "I understand. I don't expect perfection. I expect diligence."

"How dangerous is she to us?" Judit asked.

Anastasia took another sip of wine and reached over to the table to refill it. "I'm afraid she must be dealt with."

"Is that necessary? She's just a kid. She has no influence. She can't be sure what she saw. No one listens to her or takes her seriously."

"Berin might."

This simple answer brought the argument to a halt, but Judit was torn. She had killed many times over, but the thought that she would be asked to remove the young girl filled her with self-loathing.

Anastasia, as if reading her thoughts again, reassured her. "Don't worry. It won't be you. We must keep you clean and away from such things, focused on higher duties."

Judit nodded. Her path had been carefully constructed by Moscow. She would be a heroine of the coming war between Arabs and Jews and, from that public status, elevated to office. There she would orchestrate the special relationship between the new nation and the Soviet Union. The Americans would be apoplectic, but only Anastasia, Molotov, Beria, and perhaps Stalin would know the truth about Judit.

Now, because of one small error, a naive girl threatened to unbalance an entire geopolitical plan. To Judit, it all appeared so fragile.

"And Berin?" asked Judit.

"You have your orders, your plan, your disguise."

Anastasia was referring to the simple dark Arab dress and head scarf that would cover Judit when she made her move against Berin, the disguise that would ensure Arabs were blamed. Implicit in the plan was that Judit must be seen by onlookers to be the killer. When the police investigated, it would be a Jordanian Arab woman who would be blamed.

"But we still need time to remove Ashira from the equation. We have to plan carefully so that no suspicion can fall on you. One way is for you to have a meeting with Berin when we put an end to Ashira. Knowing him, he'll be suspicious of the coincidence. So I'm afraid that when Ashira goes to meet her god, Berin will have to suffer the same fate. You'll have to be responsible. His death is too important to be left to an underling."

Anastasia swallowed the rest of the wine and returned her hand to Judit's leg. "Then, when these dark clouds have departed, we can finish what we started."

• • •

It was overcast and late in the day. In such light, Ashira was very good at being invisible. She was nondescript in many ways, ordinary in height, gait, and shape. Few saw her to be a threat as a young woman in Jerusalem, and her dark Tunisian features made her appear as much Arab as Jewish. The effect was that neither side immediately saw her as the other, and she dressed accordingly, wearing nothing that marked her as decidedly Jewish or observantly Arab. She blended in easily.

Had she been trained as Judit had been, Ashira may have been a master spy. But her only training had been a harsh life and a determination to survive. For now it was enough as she lay on her belly atop a low hillock, nestled behind a tall tuft of grass and rubble, with a small but powerful pair of binoculars pressed to her eyes.

She kept a long distance between herself and Judit. She had stayed on high ground, rooftops and embankments, using her binoculars. It had not been easy, and she had lost her target several times, having to guess her trajectory and scan furiously to find her again. But now Ashira lay looking down at a house into which Judit had disappeared.

Just weeks ago, Ashira had been enamored with the woman who epitomized everything she wanted to be—strong, committed, defiant. But the assassination of the professor had turned her reverence for Judit into rage.

Through the twin lenses of the binoculars, a lone figure appeared at the side of the house and slipped casually across the garden to the street. Ashira barely had to study the figure to know it was Judit. She had seen her enter the house an hour earlier and had been waiting patiently for her to emerge. Ordinarily, this would have been the cue to follow, but Ashira's intentions were different this time. It wasn't Judit who was important this time; it was whom Judit had been speaking to.

Ashira had confided what she knew to Berin, his approval and acknowledgment important to her in ways she didn't fully understand. He remained somewhat skeptical and seemingly unwilling to act. Shalman had revealed to him that his wife often went to places and meetings he knew nothing about. Berin had wanted to know with whom Judit was meeting when she slipped away from her apartment, and Ashira was hoping to find out now.

Ashira didn't follow Judit but waited and watched.

A further hour passed with no sign of anyone, and the light dimmed as night fell. A car, silent and still, had sat in front of the home since before Ashira had arrived. The road the house was on ran in two directions, away from Jerusalem and back toward Jerusalem, with nothing but small tracks and dusty dirt roads deviating from that path. Ashira knew that whoever came out of that house would be unlikely to head away from the city. Ashira also knew that not far down the road was a British checkpoint through which any car heading back to the ancient city would need to pass. This was her plan. But she would need to be fast.

Through the binoculars she saw a shadow of movement—not from the front door but from the side of the house. The sky was getting dimmer, and there were no exterior lights on the home nor streetlights to illuminate the scene.

The person moved slowly. Very slowly. Not creeping but with small steps. High heels on grass and stone, thought Ashira. A tall and lean woman. Ashira would have to be quick. She watched as the tall woman paused before turning slightly toward the waiting car.

This was the cue; Ashira could wait no more. She pushed herself to her feet and ran. She would have to sprint to make it to a vantage point near the British army checkpoint before the car arrived there.

Ashira carried no bag; she was light and ready to run. She left the binoculars on the dirt where she had been lying, choosing to have nothing to weigh her down except a Leica camera slung over her shoulder in a leather holster.

Her legs pumped as she sprang over the ground. The road swung a wide arc around the low hills. The car would have to pass around that arc while Ashira ran across country on a dirt path through shrubs and a small field. It was a straight line to the checkpoint.

As she ran, she could hear the faint sound of a car engine in the near distance, but she had no way of knowing if it was the car carrying the tall woman. She ran on, holding the camera close to her body with one hand to stop it flapping about and slowing her down.

Up ahead, in the fading light, she could see the checkpoint and hear the rumbling of a generator. The British imposed a curfew after dark, which added another pressure to Ashira's task. She needed to be home before curfew began, or she was in danger of being dragged to a holding cell by British Tommies.

She drew up to the checkpoint, her breath coming hard; she knew she couldn't just enter the checkpoint. She'd scoped the area earlier that day and knew exactly the spot. The dim light of dusk hid her as she crept around the checkpoint, manned by only three British soldiers, and nestled between two large sandstone rocks that concealed her yet gave her a clear view of any car that approached the boom gate.

It was difficult to steady her breathing, but she had to in order to still the image through the telephoto lens.

And then she saw the car. With the tips of her fingers, she adjusted the focus ring. The woman she saw was dark and severe but beautiful, her hair pulled back in a tight bun like a ballet dancer's. Ashira's finger hovered over the shutter release, about to capture an image of that face. In that moment a soldier stepped between Ashira's camera and the woman, blocking the view. Ashira swore under her breath and felt the urge to get to her feet and shift position, but there was nowhere to go that wouldn't reveal her presence. She had to stay wedged between the rocks. She held the camera in position, kept the focal length the same, and prayed for the soldier to move.

The boom gate rose, and Ashira swore again, trying to shift her body as far as it would go, attempting to see around the body of the soldier obscuring her view.

Finally, he stepped aside and the woman came into sight through the windshield of the car. Ashira did not hesitate and squeezed the shutter release like a sniper executing a target. Her thumb dexterously wound the camera, and she took another and another. Three, four, five in quick succession until the car had passed by.

The young woman waited, her breath slow and calm now, praying that she had what she needed to show Berin.

When the soldiers returned to their smoking and banter, Ashira slipped away. She wound the film back into the canister and plucked it from the open chamber of the camera. If she was questioned by any soldiers as she made her way back to Jerusalem they would likely confiscate the camera, and she did not want to lose the film. She took the film roll and stuffed it into her underpants, securing it between her legs, and set off back to the city.

• • •

Late into the night, Immanuel Berin swirled the photographic developing fluid in the tray in front of him. The dull red glow from the safelights overhead washed the room crimson.

He had been brought a message that something important had

arrived, and he had ventured cautiously out of his home to the secret Irgun base to meet with Raffe. The thickset fighter, soft-spoken and stoic, leaned over to whisper into Berin's ear as if afraid of being overheard, even in the underground base.

"It's from Ashira." He pressed the small film canister into Berin's hand without further explanation.

The white paper began to darken into contrasts of black, gray, and white. At first he couldn't make out the image. But then, slowly, detail began to etch into the paper—a car and windshield and figure behind the wheel. Then, slowly, a face.

With a small pair of tongs, Berin lifted the paper from the bath and rinsed it in a second tray of water, washing the developing fluid from it and leaving it dripping as he pegged it carefully to a small wire line strung across the room. He reached up to maneuver the red safelight more directly onto the photo.

He looked hard at the woman in the photo through his small round glasses. He took in her features, her tightly drawn hair, her face . . . And Berin knew who she was. The information from Golda Meir was confirmed. Berin knew now that T'homi had been right.

Jerusalem

January 27, 1948

THE CAFÉ WAS quiet and ordinary. As she looked through the window at the people seated at tables, Judit pondered the word "ordinary" within the extraordinary world she lived. The increasing violence, the tension in the streets, turned each ordinary day into an anxiety-riddled existence. Wake up safe, get through the day, go to bed. These were the tidings of a good day for most of the citizens of Jerusalem. That a café would even be open to serve coffee and food as if everything were normal seemed strange to Judit. It was a thought that she had not previously entertained, and she wondered why she would be thinking these things as she prepared to execute the order she had been given by Molotov.

She sat across the road from the café, observing with sharp eyes while she pretended to read the newspaper. At her feet was a leather bag that contained the costume and the hand grenade.

The café was one sometimes used for meetings by the Irgun; the owner was a sympathizer, and he had an upper room where they could meet in secret. This also made it the perfect place for Judit's plan as she watched for signs that Berin had arrived.

As she waited, she looked at the other people lingering nearby. Four of them were fellow Irgun, but only Judit knew that they were also MGB agents working for Anastasia.

The attack needed to be public, but Judit also needed to survive and remain disguised. For that she would need these four men to bundle her away.

The road was becoming noisier by the minute with street sellers and traffic, but Judit tuned out all other distractions.

She detected a sudden movement and tilted her head to see Immanuel Berin's lean frame stride toward the café from across the square. He was flanked by two of his bodyguards. This was all she needed. She stood and casually walked into a small alley. Once in the shadows and out of sight, she pulled an Arabic woman's full-length dress out of her bag. It had been carefully chosen. Different Arab nations wore different patterns and colors; it was important that Judit be identified as a woman from west of Jerusalem—from areas that aligned their population with Jordan.

She threw the ankle-length dress over her head. Next a headband holding in place a long scarf that fell to her waist and covered her shoulders. She drew the scarf across her face, tucking it in to secure it.

Last from the leather bag she pulled out Berin's death warrant. It was what the British called a Mills bomb. The hand grenade had a round metallic pin and a timer set to explode in seven seconds.

Seven seconds, thought Judit. Seven seconds to get away. Seven seconds to kill and not be killed. She quickly pushed the grenade into the leather bag and stepped back out into the laneway.

No longer Judit, she stood at the edge of the square, clearly identifiable as an Arab woman of Jordanian descent. From above the veil, she saw Berin seated at the back of the café with a cup of coffee in his hand.

The plan was simple—walk toward the café slowly and not in a direct line, then enter as though she were a customer. While she stood there, apparently looking for a friend, she would time the distance in seconds between herself and where Berin sat at a far table. From within the bag, she'd pull the pin from the grenade and count three seconds before rolling it along the floor and exiting immediately.

Judit knew she'd have approximately four seconds to get away from the blast and knew she would be held firm by the four MGB agents, hurried away from the chaos of the ensuing explosion.

Judit was aware of her boots on the cobblestones. They were not the boots of a Palestinian Arab woman, but she had been careful to ensure the dress was long enough to conceal them.

She entered the café, her heart beating fast. She was perspiring underneath the heavy cloth. She saw Beria twenty feet away. Through the slit for her eyes, she saw many of the customers looking at her. There were other Arabs in the café, but most were western Jews.

Berin noticed her but looked back at his companions, sharing a joke as he sipped his coffee. People moved around the edges of her vision, but Judit was focused behind her veil. She moved farther inside, moving her head as though looking for somebody. The café proprietor came toward her, an avuncular smile on his face.

Judit put her hand in her bag and felt the grenade inside. And then she saw Shalman. He seemed to appear like an apparition at the edge of her sight. But his gait, his body, the way he moved and held himself were as familiar as her own shadow.

Her hand, moving of its own accord, slipped around the grenade in the leather bag, and her thumb searched for the ring of the weapon's pin. She had practiced a dozen times how to pull the pin with one hand. Even as she tilted her head to see her husband walking toward the café, muscle memory took over and her thumb penetrated the ring of the grenade's detonator that would start the seven-second timer.

Her heart stopped. Berin set down his cup. Outside the café, the four MGB agents tensed, ready for the signal. But Judit found she could not take her eyes off Shalman and the bundle on his hip: Vered.

Her thumb was in the pin of the grenade, and with almost imperceptible movement the grease was dissolving the friction that held it in place as her thumb began to pull. She continued to look at Shalman coming nearer to the café. Oh dear God, the grenade's blast would blow out the window, and its fire and shards would engulf her husband and daughter. She couldn't do it. She turned and walked hurriedly out of the café.

Behind her, Berin turned back to his coffee, thinking no more of the strange woman who had obviously thought better of entering a café frequented by Jews. One day, he thought, this might be a land where no such racial hatred existed. One day.

Shalman walked with his daughter past the café and didn't even notice the Arab woman striding rapidly away. Nor did he notice the way four men were watching her cross the road.

Two suburbs away, Anastasia Bistrzhitska sat on a bench in a park and watched a young woman walk toward a bus stop to join half a dozen other people waiting for the arrival of an Egged bus. The young girl was Ashira.

Anastasia looked at her watch. Years of patient practice forced her to remain calm. She sat there, pretending to read the newspaper, while her eyes were looking directly ahead at the bus shelter.

She heard a car's wheels squeal as a vehicle rounded a corner at high speed. She looked up cautiously from the paper at the car; it had been chosen carefully. An aging stolen Ford pickup with three men sitting cross-legged in the back, holding on to the sides as it rounded the corner and gathered speed.

It screeched to a halt opposite the bus stop, blocking Anastasia's view. But Ashira got to her feet in sudden horror as the three men, dressed like construction workers in red-and-white-checkered keffiyehs, dusty jackets, and trousers, pulled machine guns from underneath blankets. They fired volleys of bullets at the men and women waiting for the bus. The screaming from the nearby park joined with the screams of those at the bus stop. Men and women threw their hands up in a vain effort to defend themselves, but the bullets tore into their heads, chests, and stomachs. Before they fell to the ground, they shuddered like marionettes while the three men posing as Palestinian Arabs continued to shoot at them. The Israelis' bodies twitched and trembled as more and more bullets hit them or ricocheted off the ground.

As death overtook her, Ashira looked at the men shooting at her as a bullet wound in her chest pumped her lifeblood onto the ground and light dimmed in her eyes. As her blood mingled with the history of Jerusalem, the truck accelerated away.

Only Anastasia knew where the truck was going. The problem of Ashira had been removed, and at the same time revenge attacks against the Arabs had been assured. Just as the British had taken control of chaos in Palestine after World War I, so, too, would Russia become the dominant power in the chaos of the war to come.

Jerusalem
February 2, 1948

A GREAT SADNESS descended upon the young men and women Irgun fighters. Though daily surrounded by death and destruction, they had long held to being persistently upbeat and positive. But the North Jerusalem group, led by Immanuel Berin, had just attended the funeral of one of their own. Ashira had been cut down in a hail of bullets in a senseless attack by Arab gunmen on civilians at a bus stop. The fighters left the cemetery in a state of rage.

Judit looked at the ground and tried to feel some degree of emotion. She told herself it was tragic that the girl had died. If only she hadn't tried to be so smart, so inquisitive, she'd still be alive. Yet in the game that she and Anastasia and others were playing, individuals would suffer to ensure a better future for everyone. A future she could shape and control.

As Judit listened to the words of the rabbi at the graveside, vapid words that in essence were meaningless, she thought back to her days in Leningrad and her lessons in Maxist philosophy. A person's nature isn't abstract, a characteristic of a particular individual; it is the totality of all the social relationships . . . so society and how its future was created were more important than any one person, even a young woman like Ashira. No matter how tragic Ashira's death, all that mattered was the society Judit and Anastasia and her mentors in Moscow were trying to create for Israel and for the world.

Judit had grown up in a home where violence was a nightly visitor; in the Soviet Union, it was so common to see starving people fall down dead in the streets that nobody bothered to glance down. She would make sure this never happened in the new Israel. She would create the future regardless of how many hapless people were hurt.

Without the Soviet Union as Israel's backer, the fledgling nation wouldn't last ten minutes in this sea of enemies. Ashira was the price to pay for that future. Judit waited for Immanuel Berin to begin the Irgun meeting. He looked directly at her in the silence before he spoke. She had missed her opportunity, though he was unaware of the attempt. Ashira had died for the greater good, yet Judit had aborted the killing of Berin to save her own family. The cold logic of spycraft told her that she should have gone through with it. But how could she kill her own daughter and husband, regardless of what Anastasia or Molotov or others might think? Surely some individuals were more important than the future of society.

Judit shrugged off such thoughts. She would rendezvous with her handler soon enough and would put forward her plan to try again for the death of Immanuel Berin. Judit kept her eyes on the floor and raised them only when Berin announced to the group that an assault was being planned on the recently militant village of Ras Abu Yussuf, in a quiet valley nearby. She knew this village, knew it was a place her husband often went to dig in the earth for his stupid statues and coins.

"The village is in the back blocks, but the local Arabs have recently taken up arms and are leading terrorist parties against nearby kibbutzim. They're firing from hillsides into the kibbutz, and Jewish children have been killed at kindergarten. There are good grounds to think that it was this village whose men killed Ashira," Berin said.

It took under half an hour for him to conclude the meeting, give instructions on what guard or assault duties each would undertake in the next few days, and clear the room. The twenty Irgun members left individually or in twos in different directions, keeping a close eye out for British troop carriers or the occasional tank that rumbled through the narrow streets close to the Old City of Jerusalem.

Judit opted to walk alone, south and then east. She quickly doubled back on herself and, using the shadows cast by trees, walked ten blocks to the building where she had arranged four days earlier to meet with Anastasia.

She walked along the side of the road, staying close to the garden fences, stopping often to glance behind to see if she was being followed. But at night in Jerusalem, people rarely came out on to the streets. Before she walked down the alley that led to the back lane servicing the gardens of the four terraces in the row, Judit checked again to see if she was being followed. She was the only person on the street. She slipped into the lane and quickly walked to the back of the safe house.

It was when she entered the garden that she knew instinctively something was terribly wrong. The door to the kitchen, which led into the back rooms, was ajar. An agent of Anastasia's pedigree never would have done something so careless. Judit weighed the situation: She could leave immediately, but then she'd never know how things were; or she could enter the house and risk whatever might be waiting. She drew a knife from inside her coat and held it by her side, ready to strike.

Judit pushed gently on the door. Hiding behind the doorpost, she looked into the darkened maw of the kitchen. The moon illuminated only part of the room, but she could see well enough to know that the room was empty.

And then the smell hit her. It was the smell of death, of decay. It was accompanied by the buzzing of dozens of flies. She had heard that sound, smelled that stench, a hundred times, passing bodies on the streets of her childhood in a Moscow summer. It was the acrid smell of dried blood, of body fluids that had leaked out of wounds, of trousers or dresses stained by piss and shit that had seeped out from terror.

But Anastasia's safe house always smelled of roses and irises and lilies or whatever was in season. Judit walked into the kitchen, gripping the knife tighter. The farther she walked into the house, the worse the smell became and the louder the buzzing of the flies.

Keeping the lights off, her back close to the wall, she inched forward, feeling her way along the hall and into the front room. She knew all too well that there was a dead body in here.

She stood stock-still on the periphery of the room, looking around, trying to get her eyes used to the darkness. The heavy curtains were drawn over the windows. There was no warmth in the room, no living presence, just the reek of decay. Hearing no movement, Judit hoped it would be safe to turn on the light. She felt for the switch, and the moment she pulled it down, she saw a gargoyle sitting in the armchair. Dead eyes staring perpetually at the drawn curtains, mouth—what remained of a mouth—just a gaping wound. Dried blood, once bright red and now a dun-colored brown, had dripped onto the woman's chin and breast and stained her yellow dress.

Anastasia Bistrzhitska's body sat in the armchair, her hands tied at the back and her body tethered. She didn't appear to have struggled. Somebody had placed her there and shot her up through the mouth, the bullet exploding in her head and splattering her brains and skull over the back of the chair and onto the ceiling and floor behind her.

Judit looked at the woman she once loved as a friend, as a mother, and felt sick. She felt the gorge rise in her throat and ran toward the kitchen, banging her shoulder on the doorpost as she rushed down the hall. She vomited into the kitchen sink once, then again, and finally retched nothing but bile.

She ran the cold-water tap and washed her mouth, face, and hands. She gulped volumes of water and threw up again. And then her training kicked in. She had to remove herself immediately. Any thoughts she had of untying Anastasia, laying her friend to rest in the cold earth of Jerusalem, were for another time and place. Now it was her own survival.

Judit's mind raced over the possibilities of who had done this to Anastasia. Arabs? Unlikely. They were known for random attacks and sniper fire, not strategic assassination. British or American? Possibly. If Anastasia's cover was blown, she could well be a target for Allied forces looking to leverage the selfsame influence in the region after the war to come. Who else could it have been? Had the Irgun leadership uncovered their plot? Had Berin ordered the assassination? If so, it would be only a matter of days before they found and tried to eliminate her.

She had to get in touch with her Russian control, to find somewhere to disappear. And then it dawned on Judit that Anastasia had deliberately kept her as the sole protégée. She'd never introduced Judit to any other people in the MGB hierarchy. It was a weakness they'd discussed once, but Anastasia had dismissed it with a casual wave, assuring Judit that she'd always be there for her special little dove.

Judit was alone, with nowhere to run and no one to call for help. Her only move now was to see the mission through, to kill Berin before he killed her.

Judit arrived outside her apartment building after midnight. The journey by foot from the safe house to where she lived normally took under half an hour, but after what she'd seen of Anastasia, she was more cautious than ever.

Certain there was nobody outside or inside her building who would do her harm, she unlocked her front door as quietly as she could, and with the door just ajar, she listened for any sound from within. It was as quiet as a grave, but she walked in wearing only her socks, turning on no lights, and tried to sense any presence in the dark. She clasped her knife tightly in her sweating palm.

The door to her bedroom was open, and she saw Shalman lying in their bed, fast asleep, with Vered's cot close beside him. She watched him silently in the darkness, feeling the deepest imaginable regret that what could have been such a happy life with a lovely man and a beautiful child in a new and exciting country should have come to this. It was at that moment, looking at him peacefully asleep beside their innocent daughter, that she understood how much she had cost those she loved: her mother, brother, and sister by her absence, her husband and daughter by the neglect that resulted from her actions.

Judit felt giddy. She grasped the handle of the door to steady herself and felt that she was on the edge of madness. Not even tears would come to relieve the dam inside her head, a pressure about to burst.

She breathed softly but deeply, using her training to control her thoughts. To think logically, to see the big picture, and not the small inconveniences. But nothing could prevent her from looking at Shalman and seeing his innocence, his openness and goodness. It was what had drawn them together and what had torn them apart.

She saw him stir and then heard his soft, sleepy, half-awake voice. "Judit?"

"Yes," she whispered. "Sorry it's so late. Look, darling, don't get out of bed. I have to go somewhere urgently. It's a big deal. We're all mobilized. I have to take some clothes with me. I hope to be back in a week, when I've sorted out what's happening."

"But a week . . . What is it? Are the Arabs—?"

"Yes, shush, now. Don't wake Vered. Big attack. We've got early intelligence. Big meetings tonight."

She walked into the bedroom and, in the darkness, opened a suitcase and threw into it some underclothes, a couple of dresses, and a hairbrush.

"Shalman, I have to go immediately. I'm so sorry. I love you. I've loved you from the moment we were on that stupid roof together. You were such a *nebbish*; you were so innocent and unworldly, and clean and pure, and I loved you to bits. And I love Vered. Tell her that when she wakes. Tell her Mummy loves her with all her heart. Tell her—"

"Judit? What's wrong? You're almost in tears. What's happened?"

"I told you. There's a big—"

"Judit. Stop it. Some men were here tonight, asking where you were. These men had guns and were very serious. They told me they needed to find you for a mission, but I didn't believe them. What's going on? What are you up to? Vered was crying because of the men. They wouldn't tell me who they were or where they were from, but—"

She sighed. She sat on the bed. "I have to go, Shalman. I can't tell you anything, but I hope we can see each other again. Don't ask me questions. Just accept that there's more to me than you know. And the less you know, the better. But one thing I have to tell you. Tomorrow or the day after, the Irgun is going to go into Mustafa's village. They're going to shoot the place up. They're going there to teach the villagers a lesson. People are going to be killed. I'm telling you this because Mustafa once saved your life, and now you can save his. Don't tell him the details; just get him and his parents out of there for a couple of days. Just do it. Don't ask questions—just do it."

And with that, she left the apartment without kissing him or touching him. She left Shalman sitting in bed, wondering how his life had become such a minefield of unanswered questions.

He looked over to Vered, who was stirring. It was as though the little one sensed that her mother had been and gone, had left their apartment, departed her life.

Shalman was suddenly wracked with an overwhelming feeling that something monumental had just happened; that despite the intensity with which he loved his wife, their brief, extreme, passionate, insane marriage was over; that he'd never see her again; that despite her vows and commitment, she'd walked out of his life, and from that moment on, he'd never know her touch, her softness, her strength, her smell, her taste ever again. He closed his eyes in a torrent of grief and realized in the darkness that he couldn't remember her face.

The feeling of bottomless sadness stayed with him as he sat up in bed all night, staring into the black void.

Foothills of Jerusalem
1099

NIMROD THE DOCTOR and Simeon the new and anxious treasurer stood still in the burning heat of a Jerusalem summer. The tympani of insects flying through the air, gripping the bark of trees, and feeding on the dry grasses was deafening. It had begun the previous year and accompanied them on their slow progress south. The incessant noise had diminished at the seaport of Joppa, but as the army walked inland and began to ascend the hills that led to the city of Jerusalem atop the King's Highway, the noise of insects became louder and louder until it was again deafening.

Nimrod and Simeon stood amid the parched bushes and dead grasses of the foothills of the holy city of Jerusalem and stared. Like a crown on the head of a monarch, the city of David, of Solomon, of Judah the Maccabee, of Herod the Great, of Jesus of Nazareth, and now of the Fatamid Muslims, stood proud and eternal. Crescents of mosques, crosses of churches, and stars of David atop synagogues were the rooftops of the city. The buildings of worship stood side by side with unadorned white stone houses, where the population of the holy city lived.

The two men gazed in wonder at the white walls, and neither moved, neither said a word. Their breath came in short and shallow gasps, as though they were confronted by the most beautiful vision they'd ever seen in their lives.

And they were not alone. Thousands and thousands of crusading soldiers, the barons, earls, chevaliers, archers, lancers, foot soldiers, and peasants, all were awestruck by the city that had woven itself into their dreams night after night through the long march from Paris.

The vast host of men wept, even as the tears running down their cheeks dried in the arid air. Some of the men stripped off their tunics and stood naked, beating their heads and chests in expressions of an emotion none had previously experienced. Some of the men fell to their knees and wailed into the ground, incapable of finding words or actions to express their feelings.

Henri Guillaume, duke of Champagne and count palatin of Meaux and Blois, sat astride his charger and surveyed the scene. He, too, was strangely affected by the sight of the city of Jerusalem, though not moved to tears. When he'd first set eyes on Constantinople, a beautiful city set above the shining blue waters of the Sea of Marble, the Bosporus, and the Dardanelles, he'd been moved by its beauty but nothing more. When he and the other barons and dukes laid siege to Antioch, he hadn't even noticed the splendor or antiquity of the city; it was simply a citadel to be overcome by force for the wealth it contained.

Even here, at the foot of Jerusalem, Duke Henri felt none of the emotion of his army, but he did experience the ghosts of its history. He closed his eyes and shook his head, and when he opened them again, Henri saw a city housing an enemy to be captured; a city to be wrested from the hands of the infidel Jew and Mohammedan and reclaimed for its rightful owners.

Yet he couldn't help but feel some mystery about the place. There were voices in his head that drove him and visions in his eyes that confronted him; he knew he had to remain silent, keeping his hallucinations to himself.

The duke kicked his horse's flanks and drew level with Nimrod and Simeon. He pointed to the prostrate and weeping men arrayed before him. "What is this that seizes my men and makes them wail like women?"

Nimrod, ever patient but surprised by the question, looked up at the duke and shielded his eyes from the glare of the sun. "The Greek doctors of old believed that a woman's womb, her *hysterika*, moved inside her body. This led to an excess of emotions, which philosophers called hysteria." Nimrod turned back to the huge walls before them. "While these are men," he said, "perhaps something similar is at work in those viewing the holy city for the first time, a kind of hysteria that spreads from one to the other until it affects all the men who are here." Nimrod finished the thought with a simple shrug.

Simeon, ever watchful, as if living on borrowed time, looked around at the army. He had been to the city, knew its walls from his youth, knew many of its secrets, but had little time for religious fervor. In his travels as a merchant, he had seen many faiths, and none had served him well. The business of trade put food on his table, and he was baffled by the response of the Christians around him. "Perhaps what your army feels is simple exhaustion after such a long journey, or perhaps there is something more."

"Never just one answer with you Jews, is there?" said the duke, his tone dry as the air around them, but Nimrod ignored the jibe.

"For two thousand years, people have lived and died in that city for the love of their God, be He Yahweh, Jehovah, or Allah. These three great creeds are centered on this very place. It is the home of the Jews, the Muslims, and the Christians. It is, my lord, the center of the world."

Duke Henri sniffed and looked up at the city. "It is a city occupied by a godless infidel called a Mohammedan who performs his heathen ceremonies here, where only Christians should be allowed to worship," he said firmly. "The Mohammedan and the Jew defile the place!"

Facing the holy city, Nimrod found a courage that he rarely had, enabling him to speak plainly. "Jesus was a Jew, my lord. And to the Mohammedan, Jesus is revered as a great prophet. The center of the world is perhaps not so simple as you may think."

Duke Henri scoffed. "You can keep your religions and your faiths and your sanctity and your goodness. It's the gold I want, and not the gold of eternity—the gold of now!"

Henri wheeled his horse around and rode away, leaving Nimrod and Simeon alone with the view of Jerusalem's massive stone walls.

"It is now a siege. And with walls such as those, it will be sickness, disease, and starvation that take the men long before the sword and the arrow." Nimrod shook his head and turned to follow his lord.

• • •

"Idiots! Crook-pants! Dankish pottle-deep puttocks!" The duke roared so naturally that it seemed his normal manner of speech; neither Nimrod nor Simeon was much affected by it anymore.

The duke continued to rant. "Not one stone, not a single pebble, has been taken down from those walls in the two months since we arrived and laid siege! Twelve thousand Crusaders, lancers, ballisters, archers, and catapulteers and still the walls stand! And now a gaggle of addle-brained malcontents say that they've seen a vision of Bishop Adhemar and want me to blow a trumpet to bring down the walls like those of Jericho!"

The stalemate of the siege had stirred a cauldron of rumors, inflamed by the fervent and deluded. The vision of Bishop Adhemar was just the latest.

The duke's voice dropped to a cold rasp, and he extended a finger at Simeon. "You said that there was great treasure waiting for us in Constantinople and in Antioch. And what did I get? Nothing. Trinkets."

This was not the first time that the duke had mistaken Simeon for old Jacob. Duke Henri often referred to him as Jacob. Simeon, for his part, had learned not to correct his master. Like Nimrod, he was all too aware of the illness slowly eating the duke's mind.

"The other dukes and nobles looted the mosques and were weighed down by fabulous riches; I followed your advice and took the synagogues and the houses of the Jews and came away with little. How do I know that Jerusalem will be different?"

"My lord, in Constantinople and in Antioch, you took a vast fortune. By our estimate, it accounts for the equivalent of two years of income from your lands," insisted Simeon.

"Two years! I could have been shafting whores in France for the next two years and still earned as much. Yet I've ridden halfway around the folly-fallen world, been laid low with pox that you cannot cure"—the finger of blame shifted from Simeon to Nimrod—"and spent a fortune feeding and arming the laziest and most cowardly army any duke has ever sent into battle! And my saddlebags remain empty. Where is all the money and jewelry of the Jews that should now be mine?"

"Jerusalem will be different, my lord," said Simeon, trying to calm the duke.

"How so, Jew?"

"Because in Constantinople and Antioch, the Jews were in a degraded condition. They were a community made poor by the Muslims' taxes and by the hatred of the Christians. In Muslim lands, my lord, Jews are considered *Dhimmi*, or non-Muslim residents, and subject to a special tax called *jizya*, which has been a great impost and has damaged their chances to attain wealth. But the Fatamid dynasty has ruled this land for nearly a century and a half, and they are, for the most part, benign rulers. Jews, Christians, and Muslims are free to follow their own faiths without interference. So the reports that reach me, my lord, say the Jews of Jerusalem are indeed wealthy."

The truth was that Simeon had no way of knowing if what he said was true; it was conjecture at best. Yet the frailty of the duke's mind, the growing discontentment in the army, the long stalemate of the siege, all prevailed upon him to lie. The simmering hatred of the Christian invaders toward any "nonbelievers" was palpable. The duke protected his Jewish advisers for now, but should something happen to the duke—either physically or financially—the fate of Simeon and Nimrod might be sealed. The hopeful lie Simeon told the duke was a ploy to keep the man focused and to keep up the morale of his army.

Duke Henri pondered the words of his treasurer. "You had better be right or else make your peace with your god!" He flung open the tent flap and looked out toward the city walls. "But I'll not fall to foolishness of trumpets and visions. I will find a way to breach those walls." The duke raised his voice once more to summon his captain. "Roux!"

The duke needn't have yelled, as the gaunt red-headed man was never far away. He quickly appeared in the portal of the tent.

"I want you to gather ten of your best men. No horses. We go on foot."

Roux looked puzzled by the order and glowered at the two Jews behind the duke. "Where are we going, my lord?"

"There is a way. There must be a way inside. And we go tonight to find it."

"My lord, the Genoese siege engines will not arrive until tomorrow. Proper siege engines made of the finest wood and tempered iron. Surely we must wait?"

"No. No. No. We will go now! Ten of the best, and we will find another way. If we wait, we will lose. They . . ." The duke cast his arm wide to take in the tents of the other lords, his rivals, encamped nearby. "They will take what is mine and what the Jews have told me awaits inside those walls."

These words brought the twisted glare of Roux back to Simeon and Nimrod.

"We will reconnoiter the perimeter of the city under darkness and find the weakness of these walls."

Roux knew there was no arguing, and moreover, he saw the misguided order as an indicator of the duke's failing faculties. At first it had been only Nimrod who had seen the duke's syphilis spread from his loins to his mind. But the paranoia and hallucinations had become harder to hide, and Roux now saw opportunity in his lord's demise.

"Go. See to the men," ordered the duke, and Roux left quickly.

The duke turned back to Nimrod and Simeon. "Yes. I shall find a way. I shall find a hole in the wall."

"But my lord—" protested Nimrod.

"I shall find a way, and you, my good doctor, will come with me. I want a doctor and a Jew by my side when I find a portal into the city."

• • •

Though there had been no arguing with the duke, Nimrod and Simeon had argued. Simeon insisted on coming to scout the walls, but Nimrod refused outright. The debt that Simeon felt he owed the older man was too large for him to remain behind. The danger in what the duke had proposed was obvious, and yet Simeon could not in good conscience let his friend go without him.

But as was often the case with Nimrod, argument became philosophical examination, only this time his voice was filled with a strange sadness.

"These may well be our last days, Simeon. And I have spent them as I have spent my life: in books seeking knowledge and wisdom. I have been reading the philosophies of the Gaonim, the wise Jews of ancient Babylon. They lived, like we do, under the rule of others—we under Christians and they under the Abbasid, followers of Mohammed. Perhaps it is that otherness that creates wisdom. Their work brings me much consolation. These Gaonim were the great minds of our people, and they changed the way we think. Unlike the Christians, they didn't encase their faith in a golden casket, making it immutable. Instead, they looked at how it might adapt and change and be renewed with thinking, as thinking itself changes. But these Christians who are our earthly lords, they're unwilling—no, incapable—of changing. They even find thinking difficult."

"Is this what we've come to, then?" asked Simeon. "Is this now our lot? To die with thousands of others in the madness that will be the end of this city as its walls are breached by the siege engines?"

"We can't stop them. An entire city can't stop them. This has always been the end of our road. I foresee great slaughter in the coming days, and I am prepared to die rather than carry back to France the awful truth of tens of thousands of Jews and Muslims slaughtered by these Crusaders. I would—I will—rather die."

Simeon was not resigned, and so as Duke Henri, Michel Roux, the ten chosen soldiers, and Nimrod slipped out of the camp under cover of darkness, Simeon, son of Abel, followed them.

· · ·

The small group of Christian soldiers and one slow-moving Jewish doctor circumnavigated the outer walls of the holy city of Jerusalem. The soldiers carried only swords, leaving behind shields and spears to keep their movement light and swift. Yet they were aware of their vulnerability to the guards who walked the ramparts above and, as a result, moved nervously along the path led by Duke Henri.

The darkness of the night sky and the perpetual shadows of the city's massive walls gave them some comfort; the lights of the torches burning atop the walls cast no illumination this far below. For hours they had been searching, not knowing what they were supposed to be searching for. The duke simply kept repeating, "There must be a hole in the wall."

Michel Roux's narrow eyes darted like a wolf's as he followed the duke. He also kept peering back at Nimrod, shuffling along behind, as if stalking prey. When the party rested, Nimrod heard murmurs of scorn among the soldiers that a "Christ killer" was among them and they were dismayed that their lord seemed to maintain such faith in Jews who, like the Muslims, corrupted the holy city. Such words could not hurt Nimrod, but the implications of darker actions quickened his heart.

The journey around the walls seemed to drag on endlessly into the night. The men were silent save for the creak of their armor and weaponry. But Nimrod could hear the duke muttering to himself; he feared the demons of his lord's addled mind now had free rein.

"The bones will lead us . . . we should follow the bones . . ." mumbled the duke, and urged the troop, with exaggerated hand movements, to follow him down a small hillock. Then, with little warning, the duke let out a scream, guttural and incoherent, and broke into a run. The men were bewildered that such a mission of stealth should see their leader make such a racket.

Nimrod watched the duke take off. His form was quickly swallowed by the shadows. Without thinking, Nimrod set off after his master.

Was it loyalty that set him running? Was it fear of being left behind with the anti-Semitic soldiers and the cold and brutal Michel Roux? Whatever it was, Nimrod found himself focused on following the sounds of the duke in the darkness.

Back at the top of the small rise, the soldiers looked at one another in bafflement. Roux quickly took charge and ordered them all to stay where they were. He alone set off into the dark after the duke and the doctor.

Jerusalem

February 6, 1948

SHALMAN SAT IN the same small room, forearms on the same simple wooden table, where he'd sat when Immanuel Berin snatched him from the street to question him about Judit's activities.

Now he faced the stern Irgun leader with a very different weight on his heart. He had asked for this meeting with Berin and had been brought, blindfolded, to the secret headquarters.

Shalman prayed that Berin would ask the questions and he could tell the truth. But Berin was not so forthcoming; he sat calmly waiting for Shalman to say why he'd asked for the meeting.

Shalman swallowed and wiped his brow. He felt torn in two. He was now certain what Judit was, what she had done, and more pressingly, what she was going to do.

The world around Shalman was a powder keg. War was inevitable, and Shalman was resigned to it. But retribution, revenge, killing to exert fear, this was what troubled Shalman's soul. He had killed, he had fought for what he believed in. He had defended his home and his right to a home. But every death had weighed on him, every widow was his wife, every orphan his child. Worst of all was the image of an Arab boy in flames on an airfield. His soul was tortured every day by what he'd done. He could not bring back those he'd killed, and he could not stop the war and whatever would follow, but Shalman felt there was at least one thing that he could prevent.

To do it, he would have to betray the woman he loved and the mother of his child. Shalman knew the price.

"I've seen Judit."

Berin's expression didn't change. "When?" he asked.

"Last night. And now she's gone. I don't think she's coming back. I think she's escaping. Is it you she's escaping? What's going on?"

Shalman's answer told Berin that Judit had found Anastasia's body and the message had been received.

Shalman tried to read Berin's face, but it was an impassive mask. The information garnered in the Russian deal by Golda Meir had given Berin the names of the MGB assassination squad. Some had already been dealt with. Soon it would be Judit's turn.

"Where is she now?" asked Berin, his voice hardening.

"I don't know," Shalman told him. "I just don't know, but she has to be stopped. You have to stop her. She's doing things that are—" He couldn't continue.

"We know," said Berin softly. "We know all about her. You know she's a spy for the Soviet Union, don't you? She was working for Moscow Central, for the NKVD and then the MGB."

The expression on Shalman's face spoke volumes.

"Come on, you don't expect me to believe that you knew nothing," said Berin.

Shalman opened his mouth to speak, but he was speechless.

"You poor bastard. You knew nothing? Didn't you even suspect?"

"I . . . When she went out at night, I thought . . . I never met her friends, but . . ." He sank back into silence.

"You'd better leave," said Berin.

"Not until you tell me about my wife. My wife! I have a right to know."

Immanuel Berin shook his head. His thoughts were in Vienna, long before the war, long before the *Anschluss*, to a city of light and laughter; to a family who lived in a beautiful three-story home in the Kaerntner Strasse: He was a young psychiatrist and she was a beautiful young Jewess, her family scions of Viennese society. They were so happy. And at some stage, Shalman and Judit had been happy.

How could Berin tell him the truth? How could he tell this decent, gullible young man that his wife was a merciless assassin who'd been responsible for the murders of innocent and important Jews?

"Go, Shalman. Just go."

The young man sat there staring at Berin. Tears were forming in his eyes. Slowly, he stood and turned to leave. To return to a home he'd made for a family but now occupied only with a little daughter. Berin felt an awful draining sadness flood through his body as he watched Shalman leave. He knew that very soon, they'd find Judit and execute her for her crimes. Just as the Nazis had executed his own wife and children in some death camp. When would it all end? he wondered sadly.

Central Museum Building
16 Rothschild Boulevard, Tel Aviv
May 14, 1948

THE INVITATIONS TO attend the meeting had been sent out by courier, and the message on the envelopes was "Top Secret."

They'd been sent to dozens of the most prominent Israelis, leaders in politics, academia, local government, the newspapers, and the editor and senior reporter of the new Israeli radio service, Kol Yisrael. All had been invited to hear the reading of the recently completed declaration, one day ahead of the United Nations decision to vote for the partition of the Palestinians and the Jews. The reason it was so secret was David Ben Gurion's fear that if the British found out about the meeting, they might attempt to stop it. The other reason he and Golda Meir and others were wary of a crowd was because the Arab armies, poised to begin their massive invasion the moment the vote was taken, might misunderstand the import of what was about to be done in the Tel Aviv museum and roll across the borders a day early.

Of course, it didn't work, and at half past three in the afternoon, those invited were forced to fight their way through the massive crowd of expectant onlookers standing on the streets outside the museum, waiting for the beginning of the top-secret event.

Ben Gurion got out of his car. "How the hell did they find out?" he snapped at his police protection officer.

With a wry smile, the policeman shrugged. "They're Jews. How do you stop them from finding out?"

He entered the hall to begin the meeting at four o'clock so delegates could be home in time for Shabbat. He saw that Kol Yisrael had already set up microphones on the tables, so that this, their inaugural broadcast, would herald the way Israel wanted to be seen and heard, in public, in the light of day, open and transparent before the whole world.

Ben Gurion looked at his watch, banged his gavel on the table, and began to speak but was immediately interrupted by the 250 delegates bursting into the national anthem of Israel, the *Hatikvah*. He wanted to bring down his gavel—the time and political pressures were enormous—but when he heard the amassed voices singing, he could barely speak. He listened to the words and joined in.

> *As long as in the heart, within*
> *A Jewish soul still yearns,*
> *And onward, toward the ends of the east*
> *An eye still looks toward Zion;*
> *Our hope is not yet lost,*
> *The hope of two thousand years,*
> *To be a free nation in our land,*
> *The land of Zion and Jerusalem.*

Men and women stopped singing, and the hall descended into silence as people turned and hugged. Clearing his throat of emotion, Ben Gurion began to speak. "This scroll establishes the State of Israel. We have come on a long, long journey, a journey which has taken us two thousand years to complete. So let me read to you the agreed text." He cleared his throat again and, like a town crier, began in a stentorian voice:

"The land of Israel was the birthplace of the Jewish people. Here their spiritual, religious, and political identity was shaped. Here they first attained statehood, created cultural values of national and universal significance, and gave to the world the eternal Book of Books.

"After being forcibly exiled from their land, the people kept faith with it throughout their Dispersion and never ceased to pray and hope for their return to it and for the restoration in it of their political freedom . . ."

He looked up from the scroll and realized that half of the delegates sitting around the hall had tears running down their cheeks.

Immanuel Berin was sitting in the audience with tears streaming down his cheeks. Though he, more than most, realized the coming trauma from this declaration, of the war just hours away, it was the culmination of all his yearning, all his hopes.

Hatikvah meant "The Hope." The Jews had hoped for thousands of years that they could be a free people in their own land, free of hatred, free of fear. One day it would come about. Not today, when the declaration was read, but when the war was won.

As the assembly sat, Berin repeated to himself in profound silence the last words of the anthem—to "be a free nation in our own land, the land of Zion and Jerusalem." Not tomorrow, when some distant international body in New York determined it, but in the future, when Jews and Arabs sat down as equals, as brothers and sisters, in peace and harmony.

Holy City of Jerusalem
July 8, 1099

NIMROD RAN FOR what seemed like a thousand steps, stumbling blindly in the dark, aware that at any moment his foot could fall into a rabbit hole and snap his leg. Up ahead he heard a noise, not the deep-throated yelling of the duke but, rather, a different voice—higher-pitched, more melodic. Nimrod was surprised by the sound, so he kept moving in that direction.

Then came the sound of metal upon metal, a harsh clash of iron that echoed through the air. These new sounds gave Nimrod a clear bearing, and he homed in on the source. With a few more steps, he had moved out of the shadow of the walls, and the dim moonlight filtered over the ground to bring the figures before him into relief.

Duke Henri stood with his sword raised high above his head and his mouth open in a roar. In front of him was a smaller, more nimble Arab warrior—presumably a scout returning from spying on the Crusader camp. The dark-skinned man held a scimitar shaped like the crescent moon atop a mosque. His clothes were lighter, his armor simpler and more flexible, his weapon faster and more agile. The Arab judged the huge armored figure of the duke, the breadth and weight of his sword. The Crusader might be slow and clumsy, but one hit would be enough to cleave him in two.

The duke's yell was a prelude to a charge, and his broadsword swiped down in a wide arc aimed at cutting the Arab into two. The Arab saw the attack coming and pivoted aside, spinning on his toes and bringing his scimitar whipping about in an arc parallel to the ground. The curved blade slashed across the duke's back as his momentum carried him forward and past the Arab warrior. As sharp as the scimitar was, it glanced off the chain mail, leaving nothing more than bloodless bruising.

The duke recovered and turned to face the Arab once more, broadsword extended and pointing at his opponent's heart. The Arab bent his knees to lower himself for greater poise, ready to spring in whatever direction the Crusader might expose in his next attack.

"You're a walking corpse," screamed the duke. He lunged again, this time thrusting forward, hoping to skewer the Arab on the point of his sword. The swiftness of the attack belied the duke's size, and the Arab's pivot was slower. The tip of the broadsword caught him under the arm, tore through the light armor, and sent a thin spray of blood to the ground at their feet.

If the wound caused the Arab pain, he made no sound and swiped his scimitar through the air in defiance, ready for the next pass.

The duke, spurred on by the strike against the enemy, rushed his next attack, lashing out wildly in a two-handed swing. The sword was long, but he overreached and was off balance. He stumbled as the Arab lifted his scimitar high above his head and brought it crashing down.

Nimrod saw the reflection of the moonlight on the Arab's gleaming blade, so much brighter than the dull and often rusted gray of Crusader weapons. He saw the sword slice the air and even imagined he heard the wind parting as it swished toward the body of the duke.

The Arab had aimed his blow well. He knew where the thick Crusader armor of interlocking rings of steel was weakest. The joints at the shoulders were his target, and his blow was true. The curved scimitar, made for slicing rather than slashing and stabbing of French broadswords, slipped through the rings and into the flesh and bone and sinew of the duke's shoulder.

The duke of Champagne screamed at the pain of his nearly severed arm, his lifeless hand dropping the broadsword.

Nimrod saw all this from behind the Arab warrior, saw the dark-skinned man's back arch in victory as he raised his sword for a final blow on the duke, now with no weapon or limb to parry.

Nimrod saw all this and ran. Not into the darkness or away in fright but straight at the warrior in front of him. He ran with all his might and all his speed and sent his body forcibly colliding into the torso of the Mohammedan warrior before the final blow could fall on his master's head.

The two figures tumbled into the dirt, arms and legs and feet in a melee of confusion and fury. The momentum pushed the Arab face-down on the ground but also carried Nimrod over the man's body, knocking the breath from his chest.

As Nimrod struggled to draw in air and find his way to his feet, his hands grabbed at his side and grew wet with blood. The Arab blade had somehow pierced him during the tackle. There was no time to contemplate the wound, as the Mohammedan was already standing and drawing a curved dagger from a sash at his waist. The man leaped toward Nimrod, who screamed and tried to roll away, but the Mohammedan was too quick. His knees pinioned Nimrod's arms to the ground. Nimrod saw the dagger draw back, ready to be swept across his throat, and tried to remember the Jewish prayer for those in mortal danger, but it had left his mind.

He closed his eyes and waited for the death blow. But it never came.

Instead, there was a sickening wet thud and Nimrod's eyes blinked open to see the Arab man's body on the ground beside him, his face a mess of blood and fragments of broken skull. The body of the warrior shuddered and twitched beside the prostrate Nimrod.

It was only then that Nimrod saw the face of the savior who wielded the stone that had killed the Arab. Over him, the light of the moon and stars gave just enough illumination to show the face of Simeon.

"You should be glad I never obey doctors' orders."

But Nimrod's mind raced to the fate of the duke, and he scrambled over to the body of his master lying flat on the ground, his nearly severed limb still pumping blood.

The duke's eyes focused on the faces of Nimrod and Simeon as they knelt over him. As a doctor, Nimrod knew that the end would come as soon as the duke's life force drained into the earth of Jerusalem. There was nothing he could do as a physician. The wound was of an enormity that defied any medicine or surgery.

Neither Simeon nor Nimrod knew what to say. The duke gazed at them for what seemed like a long stretch of silence, then his eyes focused not on their faces but something behind them. The two Jews turned to see what their lord was staring at.

They saw nothing at first but soon saw what the duke was focusing on. High on the hill, the city of Jerusalem was beginning to glow golden as the very first rays of dawn lit the minarets and crucifixes and the tops of the white walls.

"I see the bones . . ."

The words of the duke, whispered before too much of his blood had coursed from his body, made Simeon and Nimrod turn away from the splendor of the city.

"I see the bones. All of them. All around me . . ."

Nimrod placed a hand on the duke's chest but could find no words.

"I see the bones of all who have died. All who have fought and died."

The duke's eyes found Nimrod clearly for the last time and held him fast.

"I'm sorry . . . Tell the bones I'm sorry . . ."

And the duke died in the shadow of the walls of the city he'd come to relieve.

Nimrod felt a great desire to sit with the lord he'd known so well and for so long. To simply sit and wait for the sun to warm the dead man's face, so that his journey into eternity was lit. But a voice calling out dragged the two men from the moment.

The voice was that of Michel Roux, unmistakable and distinct. Simeon grabbed at Nimrod's clothes and hauled him to his feet.

"Come on, we have to go," Simeon said in a harsh whisper.

But Nimrod resisted. "Where? Where shall we go? We have nowhere to go and no one to trust!"

In that moment Simeon found a sense of faith that had long been absent in him. "I'd rather die inside the walls of the holy city with my people than out here with these dogs of Crusaders. For surely we will both be dead by morning, either at the hands of Roux or by a sword from those within the walls. Come with me, Doctor." Simeon pulled Nimrod up and forced him to follow. "We have to get to the tunnel!"

They scurried toward the walls, Nimrod wondering what tunnel the man was talking about. They ran into the early-morning gloom with the voice of Michel Roux behind them, baying for their blood.

• • •

Nimrod followed, too exhausted to ask Simeon to explain, the wound delivered by the Saracen beginning to hurt viciously. He pressed his hand to his side, holding in the blood that was leaking from the wound, but he could feel his head growing light. He leaned on Simeon's arm as they scrambled around the edge of the white stone walls and through the low tangled bushes and stunted trees that grew in the shadow of the city.

Was Simeon seeking something from memory or instinct? Nimrod could not tell. But the wiry man moved with purpose and focus, searching for signs that Nimrod could not see. Finally, Simeon stopped when they were well clear of the evil Roux. "There has long been rumor in my family of a tunnel into the city, an ancient watercourse," he said breathlessly. "This ancient tunnel was supposed to be used by the inhabitants. Some say my family had a hand in it, but who knows? Yet our connection has come down through generations of my family. They spoke of a watercourse built in the time of King Solomon. Few know of it, other than us Jews, and perhaps the Muslims."

Nimrod reached into his tunic to touch the medallion around his neck. Simeon saw the hesitation and his gaze moved to Nimrod's other hand grasping at his side, saw the blood seeping between his fingers. Nimrod wanted to say that such a story had been told from father to son in his own family for generation upon generation, but he was weak from the wound and found talking difficult.

Simeon continued. "They say of this tunnel that it runs beneath the walls of the city, carrying water to the pools below. If we climb up from the pools of Siloam, pray God Almighty that what is told in my family is correct, we will come into the heart of the city."

Was Simeon saying this to keep up Nimrod's spirits as he died? Or did the merchant truly know how to find the ancient tunnel? As Nimrod held the metal seal at his neck, he remembered the words written in ancient Hebrew. He knew by heart the name Matanyahu and the story handed down in his family of a builder who worked in the time of King Solomon. And Nimrod remembered the words inscribed on the seal:

I, Matanyahu, son of Naboth, son of Gamaliel, have built this tunnel for the glory of my King, Solomon the Wise, in the Twenty-second year of his reign.

• • •

When the siege engines made by the Genoese sailors in Joppa arrived and began assaulting the walls, new life was breathed into the Crusader campaign. The cheers of the soldiers could be heard throughout the valleys and over the hills as the siege weapons hurled massive rocks over the towers along with the bodies of the recently killed Saracens. Not only did these dead bodies flying over the ramparts cause horror and panic, they were a marvelous weapon for spreading disease and destroying morale.

The noise of the melee above was lost on Nimrod and Simeon as they made their way, slowly and painfully, up the ancient tunnel. They had found the entrance to the watercourse covered by a thousand years of rock slides, dirt, fallen debris, and dead vegetation, but Simeon had been right. From the pools of Siloam, the watercourse became clear when they pulled away the vegetation where the ground was wet. They slowly, painfully climbed the black and slippery tunnel up toward the center of the city.

Nimrod and Simeon were repeating precisely what Abram had done in the time of the Romans when he returned the seal made by Matanyahu, along with the woman who would become his wife, Ruth, daughter of Eli and Naomi of the Tribe of Judah.

With a millennium separating their ascent into the tunnel, the ancestor and the descendant slipped on the same ground covered in black moss and squeezed through gaps in the rock that were little wider than their bodies.

As they ascended to a larger and more open space, they felt like they'd climbed from the bottom to the top of a mountain, but in reality they had no idea how far up the city of Jerusalem they had ascended. Nimrod was growing weaker by the hour, and the blood loss, though largely stanched, had caused him to feel faint almost every step of the way.

Nimrod and Simeon, like Abram and Ruth, eventually rounded what appeared to be a bend in the tunnel and, out of the deadened silence punctuated only by footfalls and breathing, heard a noise.

But unlike the noise of the pagan conquerors walking the streets of Aelia Capitolina when Rome commanded the city, the noise that Nimrod and Simeon heard was the wailing of Jews, Christians, and Mohammedans. With the arrival of the siege engines, the inhabitants of Jerusalem understood that these were their last days and were praying together to their one God. Even the Christians believed, despite the flags with the cross of Jesus clearly displayed, that these were the end times, and chanted a prayer to save them from the onslaught.

It was only when Nimrod and Simeon, dirty, wet, cold, and aching from the climb, came to the underside of the pavement on which thousands of feet scurried above that they realized their way was barred.

The ancient water causeway had been blocked four hundred years earlier by the caliph Abd al-Malik when he'd ordered the construction of the Dome of the Rock Mosque. He'd made access to the water into a well, and the sides were so narrow, steep, and slippery that they were impossible for Nimrod and Simeon to climb.

And so, as the tens of thousands of citizens of Jerusalem were wailing in fear of the assault and the destruction of their city, just the thickness of a pavement and a depth of rock separated the two men from their besieged brethren. Nimrod and Simeon sat in the dark.

"We should return to the valley floor," said Simeon, already turning to negotiate the way down. But Nimrod's strength had left him. His hand was still pressed to his side, but the blood, once crimson between his fingers, was now black and dry and spent. His limbs were numb and thoughts drifted toward sleep. He could go no farther.

"No," he said in little more than a whisper.

"You can. We can make it back. Once the Crusaders have taken the city, we will be outside the walls and can make our escape. They won't notice us when they're slaughtering the inhabitants."

But Simeon's words were futile.

Nimrod shook his head. "I die here, my friend."

• • •

The siege assault took five days to drain the city of its strength. Flaming arrows set fire to rooftops and stables, dead bodies hurled through the air crashed through ceilings. Rocks exploded with the pounding of battering rams. Women and children sheltered from the nightmare as men died in the midst of it. With a final breach of the outer wall, the Crusaders streamed into the city.

The Crusaders screamed "Hep, hep, hep, hoorah" as they cleaved every limb from every body in their path. The words meant *Hierisolyma est perdita*, "Jerusalem is lost," an insult to all the inhabitants. The Christian men of God had ordered the Crusaders to shout it out as they entered the city. The charge and chant were led by Michel Roux, a man never driven by faith but by power and an unquenchable desire for riches. Roux led the charge with a fervor to rival any cleric, and his bloodlust fell like rain on his victims.

Tens of thousands of men, women, and children were slaughtered in a single day, an orgy of killing, rape, and theft. Nobody was spared the most hideous of deaths; nor was anybody saved to become a slave. Even many Christians of Jerusalem, fighting alongside their Muslim and Jewish brothers and sisters to defend the city, were hacked to pieces.

The destruction was total, and the impact of the pain on the city would course through its veins for centuries to come.

By the time the end had come for Jerusalem, Simeon was well away from the city and leaving the Crusaders' madness far behind him. He had sat with his friend Nimrod until the end. The man who had spared his life died in his arms.

Before his final breath slipped away, the doctor had taken a small metal seal from around his neck and pressed it into the palm of the merchant.

"Take this. It was born in this tunnel. But don't let it die in this tunnel. Take it with you."

And with that, Simeon had left the secret tunnel beneath the walls of the ancient holy city, climbing back down the steep, slippery path to emerge into the sunlight.

North Jerusalem

Shabbat morning, May 15, 1948

IMMANUEL BERIN LOOKED up from the table and tried to take in the scene so he could tell his grandchildren in years to come where he had been when the United Nations decided on the fate of Israel and its Jews. That is, if he married again when this madness was over, and if his wife was young enough to bear him a second family.

But no matter who was gathered in the room around the radio, listening to Kol Yisrael rebroadcast the vote being taken at that moment two thousand miles north in the Palais de Chaillot in Paris by the General Assembly, two faces were missing, faces that he'd never see again.

He was older than all of the others. He'd been through vastly more in his life than almost all of them, and had taken its vicissitudes in stride. In his life, he'd been to the heights and sunk to the depths. If Israel were granted nation status by the two-thirds majority of the General Assembly, all well and good; if not, then he would wait another year, and one year after that if necessary. But for these kids, it was life and death.

He looked for the face of Judit Etzion, but she wasn't there. He felt disgust when he tried to remember her face. He didn't know where she was, nor where his men had dumped her body, never to be found, nor given a burial, nor marked with a gravestone. He'd specifically told them not to tell him, so that in years to come, he wouldn't inadvertently travel there and remember her. He wanted to expunge her from his mind for all time. The others in the MGB death squads . . . well, they were just irrelevant, pawns in a geopolitical game. But Judit had a presence in his mind, in his actions, and even in the room, and he had to expunge her. She had reminded him so much of his wife, victim of the Nazis.

And as Israel's history was written, Judit would become one of Israel's fallen heroines, remembered for the good deeds she'd done to secure the nation. Known only to a small number of Israelis for the hateful, traitorous, murderous things she'd committed as an agent of the Kremlin.

He continued to be distressed by the absence of Ashira, so full of zeal and intelligence and potential to be a great Israeli in a new nation, murdered by Judit and her insane cabal for reasons he hadn't been told and upon which he could only speculate.

But all the others were there, except those who'd died in the course of the past year's Arab uprising, or had been arrested by the British and incarcerated. Proud that he'd been able to bring so many through to see this day, Immanuel listened to the voice of the reporter.

While the meeting was called to order by the session's chair at the UN, at another radio in a corner of the room, one of the young men shouted with glee, "Hey, the USA has just recognized Israel. The White House put out a statement by President Truman that says the Yanks have been informed that a Jewish state has been proclaimed in Palestine, and recognizes the provisional government as the de facto authority of the State of Israel . . . you hear that? . . . the State of Israel."

The room erupted into cheers. Only Immanuel Berin knew what was behind Truman's move—the president's friendship with Eddie Jacobson, a former partner of Truman's in a clothing store, who was still a close friend. The U.S. Department of State was against granting nationhood to Israel for fear of the war that would follow, as well as Russian intervention, but a phone call and a meeting with Jacobson, who had introduced Truman to Chaim Weizmann, changed the president's mind. Immanuel smiled and wondered whether other nations had been created through friendships, happenstance, and sheer *mazel*.

While waiting for the chairman of the General Assembly to begin the voting process, Immanuel spoke to the young men and women around him. "Last night, the British army lowered its last flag to end its mandate over Palestine. The last British troops are leaving today. Six months ago, the United Nations voted for the partition of this land into the State of Israel and an independent, secure nation for the Arabs of Palestine. We Jews received far less land, fewer natural resources, and a more fractured nation than we prayed for in all the years of our exile. Our birthright has been stripped from us. Yet we accepted the decision of the UN. The Arabs, given preferential treatment by the UN, have rejected out of hand what they were offered. For six months, they've been waging a civil war against us. But all that has been little more than a guerrilla conflict compared with what's over the hill.

"If the vote in the UN in just a few minutes is two thirds in our favor, then while we Jews are cheering our freedom, the tanks, artillery, and soldiers of five Arab countries will be coming over the hills, invading our borders, destroying our villages, killing our population in their efforts to eradicate this land and make it free of Jews—what the Nazis called *Judenrein*. Armies and air forces, some British-trained and equipped by Egypt, Trans-Jordan, Syria, Lebanon, and Iraq will invade our sovereign nation.

"Yet we sit here, knowing what's going to happen in a few hours, and pray for Russia to vote with the United States and other countries so that we can be free citizens in our own land. So should the vote go our way, brothers and sisters, let us celebrate the moment but gird our loins for the fight ahead."

He glanced around and saw every boy and girl, man and woman, staring at him. He tried to read their faces but couldn't differentiate between hope and despair. These kids knew nothing about the way Moscow had managed to assassinate so many good Jews in Palestine. Yet there was every indication that they'd vote for the creation of Israel. But he was only a psychiatrist! How could he possibly understand the Russian mind or the sort of deal that Golda Meir had made in Moscow?

Immanuel turned up the volume, and they all listened to the chairman of the General Assembly begin the process of voting. Three lists were made on three sheets of paper: one for yes, one for no, and one for abstentions. Nobody was certain until the vote came to the Soviet Union whether they had succeeded or not. When Andrei Gromyko voted with a simple yes, the room erupted into hysterical cheers.

Immanuel held up his hand for silence. There were other nations to vote. When the voting had finished, the men who had made ticks on the paper added them up quickly and compared notes. One, a farmer from the Galilee village of Peki'in, shouted out, "Two thirds. Two thirds. We've done it."

Nobody heard the chairman of the General Assembly of the United Nations in distant Paris announce the creation of the world's newest nation. The cheering and hugging and kissing in the room in Jerusalem was cacophonous.

And nor did anybody celebrating in the room hear the throaty roar of the engines of Arab tanks, Jeeps, planes, and troop carriers roaring into life on the northern, eastern, and southern borders of the State of Israel.

EPILOGUE

A hill overlooking Ras Abu Yussuf
The State of Israel
June 19, 1949

SHALMAN ETZION HANDED his two-year-old daughter, Vered, a honey biscuit and a half-filled bottle of milk. She thanked him. He loved her thin, piping voice and blew her a kiss, which she returned with determination.

He smiled when he realized that it was probably close to this spot, three thousand years earlier, that the ancient Jews, returning from their exile in Egypt, had looked with joy from hills like these into a land of milk and honey.

Shalman lay down on the blanket and looked up at the sky, a deep, almost violet blue. It was a clear sky, no longer full of angry war planes or the smoke from artillery guns or the trace of bullets whizzing through the air. It was a peaceful sky. An Israeli sky.

"How long do you think this will last?"

It was the same question that Mustafa had asked the previous week, the previous day, and just an hour ago.

"God knows, because He knows everything, and I don't," said Shalman.

"Daddy said God," piped up Vered, her mouth full of biscuit, her lips ringed by creamy white milk.

Mustafa hauled himself from lying on his back onto his elbow and looked at Vered. "Are you enjoying the picnic, darling?"

She beamed and nodded vigorously. Then she turned when she thought she heard the noise of some small animal in the undergrowth.

"Do you think the Arab armies will let up now that they've signed an armistice?" Mustafa asked.

Shalman shrugged. "There's been so much killing, so much hatred. On the one hand, I'm certain the Jews and the Arabs want this whole disaster to be over. On the other hand, the Arab leaderships have already declared that they'll never accept Israel in their midst."

Mustafa smiled. "Why do you Jews always have to have two hands? We Arabs only have one opinion, and the rest is *Insha' Allah*."

Having an ear for languages, Vered mimicked the word *Insha'Allah* but couldn't quite get her little tongue around its cadences.

Shalman smiled. "On the one hand, you saved my life; on the other hand, I saved yours. That's life."

"So life returns to normal," said Mustafa.

"Normal? If only I knew what that means. But at least the Hebrew University is starting up its archaeology courses again, which means you can enroll in your degree course, and then we can—"

"Are you crazy? They'll never accept me. I'm an Arab. A Palestinian. An enemy. No, my friend, forget that. I'm back to being a farmer, doing what my father and his father did."

"Over my dead body. There's not a single statement put out by the university authorities that says Palestinian Arabs are not allowed. If they did, I'd be the first to stand in the middle of the campus and scream from the rooftops."

"You're being naive, Shalman. Our people have just finished trying to kill your people. You don't seriously think for one moment that the Jews are going to allow us Arabs back as if nothing happened. Do you?"

Vered, listening to every word and not understanding a thing, repeated quickly, "Do you?"

"Now that the armistice has been signed—"

"Then you're an idiot, because—"

"Daddy *ijut*," said Vered.

Both men looked at her, and she beamed a mischievous smile, knowing that she'd had an impact.

"So much like her mother," said Shalman. "That, for me, is the greatest tragedy of this war—that women like Judit were the casualties."

Mustafa nodded. "I wish I could thank her for what she told you. She saved my family. We would have been killed had it not been for her."

Shalman put his finger to his lips and nodded toward Vered. "I don't speak in the past tense," he told Mustafa. "When she asks about Judit, I tell her she'll be back. How do I know?"

He said nothing more. How could he? How would he explain to his daughter what had probably happened to her mother or, to Mustafa, the complexities of a woman like Judit? He could never tell his Arab friend, nor Vered, nor anybody, what Immanuel Berin had confided to him shortly after she'd disappeared—that she was a Russian assassin who'd probably been responsible for killing dozens of innocent men and women. It was a secret that he'd take to his grave. It made life intensely hard for him. He still loved Judit, yearned for her, admired all the qualities in her that had made their love so passionate.

On the other hand, he hated her with a depth and intensity that frightened him, hated her for the way she'd ruined his life, hated her for the way she'd left Vered to grow up without a mother, hated her for her fanaticism and militancy. But he knew that he had to bury his hatred, because it would only damage Vered and those he loved if the truth were ever known.

"Do you ever wonder what happened to her? Where she's—?" Mustafa was about to say "buried" but stopped himself, remembering that Vered was a very bright little girl who would probably repeat the word, which would hurt Shalman even more.

Shalman lifted his arm and pointed into the Judean wilderness. "Somewhere out there. Along with all the thousands of Jews and Arabs and Christians, Bedouin and travelers and wanderers who have crisscrossed this land. Who knows? Remember when you and I found that skeleton in the caves near your home? Maybe one day a thousand years from now, some archaeologist will discover my Judit's bones and . . ." He fell silent.

Mustafa nodded. There was nothing more to say. All these two young men could do—one a Muslim, one a Jew; one a Palestinian and one an Israeli—was stare out into the land of Israel, the land of hope, and beyond into the land of Palestine and the eternity of history. And wonder.

ACKNOWLEDGMENTS

Pablo Picasso said, "Others have seen what is and asked why. I have seen what could be and asked why not." In the tough commercial world of publishing, the route of safety is all too often the path dictated. Not so with the stellar team at Simon & Schuster Australia, who saw the daring vision that we presented, and said, "Yes, let's do it." So to Lou Johnson, Larissa Edwards, Roberta Ivers, Laurie Ormond, Jo Butler, and Jo Jarrah go my most sincere thanks for their confidence, support, and advice.

My thanks and admiration also to Harold and Rebecca Finger for their continued backing and encouragement. And to Mike Jones, an amazing co-author, whose leaps of imagination often caused him to crash through the ceiling.

My love for their wisdom and understanding go to my wife, Eva, and children, Georgina, Jonathan, and Raffe, for bearing with me on this long journey to the City on a Hill.

Alan Gold

No one writes a book alone, and this book has enjoyed the enormous support of a wonderful circle of collaborators. We could ask for no better partners than our publishers, Simon & Schuster Australia— Lou Johnson, Larissa Edwards, Roberta Ivers, and the whole S&S team. Likewise Harold Finger, for his passion and faith. Of course, I have to thank my co-writer, Alan, for having me along to contribute to this wild project he dreamed up. Finally, and most of all, my eternal thanks and love go to Leonie for everything, always and forever.

Mike Jones

ABOUT THE AUTHORS

Alan Gold is an internationally published and translated author of fifteen novels, his most recent *Bell of the Desert*, published in 2014 in the United States. He speaks regularly to national and international conferences on a range of subjects, most notably the recent growth of anti-Semitism. In 2001 he was a delegate at the notorious United Nations World Conference on Racism and Xenophobia held in Durban, South Africa, and has addressed UN conferences and meetings, as well as speaking throughout the world to universities and community groups.

Alan is a regular contributor to *The Australian*, *The Spectator*, and other media as an opinion columnist and literary critic, as well as being a lecturer and mentor at the master's and doctoral level in creative writing at major universities.

Mike Jones is an award-winning writer who works across forms including books, screen, and digital interactive media.